# CRY LOVE

EVE GADDY

SxNW PUBLISHING

*Praise for Cry Love*

"Deftly handling past and present, weaving together storylines that will haunt you, Eve Gaddy has written a sensitive, emotional love story spiced with danger and an ugly evil. CRY LOVE will leave you both moved and satisfied. A book you will not quickly forget!"

—Justine Davis, *USA Today* Bestselling and 5-Time RITA Award Winning author

"CRY LOVE is a provocative, emotional page turner that I couldn't put down. Eve Gaddy has written a gripping love story that could be ripped from the headlines. This story has everything!"

—Katherine Garbera, *USA Today* Bestselling author

SxNW PUBLISHING



This is a work of fiction. Names, characters, places, and incidents are products of the author's imagination or are used fictitiously. Any resemblance to actual persons, living or dead, events or locations is entirely coincidental.



Cover Art by Lynn Andreozzi

Paperback ISBN: 978-1-946331-28-1

*This book is for every writer who has quit and struggled back, for every writer with a book of the heart who despaired of ever publishing it, or even writing it. Keep the faith. It can happen.*

# AUTHOR'S NOTE

When this book first started forming in my mind, I decided it would make sense if there was another Underground Railroad, but this one originating in Texas and going west or south. To my complete surprise, when I began researching *Cry Love,* I discovered that there had indeed been an Underground Railroad in Texas. It ran primarily south to Mexico, where slavery had been outlawed long before. There isn't a lot of information about the Texas-Mexico Underground Railroad to be found, but it definitely existed. Today there are still towns in northern Mexico where many of the descendants of those who came to Mexico via the Underground Railroad live. It seems in keeping with this book that a coincidence like this would happen.

# CHAPTER ONE

THEY LYNCHED HIM at dawn.

He struggled, kicking out, then digging his worn boots into the ground as they dragged him toward the tree, the huge oak standing sentinel on the front lawn. But he could do nothing against five men.

*Oh, God, no.* No, please, she pled silently, knowing it was a futile prayer. They had tied his hands, beaten him until she could see the blood dripping from his face and body in the eerie fog of the emerging dawn. Despairing, she put her hand to the window, choked out a cry as they threw him up on the horse and placed the noose around his neck.

*My love. My only love.*

CLAIRE GASPED, choked, and sat up in bed, struggling awake through a thick fog of sorrow. She raised a hand to her cheek, felt the moisture of tears.

"What the hell is going on?"

Claire Westbrook had never been a fanciful woman, not even when young and naive. Certainly not since she'd become a physician. As a trauma surgeon she dealt in gritty reality. Too damn much of it.

Yet she'd awakened in tears from a dream so real she could have sworn she still heard the screams.

Hers.

His.

Unsettling, and frankly, annoying. She didn't have the luxury of a sleepless night. She needed her rest, not to awaken breathless, heart hammering after some bizarre dream.

Her sleep had been growing progressively more restless, but it wasn't until waking up this morning that she actually remembered one of the dreams. And thank God she couldn't if they'd all been like that dream. The only good thing that had come from her restless nights was they had given her a good excuse to move out of the bedroom she shared with her husband. Glenn hadn't seemed upset to have her move, either. She wondered what was keeping them together. Not sex and not companionship, that was for sure.

Determined to get a grip, she swore not to think about the dream again. She got out of bed and lurched into the shower, turning the water on as hot as she could stand it.

It was that damned journal. The one she'd found yesterday morning, when she was cleaning out her mother's house for her upcoming move. With her father gone now for two years, Claire had finally convinced her mother she had to move to a smaller house. And Lord, was it a production downsizing her. The woman had kept stuff going back to the seventeen hundreds. Every time a family house had been cleaned out—and her mother had a lot of family—the junk had all migrated to Evangeline's. Some of it was interesting, letters from World

War I, guns from the late eighteenth century, a postcard collection dating from the late eighteen hundreds. But a lot of it was junk, plain and simple.

Then yesterday morning, Claire had found a journal, obviously antique and stuffed in among a bunch of ancient receipts, though not of the same time period. Her mother thought it had belonged to Claire's great-great-great-great-grandmother, Rachel Adams, who had lived during the Civil War.

The journal was certainly old. Claire had glanced at it long enough to read a sentence or two, and sure enough, it was dated 1859, just prior to the Civil War. Claire had never been a Civil War buff. In fact, she'd avoided the whole era, other than what she'd been forced to read in school. In the past, she'd found reading about it painful, so whenever possible, she didn't.

Despite her embargo of the Civil War era, the journal piqued her curiosity. If she were an imaginative person, she'd say it called to her. Since she was a pragmatist at heart, she merely acknowledged it was interesting. Still, she hadn't read enough of it to warrant a dream like the one she'd had. Good God, that was crazy.

Damn it, she was doing it again. Obsessing over that stupid dream was getting her nowhere. And if she didn't get her ass in gear she'd have to skip her skinny white chocolate mocha from Java Joe's. She stopped there religiously every morning before work, and some days when she was off.

Yet on the way to the coffee shop she found bits of the dream replaying itself in her head. Out of the confusing fog-like wisps, one certainty emerged.

She had no idea who he was. And he had died because of her.

THANK GOD FOR coffee, Jonas Clark thought on his way to work. And thank God there was a decent coffee shop across from the hospital. His coffee pot had broken during the move a week ago, and he'd yet to replace it.

He'd never imagined living in Texas again. Certainly not in Fort Worth, his hometown. He'd left Texas behind a long time ago and hadn't missed it a bit. But his mother had developed health problems, and she needed help. Jonas was an only child so he didn't have a choice. He couldn't do her much good from fifteen hundred miles away in Boston. Moving his mother to him was not an option, either. First of all, she hadn't completely given up hope of going back to work, though Jonas thought there was a slim chance of that happening. Still, she was settled in Fort Worth, with many friends as well as her church. She'd always said she'd been born a Texan and intended to die one.

So Jonas had started looking for jobs in the Metroplex. He'd thought he could tolerate Dallas, but instead he'd ended up in Fort Worth. An old buddy of his from medical school was a partner in a neurosurgery group looking to expand. They worked out of Shady Grove Memorial Hospital, a fairly new level-one trauma center that had opened a few years ago. The hospital, and consequently, their practice, had been steadily growing, and they were desperately in need of more neurosurgeons. Having a new one as well-trained as Jonas was a definite plus.

Jonas stood in line behind a woman who seemed vaguely familiar. Blonde, pretty, dressed in scrubs, she could easily be someone else who worked at the hospital. Probably was.

God, he needed the caffeine. His sleep had been restless

since coming to town, which was unusual for him. He put it down to the move, and maybe the stress of a new job. Except the job was fine and not particularly stressful to someone accustomed to a busy pace. But something was waking him in the night. Normally, he slept like a log when he wasn't working.

"What can I get you?" the clerk asked, pulling him out of his reverie.

He ordered a skim latte with a double shot, then followed the blonde to the take-out counter. He stepped up to get his latte just as the blonde turned around and crashed into him, sending scalding coffee cascading over his arm. "Shit," he said, and stepped back.

"Oh, God, I'm sorry. I didn't realize you were there." She looked at him a moment with the oddest expression, then put her cup down on a nearby table and ran to the counter, bringing napkins with her.

He fended her off, saying, "Just let me get my coffee."

She ignored him, dabbing at him ineffectually as he determinedly made his way back to the counter and picked up his latte. "Don't worry about it. I'm fine."

"Don't be ridiculous, you're burned. And pretty badly too." She looked up from his injured arm to stare at him a moment, clearly taking in his attire, which was the same as hers. She had the oddest eyes. One green, one half-green and half-blue. He'd seen those eyes before, but he couldn't remember when or where.

"You're new at the hospital, aren't you?" she asked. "Didn't I see you earlier this week? From a distance, anyway. I'm Claire Westbrook, one of the trauma surgeons at Shady Grove."

Because it was there, he started to shake her hand, but

found himself strangely reluctant to touch her. Why, he couldn't have said. She seemed like a perfectly nice woman, if clumsy. Still, he almost had to force himself to take her hand. Their palms met, and he felt a subtle pop. The sounds around them faded, and he was mired in quicksand. Sorrow, grief, pain flashed in his mind, and then they were gone, and he was left staring at the woman who had paled to sheet white. They dropped hands, she with as much alacrity as he did.

"Jonas Clark. Neurosurgery." Jesus, he needed more sleep. He took a big gulp of coffee and burned his tongue. What was with the Twilight Zone moment?

"I'd heard we were getting a new neurosurgeon. I guess that would be you."

"Guilty. I started a week ago."

"You came from Massachusetts General, right?"

He sipped, more cautiously this time. "That's right."

"How are you adjusting to Texas? It's a lot different from Boston." She laughed when she said it.

"I'm originally from the area."

"Really?" She looked surprised. "I wouldn't have guessed that. You've lost your accent."

He made a noncommittal sound. He'd worked hard to lose his Texas accent, but somehow he didn't think that appropriate to say to a woman whose Southern Comfort drawl reminded him of hot summer nights and fast women.

She started to touch his arm, then seemed to think better of it. Maybe she'd felt that weird little tug too.

"Look, I'm really sorry about the coffee. Maybe I can buy you a latte sometime."

"Forget it." He knew it had been an accident, but something warned him this woman was trouble with a capital *T*.

"OKAY, WHO IS Dr. Awesome?" Lanie Avery asked Claire while they were scanning charts.

"Dr. Awesome?"

"Tall, black, and awesome gorgeous." Lanie was an orthopedist Claire worked with often, as well as a friend.

Claire laughed, glancing up from the chart she was perusing to look in the direction Lanie indicated. Seeing who it was, she frowned. "Oh, that's Jonas Clark. He's the new neurosurgeon. You know, the one from Mass Gen."

"Mass Gen? Wow. He's a long way from Boston. I wonder what made him move to Texas?"

"I asked him that. He said he was from the area originally." Claire went back to the chart.

"So you've met him already. Some people have all the luck."

Claire had to laugh at that. "I bet he didn't think so."

"Why, did you have a run-in with him?"

"I don't have a run-in with every man I meet."

"Just most of them," Lanie said with a smirk. "What happened?"

Claire closed the chart and waved a hand. "It's nothing. I spilled my coffee on him this morning at Java Joe's, and he seemed a bit . . . annoyed. Not that I blame him," she added hastily. "I'm sure it hurt like hell."

"Aha, do I detect some interest?" Lanie asked.

"Hardly. I'm married, remember?"

"Married women have eyes too. Besides, Glenn's such a jerk."

"Don't start, Lanie," Claire said wearily. Her friend had no use for her husband, just as he had no use for Lanie. Part of it was Claire's fault for talking about her troubled marriage, but she had to talk to someone, and Lanie was totally loyal to her. Of course, her friend hadn't liked Glenn to begin with, and now she detested him. Claire wondered if something had happened between them, something they didn't want to tell her. If so, neither would admit to it. "And don't make something out of nothing."

Jonas Clark *was* gorgeous. But no doubt he knew that. He looked more like an athlete than a doctor. Broad shoulders, trim waist, perfect white teeth in a darkly handsome face. And what in the hell was she doing salivating over the man? That was so not like her. She hadn't done that even when she was single.

"Dr. Westbrook," one of the ER nurses called from across the room, "EMS wants to talk to you."

She crossed the room to the big central desk, where among other things was the telephone EMS used. Picking up, she said, "This is Dr. Westbrook."

"We have a victim involved in a head-on collision. Two cars, one driver is dead and the other severely injured. Also a passenger with possible broken leg and ribs. The worst is the driver, though, a middle- aged male with head injuries and blunt injuries to the chest and abdomen."

"Is he coming by helicopter or ambulance?"

"Passenger by ambulance. Driver by helicopter. We're en route now as is the ambulance. After we got him out of the car, we stabilized his spine, intubated him, and started IVs. He's unconscious, possibly due to the head injuries. Estimate arrival time in five minutes."

"We'll be ready." Claire relayed the information to the ER staff and let neurosurgery and orthopedics know they would likely be needed.

Twenty-five minutes later, after ordering a trauma panel CAT scan, Claire talked to the radiologist. "What have we got, Turner?"

"Hey, Westbrook, your trauma, Peter Moore, has got a left temporal skull fracture with an acute epidural hematoma causing mass effect and midline shift."

She frowned at the scan on the computer. "Okay, neurosurgery is on the way."

"That's great, but your other big problem is that he's got a contained rupture of his aortic arch."

"Wonderful. That's two immediately life-threatening injuries I've got to deal with. Thanks, Turner." To her mind, of the two, the aorta was the first injury to take care of.

She turned and found Jonas Clark at her elbow. "What can I do for you, Doctor?"

"Other way around. You called neurosurgery. Is this for me?" He was looking at the head scan as he spoke.

Sure she had, but she hadn't expected him to show up until she confirmed he'd be needed. Most of the neurosurgeons didn't. He was new, though. No doubt he'd change once he'd been there a while. "My patient has a hematoma you need to drain as soon as I've repaired his ruptured aorta."

He glanced at her briefly before turning back to the scan. "Bullshit."

She stared at him a moment. "Excuse me?"

He smiled and repeated pleasantly, "Bullshit. You need to fix your aorta after I've drained his hematoma." He motioned to the scan as if that settled it.

She clamped down on her temper. "If his aorta goes, he'll bleed out."

"Or he could be brain dead if I don't operate now. If the aorta is contained it can wait."

They glared at each other, and Claire opened her mouth to argue some more.

"Doctor! Doctor Westbrook! We need you in exam one." One of the ER nurses rushed up to them. "Mr. Moore's blood pressure is steadily dropping and his heart rate is going up."

Claire gave Clark a prim smile. "It looks like that aortic rupture is no longer contained. Let's get him to the OR," she told the nurse and left, well satisfied with her parting shot.

# CHAPTER TWO

A BIT MORE THAN an hour and a half later, Claire finished up her part of the patient's surgery. Jonas Clark had come in several minutes before and observed. He didn't make her nervous. She wasn't a novice, after all. But she was very aware of his presence. Fortunately, the repair of the aortic arch had gone well. As soon as she closed, Clark's surgical team started prepping and repositioning the patient for his craniotomy.

Claire didn't leave immediately, but stayed to watch Clark work. It wasn't every day she was able to see a world-class neurosurgeon perform an operation. She hoped it went well, especially since it had been unclear as to who should operate first, not that she had admitted to any indecision at the time. The patient's condition had decided for them.

"Worried about your patient, Doctor?" Clark asked her as he began.

"No, just interested. Do you mind?"

"Not at all."

He was accustomed to people observing him, she knew,

since he'd come to Shady Grove from Massachusetts General, a huge teaching hospital. She watched for some time, impressed with the man's abilities. Reluctantly, she left before he finished, knowing she had her own duties to attend to.

She went to her locker, picked up her cell phone to find her husband had called five times, not leaving a message until the last one, just a few minutes before. Glenn didn't call that many times for no reason. Usually he didn't call her at all when she was at work.

She listened with a sinking heart. "Goddamn it, where are you? Call me immediately," was the extent of his message. If that wasn't typical Glenn. Just then she was paged to the ER. She would deal with her husband later.

To her surprise, Glenn was in the ER when she got there. "About damn time you showed up," he said. His blond hair was disordered, and he'd taken off the suit jacket he habitually wore. He looked rumpled, stressed, and angry. Very unusual for him. Well, the rumpled part anyway. Stressed and angry were quite common nowadays.

"You had me paged? Why?"

"To ask you what the hell you mean by not alerting me about my father."

"Your father? Did something happen to Lawrence?"

"He was in a car accident. He's here in your ER. I didn't get a call from you. No sign at all that you even know or care. This is my father, damn it, you should have been the one to call me."

She didn't blame him for being upset about his father, but that still didn't justify his yelling at her. "I just got out of surgery," she said, guiltily aware that she could have been there sooner if she hadn't stayed to watch Jonas Clark perform his wonders. "My patient was the driver in a bad car wreck.

His passenger was injured as well. I wonder if your father was that passenger? The other driver was killed."

"I neither know nor care about the other people. I'm concerned with the treatment, or lack of it, that my father is getting. Why the hell aren't you at least overseeing things? He has a head injury, a concussion the doctor said."

Knowing there was no way to stop Glenn's tirade, Claire let him rant.

"My father's arm might be broken. Goddamn Lanie Avery is the orthopedist taking care of him, over my protests. I want her gone. I won't have that incompetent bitch putting her hands on my father."

"Oh, for God's sake, Lanie's a very fine doctor," she said impatiently. "She wouldn't be here otherwise." Claire refused to be drawn into an argument about Lanie. They'd never agree. "Never mind. I'll go check on him. Where is he?"

Glenn said no more, just turned and led the way to one of the cubicles. Glenn's father, Lawrence Westbrook, was awake and obviously in pain.

"Where the hell have you been? Why haven't I been given pain medication? Does the goddamn doctor think I'm an addict? What's taking so long?"

And as big of a jerk as ever, she thought, unsurprised. She told herself to give him the benefit of the doubt. He was clearly in pain and possibly scared, though she had a hard time believing that. "Let me look at your chart. I'm sorry I missed you, but I was in surgery. It sounds like my patient might have been the driver of your car." Almost certainly was since her father-in-law and her patient were the only auto traumas currently in the hospital.

"Peter Moore?" he asked. Claire nodded. "Damn fool. I told him to let me drive, but no."

"He's in critical condition. He's still in surgery."

Lawrence grunted. "Get me something for the pain, right now," he demanded.

So much for being concerned about his friend, she thought. Reading through his chart quickly she said, "You have a concussion, Lawrence. They have to be very careful about giving you pain medication with a head injury."

Just then Lanie came in and shot Claire a meaningful look. "I've looked at your X-rays, Mr. Westbrook. You almost certainly have broken ribs, and you fractured your radius. Ordinarily I'd put you in a soft cast and send you home until the swelling goes down, but since you'll be in the hospital for a few days because of your concussion, we can probably do it while you're here. You won't need surgery, at least."

"I don't want to stay in the hospital. Why can't I go home?"

"I'll let the ER doctor talk to you about that," Lanie said diplomatically.

Ignoring Glenn, Lanie said, "Claire, if I could have a word with you?"

Claire followed her out, conscious of a feeling of relief at leaving the room. "Do you think he has internal injuries?" she asked her friend.

"Not according to preliminary findings. It's possible further tests will turn up something, as you know. Although he fractured his radius, it's not an open fracture, so that's good news. The concussion is a bit of a worry, but you can talk to the ER doc when he comes back. I haven't seen films on that. How about the driver?"

"The aortic repair was successful. Now it's up to the neurosurgeon."

"Jonas Clark was breathing fire after you went to the OR. I don't think he liked having his patient whisked away."

"I wouldn't have either. But he got over that once the patient's status was clear. He should be finishing up soon."

"Did you watch any of the operation?" Lanie asked.

"I did. The man lives up to his reputation. He's good. Damn good from what I saw."

"He came from Massachusetts General. He should be good."

"I hope Glenn hasn't been too hard to deal with," Claire said, knowing he had likely been a pain in the ass at the least.

"Oh, he's been a peach," Lanie said sarcastically. "Seriously, other than yelling about how he didn't want me touching his father, he's been okay. Once he realized it was me or no one, he shut up." She glanced at the cubicle. "I see where Glenn gets his winning personality."

"Lawrence is a piece of work."

"*Flaming asshole* is how I'd describe him."

Claire laughed. "Yes, that works too. But he is in a lot of pain."

Lanie leveled a look at her. "And he's normally sweet as pie, right?"

"No, he's normally a jerk. Just not so blatant about it. Thanks, Lanie."

"All in a day's work. Unfortunately." Before Claire left, Lanie put a hand on her arm. "I still can't understand why you stay married to Glenn when you're clearly unhappy."

"It's complicated," Claire said, and left her.

Glenn knew how to be charming. She'd never have married him if he'd treated her then like he did now. But that didn't explain why she put up with it. Was she just chasing a hopeless cause? Or did she hate to admit failure so much that she continued to stay in a dying marriage?

HOURS LATER, CLAIRE let herself into her house and collapsed on the sofa, tossing the sandwich she'd picked up onto the coffee table. It had been a long day. Glenn was still at the hospital with his father, which suited her just fine. She'd felt a little guilty leaving, but she had to work tomorrow, and if she didn't get some sleep she'd be useless. And Glenn knew he could call if he needed her. But she didn't think he would. Given the severity of the car accident, Lawrence's tests had turned out well. A couple of broken ribs and a broken arm, while painful, were nothing compared to the trauma the driver had suffered.

Even if she could have tolerated it, Claire wouldn't be of any use at Lawrence's bedside. Lawrence didn't like her any more than she liked him. He'd had a different kind of wife in mind for his only child. A woman with more beauty than brains and who would stay home and manage their social life. Which was about as far from Claire as you could get.

Glenn hadn't exactly gotten what he'd expected when he'd married her, either. He'd known she was studying medicine, of course, but he'd been a lot more interested in her social pedigree than she had realized at the time. Claire came from a socially prominent, wealthy family, but she'd always been driven to succeed in her chosen profession. She hadn't scorned the social scene her parents had enjoyed, so much as she simply didn't have time for it.

After eating she took a quick shower, then crawled into bed and closed her eyes. Fifteen minutes later, she acknowledged she couldn't turn off her brain long enough for sleep to take over. The journal she'd brought home from her mother's house sat on the bedside table. Had it really been the cause of that dream? Surely something like that was a fluke and wouldn't happen again. She'd only glanced at the journal the first time, after all.

She reached for it, picked a page at random, and started reading. Fortunately, Rachel's handwriting was beautiful and not difficult to read except where it had faded. For the most part it hadn't faded too badly, which surprised Claire. After all it was nearly 150 years old.

***Rachel's Journal—January 2, 1859***

*I am a wretched, wretched person. Victor Lawrence came to my father and asked for one of his daughters in marriage. At first, he cared not which one. He made it clear he wanted a good breeder. My father, naturally, denied him. But when Mr. Lawrence saw the two of us, he insisted he wanted Sarah. Sarah is by far the prettier, and suffers no squint, as I do. Father denied him again, saying he would force neither daughter into marriage against her will.*

*But Mr. Lawrence said he would ruin Father and force him to leave the area. And when he found that Ben and I were to marry, he threatened Ben's livelihood as well. He says he can destroy the store, and I believe him. Whereas if Father agrees, Mr. Lawrence said he would gift Father with enough money to not only keep up the farm but to expand it. And that he would give him money for Ben and I as well. While Ben and I do not need his money, I am afraid of what he will do if he does not get his way. Sarah has agreed. And I, wretch that I am, allowed it. I said nothing in protest but allowed my darling sister to sacrifice herself for the rest of us.*

*To what misery have I sentenced my poor sister? But how can we fight so powerful a man? Perhaps he will not be as terrible as I fear. Are the rumors true? They say he is a brutal master. His slaves do not talk. They dare not. None of our servants talk to his slaves. They say he threatens to whip them to death if he hears his business bandied about. I fear a man so cruel to his slaves will be no better to his wife. Others say I am naive and that is how many use their slaves. But I cannot condone such cruelty.*

CLAIRE CLOSED THE book and set it aside. She wanted to read more but knew she'd regret losing sleep, especially since her workdays were normally busy. She closed her eyes and drifted off, thinking of two sisters on the eve of the Civil War.

***January 1859***

SARAH KNEW WHAT she had to do. Her duty, regardless of what she wanted. Victor Lawrence desired her. He had made it clear he could help her father keep his farm, or he could ruin him. As well as ruin Ben, her sister's betrothed. Her father wouldn't force her to marry the wealthy plantation owner. A kinder, gentler man than her father she'd never known. That was part of the problem, that and his abolitionist leanings. He refused to own slaves, relying instead on freedmen, those of his own he had freed as well as the few others he found, to work his fields. Around these parts such actions were viewed as eccentric at best, seditious at worst.

Sarah could not let her father sacrifice everything for her. Her sister Rachel loved being betrothed and couldn't wait to be a married lady. She was to marry Ben Adams, the man she loved, though. Soon, God willing, they would be married and have children to brighten their days.

But Rachel's betrothed owned the general store, and he depended on the goodwill and business of the plantation owners from the surrounding areas. Everyone was well aware that a man like Victor Lawrence could ruin anyone he chose. She knew Victor had threatened her father with ruin if she didn't choose to marry him. And she believed he had threatened Ben, as well. Her father wouldn't speak of it, but she could tell by his ceaseless poring over his accounts that he was worried.

Perhaps once she married Victor Lawrence, her life wouldn't be so bad. He was wealthy and could offer her whatever she wanted.

Everything but love.

If she married Victor Lawrence, her loved ones would be safe. If she resisted, ruin.

Duty won.

# CHAPTER THREE

*August Present Day*

IN THE THREE days since he'd met Claire Westbrook and tangled over a patient, Jonas had not been able to get her out of his mind. He couldn't figure it out. He was not the kind of man to obsess over a woman. Especially not a woman he wasn't even sure he liked. But for reasons he didn't understand, Claire had been on his mind. And stayed there whether he wanted her to or not.

She *was* beautiful. A knockout with long, dark blonde hair of a thousand shades, and a flawless milky-white complexion. Even in scrubs he could see she had curves for days. Okay, she was smoking. But so what? He'd known other beautiful women. Even dated a few. Besides, she was married. She didn't wear a ring, but that wasn't unusual for a trauma surgeon. No sense wearing something you had to take off and keep up with on a daily basis. His information about her marital status came from her friend, Lanie Avery. The orthopedist had mentioned something about Claire's father-in-law going through the ER the same day as Mr. Moore, their mutual patient.

Father-in-law meant she was married. Off the table. It wasn't as if he wanted to date her, anyway. There were plenty of available women, a lot of them right there in Shady Grove hospital.

There was Arianna, the radiology tech who'd made it clear from the day he'd met her that she'd be interested in seeing him outside of work. She was hot. And available. There was also Chamika, a model he'd met in Boston who was based in Dallas. Somehow she'd heard he had moved to Texas, and she'd texted him to call her. Chamika was gorgeous. Available. But he couldn't summon up the energy to do anything about it.

Poor timing, that's all it was. New job, heavy schedule. Right now, all he wanted to do was sleep. He'd been on call last night and up operating for most of it. He got in his car, the silver ZR1 Corvette that he loved like a child. At the rate he was going, the 'Vette might be as close as he ever came to offspring. Still, he was only thirty-four. Plenty of time left to tie himself down with a wife and kids. If he wanted to.

Which he didn't.

He drove out of the parking garage and nearly passed a woman leaning against her car, an eye-popping candy-cane red M5 Beamer. He slowed down, then stopped. The hood was propped open, indicating she wasn't standing there for kicks. Well, damn. Claire Westbrook, looking cool and beautiful in hospital scrubs after a night spent on call. How did she manage that?

He rolled down his window. "Need some help?"

She looked relieved. "Yes, thanks. A jump would help. I hope."

He got out, went around to the trunk, and pulled out his jumper cables. "Long night?" he asked as he connected the cables.

She rubbed her neck and groaned. "Very. How about you?"

"Yeah, it was long. I operated most of it."

"Me too. The older I get the more I wonder if I picked the right specialty. I should have been a dermatologist. Or something else nine to five. But no, I had to pick trauma surgery."

"You'd be bored in a heartbeat with a nine-to-five job."

"How do you know that?"

He glanced at her and smiled. Nine to five? He didn't think so. "I saw you operate on Mr. Moore. You're a born surgeon." Cool, collected, capable. Of course, he expected that in a hospital as well run as Shady Grove. Didn't always happen, though.

"Thanks. That means a lot coming from a surgeon of your reputation."

"I wasn't blowing smoke. I meant it." He couldn't say why it was important to him that she knew he was sincere, but it was.

She smiled. "It never occurred to me that you were feeding me a line. I'm not that insecure. But thanks for the vote of confidence."

Annoyed that she'd managed to throw him off balance without even making an effort, he said, "Get in and crank it."

It took several tries, but it finally started. Her car was seriously smoking, just as she was. Briefly, he wondered if it was hers or the husband's. Hers, he decided. It suited her perfectly. Classy and beautiful. He bet that sucker would run.

"Thank you." She propped her arm on the open window and smiled at him. "I wasn't looking forward to waiting for AAA. Last time I called them it took hours. Can I buy you a cup of coffee?" She laughed at his expression. "Decaf, so you can sleep once you get home. How about it?"

What the hell. Maybe if he got to know her better, she'd cease being such a fascination. "Sure, why not. I'll follow you."

Or maybe she'd become even more intriguing, in which case he was screwed.

The coffee shop he followed her to was a small diner on Berry Street that he remembered from his high school days. He wouldn't have thought Claire knew it, though. Interesting.

"I'm starving," Claire said after they were seated. "What about you?"

"I could eat. This place had great food when I was in high school."

"Still does." She smiled at the waitress and chatted with her a bit before giving her order. Clearly she came here often.

Jonas ordered as well and settled back with his coffee. He liked the fancier coffee shops sometimes, but what he really enjoyed was just a good cup of black coffee without any frills.

"Why did you come back to Fort Worth?" Claire asked. "I know you said you'd lived here before, but you'd been in Boston a long time, right?"

He nodded. "I did my residency there and practiced at Mass Gen for several years. Then my mother began having some health issues. I'm an only child so I came back to care for her."

"I hope it's not serious."

"It's not life-threatening. She has wet macular degeneration, and it's growing worse."

"I'm sorry. Does she still have her sight?"

"Yes, but it's getting to be more of a problem." He laughed. "According to her, she's handling everything just fine. She doesn't accept help very readily."

"Independent, huh?"

"You can say that again." She'd pitched a fit when he broke the news to her that he was moving back to Texas. Naomi had always pushed him to succeed and wanted no part of hampering his career path, or changing it in any way. But Jonas had stood firm. She needed him in Texas, and that was that. When the position at Shady Grove had opened up, he'd known it was meant to be. "So what about you? Did you grow up here?"

"I did. Lived here all my life except for college. I went to Arlington Heights for high school," she said, naming one of the large high schools in Fort Worth. "Where did you go? I'm betting we're about the same age."

He grinned. "Possibly. I didn't think a woman ever volunteered her age."

"I'm still in my thirties, so maybe I just haven't gotten there yet. I'm class of 1995."

"I went to Paschal," he said, naming one of the other big high schools in Fort Worth. "Same graduating class. We never met, though. I'd have remembered you." If she'd looked anything like she did now, he sure as hell would've remembered her.

The waitress came back with their meals, and they both dug in. Jonas wondered what Claire had been like in high school. He hadn't taken to the party circuit, but in all likelihood, neither had she. He'd been busy busting his ass in order to get a premed scholarship at a competitive college. He'd set his heart on Harvard Medical School from the time he was fourteen. Jonas was a decent athlete but not good enough to make it in the pros. Besides, his interests had always leaned more toward the academic. He'd figured out early on that academics were his ride.

"I spent high school with my nose in a book," Claire said. "I always wanted to be a doctor. I never had much interest in the social scene. Didn't see any point to it."

"Valedictorian?" he asked.

She laughed. "Yes. You?"

"By a tenth of a point," he said, smiling. "My mother worked two jobs to support us until I got old enough for a part-time job. Between that and school, I didn't have much of a social life either."

"It was just you and your mom growing up?"

He nodded. "My dad died when I was six. Mom never remarried. She said she'd had one love of her life and didn't expect to find another."

"That's really touching."

They both grabbed for the napkins at the same time. The instant their hands met, Jonas felt a jolt. Similar to the one he'd felt the first time she touched him, only more intense. Their eyes met, hers that odd combination of colors, and he was reminded again that he'd seen them before. But where?

She looked as startled as he felt. "I swear this isn't a line," he said, "but . . . did you feel that?"

Claire looked away, then back at him. "Yes. It was . . . weird."

"*Weird* is an appropriate word. I felt it the first time, too. When you spilled coffee on me."

She didn't say anything, but judging by her expression, she had too.

He put out his hand. "I'm not a big believer in woo-woo crap."

"Me neither." But she didn't give him her hand.

"Scared?"

"Not exactly." She placed her hand in his. Let it lie there, passive.

Her image shimmered. Faded. For an instant, he was somewhere else . . . *someone* else. A black boy, sitting in a diner with a white girl, holding hands. Young. Teenagers, both of them.

*"I have a bad feeling about this," he said. "You and me, nothing good's gonna come of it."*

*"Then why do you keep seeing me?" She tossed long dark hair back over her shoulder and gazed at him with oddly colored eyes. One green, one half-green, half-blue.*

*"I can't seem to help it. You're just so damn pretty."*

*She laughed. "That's a shallow reason."*

*He laughed too. "Maybe I'm just a shallow kind of guy."*

As quickly as the scene had come, it faded. Jonas pulled his hand away from Claire's. Shook his head to clear his thoughts. Weird. He didn't remember that scene ever happening. But if it hadn't been his memory, then what the hell had it been?

"I'm married," Claire said.

"I'm not." He didn't ask why that was pertinent. He knew, and obviously, so did she. His mouth ran independently of his good sense. "Are you happily married?"

She didn't answer. She picked up her fork and ate some of her omelet. "I'm married. Let's leave it at that."

So her marriage wasn't a happy one. He'd be crazy to get involved with a married woman. A married white woman at that. But damn, she was beautiful, even after all night in the OR. And that odd connection thing only made her more intriguing.

*Don't do it, Jonas,* he thought. *You're going to regret it.*

Like the boy, he had a bad feeling. But again, like the boy, she was just so damn pretty.

Hell.

***Rachel's Journal—March 3, 1859***

*Sarah came to see us today, Ben and I. Sensing her need to speak freely, Ben left us to ourselves. I am glad that he did, yet I feel so helpless. Her life simply grows worse. Her husband blames her for her barrenness, though as far as he knows, he has never fathered a child. That fact matters not to him. In his world, Sarah is at fault.*

*Sarah is at her wit's end. For while her husband prays for a child, she prays to remain childless. She wants no child of Victor Lawrence's, for fear he will hurt the child, as he does her. Sarah does not speak of it in detail, but I can see the bruises he leaves. Lord only knows what further horror is hidden by her clothes. Neither Father nor Sarah ever speak of the reasons behind this disastrous marriage, but we all know the sacrifice Sarah made and why. And I am so fortunate to have a husband who loves and cherishes me. Am I wrong to feel desperately thankful, even as my heart aches for my sister?*

***March 1859***

"OH, THANK GOODNESS," Sarah said upon spying the big black man walking toward her. "You're Elijah, aren't you?"

"Yes, ma'am." He tipped his straw hat and didn't look at her, as all the slaves had been trained.

My, he was large. "My horse has come up lame, and I don't know what to do. Can you help me?"

He shuffled his feet a bit, then said, "Yes'm." He went to the horse and felt of his hock. "It's done swole up. Look like she been kicked. Or she hurt it kickin' something."

"Can she get home pulling the buggy? Or should I unhitch it and lead her?"

"I'll lead her, ma'am. You and the buggy won't bother her

none." As Sarah started to get down, he added, "No need to get out, ma'am."

"Nonsense. She doesn't need my added weight, and I'm perfectly capable of walking." Elijah looked as if he wanted to argue but said nothing. "Well, don't just stand there. Help me down."

The big man looked even more uncomfortable at the command, but he came to the wagon and placed his hands on her waist. He picked her up as if she weighed no more than a feather, letting go of her immediately when he set her on the ground.

Then he went to the horse's head and looped the reins in his hand. Sarah scrambled to keep up with him. She looked around carefully, making certain no one else was about. She knew if anyone saw her walking side by side with a slave, or worse, if her husband saw, he would have a fit. In all likelihood, he would vent his anger on poor Elijah and then turn on her. But then, he didn't agree with Sarah that they were all God's creatures. Victor thought the slaves were no better than animals, and he wasn't very kind to them either. If she'd known how brutal he was before she'd agreed to marry him . . . no, it wouldn't have mattered. She would have felt duty bound to marry Victor regardless of his cruelty.

"You're not from around here, are you, Elijah? You sound more educated than most of the other slaves."

He still wouldn't look at her but, he answered. "Near Canada. My mother schooled me. Before I was took."

"Took? Taken from where?"

"From my home, ma'am."

"You mean from another plantation, another master?"

"No, ma'am. I was born free."

He said it proudly. Other than the slaves her father had

freed, she hadn't known any freedmen. "You and your family were free? You were stolen from your home?"

He nodded. "Yes'm. When I was twelve."

"Why, that's terrible. Unconscionable."

He shrugged. "'Twas a long time ago. But I ain't forgotten how it feels to be free. Still and all, least my schoolin' got me a better job to do."

"That's right, you take care of the accounts. Victor, my husband, said something about you just the other day. He was surprised—" she broke off abruptly, remembering the crude nature of her husband's comments.

"That a colored slave could know figurin'?" Elijah asked. "I'm sorry, Missus," he said immediately. "I didn't mean no disrespect."

"None taken." By her, at least. Victor would be another matter.

No one had seen her walking with Elijah. They were on her husband's land, and not a soul had been in sight for miles around. If she were careful, she might talk to Elijah again. Sarah didn't analyze why she wanted to see him again. She only felt as if she had found a friend.

# CHAPTER FOUR

*August Present Day*

GLENN'S FATHER STAYED in the hospital for several days due to the concussion. By the time he was released, Claire suspected the nursing staff was as ready to get rid of him as he was to leave. He put the *D* in *difficult*. Claire hadn't planned on being present to help take him home, but Glenn had specifically requested her to be there. Lawrence, in his usual pain-in-the-ass manner, had been running Glenn ragged. Glenn, in turn, had decided she needed to facilitate Lawrence's release, although she'd told him there was nothing she could do about that. Claire and Lawrence had never had the best of relationships, and since she'd quit catering to his wishes, it had grown worse.

At first Lawrence had liked her. Or at least, he'd liked her family's social position. He'd never really liked *her*, and he detested her oddly colored eyes. He'd often made rude comments about them, though she wasn't sure why they bothered him so much. Finally fed up, she'd told him she could do without seeing him if he couldn't shut up about something so insignificant. He'd backed off after that.

"Did you talk to that night nurse?" she heard Lawrence ask as she entered the room. "I don't think I need one, but if you insist, I guess I'll have her. But if I don't like her, you'll have to find another."

"We've talked about this," Glenn said. "I'm sure she'll be fine, she came highly recommended. I think you'll just need to keep her for a short while, but you'll also need extra help during the day and you'll probably need that for a long time. For one thing, you won't be driving for a while. Not while you're on the pain medication, anyway."

Glenn looked exhausted. Claire suspected his insistence on his father having a nurse was as much self-preservation as anything else. She felt sorry for him. His mother and a sister had died years before in a car accident, and Glenn was the only one left to deal with his cantankerous father. The fact that they had many business dealings together made things worse, though Glenn would never admit it.

"You're looking better this morning, Lawrence," Claire said. "Are you ready to get out of here?"

"I'd like a decent night's sleep, but as long as I'm in such pain, that's out of the question. And of course, the hospital's so damn noisy no one can sleep. Why the hell do they come in and wake you up every ten minutes?"

Claire exchanged glances with Glenn. Ignoring the latter part of his comments, she said, "Yes, broken bones are very painful. Did you have your pain medicine prescription filled?"

"My son was supposed to take care of that."

"We'll pick it up on the way home," Glenn said.

Lawrence was already sitting in the wheelchair, so she handed him his bag to put in his lap and led the way while

Glenn pushed him. As they passed the nurses station, she saw Jonas and smiled, prepared to go on by, but he stopped her. "Claire, do you have a minute?"

"Sure." She turned to tell Glenn and his father she'd catch up with them. Lawrence looked ghastly, his hands clenched white-knuckled on his overnight bag and his complexion a matching pasty white. Great, all they needed was for the man to have a heart attack. "Lawrence, are you in pain?"

"Of course he's in pain," Glenn said. "Look at his face." He bent down by his father. "Is it your head? The concussion? Or is it your heart?"

"No, I'm fine," he said. His color was coming back, but he still didn't look great.

He eyed Jonas with obvious dislike. "Who the hell are you?"

Jonas looked a little taken aback at the rude question, but answered him easily. "I'm Dr. Clark. And who are you?"

"This is my father-in-law, Lawrence Westbrook," Claire said, wanting to sink into the floor. "And this is my husband, Glenn."

Neither her husband nor his father made a move to shake Jonas's hand. Neither, she noticed, did Jonas hold out his hand. The tension was palpable and most of it emanated from Lawrence. What in the hell was going on with the man?

"Can I get back to you, Jonas? My father-in-law is being released today. I think he's anxious to get home."

"No problem. I just had a question about one of your patients." He nodded at the two men and walked off.

"Are you sure you're all right?" Claire asked Lawrence. Other than being angry, he looked fine now.

"Never mind that. Who the hell was that man?"

"He told you. He's Dr. Jonas Clark, one of our best neurosurgeons. Why were you so rude to him?"

"Black bastard doesn't belong in this hospital."

"Oh, for God's sake, can't you put your prejudice aside for once? He's a world-class neurosurgeon. He also saved your friend's life." She knew Lawrence was a bigot, which was only one of the reasons she didn't care for him. Ordinarily, he hid his prejudice better than he was doing now. "I don't appreciate your being rude to one of my colleagues."

"How dare you lecture my father?" Glenn said. "He's a patient at this hospital, a paying one, and he can say whatever he wants."

"You weren't much better," Claire said, unrepentant. Her pager went off, giving her the perfect excuse to leave them. "Sorry," she said, checking it. "I've got to get to the ER. You'll have to do this without me."

As she left, she heard Glenn say, "Are you sure you're all right? You looked like you'd seen a ghost."

"I did," Lawrence said. "The ghost of a black bastard I never thought I'd see again."

*COINCIDENCE, THAT'S all it was,* Lawrence told himself. There was no reason to flip out simply because a man looked like someone long dead.

There was no denying that Jonas Clark bore a strong resemblance to Calvin Davis. If Lawrence's memory wasn't playing tricks on him, and he didn't believe it was, Clark looked like a grown-up version of Davis. Maybe he was related to the bastard. And if he was, so what? Maybe nothing, but . . . better to know than to sit around wondering.

"Dad, are you all right?" Glenn asked. "You really gave me a scare in the hospital."

"I'm fine. I need a pen and paper."

"Both are in the glove compartment."

After opening the compartment, Lawrence reached in and pulled out paper and pen. He made note of what he wanted, then folded over the paper. "I want you to give this to my assistant right after you drop me off."

"Don't you want to just call him?"

"Goddamn it, can't you do one simple thing I ask? Give this to Leon. And tell him to hurry. I want this information yesterday." He wanted to know everything there was to know about Dr. Jonas Clark. His family, his history, everything. Knowledge was power, he'd always said. With any luck, he'd find out that Jonas Clark bore absolutely no relation to Calvin Davis.

"What's this about?"

"None of your business. Just give Leon my note."

Glenn sighed heavily. "All right. I'll see to it as soon as I get you settled. The nurse should meet us at your house in about an hour."

Now Lawrence simply had to wait until his assistant came through with the information. No reason to be concerned about something that happened more than fifty years before. Why worry simply because Jonas Clark looked like Calvin Davis would have looked had he lived past the age of eighteen?

JONAS DIDN'T HAVE time to think about anything other than work until he went home that evening. But as he lay in bed waiting for sleep, the scene with Claire and her husband and father-in-law came back to him. It wasn't as if he'd never had to deal with bigotry before, but he wasn't even Lawrence Westbrook's doctor. The man's reaction seemed excessive and out of place. As if he'd conceived an instant dislike for Jonas when Jonas was positive they'd never met before.

So why did he have this weird feeling that he knew the man?

*Fort Worth, Texas, September 1968*

CALVIN DAVIS INTENDED to get the hell out of Fort Worth, Texas, and he didn't mean to go by way of Vietnam. No, his ticket out was college deferment. Basketball, to be exact. Calvin was good, and he knew it. He intended to be so good that the University of Southern California would give him a free ride.

He had competition, yeah. But not only was Calvin good at basketball, he was a damn good student. And he should be hearing any day about his scholarship. Then he'd be out of Texas and out of the damn draft.

He was so busy dreaming about his scholarship he almost missed the pink '55 Caddy by the side of the road. He knew that car, and he knew that girl. Trouble, in the guise of a sexy brunette by the name of Isabel Cantrell. Every guy in school wanted to date her, and not many of them had managed to make it happen.

Isabel didn't date black guys. She didn't date many white ones, either, but when she did go out it was with someone her daddy would consider her social equal.

Her father, Buster Cantrell, owned Westside Bank, the largest privately owned bank in Fort Worth. Buster Cantrell had made a name for himself as the meanest son of a bitch Fort Worth had ever produced. And he didn't like colored folk, not one little bit. So it wasn't surprising that Isabel wouldn't date a black guy. Her old man would kill her if she did. Not to mention what he'd do to the boy.

But she was stuck by the side of the road, and there wasn't a soul in sight, and he'd bet his last nickel she didn't have idea one how to change that flat. So he pulled up behind her and got out. It wouldn't be right to ignore her. Besides, his mother had drilled it into his head that you never passed by a person in need without lending a helping hand.

"Need some help?"

Relief chased nerves across her face. Relief someone had stopped, nerves that it had been a black guy? It annoyed him —partly because he had to admit he'd had a fantasy going about her ever since he'd first set eyes on her. But he wouldn't hurt her, or any woman. She didn't know him, though, so she might not realize that.

"I have a flat," she said. "I'm Bella Cantrell. Don't I know you?"

Bella. It suited her, better than Isabel did. "Not really." He shrugged and added, "But I go to Paschal, too."

"I know who you are," she said, happy with her discovery. "You're Calvin Davis. Basketball. Our star guard."

Okay, that made his chest stick out a little. "I wouldn't say that." But he was glad she had.

"I would. I've watched you play. You're amazing."

Embarrassed, he ignored the flattery. "What's the problem here?"

"I don't suppose you can change a flat?" she asked, gesturing at the rear tire.

He gave her a look and said, "I need the trunk opened."

She went to the trunk and opened it. "I hope everything you need is in here, because I've never had to change a flat before."

No duh. Calvin felt her watching him as he muscled the spare out, then went for the jack.

"It was nice of you to stop. I've been sitting here half an hour and no one else has been by."

"What are you doing all the way out here anyway?" Calvin asked. He'd been coming back from his job in Grapevine but not many people traveled this road. "You're pretty much smack in the middle of nowhere."

She hunkered down beside him, which was pretty interesting since her skirt barely covered her butt. "Running away," she said easily.

He shot her a glance. "No shit?"

She laughed. "Well, no, but I wish I had been. I had a fight with my father, so I did what I always do and got as far out of town as I could. He doesn't like me to drive out of the city limits, so I do it to tick him off."

It wouldn't have surprised Calvin if her old man had sent the cops after her. "What was the fight about?" he asked, not really expecting her to answer. But she did.

"College. He wants me to go to TCU and live at home and I want to go anywhere else *but* there. I am not living with him. Not any longer than I absolutely have to."

"Good luck. You don't get along with your daddy, huh?"

"Nobody gets along with Buster Cantrell. Especially not his children."

He'd taken off all the lug nuts by now, and she held them, watching him closely as he took off the flat and put on the spare.

"My sister Sophie doesn't get along with him, either," she continued. "But she's better at hiding it than I am."

Calvin snorted. "No offense, but you live like a princess. Kinda hard to feel sorry for you."

"You have no idea," she said bleakly. Then she shook it off and added brightly, "Haven't you heard? Money doesn't buy everything."

"Maybe not, but it buys a hell of a lot." He thought about his mom working three jobs to support them when he was younger. Until he managed to start bringing in some money and she was able to quit one of them. Yeah, money would help.

"What's your dad like?" Bella asked.

"I don't know." He shrugged. "He took off when he heard my mom was pregnant."

"I'm sorry."

"No big deal. My mom's enough." He grinned, thinking about his mother. Fay Davis made damn sure he toed the line. Bella handed him a lug nut, and swear to God, his hand tingled where she'd touched it. Startled, he met her eyes. She'd felt it too, he could tell by her expression. Weird.

They talked some more, Bella telling him more about her plan to escape. He didn't say it, but he didn't think she had a hope in hell of getting out from under her old man's thumb. He finished up, conscious of a feeling of regret that she'd be driving off and out of his life. "That should last you until you can drop the flat off at the gas station."

"Thank you so much," she said, wiping her hands on the back of that tiny skirt. She held one out to him, and he took it. And damn, there it was again. That feeling of . . . connection. He got lost in her eyes. They were different, like nothing he'd seen before. One green, the other half-green, half-blue. Weird, but beautiful.

He knew for a fact he hadn't seen them before, so why did they seem so familiar?

"Calvin?" she said. "Would you like to go to a movie with me Friday night?"

No girl had ever asked Calvin out. Oh, they'd made it plain they wouldn't mind going out with him, but no one had ever dared to actually ask him. And sure as hell no girl like Isabel Cantrell. A white girl. A rich white girl.

Calvin shook his head. "I'm sure your daddy would love that." And it hit him, left a nasty feeling in his gut. "You'll have to find another way to get to the old man."

She flushed, then grew angry. "That isn't why I asked you."

"Sure it isn't."

"It isn't," she insisted. "Don't you feel it?"

What he felt was pissed.

"Don't you feel the connection? I mean, I know it's the first time we've ever talked but I feel like I know you. And you know me."

Maybe he did. "That doesn't mean I'm going out with a white girl whose father thinks blacks are one step lower than dog shit."

"I'm not my father. And he doesn't have to know. We can go to a drive-in or something."

He was crazy to even consider it. But damn, she was pretty. She obviously wanted a little walk on the wild side. A colored boy dating a white girl . . . risky. Very risky. Was he willing to take the chance? If her father found out, he'd get the hell beat out of him. At least. She smiled at him, waiting for an answer.

"I'll meet you at the Twin. Do you know it?" he said.

"No, but I'll find it."

He gave her the address. "Nine o'clock, Friday."

She smiled. "See you there," she said and slid her sweet little butt into that pink Caddy. He watched as she pulled out and drove off, giving a little wave of her hand out the window.

Oh, man. He bet dollars to donuts she wouldn't show. But if she did . . . . This date had *mistake* written all over it. He knew he'd be there.

But would Bella?

# CHAPTER FIVE

*September Present Day*

CLAIRE SMILED AT Jonas as he walked through the ER. Since their impromptu breakfast, she'd thought about him a lot. Her odd dreams had increased in number as well. She wondered if there was a connection, but didn't see why there would be. It wasn't as if she were dreaming about Jonas, after all. No, she dreamed of people she didn't know. People who had lived in a previous century. A woman named Sarah and a man named Elijah. A man who happened to look astonishingly like Jonas.

How weird was that?

"Admit it," Lanie said. "You're hot for the man."

"Hot for who?" Claire asked, though since she'd just been gazing at Jonas like a lovesick puppy, she didn't need to ask.

"You know who. Dr. Jonas Hottie."

Claire shot her an annoyed look. "I am not hot for anyone, least of all Jonas Clark. I merely said he was good looking." Why she'd admitted that much to Lanie, she didn't know.

Lanie's memory was phenomenal. She never forgot anything, even if you wished she would. No, make that *especially* if you wished she would forget.

"I'll say. All the single women are making plans to snare him. And some of the married ones." She smiled. "He's into you, too. I can tell."

"I'm married," Claire reminded her. "Besides, I hardly know the man." She refused to tell Lanie about the breakfast she and Jonas had shared. Lord knows what her friend would make of that outing. Claire wasn't sure what to make of it herself. It had been a perfectly innocent meeting, so why did she feel guilty?

Because she wanted more?

Jonas seemed strangely familiar, but she was certain she had never met him until recently. Not in high school or anywhere else. Determinedly, she went back to her charts, unsuccessfully trying to ignore her friend as well as the questions swirling about in her head.

"Sometimes you just know. Instantly. That's the way I felt about Joe."

Claire glanced up and glared at her. "What part of *I'm married* don't you get?"

Lanie waved a hand. "Unhappily married."

"Regardless, I've never cheated and I don't intend to start now. All this is beside the point, anyway. Jonas hasn't made a move on me or anything approaching it."

"Oh, please," Lanie held up a hand, interrupting her. "It doesn't take a genius to read between the lines. He's interested. You're interested. You've been unhappy since the day you married Glenn Westbrook. Do something about it."

"All marriages go through rough patches."

"Honey, as far as I can tell, you've never had much of anything but a rough patch."

Claire closed her eyes. "If I admit that there are problems, then I have to do something about it."

"So?"

Do something. Like ask for a divorce? It wouldn't be the end of the world. But it would mean admitting defeat. Admitting she'd made a colossal mistake.

Lanie continued impatiently. "Claire, you made a mistake. People do."

"I don't see how I could have been so wrong about Glenn. About the two of us."

"What's he done now?"

It was what he hadn't done. When they'd begun having problems early in the marriage, Claire had suggested counseling. Glenn had vetoed it then, and every other time she'd suggested it. By now their marriage was so bad that Glenn hadn't touched her in months. Not that she wanted him to, but it was hard to try to save a relationship when you slept in separate bedrooms and neither party seemed interested in fixing that. She'd been the one to move out, but he hadn't argued.

"The marriage isn't working," she finally admitted. "Hasn't in a long time."

"Is this because of Jonas?"

"Of course not. I told you, there's nothing between Jonas and me." Which was a big fat lie. There was clearly something there. She just didn't know what. He was so damn familiar. Sometimes she even felt as if she knew what it was like to kiss him, which was clearly insane. "Have you ever experienced déjà vu?"

Lanie accepted the apparent change of subject. She must

have decided she'd pushed Claire as far as she should for one day. "Sure. Why?"

"No, I mean, a real déjà vu." She tried to explain that it wasn't the same as those nebulous experiences everyone has and calls déjà vu. "I'm talking about a feeling, no, a knowledge, that something has happened before."

"Everybody has those, Claire."

Clearly she wasn't getting through to Lanie. "This is different." She couldn't explain it, but what she was experiencing was unlike anything that had happened to her before.

"Does this déjà vu have to do with Jonas?"

She nodded. "I feel as if I've known him before."

"You said you both grew up around here. Maybe you met him. When you two were younger."

"No. I'd remember. I think he would too. But damn, I feel as if I know him. Really know him. Not just casually, either. Like we were involved." *Lovers.* "It's a spooky feeling." Made even spookier by those dreams she'd begun having. Dreams of a place and time long ago, and a man who looked so much like Jonas. Waking up with tears streaming down her face. A sorrow too deep to bear.

She was going crazy. Obviously.

***Rachel's Journal—April 2, 1859***

*Many people down here have heard of the Underground Railroad. But they think of it as a northern thing. Very few, besides the slave catchers, realize there is another Underground Railroad. One that runs from Texas to Mexico. Many Southerners think it is wrong to help people escape the bonds of slavery. They cite disaster for plantation owners and have many reasons to justify the owning of another human being. Perhaps it's my father's influence, but I cannot believe this is right. And my dear husband, Ben, agrees. But then, he comes from the North, where slavery is not tolerated as well.*

*How did I get involved in such a thing? Through my father. By chance, when I discovered him helping a slave to flee. He swore me to secrecy, would not even let me tell my sister, Sarah. But the time has come to talk to Sarah. I know she feels the same as I do. We have talked about the evils of slavery. How she can live with that monster of a husband, I do not know. I curse the day Father—and I—allowed her to marry him.*

*But we need help, and Sarah can offer it. Her husband's plantation sits in a strategic location. Add to that the fact that Victor is often away, and it is perfect. Yet I do fear for Sarah if she were to be caught offering help to the slaves. Would Victor harm her, his own wife? It must be up to Sarah to decide if it is worth the risk.*

Reluctantly, Claire closed the journal. As fascinating as it was, she needed to get to sleep. A dreamless sleep, preferably.

***April 1859***

"RACHEL, WHAT IS IT?" Sarah asked as soon as the servants left the parlor. "I'm happy to see you but you usually let me know you're coming."

"I had something to talk to you about and I wanted to make sure Victor was not home when I did."

"You saw him in town, I take it."

"At the store." Rachel rolled her eyes. "Never mind him. I wanted to talk to you about something important. More important than anything else we shall ever do." She looked around and not seeing anyone, lowered her voice. "Not that I expect your slaves will talk, but we must be careful."

"Careful about what?"

"Have you heard of the Underground Railroad?"

Sarah stared at her. "Of course I have. That's what they call it when they help slaves get away. Up north. What has that to do with us?"

"It's not only up north. We have one right here in Texas too. Only most of our slaves go west, or south to Mexico."

Rachel and the Underground Railroad? Sarah had never imagined such a thing. Their father was sympathetic to the abolitionists, but would he go so far as to be involved in smuggling slaves to freedom? "Rachel, are you involved in this? Does Ben know? Are you crazed? They hang white folks who help the darkies escape."

"You know Father is sympathetic to the slaves."

"I know, but I did not know Ben was."

"Ben is an abolitionist. He has been since before I married him."

"Ben is—your husband is an abolitionist?" Rachel hushed her, and she lowered her voice. "Good Lord, does Father know?"

"Yes, of course he does. We have all been helping the slaves for some time now. But we need more help. And I thought of you." Another quick glance at the door to the parlor. "Father and Ben do not know I came to ask you. They never would allow it. They fear your husband."

"With good reason. You know what he's like. I can't. Rachel, Victor would kill me if he found out." She thought of how Victor had reacted to her intervention when he "disciplined" one of his slaves. He'd given the man twice as many lashes. She'd learned not to interfere, only when she knew Victor was gone would she check on the slaves and do what she could to help them. But escape? No matter her personal beliefs, she couldn't afford to help escaped slaves.

But how could she not? It was the moral thing to do. How

could she stand by while all sorts of atrocities were committed, many of them by her own husband. What if she could help?

"What would I need to do?"

Rachel grasped her hand and squeezed. "I knew I could count on you."

"I'll try, but we can't let a whisper of this get out to Victor." To find his wife helping fugitive slaves and abolitionists. She didn't want to imagine his reaction.

But she never had believed in the slave trade, never believed a person had the right to own another. No matter what Victor and his like said, the color of skin didn't make a person an animal. And nothing could ever, in her opinion, make slavery right.

*September Present Day*

JONAS COULDN'T SHAKE the feeling that he knew Claire. Especially since their breakfast together. But try as he might, he couldn't remember meeting her. That feeling sure as hell didn't stop him from wanting to know her better. If anything, it made the desire more urgent. He wondered what it would be like to kiss her. If he touched her again, if he kissed her, would he have another of those weird . . . well, shit. He didn't even know what to call the thing that had happened at breakfast. A flashback? But he hadn't been the one sitting there in the diner. And the girl—it hadn't been Claire sitting across from him.

Okay, he'd had some sort of odd déjà vu—flashback thing. Even that bothered him to admit. He was a doctor. That sort of thing was for flaky people who believed in a bunch of psychic crap and the like. He was a scientist. A believer in what you could prove. Give him a scalpel, let him cut into a brain, and he was good. Sure, things happened that you couldn't explain in medicine as well as life. Déjà vu? No fucking way.

He'd been dreaming a lot lately. Generally he remembered his dreams but these were just out of reach when he awakened. He'd wake up feeling disturbed with only flashes of memory about the dream. A young white girl. A young black boy. The teenagers from the diner. But that was all that stayed with him.

He'd never had strange dreams until recently. He didn't care for it. Not one damn bit.

But none of that really pertained to his current dilemma. Claire Westbrook was married. Unhappily married, that was clear. God knows, he didn't want to be involved with a married woman. He'd been there, done that once before. Leslie had sworn she was getting divorced, and he'd been fool enough to believe her. She hadn't, of course. The whole affair had been an unmitigated disaster. One he sure as hell didn't intend to repeat.

Therefore, until and unless her status changed, he needed to get Claire out of his mind. He knew just the way, and the woman, to do it.

*GODDAMMIT, WAS nowhere safe?*

Jonas stared at the trio of people headed toward his table. Claire, her husband, and some other man. Claire looked beautiful, as usual. In scrubs she was pretty. In street clothes, a sleek, sleeveless, short black number, she was a knockout. She looked as startled to see him as he was to see her.

This was carrying coincidence too far. Why did Claire and her husband have to choose the very restaurant Jonas had decided on in his quest to get the damned woman off his mind?

Claire said something to her husband, who shot Jonas an ugly glance before turning away. She came over to his table while her husband and the other man went to their own table.

"Hello, Jonas. No, don't get up."

Ignoring her, Jonas stood and introduced his date, Chamika. "Chamika Rollins, Dr. Claire Westbrook."

The women shook hands, and Jonas continued to stand. "Do you eat here often?" he asked.

"No, Glenn's client suggested it. He says it's excellent."

They chatted briefly. She smiled at Chamika and said, "I won't keep you. Good to see you, Jonas."

Jonas watched her go. *What are the odds*? he asked himself.

"It's none of my business," Chamika said when he sat down, "but did you two date? In the past?"

Surprised, Jonas turned to her. "No, we're colleagues. I've only known her a few weeks. Why do you ask?"

Chamika shrugged an elegant shoulder. "It feels like there's something going on between you two. Big-time vibes. I thought she might be an ex."

They went on to talk of other things, and Jonas did his best to keep his attention on his date and off Dr. Claire Westbrook. For the most part, he succeeded.

"The restaurant was wonderful," Chamika said when he took her home. "Is it new?"

"No, it's been here a long time." He parked at her apartment. Nine thirty, and it was still hot. It was fall, for Chrissake. Wouldn't the heat ever end?

"Would you like to come in?" Chamika asked Jonas.

Code. They both knew what she meant. They had gone out a few times in Boston, but for one reason or another they'd never made it to the bedroom. He wasn't sure why. At first, she'd been the one being cautious. Now he was. Unlike most of his single friends, he didn't take every woman he dated to bed. Maybe most of them, but still. Chamika was a beautiful woman. Tall, black, gorgeous. Any man would be lucky to have her in his bed. She had brains to go with that beautiful body, too. She said she didn't intend to stay a model forever and was socking away her earnings to start her own agency.

Why was he being even more cautious than usual? He liked Chamika. A lot. He'd decided nothing was going to happen with Claire, which left him free to take advantage of a relationship with a very desirable woman. He took Chamika's hand and followed her inside. Kissed her at the door. And again as she led him toward her bedroom. He backed her up against the bedroom door, filled his hands with her breasts and looked into her eyes. Dark, beautiful, inviting.

He closed his eyes for a moment and saw another woman's eyes. One green eye, one half-green, half-blue. Claire's eyes. Damn it!

His beeper went off, meaning the hospital wanted something. He'd much rather answer to a pager than phone calls. Instead of being pissed, he had an overwhelming feeling of relief. He dropped his hands and backed away. "Sorry," he muttered and checked the number.

"Is that the hospital? I thought you weren't working tonight?" She hadn't bothered to adjust her clothes. She looked gorgeous, and sexily rumpled. Oddly enough, it wasn't doing a thing for him.

"I'm back-up call. Dr. Zekial must have caught a case." He could probably take care of things with a phone call, but Chamika didn't know that. "Sorry. I have to go in."

Chamika didn't pout. She was too classy for that. Besides,

she probably didn't realize that their relationship was going nowhere.

But he did. And Claire Westbrook was the reason why.

GOD, CLAIRE HAD thought dinner would never end. Glenn's client had spent the night not so subtly hitting on her. Glenn hadn't even noticed, or if he had, it hadn't bothered him. And if that wasn't bad enough, she'd had to spend the evening trying not to watch Jonas with his date. Chamika was a very beautiful woman who had to be a model. Normal women didn't look that good. Claire wondered if they were serious.

*Not your concern*, she told herself.

She changed into her pajamas, a T-shirt and soft, baggy pants, then went to the kitchen, trying to decide between a cup of Sleepytime tea or something stronger. She sighed and reached for the tea. Another glass of wine would only give her a headache.

"Since when are you best buddies with a black man?"

She turned around to see her husband standing behind her. He'd had several drinks tonight and looked it. He'd ripped off his tie and unbuttoned the top two buttons of his dress shirt. His eyes were bloodshot, his expression peevish.

"Excuse me?"

He gestured with the drink he must have poured when they got home. "It doesn't look right."

"What doesn't look right?" She was truly baffled.

"You're married. And white. It doesn't look good to have you cozying up to a black man."

"You mean Jonas? Jonas Clark?"

"Yeah, that's him. The black son of a bitch I met in the hospital."

"I wasn't cozying up to him," Claire said. "He's one of my colleagues and I merely stopped to speak to him. Besides, I hardly think a conversation with a man and his date in a restaurant constitutes *cozying up*."

"You're my wife," Glenn said pompously and took a slug of his drink. "As such your behavior should be exemplary. Harold Brimmer is an important client. A married white woman hanging around a black man is not something I want my clients to see."

"Are you kidding me? Did you seriously just say that?"

"I don't think it's too much to ask that you behave with some decorum. You are my wife."

"Not for long if you continue in this vein."

His eyes flashed, and he took a step toward her. "Don't push me, Claire. Why do you think my client was hitting on you?"

"So you did notice that. I assumed because Harold Brimmer is an ass. And because you, my husband, didn't do a damn thing to stop him. Or even try to discourage him."

"He thinks you're a slut. I'm beginning to wonder as well."

She stared at him incredulously. "You've lost your mind. All this because I talked to a man in a restaurant?"

"It was the way you did it. To make matters worse, you stared at that black bastard like a lovesick whore through the rest of dinner. Jesus, I could have killed you." He slammed his empty glass down on the kitchen table.

"Are you channeling your father? When did you become such a bigot? This conversation is absurd, not to mention, extremely offensive to me."

He grabbed her arms and shook her. "Goddamn it, I won't

have it. You're my wife and you should show me some respect."

"Let go of me right now." He'd never laid a hand on her before, but for the first time she wondered if he would hurt her.

His eyes narrowed, and his grip tightened. "Let go," she repeated softly. "Unless you want me to see a divorce attorney tomorrow."

He dropped his hands, slowly. "Don't be such a drama queen, Claire." He left the room.

Claire drew in a shaky breath. She'd never before mentioned divorce, but Glenn had never before behaved like a jealous fool. What in the hell had come over him? Acting as if talking to a man was a crime. He'd witnessed two conversations between her and Jonas. Two very brief, very public conversations. He had no idea of the breakfast she'd shared with Jonas, or of the connection she felt to the man. No idea how attracted she was to Jonas Clark.

To all outward appearances, they were colleagues, nothing more.

She was married to an irrational bigot. And she was so clueless, it had taken her six years of marriage to realize that fact.

# CHAPTER SIX

AS SOON AS HE left Chamika, Jonas called the hospital and took care of his page. As he'd thought, he didn't need to go in. He went home, turned on the TV, and thought about Claire. Damn, why did she intrigue him so much? What was it about her? He lay down on the couch and since the movie was boring, closed his eyes and fell asleep.

***September 1968***

"THERE'S A LAKE I found one time when I was hiding from my father," Bella said. They'd met in one of their usual places, a small park where he could leave his truck and drive around with Bella. Or just stay in her car and talk, which is what they were doing now.

"What lake? Eagle Mountain?"

"No, it's small. Not much more than a pond, but I call it Dream Lake. It's not far from here. Near the Trinity River, not far from downtown."

"Do you run away from your old man often?"

"All the time. When I was little I wanted his attention. Now I wish he'd go back to ignoring me."

"What does he want you to do?"

She laughed. "Be a good girl, marry a suitable boy, and raise little Cantrells."

"They wouldn't be Cantrells, though, would they?"

"To him they would. Besides, I wouldn't put it past him to pay my future husband to change his name to Cantrell. But I don't want to talk about him. Let's go to the lake, Calvin."

Alone with Bella at the lake. Yeah, that sounded like trouble. But tempting. God, so tempting. He shouldn't, but he found himself wavering. "When do you have to be home?"

"I told him I was spending the night at Gail's. But her parents are gone so I can get there whenever I want."

"Does Gail know about us? Does she know we're dating?"

"She knows. She thinks it's exciting."

"She doesn't care that I'm black?"

"Gail isn't prejudiced. She says she has abolitionists in her heritage, and they'd rise from the dead if she was prejudiced."

"Have you thought about what will happen when your old man finds out?" He didn't think the old man would kill him, but he couldn't be completely sure.

"Calvin, don't you want to be with me?"

"Yeah."

"Then stop questioning everything. Stop worrying so much. We'll work it out." She took his hand, then glanced around, though the park was deserted at this hour. Then she leaned in and kissed him.

He was lost. God, how could it feel so good, so different with Bella than with any other girl? Why did she seem so familiar? Like he'd held her before, kissed her before. And more.

"Do you ever have déjà vu?" he asked her when the kiss ended.

"You mean when we kiss?"

"Yeah."

"Every time. Funny, isn't it? I didn't know you felt it too. I was afraid to say anything. Afraid you'd think I was silly."

"If you are so am I." He kissed her again. Slid into her mouth like in a dream. Like coming home.

"I have a blanket in my trunk."

"I don't know, Bella. Maybe we shouldn't."

"Sometimes I think you're scared of me, Calvin. Not just of my dad, but of me."

He couldn't argue. She terrified him. It scared him that because of her he'd ignore his opportunities. That he'd never get out of this place, unless he did it by way of 'Nam. And he wasn't going there. Slowly, he said, "The way you make me feel . . . I've never felt this way before."

"Neither have I." She looked at him and smiled. "Maybe it's fate. Do you believe in fate, Calvin?"

***October Present Day***

SOMETIME DURING the night, Jonas exchanged the couch for his bed. He woke with the same feeling he had nearly every morning now. Knowing he'd dreamed but not remembering what the dreams were about. What the hell was going on? He was a man who liked to be in control, and nothing about these dreams was controllable, including whether he remembered them or not.

They're just weird dreams, he told himself. No reason to get bent out of shape over a dream he couldn't even remember.

TWO DAYS LATER, Lanie had a party.

Jonas hadn't intended to go, and in fact, wasn't sure why he'd come. Probably because Lanie, part bulldog if he'd ever known one, had twisted his arm until he'd agreed. Not that he minded parties, he just hadn't been sure that a roomful of people he worked with was exactly what he needed on his night off. Although, he'd met Lanie's boyfriend, Joe Montlake, an orthopedist who worked independently out of Shady Grove as well as another hospital. He seemed like a decent enough guy, for a Mavericks fan.

But mostly he'd gone because he knew Claire would be there.

"Hi, Jonas. Glad you made it. Lanie wasn't sure you would."

*Speak of the devil.*

He turned to look at Claire. She was wearing a short skirt and a silky blue top that hugged her breasts and emphasized the odd colors of her eyes. It was a good thing she wore scrubs most of the times he saw her, because she was dangerously hot in non-work clothes.

"She threatened dire things if I didn't come."

"Really. Like what?" She took a sip of her wine and smiled, waiting for his answer.

"She didn't specify. Just promised I'd be sorry."

Claire laughed. "Knowing Lanie, you probably would."

"Is your husband with you?" His brief encounter with Glenn Westbrook the other day hadn't impressed Jonas, but he gave the man the benefit of the doubt. Lawrence Westbrook was another subject. Jonas could do without seeing him again. The older man had touched a nerve, though

Jonas had come up against bigots before. The most disturbing thing about that meeting had been the feeling that he knew him. Lawrence, not Glenn. Absurd, but there it was.

He brushed the thought aside as Claire responded to his question.

"No. Glenn and Lanie can't stand each other. They're rarely in the same room voluntarily."

"Wasn't she his father's orthopedist?"

"Yes. Much to their mutual irritation. Glenn nearly had a cow until he figured out he had no choice."

"Are you and Lanie close?"

"Very. She's my best friend."

He raised an eyebrow. "That must be tough to have your best friend and husband dislike each other so much."

She shrugged. "Glenn's not big on socializing with my friends anyway. He's a real estate attorney and he often works evenings." She looked over at the table, teeming with food. "Have you had some of the shrimp? It's great."

"I was about to go over there."

"If I can have everyone's attention, we have an announcement," Lanie's boyfriend, Joe, said.

Joe took Lanie's hand and smiled at her. "Lanie has agreed to marry me."

After a lot of whistling and cheering and backslapping and kissing, Jonas looked at Claire. She was watching her friend with a curious expression on her face. Happy, but wistful at the same time.

"What's wrong, don't you like engagements?"

"Of course I do. I'm happy for them."

He simply raised a brow.

"I am," she insisted. "I'm—oh, hell," she muttered and took

another sip of her drink. "If I tell you something, you can't repeat it."

Jonas crossed his heart with a finger and waited.

"I'm jealous. Oh, not because she's marrying Joe. They're perfect for each other. But they're so happy . . ." her voice trailed off.

"And you're not." She didn't have to hold up a sign for him to get that.

She sighed but didn't agree or disagree. "It's not something I talk about often. Or to casual acquaintances for that matter."

"Is that what we are?"

"I don't know. What are we?"

"Friends?" he hazarded.

"We don't know each other very well."

"We could change that." Of course, he didn't want to be her friend. He wanted more.

"I could use another friend," she admitted. "One who's more objective."

Objective? Him? About Claire's husband? Right.

"Lanie isn't rational on the subject of Glenn," Claire continued. "She doesn't understand why I don't divorce him and get on with my life."

"At the risk of being too much like her, why the hell don't you? You're clearly unhappy." From what little he'd seen of her husband, he didn't blame her.

"Have you ever been married?"

"No."

"It's not that easy to admit you made a mistake and possibly should never have married someone. I made vows. They meant something to me." She was quiet a moment and added, "I keep thinking things will get better."

"And how's that working for you?"

She laughed unhappily. "Not well. He won't admit there's anything wrong." She looked at her glass, which was empty. "But you didn't come here to hear my marital woes. And I need another drink."

"Coming right up." If she needed a shoulder, he thought as he refilled her glass, he was willing. Even if it probably wasn't a good idea to offer one to the woman you wanted to take to bed.

But if she got rid of the husband, then that was one big obstacle out of the way.

"THE PARTY'S WINDING down," Jonas said to Claire some time later. "Do you want to go get a drink? A cup of coffee or something?"

She shouldn't. She really shouldn't. She'd already spent most of the evening with him. God, if Glenn got wind of that no telling what he'd do. But she was so enjoying being with a man who talked to her, who listened. Who seemed to appreciate what she had to say.

Unlike her husband.

"Just coffee," Jonas added with a smile.

"All right. There's a place not far from here. La Costa."

"Mexican? For coffee?"

"It's a little bit of a dive, but they have good coffee. Good food, too. It's open late. We used to go there when we were kids. Didn't you?"

"Maybe the white kids did but my friends didn't."

"Where did you go?"

"Ol' South Pancake House. Or if we were trying to score drinks, the Bluebird Lounge."

She laughed and shook her head, then gave him the address. "I'll meet you there."

On the way she asked herself why she felt so guilty. She was meeting a friend for coffee. A very attractive friend of the opposite sex. Claire didn't cheat. At least, she never had before. She'd never been tempted, no matter how unhappy she'd been.

Until she met Jonas.

Jonas had arrived before her and gotten them a table in the corner. They'd both ordered decaf coffees.

"They make a mean margarita, too," Claire said. "But I had my limit at the party, and I have to work tomorrow."

"Yeah, me too."

"Do you ever wonder what would have happened if we'd met back when we were in high school?" Claire asked Jonas. "Maybe we did meet and just don't remember it."

"No. I'd have remembered you." He looked her over and smiled. "Someone who looks like you? Oh, yeah, I'd remember you."

Claire laughed. "Flatterer. How do you know what I looked like in high school?"

"What did you look like, Claire?"

"Younger. Chubbier. But pretty much the same." She sipped coffee. "I'm positive I'd remember you, too. Do you look a lot different than you did in high school?"

He grinned, his teeth a flash of white. "My hair's shorter and I've filled out but basically I look the same."

"Were you a jock?" He sure looked like an athlete.

"Nope. I played basketball my freshman year, but there were others a lot more talented than me. I decided hitting the books was my ticket, not sports."

"You could have done both. Joe, Lanie's fiancé, was a football star in high school and college. I don't know why he didn't go pro. I guess he decided medicine suited him better."

"That's what I decided. Speaking of your friend Lanie, why do she and your husband dislike each other?"

She set down her cup and grimaced. "Dislike is a mild word. They detest each other."

"Do you know why?"

"No. Neither of them will say. Although they're both outspoken about their feelings, they won't tell me why. Lanie's especially vocal. Glenn says she's trying to undermine our marriage." She laughed unhappily. "I told him we were doing that without anyone's help." God knows that was true. "I've always wondered if—" she broke off and shrugged. What was it about him that made her so chatty? She was never this open with people she didn't know well. Or people she knew well, for that matter.

"If there was more to it," he hazarded. "Can you pinpoint when she started hating him, or has she always disliked him?"

"Funny you should ask that. Shortly after we married, we were living in San Antonio. Glenn was going to law school. Lanie came to visit and stayed with us. I was a resident, and you know what those hours are like. I went to bed early. Lanie left the next day. She was supposed to stay but she said she had an emergency come up."

"That's when it all started?"

"I think so. I don't remember it being bad before that. Maybe I never noticed, though."

"You're thinking he hit on her and she shut him down."

"I think he might have. It makes sense." She'd tried to ignore her uneasiness, but she'd always wondered. "Why wouldn't she tell me, though? Do you suppose she thought I wouldn't believe her?"

He shrugged. "It happens. Maybe she was afraid it would wreck your friendship. Was he drinking?"

She nodded. "They both were. I didn't because I had to work the next day. I went to bed early and they stayed up and drank. I didn't think anything of it." At the time.

"Are you sure it wasn't the other way around? Maybe Lanie did something she's not too proud of."

"No, not Lanie. She would never betray me. Drunk or sober."

"But your husband would."

She didn't answer. But then, he hadn't voiced it as a question.

"Maybe he threatened her," Jonas continued. "Threatened to screw with your friendship if she told you."

"I don't know. I just don't know."

"You could ask her. But really, why does it matter now? Your problems with your husband are in the here and now. Not something he might or might not have done years ago."

"True, but it would prove again how wrong I was about him."

"And you need proof you were wrong? Before you can do anything?"

Claire shrugged but didn't answer.

"Why now?" he asked.

"What do you mean?"

"I'm sensing this isn't a new problem. So why now? Has he done something recently that pissed you off?"

Claire bit her lip. "Not pissed me off. Not exactly."

Jonas waited, saying nothing.

"We haven't been getting along well for a long time. He's been especially strange since we ran into you at the hospital. And again after dinner the other night, he . . . damn, I don't know what came over him. He flipped out over me talking to you. He became totally, irrationally jealous."

"Jealous of me? Of you and me?"

She nodded.

"That is weird. Especially since I was there with a date."

"I pointed that out."

"Did you tell him there's nothing going on between us?"

"Yes." She met his eyes. "Even though that's a lie."

There was a long silence before Jonas asked quietly, "Is it?"

"You know it is," she said. "Every time we touch, something happens. There's a connection between us. We both feel it." She put out her hand and waited.

He took her hand. Rubbed his thumb over her palm. She met his eyes and lost herself in them.

Oh, yes, they were connected. She didn't know how, she didn't know why, but she was absolutely sure that she and Jonas Clark had known each other before.

JONAS WAS NOT a fanciful man. In fact, more than one woman had told him he had an amazing lack of imagination. So if it wasn't his imagination, what the hell were these weird moments he had whenever he touched Claire? Flashes of feelings he couldn't pin down. Flashes of dreams, the dreams he'd had almost nightly since he'd met Claire.

They're just dreams, he thought. So why couldn't he remember them? Why was the only thing he remembered a couple of teenagers, one white, one black? He couldn't even remember their names.

It was enough to make him not want to sleep. Which was ridiculous. He wouldn't allow some weird moments and even weirder wisps of dreams to bother him. He got into bed and willed himself to sleep, but his last conscious thought, despite himself, was of Claire's eyes. Beautiful. Different. He knew those eyes. . . .

*October 1968*

"BELLA, WHAT ARE you doing here?" Calvin hadn't realized she even knew where he lived, much less expected to see her show up at his house.

"I didn't know where else to go."

Even with the porch light on, he couldn't see her clearly. The rain was coming down in sheets and she was wrapped up in a hooded raincoat that enveloped her entire upper body. Before he could decide what to do, he heard his mother behind him.

"Let the girl in, Calvin. I know I taught you some manners."

Great. He wasn't ready for his mom to meet Bella. He doubted she'd approve of him dating a white girl. Especially one related to Buster Cantrell. His mom considered the wealthy banker to be one of the dregs of humanity.

"No, thank you, Mrs. Davis," Bella said. "I don't want to impose."

"No such thing. Come on in, child." Fay was already drawing her inside. "Let me have your coat."

Bella took it off and gave it to her, then stood shivering, looking like a drowned rat with her hair hanging down her back in a sodden mess. She must have gone out in the rain before she put on her coat.

"Go get the child some towels, Calvin. And bring a blanket, too."

"What's wrong, Bella?" He did as his mother asked, running to the bathroom quickly and returning with the towels. As Bella dried off, he grabbed a blanket from the couch and wrapped it around her. She'd yet to look at him. As he led her into the den, she raised her head, and he got his first clear look at her face.

He couldn't stop the gasp. Or the suspicion that he knew what was coming. His mother said nothing, simply took her arm and allowed her to sit on the ancient sofa.

"My father's not happy with me." The entire left side of her face was swollen, her eye already purpling. Her beautiful eyes, bruised and battered.

Calvin felt a helpless rage that her father could use her so, and that Calvin couldn't do a damn thing about it. "Why? Why did he do this?"

Still quiet, his mother didn't speak, but left the room to return with a bag of frozen peas. "This will keep the swelling down," she told her, then sat on her other side. "Unless you think we need a doctor."

Bella shook her head. "No, it's just bruises. Nothing I haven't had before," she added bitterly.

"What can we do to help?" Fay asked.

If his mother was surprised that an unknown girl, a white one at that, had showed up at their house asking for help, she didn't reveal it. But he wouldn't put it past Fay to know about him and Bella anyway. Fay Davis had channels. She knew about everything, or almost everything, that went on in the community. The black community, anyway.

"Nothing." Bella shivered convulsively. "No one can do anything. We've been going round and round about college. At first he was convinced I should go to TCU and live at home, but now he's decided I have to go to Sarah Lawrence. I've begged and begged but he doesn't care what I want."

Calvin started to ask if her father knew about the two of them, but on the chance that his mother didn't, he changed the question. "Has he heard something about you? Something that upset him? Is that why he wants to send you so far away?"

"No," she shook her head vehemently. "If he knew about you and me he'd kill me. He wouldn't just slap me around. Tonight he hit me because I told him I wouldn't go to Sarah Lawrence, I'd run away first. So he said we'd see about that."

Fay looked at Calvin with an expression that let him know he was in for it later. But he couldn't be concerned about his mom now. Right now he was sick with worry about Bella.

"Does he do this every time you don't do what he wants?" Calvin asked.

"Every time." She looked up at him, her eyes brimming with tears. "I don't want to leave you, Calvin."

"You don't have to," Cal said, regardless of his mother's presence. "We'll figure something out."

It wasn't an empty promise. Cal was going to do anything necessary to make sure Bella didn't have to live with that child-beating bastard for long.

# CHAPTER SEVEN

**October Present Day**

FORTUNATELY, GLENN had gone to bed when Claire returned home, so she didn't have to deal with him. She was still uneasy over the time she'd spent with Jonas. When she touched him—it wasn't normal. These feelings she had for him were not reasonable. And while Jonas hadn't said anything at the restaurant, she knew he'd felt something too.

But he wouldn't speak of it. In fact, he'd made an excuse to leave shortly afterward. Because he was uncomfortable?

That damn journal beckoned her. It was almost as if it had a mystic force to it, one that drew her in. She was tired. She didn't need to read more and chance . . . dreams.

*You're a doctor, a scientist,* she berated herself. *It's just a fluke. Read the damn thing. Nothing strange is going to happen.* She picked it up, cracked it open at random. The words jumped out at her.

***Rachel's Journal—April 18, 1859***

*Sarah came to me today in tears. Her husband, Victor, had her servant whipped.*

*She tried to stop him and received a fist in her face for her trouble. He said Celia, her servant, had sassed him. He said she was lucky to only receive five lashes. We all know Celia would never have dared sass the man. He revels in his power over those more helpless than he. Victor Lawrence has no compunction harming slaves, treating them as animals, or worse. It is rumored he has killed more than one slave, and no one has ever called him to account. Oh, how I abhor this world of slavery! If Victor knew that Celia was a freedwoman he would likely kill her. How Sarah keeps such secrets, I do not know.*

Claire closed the journal. And slept.

***April 1859***

"YOU ALWAYS SEEM to come to my rescue," Sarah told Elijah. "This is the second time Peaches has come up lame, and here you are."

He didn't say anything, just knelt down by Peaches's head and picked up the horse's foot to look at her front hoof. "There's a stone in her hoof. I'll see to gettin' it out." He got up to pull some sort of tool from his pocket and then knelt again beside the mare.

Sarah knelt down beside him. "Poor thing. I didn't notice she was limping until a short while ago. I hope I didn't make it worse."

"Came out too easy to have bothered her long. She coulda' just picked it up. She be fine." He rose and patted the mare's neck. Peaches nickered and nudged him. Elijah laughed. "No apples today."

It seemed a familiar routine. Sarah wondered how much Elijah stayed around the stables. She liked how gentle he was with the mare. Clearly, he knew and liked horses. She tried to rise and stumbled against him when her weak ankle buckled. "Thank you," she said as he steadied her.

He was staring at her, at the bruise on her face. She knew he wouldn't ask. Wouldn't dare to, so she told him. She was beyond embarrassment over what her husband did. She'd had too many episodes to care. Besides, Elijah wouldn't tell anyone. "My husband gets angry at my clumsiness. I turned my ankle this morning and dropped the corn pones."

He had averted his eyes, but at this he looked at her. "Your husband beats on you?"

"He doesn't consider it beating. That he reserves for the slaves who displease him. But I'm sure you know that. He's had you whipped before, hasn't he?"

Elijah shrugged. "Jest the once. When I was new here."

"This—" she pointed at her face, "he merely considers a reminder not to be so clumsy."

"A man shouldn't lay a hand on a woman."

"If it comes to that, a man shouldn't whip slaves either." Or own them, but that was another subject. One she couldn't get into with this man. No sense making him yearn for a freedom he'd never have.

"No, ma'am."

"Can she pull the wagon?"

"I reckon."

"We'll have to lead her." She swept up her dress hem, prepared to walk.

"No, ma'am. You can't walk. Not with that foot. I'll lead her, you set in the wagon."

"Nonsense. My ankle is fine now."

"No, ma'am, it ain't fittin'."

He was right about that. But she felt they were safe on her

husband's land, as long as they were far from the house. "Elijah, no one is out here. I'll get in the wagon once we near home. How would that be?"

He hesitated a moment, but made no further protest. Try as she might, she couldn't help limping. She studied his profile. "Did you have schooling, Elijah? Did you go to school, or was it only your mama who taught you? Before you were taken, I mean." She strongly doubted he'd had any education since he'd been separated from his family. Most folks didn't hold with educating slaves.

"Jest my mama. She was a teacher. She held school at our house. Taught me and the others to read and write and cipher."

He stopped walking abruptly. "You be limpin', Missus."

Sarah sighed. "I thought I could walk, but you'd better help me back in the wagon."

Jonas helped her in, but she laid a hand on his arm before he could start to lead Peaches again. "You must miss them very much. Your family, I mean."

"'Twas a long time ago."

His eyes were brown. Deep and beautiful. "I'm sorry. No one should be ripped away from family that way."

"No, ma'am." He sounded resigned. But then, he'd had years of slavery to come to terms with his loss.

She couldn't imagine what it would be like to be wrenched from all you loved. To be thrown, terrified, into a whole new way of life. A world of beatings and pain and hunger. A world of slavery.

It wasn't right. But what could she do to change it? She was forced to pretend that her own dear maid, Celia, was a slave, though she never had been, nor any of her family. Victor wouldn't have stood for his wife having a freedwoman in her employ, so she simply hadn't told him.

Before she came to know Victor, she had hoped to convince her husband to follow her father's example and free his slaves.

She knew better now.

*October Present Day*

A FEW DAYS LATER Claire met Lanie for a drink at 8.0's in Sundance Square, a favorite of the locals. Since it was October and the weather was mild, she took a table outside. The patio was lighted and tables were scattered everywhere with lights in the trees and hanging from the stage. There was often live music, though it was too early yet for that. The place ran to a younger crowd than hers, especially late, but she liked it early in the evening.

She thought about the dreams she continued to have. The man in the dreams looked so much like Jonas. The last dream she remembered had been the night of Lanie's party. After she'd been with Jonas. But was Jonas the trigger or was it the journal?

Or was she simply losing her mind? As much as she told herself it had to be coincidence, the dreams still bothered her. They seemed so real. Particularly the first one. The one she had periodically now.

But then, who the hell wouldn't be bothered dreaming of a lynching?

"Hi, Claire, sorry I'm late," Lanie said, taking a seat. "I'll have a white wine," she told the waitress. "House is fine."

"No problem. It's nice out tonight, so I didn't mind waiting." She took a sip of her wine and asked, "How is Joe? Have you two set a date yet?"

Lanie's face softened. Her friend was happier than Claire had ever seen her. "He's good. We're thinking about Christmas. We can both take some time off. Have an actual honeymoon." She fiddled with her napkin. "He wants me to join his practice."

"Are you going to?"

"I don't know. I'm a little afraid working with him might be too much togetherness."

"You've been making noise about wanting a change. Here's your chance."

"What if we don't like being around each other all the time? For work, I mean."

"You worked together at the hospital."

"It's different in private practice. But I'm thinking about it." She drank her wine. Tossed long, dark hair back over her shoulder. "How is Glenn's father doing?"

"Glenn and I don't talk about it much, but I assume he's doing all right or I'd have heard. I've stayed away. I feel a little guilty, but honestly, the man is such a jerk."

"Like father, like son."

Which seemed the perfect opening. "Why do you and Glenn hate each other? Don't give me your standard bullshit answer, either. Don't you think it's time you told me?"

"Be careful what you ask for."

"Because I just might get it?"

Lanie sighed and sipped more wine. "I don't want to make trouble between the two of you. And it will. Trust me on this."

"How can I when I know you're keeping something from me? I find it strange that neither you nor Glenn will tell me what happened. It was when you came to see me in San Antonio, wasn't it? When Glenn and I were first married."

Lanie shook her head. "You don't want me to go there, Claire. You really don't. It was years ago. Let it go."

"My marriage is on its last legs, anyway. Nothing you say is going to change the way things are going to play out. But I need to know. Just tell me."

Lanie looked startled. "Your marriage is over? When did this happen?"

"It isn't over, exactly. I haven't filed yet. But I'm going to." Soon. There was no point delaying any longer.

"Does this have something to do with Jonas?"

"Why would you ask me that?"

"I saw you with him at the party. Besides, every time I'm near the two of you I get the vibes. Don't deny you're hot for him. That won't fly."

"We're getting off the subject. You and Glenn, Lanie. What happened? Why do you detest each other so much?"

Lanie sipped her drink. Put it down and fiddled with the glass. Finally she said, "You'll hate me if I tell you."

"No, I won't. I could never hate you."

She stared at Claire for a long moment, then nodded as if satisfied. "Yes, you will. But I owe it to you anyway. You're right, it was when I came to see you in San Antonio. Years ago, but neither of us has forgotten. You went to bed and we continued to drink. A lot. I swear, Claire, I didn't lead him on, no matter what he says."

Even though she'd been expecting to hear that or something similar, Claire's heart sank. "Glenn made a pass at you."

Lanie nodded. "I was so surprised, and I guess I'd had enough to drink that I didn't react at first. I let him kiss me. Or I didn't stop him. However you want to put it, we kissed. I can't tell you what a shit that makes me feel like. From that viewpoint, I did lead him on. But then I told him to stop. To forget it. He didn't take rejection well. I guess he's always been afraid I'd tell you."

She wasn't shocked. Bothered, yes, but not surprised. In fact, she'd wondered if something of the sort had happened to explain the depth of their antipathy to each other. "Was it just the once?" Once, she could forgive her friend, but more than that would make it much harder.

Lanie shook her head. "No." At Claire's exclamation of distress, she rushed to add, "It was the only time anything actually happened, but not the only time he tried. He thought because I let him kiss me that first time that meant I would give in. That I wanted him, too. Claire, I swear I'd never do that to you."

"I know." No, Lanie wouldn't cheat with Claire's husband, but she hadn't told her he'd come on to her, either. Not exactly blameless. "Go on."

"I had a hard time convincing Glenn I wasn't interested. The third time, I threatened to cut off his balls and tell you. He finally believed me. He hasn't bothered me since. In fact, he's hardly spoken to me since."

"Why didn't you tell me?" She couldn't decide if it hurt her or angered her more, that Lanie had said nothing and had let her go on believing that she could save her marriage. If Glenn had been cheating since the beginning, that didn't say much for the strength of their marriage.

And Lanie, her best friend, had let her believe a lie for six years.

"You'd only been married a couple of months. You were madly in love. At that time you acted like you thought he hung the moon. Would you have believed me?"

Six years ago. It seemed a lifetime. "We'll never know, will we? Because you chose not to tell me."

Clearly upset, Lanie continued. "I've always felt guilty for not saying anything. I was afraid to risk it. He said if I did, he'd tell you I came on to him. You wouldn't hear a bad word about Glenn back then. I didn't want to lose our friendship."

"So you let me go on believing in a man who was already cheating on me? Hell, he could have cheated on our honeymoon and I wouldn't have known it."

"He said he wasn't. He said it was my fault, that I was a tease. That he'd never have approached me if I hadn't led him on." She laughed harshly. "I'll admit, I thought he was charming at first. And he is good looking. But I wouldn't have done anything. He's your husband."

A horrible thought occurred to her. "Did he—oh, God, Lanie, he didn't try to force you, did he?"

"No. Nothing like that. I couldn't have stayed quiet if he had. He was just persistent. Until I set him straight." She signaled the waitress for two more drinks. "I know I should have told you. But the longer I put it off, the harder it was. And you've never come out and said before that you thought your marriage might be over."

"I've been trying to deny it for months."

"Do you think he's been fooling around on you all along? Wouldn't you have realized it?"

"I don't know. You know how weird my hours are. He works a lot too. Goes to a lot of social functions without me." She put her face in her hands and groaned. "God, what a fool I've been."

Lanie bit her lip. "There's something else. Something worse."

"Worse? Worse than my husband making a pass at my best friend and no one saying a thing about it?"

"Claire—"

"Just tell me," Claire interrupted. She didn't want to hear excuses. She wanted to know the truth.

"I saw Glenn with a woman, a couple of weeks ago. In a restaurant. He didn't see me."

"With a woman as in a client? Or something more?"

"She could have been a client." Lanie sounded unsure. "But they seemed awfully close. I followed them when they left. I told Joe I was going to the restroom, but I watched the two of them out the window. He kissed her, Claire. Not just a friendly kiss, either."

Claire simply stared at her for a moment. "Goddamn it, Lanie, why didn't you tell me? Even if I could understand the first time, surely when you saw him with another woman you could have told me. You know we've been having problems. How could you keep quiet?"

"What if I was wrong? What if it was nothing? I wanted to, but you said you wanted to work things out."

Sure she had. Months ago. Not anytime lately. She pushed that thought aside to concentrate on the latest bit of news. "Did it look like nothing?"

Lanie looked down at the table. "No. I'm sorry Claire."

How could Lanie have kept something so important from her? Not once but twice? Obviously, Claire didn't know either her husband or her best friend.

"What are you going to do?"

She looked at Lanie. "Divorce him." Which she might have done years ago, if Lanie had been honest with her.

"I'm so sorry, Claire," Lanie repeated. "I was wrong not to tell you."

"Yes, you were."

"I knew you'd hate me when the truth came out. That's why I never said anything."

"I don't hate you," Claire said wearily.

"You're angry."

Her temper snapped. "What do you expect, Lanie? That I'd just blow it off? Tell you it doesn't bother me that you lied to me for years? I'm not that noble."

Tears welled up in Lanie's eyes. "If I could go back and do it over I would. I'd give anything to change—"

"Spare me," Claire interrupted. "You wouldn't say a word and you know it. You proved that when you didn't tell me about seeing Glenn and another woman two weeks ago."

"I was going to say something. I wanted to, I just . . . I didn't know how. I didn't want to make matters worse."

"Didn't want to make it worse? Worse than my husband cheating and me being clueless? You know what I've done to try and save my marriage. We've talked about it often enough. Yet you just sat there with your mouth shut while Glenn made a fool of me. More than once."

"Oh, Claire, that's not true. He's the fool, not you."

"I don't want to discuss this anymore." *And sure as hell not with you,* Claire thought but managed not to say it.

"Do you want me to leave?"

Claire could hardly look at her. She felt betrayed by her friend's silence. "Yes."

Lanie paled but nodded. She reached for the check.

"Leave it," Claire said.

Lanie ignored her and put money on the table. "I'm sorry, Claire. More than I can say."

Claire didn't respond. She didn't want to talk to Lanie at the moment and wasn't at all sure when she'd be ready to. She watched her go with mixed emotions. The failure of her marriage was not her friend's fault. But Lanie's silence was a betrayal all the same.

# CHAPTER EIGHT

CLAIRE STAYED AT the bar, unwilling to go home and risk running into her husband. She simply wasn't ready to see him. Putting it off served no purpose, but she wasn't sure this was an appropriate time to tell him she was leaving him. Or even to talk to him, for that matter. She knew he was spending a lot of time with his father. That had to be stressful.

But so what? After what he'd done, why did he deserve her consideration? *What you think he's done,* she corrected herself. Claire wasn't even sure if Glenn was committed to the marriage anymore. If he were having an affair, then he couldn't be very serious about making the marriage work. But one kiss didn't mean he was having an affair. She'd thought about kissing Jonas, and she wasn't cheating.

But she was tempted.

Glenn had certainly never suggested counseling. In fact, when she'd brought it up, he'd told her he wasn't airing any personal issues with a damn shrink. Nothing Claire had said made a difference. He wasn't interested, therefore she could lump it. Claire hadn't pushed him, not after the first few attempts. What she'd been waiting for, she didn't know.

She looked up from contemplation of her empty glass and saw Jonas Clark heading her way. Well, thank God and speak of the devil. Someone to take her mind off her problems.

"How is it that in a place the size of Fort Worth we keep running into each other when we're not at work?" Claire asked. Not only did she see him at the coffee shop, almost daily now, but recently she'd run into him at the grocery store. Obviously, he didn't live too far from her.

Jonas took a seat at the small table. "Similar interests? I heard about this place but hadn't been yet. How's the happy hour?"

Claire glanced at her watch. "Hate to tell you but you missed happy hour by an hour and a half."

"Yeah, but I'd already decided to try out the place."

"They have lots of specialty drinks. Good margaritas, too."

"Not much for those." The waitress came up just then, and he ordered a draft beer. "Claire, can I buy you another glass of wine?"

"No, I've had two. I won't be able to drive if I have another."

"I could give you a ride."

Their eyes met, and he smiled. God, that offer was tempting. And not just for the wine. Really, why shouldn't she?

*Because, you idiot. You're still married, and he is too damn tempting.*

"Thanks, but it will be too hard to get my car in the morning," she said. "Especially since I have to go to work. I'll have a diet tonic water," she told the waitress.

"Bring us some chips and queso, too," Jonas said. "Unless you'd like something else."

"No, that sounds good. I'm hungry and I could use some food."

They talked medicine, hospital gossip, sports. They clashed over sports since he was a San Antonio Spurs fan and Claire was a die-hard Dallas Mavericks fan. But they both liked the Rangers. It was such a relief not to think about her disastrous marriage or her anger with Lanie. Even if only for a short time. Claire couldn't remember having had such a nice time with a man since . . . before she was married.

Oh, God, was she in trouble.

Sometime later Jonas asked Claire, "Can I ask you a personal question?"

"Depends on what it is. Shoot. I'll probably answer."

"Did you say no because you thought your husband would lose it if I brought you home?"

"No. Absolutely not. I wouldn't care if he did."

"Trouble?"

"You could say that." She contemplated the chips before looking at him. *My husband's having an affair,* she thought. *At least, I think he is.* But she wasn't ready to tell Jonas all of her marital woes. "I guess women tell you all the time that you are damn good looking."

Jonas laughed. "Way to change the subject. No, I can't say they do."

"Well, you are, and I suspect you know it."

"All you have to say is 'I don't want to talk about it.'"

She sighed. "The problem is, I'm afraid to talk about it. I'll just get angrier and do something stupid."

"Define something stupid."

*Have an affair with you,* she thought. Stupid, or at the least, ill-advised. Even if she filed for divorce—no, especially if she filed for divorce— then having an affair with Jonas would not be a good idea. Not until the divorce was final. And why the hell was she thinking about having an affair when she hadn't even filed for divorce yet?

Because Glenn had? No, her feelings about Jonas had nothing at all to do with her husband.

"Your eyes are amazing. So expressive."

"You mean weird. I've been told that often enough."

"Not weird. Just different."

"My husband says they're the strangest eyes he's ever seen. And he doesn't say it in a complimentary manner."

"Seems an odd thing to say to your wife."

"He calls it being honest." She snorted. Oh, yeah, he was honest all right. Honestly having an affair?

"Sounds like you need to talk."

"I don't know." She gave him a rueful smile. "You must be sick of hearing about my failing marriage."

He studied her a moment, then smiled. "I'd rather hear about your divorce."

She sucked in a breath. "That's blunt."

"But true," he corrected. "Sounds like you need to make a choice. End your marriage or try to fix it. The indecision is what's really killing you."

"You're right. But I'm not indecisive. Not anymore."

He looked at her for a long moment. "So which is it, Claire? Fix it or end it?"

She drew in a deep breath and let it out. "End it."

"Are you sure about that?"

"I'm sure." And she was. Surprisingly, after so much anguish, she was certain now of what she wanted.

"Do you still love him?"

Slowly, she shook her head. "No. And he doesn't love me either." She hesitated. What the hell. She needed to talk to someone. Lanie was out for obvious reasons, so Jonas won by default. "I think my husband's having an affair." She laughed unhappily. "God, it sounds so pedestrian."

"You think? Or you know?"

"I don't know for a fact. But I'm about ninety-nine percent certain. We've been having problems for a long time now. Tonight I heard something that makes me believe he's been playing around. Possibly since the beginning."

"Is that why you decided on divorce? Because you think he's cheating?"

"Not the only reason. The final reason in a long list." She met Jonas's eyes. "My marriage was over long ago, I just couldn't admit it. I want to move forward, to be happy again. I want a life, not to hang around trying to save a marriage that's broken beyond repair. A marriage my husband won't even try to save."

"You're angry. You might change your mind when you've cooled off."

"No, I won't. I'm finished." The relief of having made the decision was almost overwhelming.

Jonas studied her for a long moment before he spoke. "I'm not into revenge sex. Not with you."

That shocked the fool out of her. "I never said—Good God, Jonas, I never implied I wanted to have revenge sex with you."

"You never said it," he agreed. "But you've thought about it."

Damn it, he was right. She couldn't deny she'd thought about sleeping with Jonas. And the damn dreams didn't help. She was beginning to get those emotions of the people in her dreams mixed up with the reality of her everyday life.

Should she admit her feelings, though, or avoid the subject and act as if he'd never said anything? Be a coward or face it head-on? "I have thought about being with you. But not for revenge," she said truthfully.

He looked skeptical. "I was involved with a married woman once. I swore I'd never do it again. The whole affair was a fiasco."

"Did she break your heart?"

"No. But she bruised it pretty damn badly."

"What did you mean, not with me?"

He was quiet so long she thought he wouldn't answer. "I don't want to have a rebound affair with you, Claire," he finally said. "I want more. A lot more."

Oh, God, how did she respond to that? "If we get together it won't be about revenge."

NOT ABOUT REVENGE. Did he trust that, trust her? Strangely enough, he found that he did.

He took her hand. Rubbed his thumb over her palm. For once, nothing weird happened. "We have a connection. Neither of us can deny it."

"No, I can't deny it. But I don't understand it, either. Do you?"

He looked deep into her eyes. She shimmered as if she weren't there at all. As if he weren't there. . . .

*We know what we're doing, Mama. We love each other.*

He heard the words crystal clear in the night. He didn't know how, or why he heard the words, but he knew who voiced them. The boy in his dreams.

"Jonas, where did you go?"

He came back to himself with a bang. Jesus. What the hell was going on with him?

"You looked like you were in another world. What happened?"

"Nothing." Nothing he could tell Claire about, or anyone else. How could he explain he was hearing voices? Voices from his dreams. God, he was losing his mind.

Claire looked at him searchingly but didn't pursue her questions. She glanced at her watch. "I need to go. I've got an early day tomorrow."

"Let me pay and I'll go with you."

"You don't need to pay my bill. Or walk me to my car, for that matter."

"I want to," he said simply.

He held her hand as they walked to the free parking garage down the street. It was a test, of sorts, to see if he could touch her and not have some weird-ass vision or worse, auditory hallucination. So far, so good. They didn't talk. He was thinking about kissing her. He didn't know what Claire was thinking.

*You are a dumb-ass,* his saner self argued. *You're walking into a disaster. Getting involved with a married woman—again. A married white woman. Yeah, that's smart.*

"Jonas? Here's my car."

Which he'd have seen if he'd been paying attention. "Sorry. Wasn't thinking." About her car, at any rate. He let go of her hand so she could find her keys.

He waited while she clicked her key fob to unlock her car door. "Will I see you at work tomorrow?" she asked.

"No, I have the day off," he said.

She smiled at him, standing with her hand on the open door. "Well, thanks. And thanks for the advice. It sounds simple. Somehow, though, it isn't that easy."

"I never said it was easy." And neither were the two of them. No, nothing easy about this relationship.

The night was cool, a little bit of fall finally in the air. The parking garage was deserted, quiet, the sounds from the street and the clubs muted. As if there were only the two of them and not another soul existed. To hell with it. He put his hands on her waist and drew her closer.

She didn't resist but let go of the door, put her own hands on his shoulders and gazed up at him with those beautiful, unusual eyes.

"This is a mistake," she said.

"Probably."

"I don't care if it is. Do you?"

He smiled and bent his head to hers. Laid his lips on hers and kissed her. Slowly, a sip, a nibble. Traced his tongue over her lips and slipped it inside her mouth as they parted. God, she tasted sweet. Hot. Spicy. Her arms crept up around his neck and tightened. He deepened the kiss, pulling her closer until they were touching from lips to thighs. Her body was soft, giving. He wanted to sink into it, into her. Their tongues touched, retreated, stroked each other.

He wanted to boost her onto the hood of her car and strip off her panties. Wanted to push her to the edge and watch her come apart in his arms. Wanted to lose himself in her, feel her heat, feel her softness.

Jesus. From a kiss?

He released her and stepped back. Claire looked dazed. It soothed him a bit that at least she hadn't been unaffected. But he couldn't remember the last time he'd shot into overload so quickly. Maybe as a teenager. But this was different. Claire was different.

Maybe he should rethink his position on revenge sex.

They stared at each other. Claire got in her car and drove off without another word.

He walked to his car, aware of a nagging question in his mind. Why had kissing Claire, a woman he knew damn well he'd never met until a few weeks ago, been so eerily familiar?

# CHAPTER NINE

JONAS KNEW HE was in trouble. *She's married,* he thought. *Off-limits.* He had no business kissing her. Sure, she said she was getting divorced, but he'd been burned before. He didn't intend to go through it again.

Besides, he was sick and tired of the dreams he was having, the ones he couldn't remember. Except when he touched Claire and then snippets of them invaded his waking thoughts.

Goddamn it, he was stronger than this. If Claire did get a divorce, then great. Otherwise, he was keeping his distance. From now on. Now if he could just sleep without having one of the damn dreams. It would be different if he could remember. . . .

***October 1968***

"WHO IS YOUR DADDY, child?" Fay asked.

*Oh, no, Mama, you don't need to get into that.* Calvin shot Bella a warning glance but either she didn't see it, or didn't care.

"Buster Cantrell, ma'am."

Fay didn't say anything, but she turned and gave Cal the death glare. Meaning, *what the hell are you thinking, boy*?

He wasn't thinking. Or if he was, it was how he could help Bella.

Fay took Bella's hand and patted it. Bella was crying now, and his mother did one of the things she did best. She soothed her, simply by taking her hand. "Can't your mama help, child?"

Bella shook her head, mournfully. "She died two years ago. Ever since she died, Daddy's been getting worse. With me and my sister."

Fay didn't speak, just waited for Bella to go on.

"He's been trying to force me to date a boy he likes. One he approves of. Larry works for him. He follows my father around like a puppy and does everything Daddy tells him. I guess that's why my father likes him." She wiped her eyes with her other hand. "Anyway, I made Daddy mad when I wouldn't date Larry, and then when I told him I wasn't going to Sarah Lawrence, he went bananas. So he hit me. And when I still wouldn't say I'd go, when I threatened to run away, he hit me again and locked me in my room. After he left, I climbed out the window."

"How are you planning on getting back in?" Cal asked.

"Back through the window. Don't worry, this isn't the first time I've done it."

Fay frowned, still patting Bella's hand. "You don't think you could do one of those things? Let your daddy have his way? At least about something."

Bella looked at Cal. She didn't need to say anything. Her feelings were there for anyone to see.

"I was afraid of that," Fay said. "You two young people are asking for a world of hurt."

"We know what we're doing, Mama. We love each other." Not the way he'd planned to tell her, but might as well be up front about it now.

"No, you don't know what you're doing. You think you do. But you have no idea what trouble you're asking for. You young folk think things have changed, but they haven't. The sight of the two of you together could cause a riot, even now."

"You're exaggerating, Mama. Civil rights, remember? Times have changed. Laws have changed."

"People haven't," his mother said bluntly. "What will your daddy do if he finds out about you and Calvin, Bella?"

Bella looked at Cal when she answered. "Kill us both."

***October Present Day***

CLAIRE COULDN'T STOP thinking about Jonas on her way home. He'd kissed her. That was all, a simple kiss. Yet it felt like so much more. Was she falling for him? She hardly knew him.

Except that she did know him. Very well.

*How? How did she know Jonas when they'd never met until a few weeks before?*

She pushed that concern aside. Now that she'd finally decided to ask Glenn for a divorce, she had to think about the logistics of ending the marriage. She needed to tell him her intentions before she called a lawyer and filed. She wouldn't feel right springing it on him, even though he was bound to know by now how unhappy she had been. Maybe he wouldn't fight her. After all, he was as unhappy as she was with the marriage.

But Glenn had never mentioned divorce. Something kept him with her, and she wasn't certain what it was. In the beginning he'd believed her family connections would help him with his real estate law business as well as socially. Before he'd realized that Claire had no interest in the social circles her parents moved in. Claire had been a disappointment to Glenn on a number of levels, her lack of social ambition being only one of them. Yet he'd never indicated he was through with their marriage.

Unless you counted being unfaithful.

Kissing Jonas had influenced her to finally act, she couldn't deny. But the problems in her marriage long predated her ever meeting Jonas. Even if nothing worked out with Jonas, she owed it to herself to end her sham of a marriage.

Tomorrow was soon enough to talk, though. It was late, and she was too confused by everything that had happened.

She let herself into the house quietly, hoping her husband was either gone or asleep.

"Where the hell have you been?" His words rang out like bullets as he got up from the couch and walked toward her.

*Great.* "I was having a drink with a friend. Now I'm going to bed."

She started past him, but he grabbed her arm. Not only could she see the glass on the table, but she could smell the liquor wafting from him. Lovely. Glenn had been drinking a lot lately, and he wasn't a happy drunk. He became belligerent and abusive. Verbally abusive, anyway, as he'd been the other night after dinner.

She tried to jerk her arm out of his grasp, but he held on tight. "Who were you with?"

"Let go of me." He was stronger than she'd realized. His fingers hurt, digging into her skin. She wasn't afraid. Not really. He'd never been physically violent with her, though he'd come close a few times. Verbal abuse didn't count.

Did it?

"Not until you tell me who you were with. I know it wasn't that bitch Lanie because she called here looking for you when you didn't answer your cell."

Claire had turned it off at the bar and had forgotten to turn it back on. Not that she'd have answered a call from Lanie anyway. "I have other friends. Now let go of me. I'm going to bed."

"Friends. That's rich. You were with a man, weren't you? That black doctor."

He said the word *black* as if it were a curse word. She couldn't understand what had set him off about Jonas when as far as Glenn knew, she hardly knew Jonas. Maybe Glenn sensed there was more to the relationship than appeared on the surface. But he couldn't know how much she thought about Jonas.

Or that she'd just kissed him.

"Who I spend my time with is none of your business."

"It goddamn sure is. Do I need to remind you, you're my wife?" He shook her hard enough to rattle her teeth. "One of my friends saw you with him, weeks ago. At breakfast. At a diner, for God's sake. You're fucking him, aren't you?"

Claire was so surprised, she simply stared at him. Finding her tongue, she lashed out. "I'm not the one cheating. Which is more than I can say for you." His smile was mean and ugly. He released her to pull out his phone. "So you're not cheating? The loyal wife, are you?" After punching a button, he held out the phone for her to see. On the screen, close up and crystal clear, was a picture of her kissing Jonas in the parking garage, not an hour before.

Her stomach rolled. "How did you—Did you have me followed?"

"That's right, bitch. I didn't believe you could stoop so low, not until it was proved to me. A picture's worth a thousand words." He grabbed her again, squeezing her arms so hard she struggled not to whimper. Not to give him the satisfaction of knowing how much he frightened her.

She twisted and tried to jerk away, but he held on tight. "Let go of me!" she cried, desperate to get away.

Glenn turned her loose suddenly. She stumbled, and his fist slammed into her cheek. Before she could recover, he punched her in the mouth with his other hand. Crying out, she crumpled, hearing his words from a distance as she huddled on the floor in shock.

"Whore! Did you think I wouldn't find out?"

He kicked her, once, twice.

She drew herself into a ball, trying to become a smaller target. *This can't be happening to me. Oh, God, no. Who is this man?*

"Goddamn you, Claire, how could you let him touch you? Bad enough you're fucking around on me . . . but with a *black* man?"

He towered over her with his fists clenched. Her cheek throbbed. Her eye and her mouth hurt, swelling already. She touched her face, then looked at her hand, shocked to see blood. Her side hurt too, a sharp pain. Had he broken a rib when he kicked her?

Glenn continued to rail at her, shouting vile accusations and foul threats, growing more furious by the second. He paced away, picked up his glass and drained it, then threw it against the wall and cursed her viciously as it shattered.

Claire staggered to her feet, holding her purse in front of

her like a shield. She was ready now. If he came close she was going for his eyes with the keys clutched in her hand.

His cell rang, distracting him for a moment, and she took her chance and ran for the door. Knowing if she didn't get away, she was in for worse. Much worse. He lunged for her but she evaded him, flung open the door, and ran outside.

He shouted something after her, but she had no idea what and didn't care. Ignoring the pain, she flew down the steps and across the circular drive, slid inside her car and locked the doors, thanking God she hadn't parked in the garage as she sometimes did, but instead had left her car out front. She glimpsed Glenn coming after her, his face contorted with rage. With shaking hands she started the car and peeled out.

Claire had seen enough domestic violence in her work that she hadn't hung around to find out what else Glenn might do. He was so angry. Unbalanced. And drunk. But that picture. Oh, God, the picture. Even though she knew that it had only been a kiss, she looked guilty of worse. *She* looked unfaithful, when Glenn was the one cheating.

But that didn't justify him hitting her. Beating her. Nothing did.

For a long time she drove around aimlessly. Dispassionately, she realized she was in shock. Her face hurt, her cheek felt sticky with blood. Her ribs throbbed like a bitch. She should go to the hospital. Let them record what had happened. Because she sure as hell intended to file for divorce tomorrow.

But God, the hospital. Where she worked. How humiliating to come in as a victim. She wasn't sure she could do it.

But she had to. She dealt with abuse victims in the ER. She knew the worst thing she could do was ignore what her husband had done. Pretend it never happened, explain it away? Hell, no.

She fished her phone out of her purse. Keyed in the hospital's number. Identified herself and asked for Jonas's number. She hadn't realized what she meant to do until she did it. She had no business running to Jonas, but she didn't care. She needed him.

"'Lo."

"Jonas, it's Claire."

"What's wrong?"

She sounded shaky, she was sure. Totally unlike herself. "Can I . . . can I come see you? Are you at home?" She'd called his cell first, thinking that was the surest way to get hold of him.

"Yeah, I'm home. What's wrong, Claire?"

"I'll tell you when I get there."

Jonas gave her an address, at an apartment complex not far from her house. Hopefully Glenn had given up on her and hadn't managed to follow her in his car. If he had, she hoped the cops had stopped him for DUI.

Jonas didn't say anything when he opened the door. Just took a long look at her face, then pulled her inside and wrapped his arms around her. She cried out, and he released her immediately. "What happened?"

"My husband. He . . . I . . ." Claire broke down. Tears poured down her cheeks, and she choked back sobs.

"Goddamn it," Jonas said, and took her back in his arms. Very carefully, very gently.

"I'm sorry," she said, clutching his T-shirt and burrowing against his chest regardless of the pain. "I feel like a fool."

"Hush." He held her, let her cry, smoothed her hair, and patted her back. "Let's get you to the hospital. You might have broken bones."

She drew back, attempted a calm she didn't feel. "No. Just

bruises." Unless she had broken ribs, but there was nothing to be done for that. She hadn't punctured a lung, she was breathing too well for that to be the case.

"Why did he do it? Did you ask him for a divorce?" he asked grimly looking down at her.

Unable to speak, she shook her head. She couldn't stop the tears from starting again, though she made the effort. "I'm sorry," she repeated.

"Don't apologize. It's not your fault. Come here." He led her to the couch, made her sit, and left the room, returning with a damp washcloth and a couple of soft, cold compresses.

"I need to take a picture before we clean you up."

She shook her head. "No."

"If you decide to press charges you'll need proof. They'll take pictures at the hospital but it won't hurt to have more for backup. Where's your phone?"

Her phone. She closed her eyes, remembering the picture of her and Jonas on Glenn's phone. Glenn had her followed. And she'd led whoever it was straight to Jonas's door. Unless she'd lost him in her aimless driving around, but that was too much to hope for. She hadn't been thinking of evasion. She'd have been an easy target to tail.

Too late to worry about it now. And Jonas was right. She might need proof of Glenn's actions. She pulled her phone out of her purse and handed it to him. "Go ahead."

He snapped a couple of pictures, then sat beside her and gently washed the blood away. Then he handed her the compresses.

She took them thankfully, wincing again as she placed one against her cheekbone, the other on her mouth. "I'm a cliché. Not only clueless and betrayed but now abused. God!"

"Can you tell me about it? Where else are you hurt? Your ribs?" He looked so angry. So concerned. Guiltily, belatedly, she realized how her actions might affect him.

"I shouldn't have come here. Shouldn't have dragged you into this mess."

"Claire, stop it." He covered one of her hands with his. "Tell me what happened."

She put down the ice pack on her mouth. "You don't understand, Jonas. Glenn has a picture. Of you and me kissing. He'd been having me followed and he—I guess it was a private investigator—took a picture tonight. Now I've led him straight to you." Agitated, she clutched his hand. "I wasn't thinking, I just . . . I knew you'd help me. Now you're going to be dragged into this nastiness whether you want to be or not."

"I've been involved since I met you. Things get ugly, we'll deal. Talk to me."

Claire dragged a shaky hand across her forehead. "I walked in and Glenn was waiting for me. Drunk. He's a nasty drunk. We argued. He showed me the picture. He accused me of . . . of cheating on him. With you. And then he hit me. Kicked me." She stopped, drew in a breath. "God, I thought he was going to kill me. I didn't wait for more, I ran the first chance I got."

"Good. You did the right thing."

"He's never hit me before." Jonas didn't say anything. "You believe me, don't you?" It was important that he believe her, that he know she wouldn't stay with a man who abused her. But she had, she realized. Verbal abuse, but abuse nonetheless.

"Claire, you're not the one at fault."

"I wouldn't have stayed if he'd ever touched me, but he hasn't." She closed her eyes. She'd seen signs, but she'd ignored them. Hadn't really believed the man she'd married could physically hurt her.

"What made him think we were together? Enough to have you followed? It's like dinner the other night. It seems irrational."

"Not this time. Not really. A friend of his saw us having breakfast together. The morning you helped me with my car. I don't think Glenn learned of it until recently. So he had me followed. Tonight, when I got home, he showed me a picture on his phone. It was tonight, Jonas, at the garage. We were kissing. Now he thinks I'm sleeping with you."

Anger showed in the hard line of his jaw. "So he beat you."

"I—" She started to downplay it but stopped herself. "Yes." And he would have done worse if she hadn't managed to get away.

"A man shouldn't lay a hand on a woman in anger. Ever. No excuses."

*A man shouldn't lay a hand on a woman.* Another man in another time had said the same thing. Oh, God, she really didn't need to go there. Not now, not tonight.

"I can't believe this is happening to me. I never imagined anything like this. Glenn is . . . he's got a mean temper but he's never been physically violent before."

"Yeah, well, he is now. What are you going to do?"

"File for divorce. I'll call a lawyer in the morning. As soon as I get a chance. I'm working, of course." Calling in sick wasn't an option. Not unless she really was dead and dying.

"You need to report what happened. Have your injuries treated. Let me take you to the hospital."

"No," she said adamantly. "I can't go to the hospital. I work there. How embarrassing. Humiliating. God."

"Claire—"

She interrupted him. "I'm okay. It's only bruises. Nothing's broken. I'd know."

"We'll go to a different hospital. We don't have to go to Shady Grove. You should document this attack. Christ, Claire, you said yourself he could have killed you."

"Attack." She shuddered. "It's so sordid."

"No, it's wrong." He touched her cheek with gentle fingers. "And it's not your fault. Not in any way."

HOURS LATER, JONAS and Claire returned to his car. He'd taken her to another hospital, one in a suburb of Fort Worth. Regardless, he suspected word would be out at their own hospital by tomorrow afternoon at the latest. Claire's face announced what had happened. She wasn't moving well either. Although she had no broken bones, her husband had bruised her ribs when he kicked her. The son of a bitch had done a number on her.

Jonas started the car but didn't pull out. "Obviously, you can't go home. Do you want me to take you to a friend's? Or a hotel?"

Claire huddled against the door. He wanted to pound on her shit of a husband and see how he liked being used as a punching bag. See how he handled fighting a man instead of whaling on a woman like the chickenshit he was.

"Can I stay with you? Just for tonight?" Her voice shook. She sounded scared, exhausted.

Hearing her sound so unlike the confident woman he knew just made him more determined to see that Glenn Westbrook got what was coming to him. But in the meantime, Jonas had to do what was best for Claire. "Your husband is probably still having you followed. You'd be better off staying somewhere else. What about your friend Lanie?"

"I don't . . . I don't want to see her. I can't talk to her. Not yet."

So, she was angry with Lanie, too. He wondered why. "Then a hotel. If you stay with me it will just give him more ammunition to use against you."

"I don't care. He's already got a picture of us kissing. What difference does it make what I do now?"

"It will make the divorce more difficult. Uglier."

She laughed humorlessly. "Glenn's a lawyer. Most of his friends are lawyers. It was always going to be ugly. You heard the cops."

Jonas frowned. The cops they'd talked to at the hospital had been anything but helpful. The conversation had been intensely frustrating, at least to Jonas and Claire.

"Were you fearful for your life?" one of the cops had asked.

"I . . . yes . . . no." Claire looked down, pleating the blanket on the gurney with nervous fingers. "I don't know. I was scared. He's never hit me before."

"Look at her face," Jonas said. "Of course she was afraid. She's in shock."

"Sir, we'd appreciate it if you let the lady speak for herself."

Jonas had shut up, but he'd been pissed. Still was. It was plain to him what way the conversation was going, and it wasn't in Claire's favor.

"I still can't believe them. Their job is to help victims, not the abusers."

"They were just telling us what happens, in their experience. They've had a lot of experience with domestic violence. This is nothing new to them."

No, they'd seen it all before. The two men had taken Claire's statement but had implied pressing charges was pointless. Claire and Glenn were married, it was a first offense, regardless of the fact that she looked like a mugging victim. The cops also made it clear they believed Jonas and Claire were more than the friends they claimed to be. Then, when they heard her son-of-a-bitch husband was a lawyer, they really didn't want to bother.

Claire hadn't argued. She hadn't filed charges, either. He couldn't really blame her. Jonas suspected she was barely holding it together.

But Claire staying with him? Bad idea, on more than one level.

"Jonas?"

She was waiting for an answer, and no matter what he wanted, Jonas had to do what was best for Claire. She wasn't thinking clearly, so he would.

"You can't stay at my place. We'll go back and get your car so you can go to work tomorrow, and then I'll take you to a hotel. After those painkillers, you shouldn't drive. I'll get a cab home."

She was quiet a moment. "I understand. I shouldn't have asked. I shouldn't have come to you at all."

He had to work not to grind his teeth. "That's not what I'm saying. I'm glad you called me. That you let me help. But you still can't stay with me."

"I shouldn't have involved you. I know, I . . . I didn't know where to go."

"That's not the problem," he said, trying for patience. "A picture of us kissing and you spending the night at my place are two entirely different things. You can explain away a kiss. Staying with me implies a lot more. You don't want to give your husband any more ammunition, especially if you're going to file for divorce."

"If?" Her voice rose with anger, and she straightened. "You're damn right I'm filing. I was sure before this happened, but now . . . God! Do you think I'd go back to him after he hit me? After he beat me?"

"No, but women do." He shrugged. "The guy apologizes, gives her gifts, promises not to do it again. It happens."

"It isn't going to happen to me. I'm done."

"Then you need to be careful. A divorce attorney will tell you your best course of action."

She slumped against the door. "You're right. You're being reasonable and I'm being emotional."

"You have cause to be." He covered her hand and patted it. "I'm glad you came to me," he repeated. "I'm just sorry for the reason."

"Yeah, me too. Would you mind taking me to a Target or something before we find a hotel? I sure as hell can't go back to the house yet. I need something to wear to work tomorrow. And some makeup."

Jonas was fairly sure the makeup wouldn't hide much, but he didn't say so. Instead, he drove her to Target.

SHOPPING WITH CLAIRE was not an experience he wanted to repeat, he thought as they left. At least, not when she had an incipient black eye.

"I thought the checkout lady was going to clock me," he told Claire as they walked to his car.

"She thought you were the one responsible. I'm sorry."

"Quit apologizing to me. None of this is your fault."

"Do you know she slipped me the address for a shelter? I didn't know whether to laugh or cry. God, I feel so . . . so *stupid.*"

"Why? Because your husband's a sick bastard?" He opened her door and helped her get in before going around to the driver's side.

"No, because I never realized he might hit me," she said when he got in. "Glenn has been verbally abusive in the past. A lot, lately. But I never thought it would escalate to physical violence."

"You trusted him. He betrayed that trust."

She stared out the window. "He thought I had been unfaithful. That's what set him off, made him so crazy."

"But you weren't." She wouldn't look at him. "Claire, look at me." When she did, he continued, "Even if you had been, it doesn't make hitting you okay."

"How do you know I haven't cheated on him? Just because we didn't? Maybe I'm the kind of woman who's had tons of affairs."

He hid a smile. He'd never met anyone less likely to be a serial cheater. "Have you?"

"No. But you don't know that."

"Yes, I do." He started the car and looked at her. "I know you, Claire. I don't know why I know you, but I do." She didn't have a response. He changed the subject, which was beginning to piss him off anyway. He hated what her husband had done to her, but he didn't like all these touchy-feely emotions he was having, either. They made him uncomfortable, just as his growing feelings for Claire were making him twitchy.

Once they went back to his place and switched cars, he asked her, "Where do you want to go? Someplace near work?"

"Take me to the Worthington," she said, naming one of the ritzy downtown hotels.

"You sure?" Very nice and very expensive.

She smiled grimly and held up a platinum card. "I happen to have Glenn's credit card. Seems like the least he can do is put me up at a decent hotel."

# CHAPTER TEN

FORTUNATELY, THE night clerk at the Worthington was female and quite sympathetic. Claire didn't bother pretending she'd had an accident. Tomorrow at work she would, but for now she could be honest. When Claire specified that her husband was not to be given a key or even told which room she was in, the woman had nodded grimly. "I'll make a note of it. Don't you worry, I've been there, too. Women need to stick together."

"What happened to yours?" Claire asked.

Glancing around, she saw that no one else was close enough to hear. She smiled broadly and said, "Son of a bitch is in jail, where he belongs. On something unrelated, but at least he's away from me and my kids. And not likely to get out any time before the end of the century."

Once in her room, Claire washed out the new underwear she planned to wear tomorrow. She could change into scrubs once she reached the hospital, but she had wanted something different to wear so it wouldn't be so obvious she hadn't changed clothes from the day before. Not to mention, she had blood on her shirt, so she washed that out too. She'd bought several things, toiletries and clothes, as well as a small suitcase to put them in, so she wouldn't look quite so out of place when she checked in to the hotel.

She very carefully didn't look in the mirror. Tomorrow was soon enough to deal with what she looked like. She'd hit the ice machine first thing and filled up the plastic bags the clerk had provided for her face. It couldn't hurt, she decided, and she lay down on the bed with washcloths and ice packs covering her bruises.

Her ribs hurt like hell, even though she'd taken prescription pain meds at the hospital. She'd hurt worse tomorrow, she knew. She would make do with OTC pain relievers for the rest of the night, since she had work tomorrow and couldn't afford to be groggy.

Tomorrow she'd also have to decide whether to try to force Glenn to move out or move herself. Even if she left, she needed to pick up some things, but she sure as hell didn't want to go when Glenn might be there. But since she couldn't say for sure if he'd be there or not, she should take someone with her. God knows what Glenn would do when he found out she was filing for divorce. She wasn't taking any chances that he'd hit her again, though. The beating she'd suffered that night had been more than enough.

She couldn't sleep. Exhausted as she was, she kept seeing Glenn, furious and towering over her. Felt him punch her, kick her. Remembered cowering on the floor like a victim. Hell, she *was* a victim. No other word for it. God, she hated that label.

So she thought about Jonas. How kind he'd been. He'd taken care of her. Hadn't blinked when she showed up at his door. He made sure she did the right thing, the smart thing, when she'd have done something foolish. Like stay with him.

Why was Jonas so familiar? Even more disturbing, why did he look like the man in her dreams?

*April 1859*

IT WAS ODD, Sarah thought, that the only times she felt truly alive were those moments she snatched with Elijah. She'd run across him while she was out seeing to the tenants. No one was nearby, so she had climbed down from the wagon and convinced him to talk to her while they led her horse.

"Why haven't you tried to escape yourself?" Sarah asked Elijah. Since becoming involved with the Underground Railroad, Sarah had discovered the many others who were part of the underground. Elijah among them. "Why do you help others, but not yourself?" Sarah couldn't understand anyone being so selfless, at least without a reason.

"I reckon I will. Someday. But—" he stopped and looked off in the distance. She could tell he was thinking about something. Someone.

"Long time ago, I tried to help a woman escape," he finally said. "We was both plannin' on goin', but I got held up. They didn't know it was me who was s'posed to go with her. They caught her, but she wouldn't tell 'em nothin'."

"What happened to her?"

"Sold her. After they took the lash to her. Don't know where she is. Dead, I reckon."

He said it so matter-of-factly, it broke her heart. "Did you love her?"

He looked at Sarah then. "Slaves don't have no feelings. Don't you know that?"

"Oh, Elijah." She touched his arm. His skin was soft, warm

from the sun. She felt the muscles bunch beneath the skin. "Tell me. Did you love her?"

"Never got the chance. Might've, though." His smile flashed, white teeth in a dark face. "She was shorely pretty."

"Have you . . . do you have a wife?" No business of hers if he did. But she realized she didn't want him to. Didn't want to . . . share him. Oh, Lord, what was she thinking?

"No ma'am. Not allowed to. The master don't hold with slaves marryin'."

"That doesn't stop them. I know, Celia's told me."

"Don't have a wife. Don't intend to. Not 'long as I'm a slave, and she would be too."

"We're getting closer to the house. I should probably get back in the wagon in case Victor sees us." He wouldn't approve of her walking beside Elijah and talking to him just as she would a white man. But then, he didn't like her talking to white men, either. Or anyone, really.

Elijah put his hands on her waist to help her up into the wagon. As he held her a little longer than necessary, they both stared at each other. She felt it, and wondered if he did too. Some sort of connection. As if fate had spoken.

Fate. Why did it sound so tragic?

*October Present Day*

UNSURPRISINGLY, JONAS had a hard time getting back to sleep. He didn't regret kissing Claire, but he sure as hell regretted her slime of a husband finding out and using it as an excuse to beat the crap out of her. He'd been sorely tempted to pay the bastard a visit and see how he liked dealing with a man. But Jonas knew that while punching the bastard might have given him satisfaction, it wouldn't help Claire. Eventually, he slept.

*October 1968*

"CALVIN?"

"Yeah." They were snuggled together on a blanket, out at Dream Lake. Bella's favorite place. The one place they could relax and be together without worrying about who might see them.

"I love you. Being with you makes me so happy."

"Why do I hear a *but* in there?"

"No *but*. Sometimes I'm just afraid it won't last. Because we're too happy."

"Don't borrow trouble." He had those same concerns, but he didn't see any point in telling Bella so.

"You're the one who's always worried about what we'll do if my father finds out about us."

His arm tightened around her. She rested her head against his chest, so trusting. "Your father's a scary guy."

"Is that why you won't make love to me? Because of him?"

Calvin groaned. God, he was so tired of being strong. Of resisting her for her own good. "Bella, we've talked about this. You're a virgin."

"So? What difference does that make?" She rose on her elbow to look at him. He saw mischief in her eyes by the light of the moon. "Besides, you're a virgin too."

"It's different for guys," he said gruffly. Why he'd admitted he'd never done it, he didn't know. "You need to be sure. I don't think you are."

"Maybe you're the one who isn't sure, Calvin."

"Maybe I'm not." But that wasn't true. If there was anything Calvin was sure of, it was that he loved Bella Cantrell and wanted to make love to her. And he would, when the time was right.

Right now he'd go on being strong. For her own good.

*October Present Day*

"I CAN'T IMAGINE why your doctor's appointment is at the crack of dawn," Glenn said to Lawrence. "Didn't they have a later time?"

*Crack of dawn, my ass.* "I asked for the first one so the damned fool doctor wouldn't get busy and make me wait forever. The later in the day your appointment is, the more likely you are to have to wait."

"You might have considered that I have to get up even earlier, as well as take time off work. Next time have the nurse drive you."

Lawrence ignored his son's griping. At least he was home, where he could sleep in his own bed, eat decent food, and not have to listen to the damned idiot in the other bed moaning, snoring, and worst of all, talking incessantly.

Swear to God, if he'd had a gun he'd have shot the noisy bastard.

He glanced at Glenn, then took a closer look. Even for an early morning, he looked rough. "You look like shit. What happened to you?"

Glenn scowled. "Nothing." He muttered something that sounded like "goddamn women."

"So it's Claire. What did she do now? Come on, spit it out."

Glenn's jaw worked. His hands tightened on the steering wheel. "The bitch is having an affair. I found out last night."

"So? It's not like you've never had a little on the side. Forget about it. She will soon enough."

Glenn's scowl grew darker. "She's my wife. I won't have her cheating on me. Goddamn it, I won't put up with it."

There must be more to it. Or maybe there wasn't. Glenn had never liked to share, and Claire *was* his wife. "Does she want a divorce?"

He laughed harshly. "We didn't get into that. She's having an affair with Jonas Clark. That black bastard she works with." His hands tightened again on the wheel, and he jerked it to the left. "Christ, I still can't believe it."

"Watch out!" Lawrence commanded sharply. Not that he blamed the boy. Cuckolded by a nigger. Shit. Jonas Clark. He made a mental note to call his assistant and light a fire under his sorry ass. Leon still hadn't given Lawrence any useful information about the man. Threatening to fire him should do the trick.

In the meantime, his son needed his help. Damn, it was never ending.

"Do you want a divorce?"

"No! And I'm sure as hell not having my wife leave me for a black man. Good God, that would make the gossip columnists cream their pants. Not to mention, think of how it makes me look. A fool. A cuckold."

"Don't give her a divorce then. What's the problem? Talk her out of it. Or if that doesn't work, you're a lawyer, you should be able to manipulate the system."

"It's not that easy. If she wants a divorce, she'll get it. Eventually."

"Why is she hot to divorce you? Just because of the nigger?" Glenn didn't answer, but Lawrence knew his son.

"What did you do?" No answer. "You didn't kill the bitch, did you?"

Glenn shot him a furious glance. "Shit, Dad, of course not. Would I be calmly driving you around if I had?"

Calm was a matter of opinion. "Then what happened?"

"I . . . when I saw the picture of Claire with that bastard, I lost it. Him with his hands all over her. She was actually kissing the son of a bitch. I . . . didn't react well. I was upset."

Probably drunk too, if Lawrence knew his son. And he did. "Christ Almighty," Lawrence said, disgusted. "You hit her. You know you have to be careful about that sort of thing."

When he was younger, before he married, Glenn had gotten "upset" when his then-girlfriend dumped him. That episode had cost Lawrence a pretty penny to buy the girl off. But he'd thought he'd put the fear of God in his son after that. Maybe he was wrong. After all, Glenn could have bought off any number of women Lawrence didn't know about in the years since.

"How bad is it? Did you break anything?"

"Break anything?" He snorted. "I barely touched her. I slapped her around a little, yeah. But she ran out of the house squawking like I was going to kill her. That won't look good if it comes out."

The boy had never been able to control his temper. He got that from his mother. "You're sure that's all you did? Nothing lasting?"

Glenn shrugged bad-temperedly. "She might have a bruise or two," he conceded.

Lawrence knew he wouldn't admit to anything more, regardless of what he'd actually done. "You said you had a picture of the two of them together. You had Claire followed? By a PI?"

Glenn nodded. "Yes. He was still on the job when she took off."

"Where did she go?"

"Where do you think? She went to him. Her lover, Jonas Clark. He took her to some rinky-dink hospital. God, making a federal case out of nothing." He slammed his hand down on the steering wheel. "She deserved worse than I gave her, the cheating whore."

No doubt. Lawrence was silent, considering the options. "Did anyone see her between the time she left your apartment and when she got to Clark's place? Besides the PI, I mean."

"No. He said she drove around a while and then went to Clark's."

"And went from Clark's straight to a hospital?"

"That's what he said. Why?"

"The cops never came to you?" he persisted, ignoring Glenn's question. "Did she press charges?"

He shrugged. "How should I know?"

"You'd know it if she pressed charges, for Christ's sake." Good God, did he have to think for the boy as well as everything else?

"Nobody came to the house," Glenn said sulkily, "so I doubt she filed a complaint."

"Good. We can use that. Where did she go after the hospital? Back to Clark's? Did she stay there?"

"No. They switched cars and he took her to the Worthington. On my money, I'm sure. Bitch."

"Here's what you're going to do. Deny everything."

"What do you mean, deny everything? Claire sure as hell knows it was me who slapped her around."

"Claire knows but no one else does," Lawrence said. "It's

your word against hers. And the PI can back you up. If you pay him enough."

Glenn thought about that, then started to grin. "My word against hers. I like that."

"Is this the first time you hit her?"

"I told you, it was barely a tap."

"Answer me."

"It was the first time."

"Thank God for small favors." Lawrence went on to explain Glenn's course of action. Once Glenn shut up and listened instead of interrupting, he agreed it was the way to go.

In the meantime, Lawrence needed to know if Jonas Clark was any relation to Calvin Davis. Clark was a dead ringer for the bastard. Older, of course, but still the image of what Davis would've looked like.

If he'd lived past the age of eighteen.

Jonas Clark might find out he too had made a big mistake, going after a white woman. Especially one connected to Lawrence Westbrook.

Calvin Davis had sure as shit learned not to cross him.

# CHAPTER ELEVEN

JONAS'S CELL PHONE woke him. Ordinarily, he'd have let it go to voice mail, especially after the short night, but it was his mother's ringtone, and he knew she'd continue to call and leave messages until she reached him. He cracked open an eye to look at the clock. What the hell was she doing calling him at 6:30 a.m. on his day off?

"What's wrong?" All he needed was for his mother to be having a crisis, too.

"Is that any way to answer your phone? What if I'd been someone from the hospital?" his mother asked.

"I know your ringtone. Besides, it's my day off. If it had been the hospital I would have told them to go—"

"Jonas Clark, don't you dare!"

Resigned, he sighed. "What do you need, Mom?"

"Can't I call my son without needing something?"

"You could but you usually don't. And why so early?" Normally when she called she had a specific reason. Naomi wasn't one to talk on the phone just to be talking.

"I wanted to catch you before you got busy doing something else. I need you to come over here as soon as you can. My dishwasher is broken. The darn thing is spurting water all over my kitchen floor."

Jonas groaned. God, not the dishwasher again. "Turn it off."

"Don't you get smart with me, Jonas Clark. You may be a grown-up man but you're still my son. Of course I turned it off, but it's plate day. My arthritis in my thumbs is acting up and I can't do it by hand. Well, I suppose I could, but I don't want to."

For reasons beyond him, once every month or so, his mother washed all her dishes, whether she used them or not. Hence "plate day," the day she washed every stinking one of her plates. It was a new habit, one she'd only begun since she retired. Forced retirement that began when she started losing her sight. "Mom, I'm not a repairman. I've told you I don't know much about fixing dishwashers."

"It's a simple request. My son, the doctor, is too good to help his mother with her broken dishwasher?"

"Your son is a neurosurgeon, not an appliance repairman."

"My son, the doctor, should be able to do his mother a simple favor. I just want you to look at it."

"It won't do any good for me to look at it. You need a real repairman." Or better yet, a new dishwasher.

"I live on a fixed income, you know. Or at least, I do now. I won't be going back to work any time soon and those repairs are expensive."

She wasn't ever going back to work, Jonas thought. At least not in the same capacity. And that was the problem.

"But if my son, the doctor, can't trouble himself to help out his widowed mother—" Naomi continued.

Jonas squeezed the bridge of his nose. Obviously, there was

more going on than a broken dishwasher. Buried in that speech was her real concern—that she might go blind. Naomi had worked for the same lawyer for as long as Jonas could remember. Roger Dennis had opened his practice as soon as he finished law school and took the bar exam. Naomi had been a teenager at the time. She'd started as his assistant and later, with her boss's help, had eventually gone back to school to become a paralegal.

It had nearly broken Naomi to admit she couldn't read the legal briefs anymore. In fact, her visual difficulties at work had led to her diagnosis of wet macular degeneration, an aggressive and often fast- moving form of the disease. Her vision had quickly declined, and Naomi had taken forced early retirement. As she put it, "A blind paralegal was about as much use as tits on a boar hog."

No words of encouragement, nothing Jonas said, or Roger Dennis either, for that matter, made a difference. Naomi had been floundering ever since she'd quit work. Jonas wondered if part of the problem was that she missed her boss. Roger was a widower now, and Jonas had thought something might develop between them since the man's wife had died. But before it could, Naomi had quit. And from what he'd been able to glean, she had distanced herself from Roger Dennis when she did it.

She refused to discuss any of it with Jonas. Or anyone else either, he suspected. Naomi had a large circle of friends, but he would bet money she downplayed her disability to them. As her disease progressed, she had become more reclusive, to the point that he wasn't sure her friends realized just how bad her eyesight had become.

He decided to address the ostensible problem first. "You know very well I would pay for the repair. Or buy you a damn new dishwasher. I've offered often enough." In fact, he had tried to move Naomi into a brand-new house as well as cover her bills, but she wouldn't hear of it.

"I don't need your charity, Jonas," she said severely. "I need for you to come look at my dishwasher."

What was the definition of insanity? Doing the same thing over and over and expecting the outcome to change? He'd had similar conversations with his mother often enough to know she wouldn't budge until she got her way. "Okay, Mom. I'll be there in an hour or so. Let me have some coffee and a shower." He sure as hell wasn't going back to sleep now.

"Fine. I knew I could count on you. If you stay a while I'll fix your favorite lunch."

"Deal."

As he hung up, he thought about Claire. He'd slept poorly, waking up worrying about her for what was left of the night. He wanted to talk to her, but if she was at work she was likely busy. He texted her instead, a simple question.

*You okay?*

*K. Sore but ok. Call u later*, she texted back.

It would have to do.

*HOLY SHIT, WHAT the hell was going on?*

A fire engine and ambulance stood in front of Naomi's house, lights flashing but sirens silent for the moment. Jonas parked and ran to the ambulance. He didn't see any flames, but there was a definite odor of smoke in the air.

"I'm Jonas Clark," he told the EMT standing by the open back doors. Jonas looked inside and saw who he assumed was his mother, lying on the gurney. "My mother—"

"You're 'my son, the doctor,'" the petite brunette interrupted. "Glad to see you. Your mother has been insisting we wait for you, but we really need to get her to the hospital."

"How bad is she?"

"She has probable second-degree burns on her arm, and we're treating her for smoke inhalation." The woman smiled ruefully. "We had to fight her on the oxygen. She didn't want it and kept taking off the mask, then when she finally agreed to use it, she wanted to wait for you."

Jonas took a deep breath. He'd been worried it was worse. Not that a fire and second-degree burns were good, but at least she hadn't had a heart attack or serious burns. He was accustomed to emergencies but not those involving his mother. Somehow, it was different when it was someone you loved.

"What happened?"

"Kitchen fire. You'll have to talk to the fire crew about details."

"Thanks, I'll do that. If I could speak to her for a moment, I'm sure I can convince her you need to get her to the hospital."

"Hey, Mom," he said after climbing into the ambulance. "What's this I hear about a fire?"

Naomi wasn't one for tears ordinarily, but he could see her fighting them as well as the telltale streaks down her cheeks indicating she'd lost that battle at least once. She attempted to pull herself together and pushed aside the oxygen mask. "I'm fine. I don't know how it happened." She coughed. "I turned my back and the next thing I knew, there was a fire on the stove and the smoke alarm was shrieking like heavy metal in a church choir."

He put the oxygen mask back on her. "You can tell me all about it after we get you to the hospital."

She pulled the mask aside again, "I don't want—"

He interrupted, firmly replacing the mask. "Don't fight me, Mom. I'm worried about you. I thought . . . God, I didn't know if you were still in there when I arrived. Please, let the paramedics do their job."

That shut her up, though she looked mutinous. He touched the plastic mask covering her mouth. "Leave that on. I'll follow in my car as soon as I've talked to the fire chief."

Naomi clutched his hand and said behind the mask, "Promise."

"Don't worry. I'll be there as quick as I can."

He got out, pulling out his cell as he watched the ambulance leave. Claire answered on the first ring. "It's Jonas."

"Hi. I was about to call you."

"My mother's on her way to the hospital," he said abruptly. "Can you watch out for her? Naomi Clark. I don't know who else is there, but I'd like you to take care of her."

"Of course. What happened? How bad is she?"

"Kitchen fire. Probable second-degree burns and smoke inhalation. I don't think it's serious, but . . ." he trailed off.

"She's your mother," Claire finished for him. "I understand. Don't worry, I'll take good care of her."

"Thanks. I appreciate it." He drew in a breath of relief. His mother would be in good, capable hands with Claire. "How are you?"

"I'm okay." She lowered her voice. "I put the word out I was in a fender bender and my air bag didn't release."

Yeah, he didn't think that would fly but saw no reason to say so. "How are the ribs?"

"I'm pretty sore. But I'll be all right."

She would, but she had to hurt. Probably barely able to move though she wouldn't admit it.

"My face looks like a Mack Truck hit me," she added, "so don't be surprised when you see me."

Damn her husband. "I'll be in as soon as I can. I'll see you then."

The firemen were wrapping up by the time he talked to them. "We arrived just as your mother had put out the fire," the chief said. "It started on the stove top. Grease fire from the looks of it." He glanced at the receding ambulance with a thoughtful look. "Any memory problems you're aware of?"

"No. But she has problems with her vision and I suspect it's been getting worse." Naomi was still young for memory issues. She'd only just turned sixty, but Jonas knew better than the chief that didn't necessarily mean anything when it came to diseases like Alzheimer's. However, Jonas was certain that her vision was Naomi's problem, not her memory. The woman remembered everything, sometimes too much.

Jonas thanked the fire crew and made sure the kitchen windows were open and locked up. One of Naomi's neighbors came over and promised to watch the house, but at this point he figured airing out the house took precedence over security. Besides, it was a low-crime neighborhood, for which he was thankful.

Naomi wouldn't like it, but they were going to have a serious talk about getting someone to help her. Daily. Although the fire was the worst, it was far from the first accident she'd had, and Jonas suspected her poor vision played a large part in all the recent accidents. God only knew how many she'd had that she'd never told him about. Naomi needed to make changes, whether she wanted to or not. She was independent to a fault and fiercely determined not to be a burden to her son. He appreciated that, but it did not make it easy to help her.

Jonas didn't look forward to the fight that was sure to come.

"CLAIRE, WAIT UP," Lanie called out.

Great, she'd successfully avoided Lanie all morning. Would have been happy to continue to avoid her for a long time to come. "I've got a—"

"Damn it, Claire," Lanie interrupted, dragging her into an unoccupied cubicle. "You can't avoid me forever. What happened to you? And don't give me that bullshit story about a car accident that's going around." She gestured at Claire's face. "I recognize what happened as well as any ER doc. That son-of-a-bitch Glenn did this, didn't he?"

"I've got a patient coming in. I don't want to discuss my accident."

Lanie studied her face closely. "Accident my ass. He hit you, didn't he? The bastard beat you up. Why? Has he done it before?"

"What part of 'I don't want to discuss this' don't you understand?"

Lanie grimaced. "I know you're mad at me. I don't blame you. But I love you and I'm worried about you."

*You should have thought about that six years ago when my husband hit on you and you chose not to tell me.* Claire's emotions, both toward Lanie and period, were incredibly tangled. No way did she want to get into any sort of dialogue right now. Especially not at work. "I can't talk about it here. Just drop it."

But Lanie could never let anything go, so Claire wasn't shocked when she continued as if Claire had never said anything.

"I thought you understood my reasons for—" she hesitated then continued "—for doing what I did. For keeping quiet all this time. But clearly I was wrong. Are you ever going to forgive me?"

Claire's patience, what little there was left of it, snapped. "Everything isn't about you, Lanie. I said drop it, goddamn it, and I meant it."

Lanie looked as if she'd been slapped. And right now Claire didn't give a rat's ass. She hurt like hell, she'd put in a call to a divorce lawyer and was waiting anxiously to hear back, and to top it off, she was in for a long, brutal day at work with no relief in sight. Lanie would either get over her hurt feelings, or she wouldn't.

Claire's pager went off. Lanie left without a word. Claire popped more Advil and went to see Jonas's mother.

## CHAPTER TWELVE

JONAS WAITED UNTIL after he'd taken his mother home and helped her get settled in to broach the subject he'd been concerned about, one he was sure Naomi would have avoided forever if she could. "Mom, we have to talk."

"What about?" Naomi asked suspiciously.

She was propped up on the couch with pillows and the TV remote; a big glass of water stood on the coffee table. She looked exhausted and . . . damn it, she looked old. Older than he was accustomed to seeing her look, anyway. She'd always taken good care of herself and usually looked a good ten years younger than her true age. Well, she didn't now. She looked every one of her sixty years. She had to be stressed to the max, though, so it was understandable she wouldn't look as good as she normally did.

"You can't continue like you have been. You need help."

"Help? What kind of help?"

"Help with daily living. More than I can give you."

"Daily living? Like I'm an old woman? I just turned sixty.

In case you missed it, that's not old these days. If you think you're going to ship me off to some old folks home, think again, Jonas Clark."

*Patience*, he told himself. "I said you needed help, not to be in assisted living. And I want to talk to your ophthalmologist. Your vision is clearly getting worse, and he needs to examine you again."

"I knew you were going to say that! That fire had nothing to do with my vision. A grease fire can happen to anyone."

"You've never had one before, have you?"

She didn't answer but she looked guilty.

Hell, he should have known. He'd suspected she was under- reporting her "accidents" and now he was sure of it. "This isn't the first fire, is it? How many have you had?"

"They were nothing," she said, evading the answer. "Everyone has a kitchen fire now and then. Just a little stove top thing."

"Mom, you know that's not true."

When she didn't respond, he said, "You're having more accidents by the day. You fell the other day, don't think I've forgotten. You tripped over something you didn't see. Which you wouldn't have told me if I hadn't happened to be here when you did it. I don't know how many times you've fallen that I haven't heard about. You're lucky you haven't broken anything yet. And that doesn't even address the cooking issue."

Naomi looked away. After a long moment she said, "You don't understand. I've already had to quit work. Now you're telling me I can't live alone. I feel like an old horse who's been put out to pasture. Useless."

"I think I do understand, at least to a degree. This condition is robbing you of your independence. You hate it, I get that."

He reached out and put his hand over hers. "You took care of me when I was young. I'd never have made it to college or medical school without you."

She sniffed. "Don't be ridiculous, Jonas. I only did what a mother is supposed to do. Mothers take care of their children. Period."

Not all mothers, he thought. "You did a hell of a lot more than simply your duty. Let me help you now. Please. If you have someone here to assist you, then you can do a lot more and still maintain your independence."

"I don't know." But she didn't sound as adamantly against the idea as she'd been at first.

"There are new treatments for macular degeneration every day. But I need to be able to talk to your doctor. To be sure we're doing everything possible to help or even stop the disease. Does he even know your son is a doctor?"

She shook her head. "I didn't want him talking to you and not to me. Talking over my head like I'm a child or something. I can take care of myself. Besides, you've been in Boston. How were you supposed to bother with my problems?"

"It's not a bother. And this is my fault. I should have been more insistent about talking to your doctor. But that changes now. All right?"

"All right. I guess you're right. It's silly of me not to talk to you about medical issues."

He should have been talking to her doctor long before now, but Naomi hadn't wanted to "burden" him. Until he'd moved back, he hadn't realized how bad things really were. His fault. He should have pushed for more information. But he was as unaccustomed as his mother was to having her depend on him. She had pushed him to succeed, pushed him to do what was best for his career and had never admitted to needing his help in the past. But that had all changed with her diagnosis.

Naomi struggled with tears. "I don't want a stranger living with me."

He'd rarely seen his mother cry. She took stoic to the extreme. "I know and I don't think that's necessary." Not yet, anyway. "We can start out with someone to come in and help with meals. Not cook for you," he said when she protested. "Help you cook. And you need a driver." Naomi hadn't driven for the last year or so, and it was getting harder and harder for her to get around. "I don't want you taking the bus everywhere. It's ridiculous. There's no reason for it when I can help you out. You still have a car. Maybe we can find a college student you like to drive and do whatever else you need help with around home."

"But they don't have to live with me?"

"I don't see why you'd need live-in help. We'll work it out, Mom. And I'm paying for it, so don't argue."

She looked stubborn, but she had to agree. No way could she afford the kind of help Jonas felt she needed.

"You're a good son. I'm just used to being the one to help." She got a faraway look in her eyes. "Everyone always came to me for help, from the time I was a teenager. Especially my family."

Her family. As he looked at his mother, her image shimmered. He heard his mother's voice, but she sounded different. . . .

*"Calvin, I'm worried about you. You're asking for a world of hurt bein' involved with a white girl."*

"Jonas, is something wrong?" His mother had gotten up and was standing in front of him, concern in her eyes and voice.

Jesus. He rubbed his eyes, trying to dispel the last of the illusion. What in the hell had happened here?

Calvin. He'd heard Naomi talking to Calvin. Her cousin. Her dead cousin. So why had Jonas heard it? Furthermore, why had it seemed as if the comment was addressed to him?

When he was young, he remembered hearing Naomi speak of a cousin she'd lost. So was all this his imagination running away with him?

Except he didn't have much of an imagination. But he knew one thing now. The boy he'd been dreaming about was Calvin, his cousin who'd been dead for fifty years.

"Jonas?"

"Nothing's wrong."

"You looked so strange. And you wouldn't answer me when I talked to you. What in the world happened?"

"Sit down, Mom. I'm fine. I was thinking about the best way to find someone to help you," he lied.

She sat back down on the couch. "I thought you just didn't want to answer my question."

"What question?"

"You really didn't hear me, did you? I asked you what's going on between you and Dr. Westbrook."

Great. Just what he needed. "Nothing. Why do you ask?"

"I may have vision problems but I'm not blind yet. That woman was beaten, never mind her saying she had a car accident. I know what a man's fist does to a woman's face. I've seen it before."

"Even if that were true, why would it have anything to do with me?"

"I heard someone ask her about her husband's father. She's married, isn't she?"

Jonas shrugged, which he supposed was answer enough.

"I saw the two of you together. You care about her, Jonas. She cares about you too. Her husband beat her, didn't he? Was it because of you?"

"Mom, you're reading way too much into the situation. You're also jumping to conclusions about something you can't possibly know anything about."

"I don't think so. Are you involved with that woman, Jonas?"

*Lie,* he told himself. "We're . . . friends," he heard himself say. "That's all. She's having some marital problems." Yeah, her husband was an abusive asshole who she was divorcing. And while he wasn't sleeping with Claire—yet—he was sure as hell involved with her.

"Friends, my Aunt Fanny. It's not a good idea. Mixed relationships just bring heartbreak to everyone."

"This is the twenty-first century, Mom. People have mixed relationships all the time."

"Movie stars," she snorted. "They don't have problems, but everyone else—normal people do."

"That's a racist attitude, isn't it? That doesn't sound like you, Mom. You're not a prejudiced person."

"I'm not racist or prejudiced. No matter what I think about the way things *should* be, I know the way they really are. The way they still are. What I'm saying is the God's honest truth. I know. Believe me, I know."

Jonas's phone rang. Claire, he saw when he checked. "I have to take this," he said, getting up and walking into the kitchen. He was just as glad. Something told him he wasn't ready to hear Naomi's story. He didn't want to know all about Calvin Davis. Not yet. Maybe not ever. His dreams were another matter. He had no control over them. He wondered if hearing more about Calvin from his mother might make the dreams easier to remember.

Maybe he didn't want to remember his dreams.

"Claire. How are you?" He wished he'd chosen another room. The kitchen looked pretty dismal with the damage from the smoke and fire. He resolved to find someone to repair the damage first thing. If the sight of it depressed him, he could just imagine what his mother would feel like.

"I'm okay. How's your mother?"

"She'll be all right. I'm working on getting some help for her. She's fighting me on it, of course. But she needs a driver and help at home. I don't see how she's made it this long without it."

"I know a college student who's looking for some part-time work to pay off student loans. She's very dependable. I'll text you her name and number."

"That would be great. Now tell me how you really are."

She was silent a moment before she answered. "Aside from the obvious, which is I hurt like hell, I talked to the divorce attorney. She's going to file as soon as we get the paperwork filled out."

"Are you going to press charges?"

"No. It wouldn't be worth it. I just want a divorce, the quickest way I can get it."

"I understand. I'm just sorry the bastard won't pay for what he did to you."

"Me too, but I'm moving forward. It's all I can do, given the situation. I've decided to pick up some of my things until we work out who's going to live in the house. It will be easier than trying to get Glenn to move out right now. I'm sure he's going to make everything as difficult as he possibly can."

"You shouldn't go alone. I'll go with you."

"No. Jonas, I appreciate the offer, but Glenn will go ballistic if he sees you. Things are dicey enough without pushing him further. And I'd never forgive myself if he hurt you."

Jonas smiled. "I'd like to see him try. Facing a man and beating up on a woman are two entirely different things."

"I don't want to involve you, Jonas."

"I'm already involved. You're not going alone."

"Don't worry, I won't. I've asked Lanie's fiancé, Joe, to go with me. We're going after work, tonight."

He'd have preferred to be with her himself, but if this was the way she wanted it, he wouldn't argue. "I'm glad you asked him. I thought you were on the outs with Lanie. When you didn't want to stay with her last night, I figured you were having problems with her."

"I am. But I'm a little desperate right now and Joe's a friend, so I asked him." She laughed. "It doesn't hurt that Glenn's always been a little intimidated by him. Not that he'd ever admit it."

"Good. Be careful, Claire, okay?"

"I will. My pager's going off. I'll talk to you later."

Jonas hung up and turned to see his mother standing in the doorway.

"That was Dr. Westbrook, wasn't it? Claire, you called her."

"Mom—"

"Do you have any idea how your voice changes when you talk to her? No, I can see you don't."

"Your imagination's running wild, Mom. There's nothing going on between Claire and me," he said firmly.

"You can lie to me but don't lie to yourself. Son, I'm afraid you're in for a world of hurt."

*A world of hurt*. Just what Naomi had told Calvin, all those years ago. Maybe Naomi was right. Even if she was, he didn't think there was anything he could do to change it.

GLENN ARRIVED JUST as Claire and Joe were finishing up at her house. One of the first things she'd packed was the journal. She didn't know why, but it was important. She knew it held answers to a lot of questions she'd had since the dreams started. Along with the journal, she packed a few boxes of mementoes, things she didn't want Glenn to destroy in a fit of rage. Her computer, some clothes, and toiletries went into a couple of suitcases. The bare necessities. She'd worry about the rest later, after her lawyer filed.

"Claire, what are you doing?" Glenn stood in the doorway between the kitchen and dining room. Clear-eyed and sober as a judge.

"What does it look like? I'm packing. I want a divorce. My lawyer will be in touch."

He took a few steps toward her, and she forced herself to stand her ground, but she was intensely thankful Joe was with her.

"What happened to your face?"

She stared at him a moment in disbelief. "You happened to it, you son of a bitch." He hadn't been so drunk he wouldn't remember. Was this an act for Joe's benefit? What did he hope to accomplish? She glanced at Joe, who was leaning against the wall with his arms crossed over his chest. Joe was a big guy, a former football player, and eminently reassuring. He appeared deceptively at ease, but she knew he'd protect her if necessary. Apparently she didn't need protection, though. Glenn seemed to want to play dumb.

"I have no idea what you're talking about," Glenn said, confirming her suspicion. "This happened last night?"

"Yes, last night when you beat the shit out of me. Call me crazy but I draw the line at physical abuse."

"Claire, you know as well as I do that I didn't lay a finger on you." His patronizing tone infuriated the shit out of her. "We argued, about your affair with Jonas Clark, but you left here without a scratch on you. Did Clark do this to you?"

"Are you insane? I'm not having an affair. And Jonas didn't touch me. In fact, he's the one who took me to the hospital."

Glenn frowned. "To Shady Grove?"

"No. I didn't want to go where I worked." She stopped herself. She didn't owe this son of a bitch any explanations. "What difference does it make where I went? I can't believe you're denying you hit me."

"I'm only speaking the truth."

"The truth? You wouldn't know the truth if it bit you in the face."

"Be reasonable, Claire." He looked so sincere, so concerned, she wanted to vomit. "We can still work things out. If your infatuation with Clark is just a temporary thing, I'd be willing to forgive you. We could try counseling. I know you haven't wanted it in the past but—"

"*Me* not want to?" She caught herself again, stopped herself from buying into his act and arguing in an endless circle. "I've had enough of this farce. And don't think anyone will buy your innocent act. I can't believe what you're trying to pull."

"I'm not trying to pull anything. I'm simply trying to work things out with my wife. You are still my wife," he added.

He turned to Joe, still propped against the wall watching them. "Why did you come, Joe? You can't have thought I'd hurt Claire."

"Somebody did," Joe said, speaking for the first time. "She says it was you."

Which she'd been forced to admit when she asked Joe for his help. She was sure he'd talked to Lanie, though she didn't know how much Lanie had told him. But she still wasn't ready to talk to her friend. Didn't know when she ever would be.

"And you believe her? You actually think I'd lay a hand on my wife?"

Joe shrugged. "Claire doesn't lie. Not that I've ever known."

"She's lying now. Because she doesn't want to admit her lover hit her. Why did he do it, Claire?"

"We're done here. Talk to my lawyer," she told Glenn. She had to leave before she exploded. She wasn't quite sure what Glenn's game was, but she realized with a sinking feeling that she couldn't prove Glenn had beaten her. The PI who'd followed her could very easily say she'd looked fine when she left her house. Oh, God, what a scandal this could cause at the hospital, especially if Glenn circulated his version of events. Talk that wouldn't be good for either Claire or Jonas. And Jonas was new at the hospital. Not many people knew him well enough to know that Glenn's story was a complete fabrication.

Jonas, whose crime had been in trying to help her.

LATER THAT EVENING, Jonas hung up from talking to Claire, relieved that at least one thing had gone right. He was grateful Joe had been with her to pick up her things, since he didn't trust her bastard of a husband one inch.

He had an early day tomorrow and needed some sleep.

Some dreamless sleep. He wondered uneasily if he'd dream again, and if so, would he remember any more of it. Goddamn it, this was ridiculous. He didn't set any stock in dreams, so why was he worried about what he would or wouldn't remember?

*October 1968*

"YOUR GIRLFRIEND called me," Naomi told Calvin.

Naomi had called and said she needed to talk to him in person, so he'd met her at the usual place, the drugstore down the street from his house. It had a counter and a few booths and served hamburgers, french fries, and shakes. Since it was in their part of town, it had no problems serving coloreds. In fact, he'd never seen a white person in the place.

"Bella called you? Why? What did she want?" That was weird. Naomi and Bella had met, but it wasn't like they were friends.

"She wanted me to tell you to meet her at your regular place. She's afraid to call your house. Afraid your mama won't like it. So she called me 'cuz she knows I'm your cousin. She knows we're close, thanks to your big blabbermouth. Why you gotta involve me in this crap?"

"We don't have anyone else we can trust. Not family, anyway." Bella's friend Gail helped her out and also gave Bella a girl to talk to about everything. But she wasn't family, and there wasn't a lot she could do besides lie for Bella occasionally. "You like Bella, don't you?"

"She's okay." Naomi shrugged, looking annoyed. "For a white girl. I wish you'd fallen for a colored girl, that's all."

Naomi didn't understand. Neither he nor Bella had a choice. They were meant to be, they both believed that now.

Their color, well, it wasn't important between the two of them. It was only the rest of the world who made things hard. He touched his cousin's cheek. "You're the best, Naomi."

"You say that now," she humphed. "Calvin, I'm worried about you. You're asking for a world of hurt bein' involved with this girl."

"I'll take my chances," Calvin said. He didn't have a choice, and he wouldn't have changed things even if he had. "Thanks."

# CHAPTER THIRTEEN

**Rachel's Journal-May 4, 1859**

*I do not consider myself an abolitionist. The word itself is considered an abomination in this part of the world. All over the South, from what I have heard. No, I believe myself to be merely a woman who believes in humanity. I cannot tolerate the way slaves are treated. I cannot tolerate the idea of owning another human being. But do I call myself an abolitionist? No. Yet while I never have, perhaps that is about to change.*

*I always knew Father was different. He educated us, my sister and me, encouraging us to read and question, to think for ourselves, at a time when most men believe women are chattel whose only use is to bear children. He came to Texas from the North, from a family most labeled as radicals even there. For if his views on women's education are unusual, his views on abolition are surely outrageous. Appalling to many.*

*Should there be war, we shall have to choose which way of life to support. But I cannot see why we cannot free the slaves and allow them to work as free men. My husband agrees, though he says I know nothing of running a plantation. (I did not point out that, as the owner of a general store, neither does he.) It seems labor is at the crux of it. Men argue that the plantation owners would be ruined if they had to pay the laborers. So they support a way of life that is, to my mind, an abomination.*

*I do not know. I only know that I am so glad my dear Ben is of the same belief as my father and I. What if Father had married me to a man such as Victor Lawrence? A cruel man who abuses his wife as readily as he beats his slaves. God, why is Sarah's burden so much harder than mine? What has she done to deserve misery while I receive love?*

***May 1859***

"I CAN HELP," Sarah told Elijah. "I can be a conductor." She'd found him in the stables, where she knew he went whenever he had a free moment. He was brushing one of the mares, crooning to the horse in that way he had.

Elijah stopped brushing and looked at her as if she were mad. "No, ma'am, you cain't."

"I can provide food, at the least. And a resting place until the slaves can be moved. I know we can find somewhere safe to keep them."

"No, ma'am," he repeated strongly. "The master will kill you." He went back to grooming the mare as if his words had settled things.

She waved aside his objection. "Obviously, he won't know. My husband doesn't pay attention to anything but the price of cotton and maize. And his hunting trips. People can come and go here without him knowing. There's a shack some distance away that the old overseer used to—" Sarah broke off, remembering the rumors of what had gone on in that shack. Of the screams of the slave women who some swore still echoed in the night. "It's vacant now," she ended hastily.

"Why you talkin' about this now?" Elijah glanced around, making sure they were alone. "If someone tells the master, you and me is both dead. If he hears you've been talkin' to me, he be mad as fire. If he hears what we talkin' about—" He broke off, then said simply, "We be dead."

"We're alone. The stable hand leaves every chance he gets. I wouldn't have spoken if I hadn't thought it safe." She took precautions when she talked to Elijah. Sarah knew as well as he did how careful they must be that no one knew of their friendship. The Underground Railroad was dangerous enough, but her friendship with Elijah was danger on an even deeper level.

Yet try as she might, she couldn't let go of their friendship. Besides, in order to help fugitive slaves she had to be able to talk to them, and since Elijah was heavily involved, she had to speak to him as well.

At least that is what she told herself.

"Safe? Ain't nothin' safe in what you're speakin' of. Anybody finds out you is helpin' escaped slaves, they'll likely kill you."

Elijah was protecting her, or trying to. But she wouldn't be sheltered any longer. Not when something so important was at stake. Not when he risked his own life to help fugitives.

"No one will dare. I'm the master's wife. Victor will decide what to do with me. He'll be angry and beat me but he won't kill me. Nor let anyone else lay a hand on me." At least, she didn't believe he would. But perhaps that was wishful thinking.

Once she'd submitted to Victor's attentions he'd not hurt her, but that first time, oh, God, the first time. She shuddered, remembering the misery of her marital bed in the early days. Victor had not been gentle, though he knew her to be a virgin. Truth be told, she thought he'd enjoyed hurting her. Once she'd learned to submit, not to fight, her husband had lost interest. He didn't come to her bed as often now. She suspected he spent his energy on the ladies of the night he found in town. All he wanted from her was a child. A child she prayed she'd never conceive.

It helped to become numb.

"Victor is not . . . a kind man. But I'm more valuable to him alive than dead." At least until she gave him a child. An heir.

Elijah didn't look as if he believed her, and his next words gave weight to that. "The master won't tolerate you aidin' fugitive slaves."

"You risk more than I do. But you're already doing it, aren't you? You've been helping since you came here, haven't you?"

He remained mute.

"Don't you know you can trust me by now?"

"It ain't you I don't trust. Ain't wise to trust most anyone these days."

"But we have to. All along the way, people have to trust. No one can make that journey alone, without help. It's a long way from here to Canada. To freedom."

"Not as far to Mexico."

Mexico. She felt foolish she hadn't thought of that. Mexico was much closer, although the border was still a far piece from where they were. But what little she'd discussed with Rachel hadn't touched on where the slaves were running to. Only that they were running from slavery to freedom. She and Rachel had only discussed what Sarah could do to help. "Are they safe there? In Mexico?"

Elijah shrugged. "Mebbe. No one comes back once they

leave. Heard stories that in Mexico folks don't believe in slavery."

A place with no slavery. It was beyond her imagination. "What happens when they don't make it? Do you ever hear?"

He shrugged, said matter-of-factly, "They mostly die. By the lash, by the noose. Some is sold off and disappear. But most think death is better than bein' a man's slave."

"Do you?"

He hesitated, then nodded. "I was born free. Was free until I was twelve. Never have learned to be some other man's property."

"Neither have I." But she was every bit as much a slave as Elijah. "They call it marriage," she added softly. "But it's not. It's slavery, just of another sort."

He snorted. "That's foolishness. Master's wife ain't no slave."

"No?" Angrily, she turned on him. "I have no choice in matters. I have to do my husband's bidding or suffer the consequences. If I defy him, I'm beaten. Or kept in my room on bread and water. He can beat me, rape me, even kill me, at his whim. I'm no more free than you, Elijah."

His eyes darkened. She hadn't meant to be so blunt, so honest, but she couldn't take it back. "He . . . he forces you?"

Elijah knew her husband hit her. He'd seen the bruises, and they'd talked about it. No one, until now, knew that he raped her. Most wouldn't consider it rape. She was his wife, after all. She lifted a shoulder. As long as she didn't defy Victor when he wanted her to pleasure him, or do anything else he bade her do, then her life wasn't too bad. When he was courting her, he'd indulged her, been proud of her beauty. Those days were long gone. Once they married he'd settled into indifference except for a strong desire to get her with child. But dear Lord, just once she wanted to feel a man's arms around her who cared for her, even loved her. A man who didn't look on her as a chattel. Someone to breed. Someone he owned, same as a slave.

"No worse than many husbands."

"It be wrong, forcin' a woman agin' her will." His voice was low and fierce.

"Victor doesn't think so. We're married. He doesn't think of it that way."

"Does he beat you often?"

"No worse than many," she repeated.

"A man shouldn't never raise a hand to a woman. That's what my daddy taught me."

Sarah didn't want to think about her own father. What agony he must go through suspecting the truth of the life she led. While the decision had been hers, her father knew she'd married Victor for him and her sister, so that they could lead a better life. And to avoid ruin by a vindictive man. The reasoning didn't matter. What was done was done.

"Let's talk of something else. Something more pleasant. Tell me about your parents. Do they love each other?" In her world, love and marriage didn't go together. Did they in his? The world he'd lost so many years ago.

Elijah smiled, nodded. "'Til death, they always said. Never knew what happened to them. Wonder if they is still free, along with my brothers and sisters, or was they all took same as me."

"Do you think they were?"

"No way of knowin'. Don't expect I ever will."

"What was their last name, Elijah?"

"Calvin. My daddy's name was Elijah Calvin."

*October Present Day*

GODDAMN IT, WHY couldn't he catch a break? Lawrence looked at the report his assistant, Leon, had emailed him. A painstakingly extensive report, complete with links to stories about Calvin Davis's murder—links he had no desire to investigate, but he obviously was going to be forced to look at them. Who would have thought that so much information about an unimportant death fifty-something years ago would still be available on the damn Internet? To Lawrence that was more of a crime than the black bastard's death.

The reason Lawrence's assistant Leon had included those links? Because Calvin Davis, that son-of-a-bitch nigger, was a cousin of Naomi Clark's. Naomi Clark, Jonas Clark's mother.

When Leon had researched Jonas Clark, he'd done it thoroughly. Not only was there a pile of crap about the bastard's education and professional life—like Lawrence was supposed to be impressed—but Leon had also delved into Clark's family history. He'd included the whole fucking family tree. Lawrence concentrated on the sixties and ignored the rest. He had vague recollections of a colored girl hanging around Bella, especially after she'd taken up with Davis, but to be honest, the little black bitch hadn't really been on his radar.

Now she was. What the hell did Naomi Clark know about Calvin Davis's death? What did she suspect? Did she believe, like most people, that Buster Cantrell had been the one to pull the trigger? A simple matter of a man protecting his daughter, and Buster then using his considerable influence to cover it up. Lawrence hoped she believed it. He didn't want to have to take care of another problem.

Surely if Naomi had believed someone else had killed the kid, she'd have raised a ruckus years ago. Or sometime in the years since. The woman had worked for a lawyer for years, so you'd think she'd have used that to her advantage. So, no, he didn't think he was in danger from Naomi Clark.

But he'd keep an eye out and an ear to the ground. Maybe call Frank Dervish. The ex-cop could see if anyone had been nosing around any cold cases. Not to mention, Dervish had been involved in the investigation into Davis's death. The investigation that had gone nowhere, thank God and Buster Cantrell's influence. And thanks to Lawrence's willingness to come to Dervish's aid over the years. Money, influence, whatever Dervish had needed, Lawrence had provided. Dervish drank like a fish, so it wouldn't be too hard to have him over, ply him with single malt scotch, and get him to gossiping. Not hard at all.

JONAS TALKED TO Claire several times over the next week, but he didn't see her outside of work. He wanted to see her, wanted to be with her, but the timing was up to her. He wasn't sure how they'd gone from a kiss to being on the verge of becoming lovers, but although neither had spoken the words, they both knew that lovers was where they were heading.

How had Claire become so important to him so quickly? A few months ago he hadn't even known her. Yet already she was an important part of his life. Important, maybe even essential.

His doorbell rang. He opened the door, surprised to see Claire, yet not, knowing she'd been thinking of him as often as he had thought about her. Knowing, feeling the connection between them.

She stood on his doorstep, looking beautiful in a thin blue

sweater and jeans. Her bruises were still evident, though they had faded quite a bit. He took her hand and pulled her inside without speaking.

They stared at each other, searching each other's eyes. He cupped her face in his hands. "Are you sure about this?" he asked, even though he knew she wouldn't be there if she weren't.

In answer she put her arms around his neck and raised her face to his. "I'm sure. I feel like I've been waiting for you forever."

So did he, but he wasn't going to think of that now. He laid his lips on hers, sank into the warm welcome of her kiss. Her mouth opened, and he stroked his tongue inside. Their tongues touched, tangled. She tasted sweet-hot, a shot of whiskey burning a fire in his blood. He left her mouth long enough to trail his lips down her neck, to taste the pulse hammering at her throat.

Claire groaned, then leaned back enough to pull her sweater over her head. She wore a peach-colored lacy bra that showcased gorgeous breasts. He wanted her out of it. He wanted her naked. Now.

She pushed her hands beneath his T-shirt and pushed it up. "Take this off. Now."

He laughed and did it. She studied him, placed her hand, warm and gentle, on his chest. Pale, so pale against the darkness of his skin. Soft against hard. He let her touch him, stroke her hands over him, but he couldn't take it for long.

*Oh, baby*. He filled his hands with her breasts and kissed her again, pressing her back against the door. Thumbed her nipples through the bra. She was hot, burning in his arms. On fire. He stripped off the bra and went to work on her jeans, still with her backed up against his door. He unfastened them and pulled them down. Claire kicked off her shoes, then gave a wiggle to help him take the jeans off completely. In moments she wore only a wisp of peach panties. He lifted her leg up and settled her against him. The thin weight of his scrubs didn't provide much of a barrier, but it was more than he wanted. He pushed against her, his cock already hard. They both groaned. Her breasts nestled against his chest, soft, so amazingly soft.

"Jonas," she gasped between kisses.

"What?" He buried his face in her throat and trailed his lips down it.

"Just Jonas. God, I want you." Her arms around his neck held him tight, as if she couldn't bear to let him go.

He cupped her face in his hands again, rubbed his thumb over her lips before he kissed her, slow and deep. "I want you too." He swung her up in his arms and carried her to his bedroom. Dropped her on the bed and followed her down. Her arms and hands raced over him, her mouth melded with his. He stripped his pants and boxers while she wiggled out of her panties. Took a moment to appreciate the beautiful, naked woman in his bed before he grabbed for a condom.

Her hands were there, helping him, stroking him, wanting him. "Hurry," she said.

He'd wanted to take his time, to caress her breasts, to learn her body, to push them both to a frenzy, but they were already there. Claire opened her legs and urged him between them, her hips lifting even as he entered her in a hard, deep thrust.

"God." She moaned and murmured his name. "Jonas," she said it on a sigh.

Her legs wrapped around him. He thrust once, twice. Said a guttural, "God," as he shoved into her a final time and exploded, her body milking him, as she cried out her climax.

It seemed like eons later when he drew back and looked at

her. She smiled, pulled him down, and kissed him. God, she was so beautiful, so. . . . His vision swam. No. God, no.

*She was so beautiful. Long, dark hair flowing over her body. Naked and trusting. So damn trusting. He'd hurt her, he knew he had, but she didn't care. She swore he hadn't and that she loved him. Bella loved him.*

*His dreams. Oh, God, his dreams.*

Jonas blinked hard. The scene faded, and he saw Claire. Beautiful, naked, *blonde* Claire. Not a girl, but a woman. A woman who looked nothing like the girl he'd just seen, the girl in his dreams. Except for one thing.

The girl of his dreams and Claire had the same eyes.

"JONAS? WHAT'S WRONG?" For a moment there he'd looked blank, completely blank. Then his expression had changed but she was hard put to classify it. Shock? Anger? A combination of both?

"No, nothing." He rolled off her and took her with him, snuggled her in his arms. "Not one damn thing is wrong. In fact, everything's right."

She sighed, content to be with him. Deciding he'd talk when he was ready, she didn't push him for answers. "Not yet. But it will be. Once I'm . . . free."

Free, as Sarah and Elijah had never been. Why was she thinking of two people who were long dead when she was finally with Jonas? She was afraid of the answer to that question, and quickly pushed the thought away.

"You shouldn't be here," he said. "But I'm glad you are."

"There's nothing he can do to me now, except make me wait longer to be free of him. And he'd do that regardless. I couldn't stay away from you any longer." She laughed. "I know we haven't known each other that long but it feels like we've known each other forever, doesn't it?"

He rolled over and kissed her. She felt him growing hard against her leg. "Jonas? Do you feel like we were meant to be together?"

He had gathered her breasts in his hands and was kissing them but he looked up at her question. "You mean, like fate?"

She touched his cheek, smiled at him. "Yes, like we're fated to be together."

"I don't believe in fate," he said after a long pause. "But I know that I want you and you want me. That's enough for me. Is it enough for you?"

She looked into his eyes. Dark brown soulfully deep eyes. It made him uneasy, she realized, to think about fate. So they wouldn't. "You're enough for me," she said and kissed him.

# CHAPTER FOURTEEN

JONAS HELD CLAIRE as she slept. She had drifted off immediately after they made love, but he couldn't sleep. Every time he closed his eyes he saw that scene from his dreams. It had to be from his dreams. Otherwise, what was it? A vision?

Absolutely not. He didn't buy into *visions*, for Chrissake.

So, it was a dream. Still, it was disturbing because he now knew he was dreaming about real people, but he had no idea why. Would he dream again? And if he did, would he remember it?

Something told him that remembering his dreams was not going to make everything all better.

*November 1968*

BELLA WAS WAITING for him at the lake when he drove up. "What's wrong?" he asked, catching her as she threw herself into his arms. She'd called and asked to meet, which was weird. She never called. She thought his mother didn't like her.

She was wrong. Fay Davis liked Bella, but she didn't want Calvin dating her.

"I don't know what to do. Oh, Calvin, everything's such a mess. It's all my fault. I should have been more careful."

"Careful about what?"

"About seeing you. Being with you. I never imagined but . . . oh, God, he saw us, Calvin."

He made her sit on the blanket she'd brought with her. "Who saw us? Your father? Slow down and tell me what happened. You're not making sense."

"It's Larry. You know my father wants me to go out with him?"

Calvin nodded. Yeah, he knew. The guy was a jerk, from what Calvin knew about him.

"So far I've been able to put him off, but he's been getting more insistent. Then today, Larry cornered me after school." She shuddered.

"What did he do to you? Did he hurt you?" If the bastard had laid a finger on her, Cal was going to break every one of them.

"No, not physically. He threatened me."

"Threatened you? About what?"

"He knows about us. He saw us kissing at the drive-in. He saw me get in your truck and he watched us." She covered her face with her hands. "It makes me sick to think of him watching us like that."

"Damn it, I knew we shouldn't have risked it."

She looked up. "We have to go somewhere. We can't always come to the lake. I hate sneaking around. I'm not ashamed of you."

Determined not to be distracted, he ignored that. "What did he threaten to do?"

"Unless I go out with him, he said he'd tell my father what he saw. And you know what Daddy will do."

"Jesus." The very last thing they needed was for Buster Cantrell to find out about the two of them.

"I told him I was just flirting. I made it sound like nothing, and that I did it to get back at my father. I told him go ahead and tell my father. That was just what I wanted." She grasped his hand. "I felt awful talking about us like that, but I didn't know what else to do."

"That's not important. You did the right thing. Did Larry believe you?"

"I don't know." She started to cry. "He said he wouldn't tell Daddy. Yet. But he looked so strange. Scary, like I've never seen him before. I don't want to go out with Larry. He gives me the creeps. I've heard other girls talk about him. They say he just wants one thing. I'm afraid of what he might do if I won't go out with him. But I'm more afraid of what he'll do if I do date him. Calvin, it makes me sick to think about."

"Don't worry. You're not going out with that scuzzball. We'll think of something." What, he didn't know. He looked down at her and saw her gazing at him with such trust in her eyes. His heart turned over. He held her close, kissing the tears from her cheeks, then kissed her mouth. She tasted salty. Sweet. So loving.

She put her arms around him and pulled him down on the blanket. "I love you, Calvin," she whispered. "Make love to me. I want you so, so much."

He groaned, resting his forehead against hers. "I love you too." He didn't know how much longer he could resist her. Or even why he should try. They loved each other. They should be together.

"Are you sure? You have to be sure, Bella."

She moved away from him and sat up. Pulled her top over her head and knelt to unzip her jeans. In minutes she was naked in the moonlight, dark hair flowing over her shoulders and breasts. So beautiful, so in love.

He was drowning, in lust, in love. He couldn't resist her, didn't want to resist her. He took off his clothes, lay between her legs. Looked down at her, so beautiful in the moonlight. "I love you, Bella."

"I love you too, Calvin." And she welcomed him home.

***May 1859***

HE WAS WAITING for her at the lake. Dream Lake, Sarah had named it. It was a pond, really, but other than the Trinity River, the only water for miles around. Sarah's heart leapt at the sight of him. For though they both waited for the slaves they were helping to escape, it seemed as if Elijah waited for her alone.

She knew some would think she was wrong to care so deeply about another man. Everyone she knew, honestly. Even her sister would believe she was wrong, though she would support Sarah's choice, whatever it was.

Even if she chose her husband's slave?

How could love be wrong? How could these feelings of joy and anticipation whenever she thought of Elijah be wrong? How could the pure happiness she felt when she was with him be wrong?

Because she was married. A loveless marriage to a man who thought more of his horses than he did his wife. Who treated his horses better than he did his wife. Who treated his horses better than he treated his slaves.

Her heart fell as reality warred with desire. No matter her feelings, she could never admit them. To do so would not only risk her own life, but Elijah's as well. And even if she counted the risk well worth it for her sake, she would not be the instrument of Elijah's destruction.

She would be his friend. Nothing more. No matter how her heart yearned for him, she could only be his friend. Even that was danger enough.

Yet friendship with a slave was nothing compared to aiding fugitive slaves. And she knew she would continue her work with the Underground Railroad no matter the risk.

"Are they here yet?" she asked, glancing around as she saw Elijah.

"No. Soon, though, God willin'." Hands on her waist, he helped her down from her horse. He let her go instantly, respectfully, but Sarah still felt the joy of his hands upon her. What would it be like if she dared ask for more?

He would refuse, and rightfully so.

A tiny kernel of hope blossomed, refusing to be daunted. One day soon she might convince Elijah himself to leave. And once he did, she could find a way to leave Victor and follow him.

A silly dream, one she knew could never be, but one she held dear nonetheless. One she wished for when her own life became too hard to bear.

*October Present Day*

"CLAIRE, WAKE UP."

She came to suddenly, staring into Elijah's eyes. She blinked, shook her head to clear it. *Not Elijah. Jonas. Oh, God.*

Jonas was looking down at her, concern in his eyes. "You must have been having a hell of a dream. Were you dreaming about Glenn?"

"Um, no." Sarah's husband, not hers. And Sarah's lover. Not hers. "Why do you ask that? Was I talking in my sleep?"

He gathered her to him and stroked her bare back. "Most of it was unintelligible, but just before I woke you up, you said, 'He won't kill me.'"

She pulled back a bit to look at him. "Oh, Jonas, no. I'm not worried about Glenn. It was just a dream. And it wasn't even about Glenn." No, she'd dreamed about someone long dead. Two people she shouldn't know anything about. Except she did.

Jonas looked skeptical. "Are you sure? If you're that worried about him, maybe you should talk to the police. I'll go with you. They can't all be like those jerks the night you went to the hospital."

She wasn't so sure about that. "Thanks, but it's not necessary." Yet. She wasn't sure how Glenn would respond to being served with divorce papers, but if his behavior when she'd gone to pick up her things was any indication, he wouldn't make anything easy. But her husband was only one of the things bothering her.

"I've been having a lot of dreams lately," she said hesitantly. "Odd dreams. Very . . . strange." She rubbed her forehead, wondering what he'd say if she told him the truth. No, she couldn't tell him what she was beginning to believe. Not yet. He'd think she was crazy.

Maybe she was.

"What kind of dreams?"

"Of another time. In the past. They're very . . . realistic." Almost as if she'd been there. *You have been there, Claire, you just don't want to believe it.*

"How far in the past?"

He asked the question sharply. Surprised, she searched his face, but she couldn't read it. "A long time ago. Over a hundred and fifty years ago. Just prior to the Civil War."

She could swear he relaxed. Which seemed odd.

"Bad dreams?" Jonas asked.

"Some of them," she admitted, thinking about the first one. The worst one. "Some of them are good, though." If you could call anything about a doomed, forbidden love good.

"What is it? There's more to it, isn't there?"

*If you only knew.* How much should she say? Would he understand? "You'll think I'm crazy."

"Just tell me."

"I've been dreaming about a man and woman who lived in 1859." She looked at him. "A black man and a white woman."

"Go on."

"She's an ancestor of mine. I found a journal when I was cleaning out my mother's house. It's been in our family for years and years. Mother had it tucked away with things from a completely different era. I'm not sure anyone has seen it or read it since the woman wrote it. So I took it home with me. I've been reading it and ever since I've been having these dreams."

"Every time you read it?"

She nodded. "And then last night, even when I hadn't read it." Again, she wasn't sure what to say. "You'll think this is strange, but I had the first dream before I ever read a word of the journal. I'd glanced at a few pages, seen the dates, but that's it. It was dated 1859. Then that night, I had the first dream. The night before I ran into you at the coffee shop for the first time."

"So this is part of the fate thing. Because you've been having weird dreams."

She frowned at him, annoyed even though she knew she must sound strange at the least. "When you say it like that it sounds ridiculous."

"I didn't say it was ridiculous. Maybe you just have a vivid imagination. You read this journal and then you dream about the woman."

"No, I don't. That's just it. I don't dream about the author of the journal. Rachel Adams wrote it. She was my great-great-great-great- grandmother. If I dreamed about her, it would make sense. But I don't. I dream about her sister. Her name was Sarah. Sarah Lawrence. I can't explain it, Jonas, but when I started that journal, when I read about Rachel and what she wrote about her sister, I had the oddest feeling. As if when Rachel wrote about her sister she was writing about *my* life. As if I knew what she was going to write next. And the freaky thing was, I was right. At least the parts of the journal that I've read. When I dream, I don't dream exactly what I've read about, but then later, I'll find an entry that corresponds to my dream."

He wasn't looking at her as if she was crazy. He had a completely blank expression on his face. Exactly like the one he'd worn before. As if he wasn't even seeing her, but something else entirely. Before she could question him, her pager went off. She reached for it and grimaced. "I'm not supposed to be working. I wonder what that's about?"

The blank look cleared. She could swear Jonas looked relieved. "Paperwork, maybe."

She picked up her cell and called in, hanging up a couple of minutes later. "I need to go sign some charts."

"But you're free after that?"

"As a bird. Unless something comes up."

"Want to spend the day together?"

She smiled, looped her arms around his neck, and kissed him. "I can't think of anything I'd like better."

CLAIRE'S DREAMS troubled him. Her dreams seemed uncomfortably similar to his even though they dreamed of different time periods. They were just dreams. Hers didn't have to mean anything, whatever Claire thought. Just as his own dreams didn't have to mean anything.

Right. So why was he dreaming about someone else's life?

A dream was a dream. It held no deeper meaning.

Jonas decided to drop by his mother's while Claire took care of business at the hospital. The new girl had started work, and so far Naomi seemed to like her. At least she hadn't complained about her whenever he called.

He walked into a scene of chaos. Naomi sat on the couch in the den with photographs and boxes spread all over the place. Maci, her helper, was nowhere in sight.

"What's going on, Mom?"

She put her hand to her chest. "Oh, Jonas, you gave me a scare. I didn't hear you come in."

"What are you doing?"

"I decided to go through my photos and organize and label them while I can still see. Just in case, you know. I'm the only one left who knows who some of these people are. Everyone should have a record of their family, and I know you don't know. You've never been much interested in the past."

Not until lately. He'd just as soon have kept it that way too, but he hadn't been given a choice.

"Some of them my mama and my grandmama marked. But a lot were just mixed up," Naomi continued. "Maci's been a big help."

He looked around and didn't see a sign of her. "And is Maci invisible?"

Naomi laughed. "Of course not. She went to pick up some more albums and boxes. Supplies to help us organize. She'll be back in a few minutes."

He moved some of the crap from the couch to the coffee table and sat beside his mother. "How is Maci working out?"

"I like her. She's young and enthusiastic." She gave Jonas a pointed look. "Doesn't treat me like a useless old fool, either."

"If you're implying I've been treating you like a useless fool—"

"Oh, don't get your panties in a wad. I wasn't talking about you. I just don't think you always listen to me."

He had to admit the charge had some merit. "I think the saying is 'don't get your shorts in a twist.' At least when you're talking to a man." He picked up one of the photos that had fallen from a pile to the floor. He started to toss it back onto the coffee table but took a second look. "Mom, is this a picture of me? I don't remember it." He was young. High school, maybe. Wearing a white T-shirt and jeans and leaning back against the hood of a fifties-era green pickup truck. His vision swam as he continued to look at the picture. A truck he remembered from . . . *Oh, God, the dreams. He knew that truck from his dreams.*

His mother's voice came from a distance. Jonas shook his head and pulled himself together. "That pile of stuff is from the sixties. I don't know how you'd have gotten mixed up in it. I haven't even started on your pictures yet. They're in a pile way over there," she said, gesturing at another chair piled high with pictures and boxes, some of it spilling onto the floor. "Let me see." Picking up her magnifying glass, she took the picture, tilted her head back and forth before finding a good angle to peer closely at it. "That's not you. That's Calvin."

Calvin. Well, shit. Of course it was. "Calvin?"

Naomi looked thoughtful, and sad. "You know who he is. I told you about him years ago. He was my cousin."

His cousin. The cousin Jonas had heard spoken of in whispers. Calvin had come to a bad end, a tragic end, was the way it had been put. Naomi hadn't mentioned him in a long time. Jonas knew it from the dreams, but now he remembered more about the stories. The whispers had been there, in his subconscious. Could that be the reason for the dreams? His subconscious had decided to go wild?

"You don't ever talk about him. Not anymore. And you sure as hell have never mentioned I look just like him."

"Calvin's been gone more than forty years. Closer to fifty. It never occurred to me you'd grown up to look like him." She peered again with her magnifying glass, then looked at her son. "You're his spitting image, though. What he'd have looked like if he'd lived. I can't believe I never saw it. Never even thought about it, which is strange. I should have seen it right off, but I guess it's been so long since he's been gone I just didn't think of it. And when you were in high school, well, it just didn't occur to me to even think about you looking like Calvin." She shook her head. "I probably did it on purpose. It always makes me so sad to think of him."

Gone. "You said he was gone. You mean dead, don't you?"

She nodded. "Still a hole in my heart where Calvin was."

"How did he die?" he asked, but he had a feeling he knew. A bad end didn't imply a happy ending.

Still looking at the photo, her expression turned grim. "He was murdered. Shot down in cold blood."

Murdered. *Fuck.* If Jonas remembered his dreams, would he remember Calvin's murder? "Was it random? Or was it a civil rights thing?" He knew it wasn't. Even though he hadn't dreamed it, or at least, remembered, he knew why Calvin had been shot.

"No, not civil rights. But it was a race thing. Calvin fell in love with a white girl. Isabel Cantrell. Everybody but her daddy called her Bella, though. Bella got pregnant and she and Calvin got married. Wasn't easy back in those days to have a mixed marriage. It had only just become legal in Texas. I helped them do it. Roger and I did."

She shook her head, covered her eyes with her hand. Her voice was thick with tears when she looked up and continued. "We shouldn't have done it. Should have known better. We should have known nothing good would come of it. Bella's daddy, Buster Cantrell, he found out the two of them were married and he shot Calvin. Killed him, though he never paid for it. No one ever did."

"There was no proof?"

"Oh, they knew who it was," she said scornfully. "Everyone did. Even though Roger and I tried to force an investigation, the police ignored us. It was early on in Roger's career. He'd just started practicing law the year before and hired me while I was still in school. So I went right to him when Calvin died, thinking he could help. Like he'd helped the two of them get married." She laughed without humor. "He tried. What investigating the police did was a joke. Cantrell money and influence made it all go away."

"So Calvin and Bella were married?" Again, something he hadn't known.

"Yes. I told you, Bella was pregnant." She sighed and looked away. "I helped them do it, God forgive me. And Calvin died because of it."

She set the picture down and drew in a breath. "Lord, I haven't thought of all that in years. Hurts too much still." She looked at Jonas and asked, "Are you all right, Jonas? You look downright sick."

Because he *was* sick. What did it all mean? He'd been having dreams of a cousin who'd been murdered. And the dreams were his own, yet from Calvin's point of view. As if he *was* Calvin. Impossible. But then the whole damn thing was impossible. He didn't believe in this shit.

"What happened to Bella? And her child?"

"I never saw her again. Bella had a younger sister. Her name was Sophie. I asked her what happened to Bella. Sophie said she died. She couldn't—or wouldn't—tell me anything else. Just that Bella died while she was still pregnant. Not long after Calvin. I don't know why, or anything else about it. Only that Bella and her baby both died."

She leveled a hard look at Jonas. "Now you know why I don't want you getting involved with that doctor. She's married. And white. I don't want anything to happen to you."

"It's hardly the same situation, Mom." He couldn't picture Glenn Westbrook coming after him with a shotgun, but the man was violent. He'd proved that when he beat up Claire.

"Isn't it?"

Calvin had been in love with Bella, for one thing. Jonas wasn't in love with Claire. They were lovers now, but that didn't mean he was in love with her. . . . Did it?

# CHAPTER FIFTEEN

PAIN MEDICINE DIDN'T work worth a shit, Lawrence thought. All it did was make him tired and groggy. He didn't like to sleep during the day. But he didn't sleep well at night, and he couldn't stop drifting off in the daytime. Maybe he could just close his eyes and rest. He didn't have to sleep, just rest, and drift off . . . .

*Lawrence couldn't believe his eyes. His date had gone to the restroom, leaving him with nothing to do but look around since the movie was too damn boring to watch. But Juliet had asked to see it, and since the girl he wanted wouldn't give him the time of day and Juliet seemed willing to give him whatever he wanted, he'd gone along with her. And then he'd seen Bella, climbing into an old Ford pickup that he wouldn't have bet a nickel she'd have set foot in. Especially not since it was parked in the colored section. Bella was with a colored kid. Sitting in his car at the drive-in. Just as if she were on a date with him.*

*But that couldn't be right. Bella wouldn't date a colored boy. Except it looked like she was. What else was she doing in his car at the drive-in if it wasn't a date? The kid was that basketball player,*

*Calvin Davis. Lawrence had never talked to him, but he had watched him play. Kid thought he was hot shit. A lot of the jocks thought that, though. But this was carrying things too far. He had no right to date a white girl.*

*Especially the girl Lawrence wanted. Other girls, like Juliet, were only good for one thing. But he'd thought Bella was different. Even Bella's father, Buster Cantrell, approved of him, so why wouldn't Bella give him a chance? Maybe he hadn't been persistent enough. If Bella would go out with him, she'd see how much better suited they were to each other than she was to some colored bastard.*

*If Buster Cantrell knew about it, then the shit would really hit the fan. Should he tell him? Not yet, he decided. First he'd see if he could use this knowledge to his advantage. Yeah, he liked that. Bella wouldn't turn him down once she knew he was on to her latest maneuver. And that he was willing to tell the old man exactly what his darling daughter had been doing.*

*He sat watching them for a while. They didn't seem to know or care that they were being observed. Bella was laughing. Leaning toward the bastard. Surely to God she wasn't going to let him put his hands on her.*

*She kissed him. Kissed that colored kid like it was nothing. Like it wouldn't make any self-respecting white person sick. Lawrence wanted to go over and rip them apart. Ask her what the hell she thought she was doing.*

*But he didn't. Instead he just watched, in silent rage.*

"Mr. Westbrook, are you all right?"

He opened his eyes to see the nurse hovering over him. The nurse he hadn't wanted but Glenn had insisted Lawrence hire, at least part-time. Damn interfering woman. "I'm fine. Damn medicine isn't worth a shit."

"Are you in pain? It's not quite time for your next dose."

The meds—or lack of them—had caused that dream. That,

on top of reading about Calvin Davis's murder on the Internet. Until he'd seen that bastard, Jonas Clark, he hadn't thought about Bella Cantrell in years. No, that wasn't true, he admitted. Every time he saw his daughter-in-law he was reminded, painfully, of Isabel Cantrell.

"Leave me alone. Of course I'm in pain, but if you can't give me the medicine then get the hell out. Why did you come in? I told you I'd ring for you if I needed you."

"You were shouting, Mr. Westbrook. Cursing. I thought you were in pain."

And so he had been. Seeing Bella in that dream brought back memories as if they'd been yesterday. Following the links on the Internet that his assistant had sent him wasn't helping. All it did was stir up a lot of memories better forgotten. No one was going to dig into a fifty-plus- year-old unsolved murder. Why would they?

AFTER SHE FINISHED at the hospital, Claire and Jonas spent the day together. They started out at the Kimbell Art Museum, then went to the Amon Carter Museum. Jonas couldn't remember ever going. Not in high school, that was for sure. He'd enjoyed the museums in Boston, but realized he'd neglected to see what his own hometown had to offer. Claire apparently spent a lot of time in them.

When they wanted a change, they went to the zoo. Now that was a place Jonas had been. He used to take dates there in high school. "What's so funny?" Claire asked him. "The elephants?"

"No. I was remembering that this is where I kissed my first girl."

"Right here, in front of the elephants?"

"Yeah. It wasn't a success, though. Her aunt happened to see us and told her mother, who grounded her for a month. She had lied and told her mom she was going to a girlfriend's house instead of on a date with me."

"Didn't her mother like you?"

"Her mother didn't like any boys. Didn't want her to date until she was sixteen. We were barely fifteen."

"Poor baby." She slid her arms around his waist and raised on her toes to kiss him. "There, now you can remember this instead."

He smiled at her but couldn't help asking, "Do you know if you're still being followed by the PI?"

"No, but I wouldn't be surprised."

"We probably shouldn't even be going out in public together."

"I'm not ashamed to be with you, Jonas. My marriage is over. Just because a judge hasn't said so yet shouldn't make a difference."

"I hope you're right. I don't want to hurt you."

"You haven't. You won't." She smiled and kissed him again. "Come on, let's go eat and then go back to your place."

They didn't speak of her husband or PIs again. After they ate they went to his apartment and made love most of the night. With every kiss, every touch, Jonas felt himself falling for her harder.

He tried to tell himself it was normal to have these feelings in a brand-new relationship. That first rush of falling for a woman. But he knew there was more to it.

He closed his eyes, knowing he needed sleep. He was tied to Claire, connected to her in a way he couldn't understand. Would the connection become clearer with time?

*June 1859*

"CELIA, WHERE IS he? Is he all right?"

"He's fine, Miz Sarah. Don't you worry about Elijah. Just a beatin', not a whippin'."

"But why? Why was Elijah beaten? Who did it?" The thought of his pain made her physically ill. Bad enough when it was one of the other slaves, but Elijah. . . .

"Mr. Bransen said Elijah sassed him." She shrugged. "It happen all the time. You know that."

Mr. Bransen, the overseer, was notorious for making up reasons to beat or whip the slaves. While it had always bothered her, she hadn't been in love with the person being beaten. Why had it taken her so long to realize she was in love with Elijah? How could she have been so blind?

But what did it matter? There was nothing she could do. She was married, and Elijah was her husband's slave.

"I want to see him."

"No, ma'am. You won't," Celia said firmly. "Master Victor will kill you."

"Nonsense. I check on all the slaves. It's my duty. And I want to see Mr. Bransen as well. While Victor is gone I have a responsibility to oversee the plantation. I won't have that man beating our slaves on a whim."

"Don't you go interferin'," Celia warned. "I don't want you to get in trouble, Miss Sarah, and that's surely where you're heading."

"Celia, I have to see him. I'm going to see him, no matter what you say."

Celia argued, but it was no use. Sarah remained adamant, and Celia reluctantly gave in.

Elijah's face was swollen where the overseer had hit him.

Sarah had no doubt he had bruises elsewhere too. She hated that she must be grateful that Elijah hadn't been lashed. The small, one-room cabin had a dirt floor, and in the corner, a rough bed of reeds lashed together, covered by a thin blanket. Someone had made an attempt to tidy the cabin. According to Celia, this was where the ailing slaves went, or those recovering from the lash. Sarah was ashamed that she was only now seeing it. Ashamed that while she and her husband lived in luxury, these people made do with so little. But Victor had deliberately kept her from seeing the slave quarters. How much else had he kept hidden from her?

"How do you feel?" she asked, kneeling beside the bed and laying a hand on Elijah's arm.

He didn't answer but looked at her maid, angrily. "Celia, have you done lost your mind? Missus ain't got no business bein' here."

"Miss Sarah was comin' whether I brung her or not. You be the fool, Elijah." She gave him a stern look, then transferred it to Sarah. She didn't quite say Sarah was a fool as well, but Sarah understood the unspoken words.

Elijah glared at Sarah though his eyes were nearly swollen shut. "Go on, get outta here. You cain't be here, Missus."

"Nonsense." Sarah gestured to Celia to leave them.

After another reproving glance at Sarah, she did as she was told, though she said pointedly, "I be waitin' outside, Miss Sarah."

Best that she did. Celia's presence gave more propriety to Sarah's tending to a slave.

"Why did the overseer beat you?" Sarah asked.

He sighed, but answered. "'Cause he could, I reckon. He don't need a reason, Miss Sarah."

"I've told you to call me Sarah."

"And I told you it ain't fittin', Miss."

"I don't care about that. There's no one here but us. You can call me Sarah when we're alone."

"Shouldn't be alone," Elijah muttered. "You shouldn't be here a'tall."

Sarah ignored that. "I came as soon as I heard. Does Mr. Bransen do this often?"

Elijah didn't answer.

"He does. I suspected so. Never mind, I will speak to him and he won't be beating our people again."

"If he don't, the master will."

Again she felt ill, knowing what he said was true. "I can't stop Victor, but I can stop Mr. Bransen." At least for now, until her husband returned. Before Elijah could say anything, or try to send her away again, she leaned over and kissed his brow.

"Sarah, don't," he said, agonized.

"No one can see," she whispered, and kissed his poor, battered mouth.

*November 1968*

"GOOD GOD, BELLA, what happened? Did your father do this?" He gestured to her face, her purpling eye and swollen mouth, but he knew there were other bruises and God only knew what he couldn't see.

She hugged him tightly, regardless of the pain it must have caused her. "Oh, Calvin, he knows. My father knows about us."

"How?" He knew even as he asked the question. "That piece of shit Larry told him, didn't he?"

She nodded, tears spilling down her cheeks. "Daddy took a belt to me. He only slapped me a couple of times, before he remembered he doesn't like to leave marks. He doesn't want the teachers saying anything. So he used the belt. Calvin, it hurt so much!"

Slapped her? The bastard used his fists on her. Worse, he used a belt, the cowardly shit. "I want to kill the bastard. Anyone who'd treat his own child this way doesn't deserve to live."

"He said a lot of horrible things. I can't believe anyone could have so much hatred in him. He said he'd kill me if I didn't give you up."

Calvin drew her close, kissed the top of her head. "I understand. You have a right to be scared." And he did understand. But his heart broke all the same.

She pushed back from him, fury in her gaze. "Do you think I'd let him break us up? I only let him think I'd obey him. It doesn't even cross his mind that I would keep seeing you."

"But how? I don't want him to hurt you again."

"He does that anyway. I love you and I'm not giving you up. We'll just have to be more careful. I might not be able to get away as much."

If he were stronger, he'd let her go. Hell, he should make her go. Yet as stubborn as Bella was, she wouldn't allow him to do that. "I love you, Bella," he said, and kissed her. Drew her down on the blanket and made tender love to her, careful, so careful not to touch her cuts and bruises. He wanted to protect her. He would protect her.

Bella. His only love.

# CHAPTER SIXTEEN

CLAIRE WOKE IN the night, thinking of Elijah. She looked over at Jonas, sleeping with the moonlight spilling over his face. The face that looked so much like Elijah's. She lay back down, sighing. What did these dreams mean? How were they connected to her and Jonas? Most of all, why was she having them?

Her restlessness must have awakened Jonas. His arm came around her. He pulled her close, kissed her, stroked her. Soon, she didn't think of anything but Jonas, didn't feel anything but happiness as he slid inside her and made her his. She slept in his arms.

***June 1859***

"ELIJAH, YOU MUST go," Sarah said. "You should take your freedom the instant there is an opportunity. You've helped enough people. Now it's time to help yourself." It wasn't the first time she'd begged him to go. But he was adamant that he didn't want to leave her.

"I cain't just up and leave. Too many folks countin' on me."

"But that isn't the only reason. You won't go because of me. That's it, isn't it?"

He gazed at her a long moment. "Never knew happiness 'til I met you. Not much happy in bein' a slave. Then there was you." He smiled, albeit sadly. "I reckon I'll stay a while."

"What if I left too? What if I went with you?"

He started shaking his head before she finished her sentence. "Too dangerous. The master, he'd hunt us down and kill the both of us."

"Then I'll go alone and meet you later. I won't let him find me. I'll leave during one of his trips. I think he's going on another soon."

"T'wouldn't be possible."

"Why? Other people leave all the time. Why couldn't I?" The more she thought about it, the more she wanted to do it. Why should she stay here, tied to a man who didn't love her when she could be with Elijah?

She would have to leave her family. Never see her father and sister again. The decision wasn't an easy one. But staying with Victor, praying every day that she wouldn't bear his child, hoping for just a glimpse of Elijah. Knowing if her husband suspected their friendship . . . . She shuddered. No, better not to think of that. Elijah had to go, but couldn't she go as well?

"You know why, Sarah. It just ain't possible."

"Perhaps you're right. But what if you leave first and then I follow?"

"Foolishness. You know it is."

Foolishness or not, she intended to try. "I'll talk to Rachel."

***November Present Day***

THE NEXT MORNING Jonas awakened before Claire. He watched her as she slept. Jonas had never felt the need to do that before with a woman. No surprise. He'd only been seriously involved twice. Once with the disastrous married Leslie, and another time when they'd both been so young that he hadn't been surprised it hadn't lasted. But he'd never watched a woman sleep before.

He was getting sappy. Emotional. Lovelorn, for God's sake. He'd fallen in love with Claire, a woman he'd known a matter of a few months.

She began to moan, then thrash. It happened so fast he didn't react at first, but when she cried out he decided he should wake her. Not wanting to startle her, he touched her shoulder, but she didn't feel it, continuing to struggle and moan, tears leaking from her eyes. He took her by the shoulder again, more firmly this time, leaned over, and spoke clearly. "Claire, wake up."

Her eyes opened, those incredible blue and green eyes swimming in tears. Eyes that looked so much like Bella's. Bella, the woman in his dreams.

Tears spilled over and ran down her cheeks. "Elijah," she whispered. "You have to go. It's not safe for you here."

Who the hell was Elijah?

"Jonas," he said firmly. "You're having a dream."

Her expression cleared. "Jonas?"

She looked so sad, so lost. He bent and kissed her, gently at first and then with more passion. Her arms came up around his neck. He slipped a hand between her legs and found her already damp, ready for him. His fingers slicked over her, and he slid first one, then another inside her. Her eyes never left his as he made her hot, hotter. Her hips thrust upward in time to his fingers sliding in and out. When she was close, he removed his hand, smoothed it over her stomach, traced it over her breasts.

She wrapped her arms around him more tightly and drew him in. Opened herself to him as he slid between her legs and pushed inside her soft, welcoming body. He pulled out, sank in again, slowly. Watching her all the time.

Her mouth opened, and she gasped as he filled her again and again, driving her to peak and trying to hold himself back. He took her mouth, thrust his tongue inside in the rhythm his body was making with hers. She was his, as no other woman had ever been.

For eternity.

Their eyes were locked on each other. Jonas groaned, spilling inside her in a torrent as her muscles contracted around him and she gasped her completion, saying his name over and over. Eventually, he pulled out and held her against his chest.

Eternity. What kind of crap was that? He wasn't even sure he believed in what they had lasting a week, much less an eternity.

And why the hell was she dreaming about another man?

"Who's Elijah?"

She rose on her elbow to look at him, her expression puzzled. "Why?" she asked guardedly.

"You called me Elijah. Before you really woke up."

She looked as if she wouldn't answer, but then she sat up and wrapped the sheet around her. Shoved her hand through her hair, pushing it back from her face. He watched it spill in a silky, blonde waterfall over her shoulders and breasts. At work she wore it pulled back, which only made it more arresting when he saw it down. Especially when she was naked.

"Elijah is the man I've been dreaming about. Sarah's lover."

Dreams of the past. Like his, except she remembered her dreams. He only remembered bits and pieces of his. "The dream that takes place in the eighteen fifties."

"Dreams. Yes. I dreamed she was trying to make him leave. But he wouldn't. She was afraid for his life." She looked at him, her eyes bright with unshed tears.

"Did the dream end there?"

She nodded. "This time. But . . . Elijah and Sarah never left."

"What happened?"

She stared at him blankly for so long he thought she wouldn't answer. When she did, the words sounded as if they'd been dragged out of her. "He was lynched. By Sarah's husband and some other men."

Jesus. No wonder she'd cried. "So you were still dreaming when you called me by his name?"

She looked away, then said slowly, "I think so." She put her hands up to her face and groaned, then dropped them to look at him. "I don't know. You look just like him. Your eyes, the shape of your face, your build." She smiled briefly. "Your smile. I had the same dream—the lynching—the night before I met you. And then when I saw you. God, it reminded me of the dream I'd just had. I think that's why I spilled coffee on you."

"That would freak you out, all right." Dreams could be explained away. They didn't mean anything other than the subconscious was working overtime.

"I don't know what it means," Claire said. "Why I'm having these dreams. But they mean something. They have to."

"Maybe. Have you been reading the journal again? Isn't

that what you thought had triggered the dreams in the first place?"

"Not in a while. I've been afraid to for fear it would spark dreams." She laughed unhappily. "Apparently I don't need to read the damn thing to have the dreams anymore."

Jonas rubbed her arm, attempting to comfort. "They're just dreams, Claire. They can't hurt you."

"I'm not so sure of that. What if they're more?"

"What do you mean, more?"

Her eyes were troubled as she looked at him. "What if the dreams have something to do with now? With you and me?"

"Why would they? They're just dreams," he repeated.

"I have her eyes. My weird eyes are just like Sarah's."

*And Bella's*. But that didn't make sense. What would a woman who'd lived in the eighteen fifties and a girl who'd lived in 1968 have to do with one another? And what would either of them have to do with Claire, a woman of the twenty-first century?

"Do you think I might find the answer in the journal?"

"Answer to what?"

"The answer to why I'm having these dreams. I think there must be a reason. I don't believe it's random." She rubbed her forehead. "I'm going to try to research them. The lovers. I know something about Sarah because of Rachel's journal, but Elijah will be harder. I don't know if he had children or not. I don't believe he did. Maybe I can find out through genealogical research."

"Do you know both their full names?"

"Yes. Sarah Lawrence and Elijah Calvin."

"Elijah *Calvin*? This dude who looks like me was named Elijah Calvin?"

"Yes, why? What's wrong, Jonas?"

*Oh, God. Calvin.*

The room shimmered, faded. He heard a pop and everything faded to black. His dreams came back to him in a flood of memories. All dreams about Calvin's life. His love affair with Bella. Her fear of her father. The two of them together, falling in love. Dreams that belonged to Calvin, not Jonas.

Claire's dreams jumbled together with his own in his mind. Bella's eyes. Claire's eyes. Elijah Calvin, who looked just like Jonas. Jonas, who was the spitting image of Calvin Davis. All three of them black men involved with white women. Two of them doomed. Murdered.

What the hell?

"JONAS, WHAT HAPPENED?" Claire was starting to worry. He looked so odd. His gaze was absolutely blank, and he wouldn't— couldn't?— answer her.

He shook his head as if to clear it. "Nothing. It's nothing."

"You checked out. Like you weren't even here. Are you all right? What is going on?"

"Nothing," he repeated, clearly irritated.

"We were talking about my dreams and something obviously bothered you," she persisted. "Why can't we talk about it?"

"There's nothing to talk about," he said firmly and got out of bed. "I'm going to shower. Unless you want it first. I'm due in at ten. What about you?"

"Not until eleven. You go ahead."

If he wouldn't talk, he wouldn't. Maybe later she could convince him to open up. Jonas could deny it all he wanted, but something was bothering the hell out of him.

# CHAPTER SEVENTEEN

AS SHE'D FEARED, Claire wound up filling in for one of the docs whose wife was having a baby. She called and asked Jonas for a rain check, promising to spend time with him when their schedules allowed. Since he was a doctor as well, Claire didn't have to defend working odd hours as she'd often had to do with Glenn. Jonas simply told her to get some rest if she could and they'd see each other when their jobs allowed.

Was it her imagination or had he sounded relieved that she couldn't see him?

At midnight, she dragged herself to the long-term hotel she'd moved to and fell into bed immediately. But sleep was a long time coming. Her mind wouldn't turn off. She kept thinking of Jonas and dreams, and forbidden, tragic love. Forbidden . . .

***June 1859***

"SARAH, WHAT ARE you doing here? It's late. Does Victor know you're here?" Even as she spoke and scolded,

Rachel pulled her sister inside. "I can't believe you're out in this weather." Rain had started coming down harder and harder the farther Sarah got from home.

"Victor's gone. Thank God. For several days. I have to talk to you, Rachel. In private." She glanced around, knowing none of Victor's spies would be working at her sister's house, but still, she worried.

"You'll have to stay," her sister said. "It's already getting dark." She drew the drapes aside to look out the window. "It's coming down in sheets now. Lord, I've never seen such a night."

"I need to get back. But that's not important." Sarah grasped her sister's hand. "Rachel, I need your help."

"Of course. What can I do?"

"One of our slaves needs to leave. Before something unthinkable happens."

Rachel left Sarah to light the lamps in the deepening gloom. The fire was burning merrily, as welcoming as Rachel herself. "I don't understand. You know we help whoever comes to us. Who is it?" She sat beside Sarah on the sofa.

"His name is Elijah. He keeps Victor's accounts."

"Oh, yes, I remember seeing him. Why must he leave?" Rachel asked.

"Mr. Bransen, the overseer, had him beaten recently. He's conceived a dislike for Elijah and it's growing worse. I'm afraid of what Bransen will do next time. And I'm certain there will be a next time." Which was one reason she'd risked coming to Rachel's on such a night.

"Can you talk to Victor? Surely if Elijah is valuable to Victor he'll step in with the overseer."

Sarah laughed mirthlessly. "I've tried. You know Victor has always been autocratic." Rachel nodded. "He's getting worse.

He won't hear any dissension, as he calls it. I can barely get out of the house to visit the tenants without him questioning me for hours. If I show too much interest in any of the slaves . . ." she trailed off. If Victor found out about her friendship with Elijah, they would both die. What her husband would do if he discovered her true feelings didn't bear thinking of.

She shouldn't have kissed Elijah, shouldn't have been alone with him, but no harm had come of it. But she wanted more. And more she could never have.

She continued, "Victor has changed. He's started beating me more. At first he wouldn't do it often, but lately it's whenever the fancy strikes him. And I can't even tell you what he does to the slaves. If he's angry, or any little thing that sets him off." She shuddered, thankful that so far Elijah had escaped the master's wrath, even if he hadn't the overseer's. "I'm afraid he'll kill me."

"Because you're barren?"

"That, and because I don't defer to him as he thinks I should."

"Sarah, I know it's hard but can't you—" Rachel halted, gazing at her sister. "No, I suppose you can't. No more than I could."

"No. Right now I'm concerned with Elijah and how to save him. How to convince him he must go."

"Convince him? I don't understand. Doesn't he want to go?"

Sarah shook her head. "He's afraid to leave. Afraid for me. He—he knows how Victor treats me."

"You've taken this man into your confidence? Talked to him about your husband? Why?"

"I'm in love with him." She said it baldly, aware it was the first time she'd put a name to her feelings. Love. Of course she loved Elijah. She'd loved him almost from the moment they met. "And he has to leave so that he'll be safe." Later, she would think about following him. Once Elijah was safe, and free, Sarah could think of her own salvation.

"You're in love with a slave?" Rachel whispered, staring at her as if she'd gone mad. "How can that be?"

"He's a man. Like any man. What difference should the color of his skin make?"

***November Present Day***

CLAIRE WOKE EARLY, staying in bed and remembering the dream. She had to get ready for work, but she could take a few moments. She reached for the journal, realizing without surprise that it had opened to the very passage she'd wondered about.

***Rachel's Journal—June 6, 1859***

*My sister is in love with a slave. I can hardly believe I've written those words, much less that they are true. Yet she told me herself, not an hour ago. I do not believe in the institution of slavery. I do not think it is right, and certainly not humane to own another human being, and I do believe colored people are human, regardless of what some say. I know they have feelings and hopes and dreams, just as I do. My beliefs are why I have chosen, along with my father and husband, to help fugitive slaves escape their dismal lives.*

*But falling in love with a slave? Set aside the fact that Sarah is married. Yes, to a cruel, horrible man. But her life, her experiences, must differ so greatly from the man she says she is in love with. She says he was born free and stolen from his home as a youngster. How terrible it must have been for him to go from freedom to slavery. I am sympathetic. Yet the problems they face seem insurmountable. To be honest, they are insurmountable.*

*Sarah says she has not acted on her feelings, indeed, knows she cannot. But I know my sister. She will move heaven and earth for those she loves. And she loves Elijah Calvin.*

*I fear for my sister. I see only heartbreak ahead for her.*

Jonas's cell phone rang late the next night. He checked it, hesitating when Claire's name came up, then let it go to voice mail. He hadn't spoken to her since she'd canceled on him a few days ago. He should talk to her, he knew. He owed her some explanation as to why he'd so suddenly gone silent. But he was having a hard enough time trying to figure out this dream bullshit himself, much less explain it to Claire.

*She's having dreams too,* he thought. *You could talk to her*. But then he'd have to admit that the dreams, both his and hers, weren't simply dreams. And if they weren't just dreams, then what the hell were they?

*Please, God, don't let me dream.* He closed his eyes and willed himself to sleep.

***December 1968***

LATE THAT EVENING, Calvin went to Dream Lake and waited for Bella. He didn't mind waiting. He liked the lake. Quiet, peaceful, and best of all, private. No one knew about it but the two of them. It was the only place they could meet, especially now that her father had found out about them. They couldn't afford to be seen together, not at the drive-in or anywhere else.

Bella showed up a little while later. She got out of her car, ran to him, and threw her arms around him. "Calvin, thank God you're here."

He caught her, held her. Buried his nose in her hair and thought how great she always smelled. Like flowers. Not too sweet, but a nice, fresh scent. He didn't know what kind, since he knew nothing about flowers. He only knew he liked it, and every time he smelled that fragrance he thought of Bella. "Of course I'm here. Why all the mystery? You could have called me. Mama wouldn't have cared."

"Yes, she does. She thinks I'm trouble for you, and I am."

"She never said that." But he was uncomfortably aware there was a lot of truth to Bella's statement.

"No, she was very kind to me. But I can't help feeling like she wishes you'd never met me." She stared up at him, looking sadder than he'd ever seen her.

He didn't doubt that. Fay had told him more than once he was asking for trouble being involved with Bella. His mother wasn't the worry, though, whatever she thought. "What's wrong? Is it your father again? Has he hurt you again?"

She shook her head. "No, it's not about him. Do you love me?" She clutched his shirt and looked up at him with desperation in her gaze.

"You know I do." He kissed her. She kissed him back but broke away long before he was ready.

"Oh, God, Calvin. I'm pregnant."

His stomach dropped. "Pregnant? A baby? Are you sure?" She couldn't be pregnant. How could this be happening to them?

She let go of him and wrapped her arms around herself. "I've been sick. Missed my period. I wasn't sure, though. So I ditched school and went to a doctor in Dallas last week."

He remembered she'd missed school one day, but when he'd asked her about it, all she'd said was she wasn't feeling well. She sure as hell hadn't mentioned she might be pregnant.

"I called them today to get the results. The test was positive. I'm not very far along, the doctor said."

"Why Dallas?"

"Are you kidding? There's no way I could go to a doctor here in Fort Worth. I couldn't risk Daddy finding out. Not after what he did when he found out about you and me."

"Doctors aren't supposed to tell anything about their patients. What you say to them is supposed to be confidential."

She snorted. "Don't be naive, Calvin. Buster Cantrell has ways of making people talk. Even doctors. Or nurses or whoever. Besides, it doesn't matter. What matters is I'm pregnant." She grabbed his hand and squeezed. "Oh, Calvin, what are we going to do?"

He couldn't think what to say. They'd been careful but obviously not careful enough. He'd known he was taking a risk making love to Bella, but they loved each other. They just hadn't been able to resist being together. He'd been strong, for her sake mostly, but he hadn't been able to refuse her forever. And he didn't regret making love to her, even if she was pregnant.

"I . . . I can't have an abortion. Don't ask me to do that."

He put his arms around her and hugged her. "I won't. I never could." A baby. A part of him and Bella. No, he couldn't ask her to get rid of it. Didn't want to. "We'll get married."

"Married?" She looked up at him, trust and hope in her eyes. "Can we?"

"Why couldn't we? We're both old enough. We're both eighteen."

"It's not our age I'm worried about. You're colored, I'm white. I'm not sure it's even legal for us to marry."

Which was just plain wrong, even though he knew that what she said could be true. "It's bound to be legal somewhere. Laws have changed. I know I've read about it. We'll go away. We'll have to anyway, because of your father. You know what he'll do when he finds out."

Kill him. God knows what he'd do to Bella. When her father found out she was pregnant by a colored kid? Then the shit would really hit the fan.

"I can't even think about him. It's too awful."

Yeah, better they didn't think about Buster Cantrell. At least not until after they were married. Cantrell couldn't do anything once Bella was legally married. Could he?

Well, yeah, he could still kill Calvin.

She clutched his shirt and looked up at him. "Do you really want to marry me? Or are you just saying it because you think you should?"

"I want to marry you, Bella." He hadn't ever dared think about it before. But they loved each other. They should be together. And now a baby. . . .

"How will we live? How will you go to college? Will they still give you a scholarship?"

"I don't know. Maybe." He thought about it for a moment, then shook his head. "No, that won't work. I'll have to get a job. I won't be able to go to school. Not with a family to support."

"Oh, Calvin, I don't want to be the reason you can't play ball. You love it."

He wrapped his arms around her, rubbed her back, held her close. "I love you more." He kissed her, those sweet lips that he dreamed about when he wasn't with her. He thought about marrying Bella, living with her, and the baby. About how to do it. It wouldn't be easy.

"We'll get Naomi to help us. She works for a lawyer, she can find out what we need to do. If we can get married in Texas or if we have to go somewhere else."

"Are you sure she'll help us?"

Bella sounded doubtful, and he couldn't really blame her. Naomi hadn't been too friendly to Bella. She thought Calvin was crazy to date a white girl. What would she think about him wanting to marry Bella?

"Naomi was so angry when I called her earlier. She didn't say it, but I could tell. I don't think she likes me."

He rubbed her back again, looked down at her, and smiled reassuringly. "She doesn't know you. And she loves me, so she'll do what she can to help us."

"I hope so. Because there's nothing I want more than to marry you and have your baby. Not even my father can do anything to stop us once we're married."

He sure as hell hoped not, but he had a bad feeling they were underestimating Buster Cantrell.

What else could they do, though? Bella was pregnant, and there was no way in hell he was going to abandon her and let her son-of-a-bitch father beat her or his child. And Calvin didn't have a doubt that he would. Cantrell had already proved himself a bully and a child abuser. No way was Calvin letting the bastard touch his baby.

Calvin was going to protect Bella and the baby. He just hoped he didn't die trying.

***November Present Day***

GODDAMN HIS SON, anyway, Lawrence thought,

watching Glenn drive away. Glenn's incessant whining about his wayward wife was getting on Lawrence's last nerve. It reminded him of the past. Of thoughts he'd buried for decades. But this talk of Claire and that black bastard was bringing up all sorts of memories. Memories he'd dealt with and put behind him years ago.

Fed up, he'd finally told Glenn that instead of whining he should grow a pair and do something about it. Make the bitch toe the line. Lawrence was a firm believer that you made your own luck, and Glenn could use to learn that lesson.

Lawrence had, after all. As clearly as if it were yesterday, he slipped back into his memories. Memories of the day Lawrence had told Bella's father just exactly what his little girl had been up to.

*Lawrence didn't like Buster Cantrell. But he wanted Bella. And if he couldn't get her one way, he'd get her another. She'd be sorry she turned him down. Sorry she rejected him—Lawrence Westbrook!—for a damn nigger.*

*"I found out something you're not going to like." Putting it mildly. Buster was going to blow a gasket when he found out who his little girl had been putting out for. The whole idea made Lawrence want to puke, too.*

*"Go on," Buster said, lighting a cigar. "What is going on with my daughter?"*

*"I found out why she wouldn't go out with me. She's involved with someone."*

*"First I've heard of it. Who is it?"*

*"His name's Calvin Davis."*

*"Never heard of him."*

*"You wouldn't have." He paused and added, "He's a colored kid."*

*Buster stared at him, then turned so red Lawrence thought he'd busted a blood vessel. "The hell you say! I ought to kill you for saying that."*

*Lawrence stood his ground. "It's true. I didn't believe it either. But I saw them together at the drive-in."*

*"My daughter and a nigger? He must have forced her."*

*"I'm sorry, sir, but she kissed him. Of her own free will, it looked like."*

*"Goddamn it! I'll put a stop to this. No nigger's going to lay his filthy hands on my daughter. Not while I'm alive."*

*"I thought you should know. I'm sorry," Lawrence repeated, trying to appear properly solemn. Inside, though, he was laughing. Calvin Davis was going to be sorry he messed with Lawrence's girl. Because if she hadn't been his girl before, she would be soon. Buster Cantrell would see to it.*

# CHAPTER EIGHTEEN

AT FIRST, CLAIRE wasn't too worried when Jonas didn't call. She knew he was having problems with his mother and his work schedule could be crazy. As a trauma surgeon, her schedule could be just as wild. She'd canceled on him the morning after their second night together. And that was the last time she'd actually talked to him. After three days of getting nothing but his voice mail, she suspected she'd been dumped.

Their last night together, she thought. Did his response have something to do with her calling him by another man's name?

A dead man's name.

Whatever the reason, her affair with Jonas hadn't been an affair. It had been a one-night stand. Technically, a two-night stand. She glared at her unresponsive cell phone.

The son of a bitch.

So much for his declaration that he wanted more from her than revenge sex. More from her than a fling. Jonas had fed her a line, and she'd been too damn dumb to see it. She'd believed him and worse—fallen for him. Smooth, seductive, she should have known he was too good to be true.

Until she sorted things out with Glenn over who would live in the house, she'd moved into a long-term hotel. It wasn't bad. Not great, but not terrible. It had a small kitchen with a stove and microwave so she could prepare food and not have to eat out every meal. There was a bed, a small table and a couple of chairs, a couch, a TV, and a high-speed Internet hookup. The necessities. But after staying in the lap of luxury at the Worthington, the small three-room apartment with its shabby furnishings and lovely view of the parking lot was pretty damn depressing.

Maybe she should move into a nice apartment and not worry about who would get the house. She wasn't attached to it, particularly. It had always been more Glenn's style than hers.

Her cell phone rang and she checked caller ID. Jonas. She thought about letting it go to voice mail, but she was really curious about what he wanted and how he would explain why he hadn't called her. Because if he thought he didn't owe her an explanation, he had another think coming.

Besides, it would be childish not to answer. She punched the answer button and said, "What?"

"It's me, Jonas."

"I know. I have caller ID."

"Are you working today?"

"No."

"Look, I know you're probably pissed, but I'd like to explain."

She barely managed not to snort. "What was your first clue? I'm not stupid, Jonas. I can take a hint."

"It's not like that. Can I come see you and talk to you? Are you still at the Worthington?"

"No, I've moved."

"Are you going to tell me where you are?"

She didn't answer. Childish, but satisfying.

"Claire, let me come see you."

She wished she could say no, but she couldn't deny him. Curiosity and, worse, just plain desire to see him won. Reluctantly, she gave him the address.

"I'll be there in half an hour. Maybe a little less, but I have to drop something off at my mother's."

She hung up, resisting the urge to fling the phone across the room. What really pissed her off was that her heart had stumbled just at the sound of his voice. That liquid gold voice, so deep and resonant it could weave a spell in moments. He'd certainly had her under his spell. So seductive it didn't matter what he said, only that he spoke in that outrageously sexy voice. How irrational was that? She wasn't a romantic. Not in the least. Certainly not about a man who'd taken her to bed a couple of times and promptly dumped her.

Oh, God. Surely she hadn't already fallen in love with him. What a disaster that would be. No, it wasn't possible. She'd only known him a matter of weeks.

*Unless you knew him over a hundred and fifty years ago.*

Impossible.

TWENTY MINUTES later, Claire heard a knock on the door. Assuming it was Jonas, she opened it before she thought about it. And immediately tried to shut it when she realized Glenn was standing there.

He lodged his foot in the door and pushed against her. "Damn it, Claire, I just want to talk to you. Don't be ridiculous."

He shoved it open, and she stumbled back. She ran across the room to the coffee table and grabbed her cell phone, holding it in front of her like a weapon. "Take it up with my lawyer. I'll call the police if you don't leave."

He shot her an annoyed look. "The police won't do anything. You don't have a restraining order against me. And you won't get one because I haven't done anything to warrant it. You're being absurd, Claire."

Absurd, was she? "So you still won't admit you beat me up." She cursed herself for being so foolish as to open the door without checking who was there. If she'd had a peephole she would've looked out, but this hotel didn't run to peepholes.

"I simply want to talk to you. No need to get hysterical." He took a seat at the table, crossed his leg, and looked around the small apartment. "God, what a dump. Why did you move from the Worthington?"

"You should know. It was too expensive to stay long term. And you canceled the credit card I was using."

"Because I thought it might help you come to your senses."

"What do you want?" How could she have loved him? Or thought she did? How could she have loved someone who would hurt her like Glenn had? In her worst dreams she'd never imagined being a battered wife. The whole thing still seemed surreal to her, except the pain she still had from her bruised ribs was as real as it gets.

"You don't have to live like this, Claire." He gestured at the room with revulsion.

"Why, are you moving out of the house? If so, tell the lawyers."

"No, I'm not moving out. But you could move back in with me."

Claire was still clutching the cell phone like a lifeline. She stared at him, but he was serious. So sincere, so earnest. As if he'd never touched her in anger. Never beaten the crap out of her. What would he do if Jonas showed up before he left? Something told her he wouldn't be so tough fighting a man. Except she didn't want Jonas hurt, or more involved than he already was. Especially now that they weren't even together.

"What part of 'I want a divorce and don't ever want to see you again' don't you understand?"

"I love you. I want you back. We can work this out, Claire."

Did he even listen? "No, we can't. You don't love me and I don't love you."

"You know that's not true. Don't give up on our marriage."

"You did that the moment you hit me. You had to know I wouldn't put up with abuse. Drunk or not, you knew."

"You're exaggerating what happened. I don't know how that man brainwashed you—"

She interrupted. "I know what happened and so do you, even if you won't admit it. We're over. Now get out and don't come here again. And stop having me followed. I'm sure that's how you knew where to find me. Nothing I do is your business anymore."

"We're still married, Claire," he reminded her. "Stop this foolish idea of divorce. Get rid of the lawyer and come back home."

"Not a chance in hell."

She heard a knock at the door. "Claire, it's Jonas."

Glenn's face darkened, and he clenched his fist. "So you're still whoring around with Clark. I'd hoped you'd gotten over it and come to your senses."

"Really, Glenn? Calling me a whore is certainly going to make me want to give our marriage another chance." She crossed the room, avoiding the table where Glenn sat and pulled open the door.

Jonas took one look at her and asked, "What's wrong?"

She said nothing, just stepped aside so he could enter.

"Westbrook," he said, catching sight of Glenn. "What are you doing here?" He turned to Claire. "Are you all right? Did he hurt you?"

Glenn stood. "That's rich. What am I doing here? I'm Claire's husband. You're the one who should be shot for fooling around with another man's wife."

Jonas's jaw tightened.

Claire stepped between them before he could do anything, such as punch out her son-of-a-bitch husband. As angry as she was with Jonas, she'd never forgive herself if he were hurt because of her. "Get out, Glenn. Next time you have anything to say to me, tell it to my lawyer. And don't threaten Jonas. He's not the problem, you are."

"I don't need you to defend me, Claire," Jonas said. "I don't hide behind women," he told Glenn, "or beat them up, for that matter."

"You'll regret this, Claire," Glenn warned. "Throwing yourself away on this black bastard. You should be ashamed of yourself. He'll dump you as soon as he's had enough. Men like him only want one thing. A white woman is nothing but a notch in his bedpost. However, I'm surprised it's lasted this long. You're ruining your life for nothing."

She grabbed hold of Jonas's arm, restraining him. "Don't. He's not worth it."

Glenn left, slamming the door behind him. Claire heaved a sigh of relief. But now she had to deal with Jonas, who had, just as her husband had said, used her and dumped her. Was she just a notch in his bedpost? She hadn't thought so. Until he dumped her so quickly.

"I've had all the drama I can take for one night. Say what you want and then leave."

OKAY, HE DESERVED that. Deserved her anger and anything else she wanted to heap on him. He felt like a shit, being put almost on the same level as her abusive bastard of a husband. When he'd first arrived she'd looked relieved, but that was clearly in response to her fear of her husband.

She didn't look happy to see Jonas now. Not that he blamed her. He knew what his actions must look like. "You don't believe what he said, do you?"

"I don't think the fact that I'm white had anything to do with it, no. But do I think I was a notch in your bedpost and all you wanted was the sex? You betcha."

Again, he couldn't blame her. He didn't know how to explain himself. When she'd told him about Elijah, his dreams had come back to him. Every freaking dream he'd had about Calvin's life had dropped on him like a ton of bricks. And those memories, coupled with everything else he'd learned, had been too much for him to handle. So he'd left her. Like a coward.

It was hard to explain something to someone when you didn't understand it yourself. When what was happening to you destroyed your picture of how the world worked.

"Did he hurt you?"

"No. He wasn't drunk. He had better control of himself. This time."

"What did he want?"

She laughed humorlessly. "He wanted me to come back. To drop the divorce. As if I would."

"It's too bad you can't get a restraining order on him."

"Yes, he pointed that out." She crossed her arms over her chest, closing herself off even further. "I don't want to discuss Glenn or my marriage. That's none of your concern."

"Yes, it is."

"Really? You could have fooled me."

As always, she looked beautiful. What he really wanted was to make love to her and forget everything else. But that wasn't going to happen. Instead, he was going to have to explain why he'd run out on her when he wasn't certain of the reason himself.

He had to talk to her about his dreams. About Calvin and Bella and murder. The whole stinking mess. Not only that, but he had to admit that somehow his crazy dreams, and hell, hers too, bore a relation to the two of them.

He didn't know how to start. How to tell her what was going on without sounding like a whack job.

"Your call surprised me," Claire said, breaking the silence. "I thought we were done."

"Because I haven't called you for the last few days."

"It was a little more than that. Try actively avoided me." Claire shrugged. "If it looks like a duck and quacks like a duck, it's a duck."

"I'd like to explain."

"Explain what? The nature of one-night stands? No, make that a two-night stand. I believe you made clear what happened between us when you wouldn't talk to me for three days."

He ground his teeth. Of course she thought he was a player. Why wouldn't she? "I didn't do it to hurt you."

"I'm not hurt," she said. "I'm pissed." She waved at a chair by the scarred table, the chair her husband had recently vacated. "Sit. Talk." She walked over to the couch and sat on the end farthest from him, watching him. "I'm waiting."

He didn't sit. Instead he paced and ran a hand over his hair. "It's not you, it's me," he finally said.

She stared at him. "Now that's original. If that's all you have to say—"

"It's not," he interrupted. He walked over to her. Studying her face, he raised a hand to her cheek and stroked a finger down it gently. "Damn, you are so beautiful." He didn't want to talk, he wanted to kiss her. To make love to her. To forget everything he didn't understand— everything he didn't want to understand.

She jerked her head away from him. "Why are you here, Jonas? You can't really think you could walk in and we would take up where we left off. I don't work that way." She paused and added, "Not with Glenn and not with you."

Man, that hurt. With all his faults, he'd never hit a woman and couldn't imagine that he ever would. Being compared to her husband in any way irritated the hell out of him. Which he suspected she knew. "I didn't come here expecting to take up where we left off. That's not why I'm here. I couldn't stay away any longer. I tried." He laughed without humor. "I really tried, but it's no use." Not seeing Claire hadn't stopped the dreams, hadn't stopped him from remembering the damn things.

"As an apology, that sucks. I thought we had something special." She winced, but continued. "Call me stupid, but I did. You apparently thought it was a fling. Which is fine, I just wish you'd been honest instead of allowing me to believe what we had was something more than the sex."

"It was more than sex. I—" He halted, paced away. "Jesus. I don't know how to explain this to you. I can't explain it to myself."

"Try," she said. "I'll start. Everything was fine, at least, I thought it was, until I called you Elijah. I told you, it was a dream. I can't help what I dream. I wish I could. It's not very pleasant being held hostage to your dreams."

"I know."

"How can you know?"

"Because the same thing is happening to me." Dreams were bad enough. He didn't know what to think about the flashbacks that happened when he was awake. Thank God he hadn't had many of those, and they had been mercifully brief. And they'd only happened when he was with Claire, touching Claire.

"What are you talking about?" She got up and walked over to him, gazed into his eyes. "You're really upset, aren't you?"

"Upset doesn't even touch it." Maybe of all people, she'd understand. After all, she'd admitted to having dreams herself, dreams that clearly disturbed her. "I've been having dreams. Dreams of another time. I only remembered bits and pieces, and not much of that. Until you told me about Elijah."

She glared derisively at him. "Let me guess. You're having dreams of the eighteen fifties."

"No. I'm not mocking you, Claire. Hear me out." She didn't speak, which he took as a sign to continue. "My dreams occur in 1968. Only they're not dreams about me. They're about someone else. A teenager. His name is Calvin." Claire made an exclamation, and he smiled sourly. "Yeah, Calvin. Like the last name of the guy you've been dreaming about. He's a black kid, about eighteen. He doesn't want to go to 'Nam, he wants to play basketball, and he wants a girl. Her name is Isabel Cantrell. He calls her Bella."

Claire had an odd look on her face. "What?"

"Just go on. I'll tell you later."

"I know it's impossible, but I—" he broke off and turned away. "I feel like a whack case." He turned back to her and said, "I think I'm channeling this kid's life. In my dreams."

"Why?"

"Because I keep seeing, no, experiencing, these scenes. They're not just dreams. It's like they really happened. Some of it did."

"How do you know?"

"Calvin was my cousin. My mother told me about him. He was in love with a white girl. Her father hated him. I'd heard whispers about this cousin, but not like the dreams. I'm telling you, it's as if I was there. No, as if I'm him in these dreams. I'm dreaming about his life, but it feels like mine." She wasn't looking at him as if he was crazy. But she still looked pissed.

"So you dumped me because I made you remember the dreams. If you didn't see me, didn't have sex with me, then you wouldn't have any dreams. Or at least you wouldn't remember them, right? No Claire, no problem."

He winced. Put like that, it sounded brutal. "I didn't dump you. I just didn't see you for a few days. To try to figure things out. I don't know why this is happening to me. You have to admit it's weird as hell. I never had anything like these dreams until I met you."

"How do you know? Maybe you've been having them for years and you've only just now remembered."

"No," he said positively. "That's not all. Sometimes I'll have a—" he hesitated. "Shit, I guess they're flashbacks. Just for an instant, but something from the dreams will come to me. And then when you called me Elijah, it *all* came back to me."

"You're serious."

"Yeah. Unfortunately." He looked at her, at those beautiful, unusual eyes. One green, one half-green, half-blue. "You have her eyes. Bella's eyes."

Claire laughed. "That doesn't surprise me. I'm kin to the Cantrells. Isabel Cantrell was a cousin of mine. I've been told my eyes come from the Cantrell side of the family. My mother still stays in touch with Isabel's sister, Sophie."

He didn't believe in coincidence, yet what was he supposed to think? "Isabel was your cousin, and Calvin Davis was a cousin of mine. A cousin I look like. Exactly like."

"So you not only look like Elijah, you look like this boy from the sixties. This boy whose life you're dreaming."

"Apparently. The other day I was at my mother's. I found a picture and thought it was me until my mother said it was her cousin Calvin."

"I have Sarah's eyes. And Bella's."

"Apparently," he said again.

"What happened to Calvin? I know Bella died young, but I don't know details. I just know it was a big tragedy and Sophie broke off all contact with her father over it. She left home the minute she turned eighteen, and didn't come back until after he died."

"Calvin was murdered. Shot. Supposedly by Bella's father, Buster Cantrell."

"Good God," she said. "Is that what freaked you out so much? Have you dreamed of being shot?"

"No. Not yet."

"You're afraid you will."

He shrugged. "Wouldn't you be?" He sat on the couch, put

his face in his hands. "I must be nuts. Fucking nuts to even consider any of this could have happened. But it did happen. If what my mother has told me is true, I can't deny that what I've been dreaming really did happen." He dropped his hands and looked at her. "Now you know why I didn't want to be around you. And why I didn't know how to tell you, or want to tell you what was going on."

She sat beside him. Touched his arm, in sympathy? Understanding? "Not really."

"Jesus, Claire, I'm channeling a kid from 1968. In my dreams. How crazy is that?"

"If you're crazy, then I am too. That's exactly what my dreams are like. I'm dreaming as if I'm Sarah. I'm dreaming her life."

"When you called me Elijah, when you told me his full name, everything came back in a rush. All those dreams unrolled like a movie in my mind. It freaked me out. Up until then I had only remembered bits and pieces. Their names, a few scenes. I could ignore it. And then, boom, there it all was. I didn't know how to deal with it. I thought I could get a handle on it if I didn't see you."

"How'd that work for you?"

"It didn't. I still don't believe in this kind of crap, and I still can't deny my dreams bear at least some relation to the past."

"Why are you here, Jonas?"

"I told you, I couldn't stay away." Maybe she was right. Maybe fate had something to do with it.

Except he didn't believe in fate.

Their eyes met. Locked. "Why?" she asked again. "Why did you come back?"

"Because I'm in love with you, Claire."

## CHAPTER NINETEEN

"I LOVE YOU," Jonas repeated. "I want to be with you."

His words flowed over her, warm, seductive. She wanted to melt, to let herself go along with whatever he said, whatever he pleased. But what she wanted didn't matter. She needed honesty more.

"When you didn't call, you hurt me. I thought you'd played me and I'd been a fool and fallen for it. Fallen for you. You seemed so sincere, and then nothing. I thought you didn't want me because I had too much baggage."

He smiled. "I'd say we both have baggage. What's a soon-to-be ex compared to losing your mind?"

"You're not losing your mind."

"God, I hope not." He raised a hand to her face, rubbed his thumb over her lips. "I never meant to hurt you. I was afraid you'd think I was crazy if I told you what was going on. Hell, *I* think I'm crazy. Why wouldn't you? So instead of telling you, I tried to avoid it. Avoid everything."

"I'm hardly one to talk about crazy. With the dreams I've been having I feel a little whacked too."

"Dreams should be explainable. But ours aren't. We can't just explain them away."

She didn't believe they were *only* dreams. Neither did Jonas, even though he wouldn't admit it yet. But they could discuss all that later. Right now she didn't want to talk. Was she a fool to believe him? To believe he loved her? Perhaps, but even so she wanted him.

She put her arms around his neck and kissed him. Gently, lightly. He started to speak, but she kissed him again, more deeply this time. Let herself sink into the kiss, into the warm flavors of his mouth, the soft, silky touch of his tongue sliding against hers, his lips rubbing over hers.

She pulled back, began undoing her buttons. He watched her, his eyes a deep golden brown, shot through with a dark chocolate. Intrigued but wary. "Don't think about anything," she said as she undid the last button and let her blouse fall to the floor. "Don't think about anything but us."

Claire stood, took his hand. Walked with him into the bedroom. Turned the lamp on low. She unbuttoned her jeans, unzipped and pushed them down her legs before stepping out of them. "Think about us. Just us." She lay back on the bed, drew him down with her as she did. "Make love to me, Jonas," she said softly.

He cupped her face, kissed her. His tongue swept inside, claimed her. His hands caressed her, helping her strip her remaining clothes and his until they both lay naked on the bed. She put her hand on his chest, so white against the deep, rich brown of his skin.

"The first time I saw you I wondered what you'd look like without your shirt. Such lovely muscles," she murmured, stroking her hand over him. "I couldn't believe I was thinking that about someone I didn't even know. I'd never had a reaction like that, not to anyone."

He laughed. "The first time I saw you I thought you were trouble. And that was before you spilled coffee on me."

She paused, her hands on his arms. "Have you changed your mind?"

He trailed kisses down her throat, took her breast in his mouth. "No. I like trouble," he said against her skin. He drew her nipple into his mouth and sucked. "I like it a lot."

Claire groaned, slid her hand down and wrapped it around him. Stroked as she felt him grow harder, bigger. His fingers played over her, sliding, teasing, exciting. "Jonas," she sighed, gasping as he slipped a finger inside her, mimicking the motions with his tongue sweeping her mouth.

He moved between her thighs and looked down at her, kissed her mouth deeply. "Tell me again," she said. "While you're inside me."

He slipped inside her, stroked gently at first, then more urgently. "I love you, Claire."

She kissed his mouth, wrapped her arms and legs around him, opened to him, loving the feel of him. Loving him.

He pushed her to the brink as he thrust into her again and again. All the sensations coalesced into a sunburst as she spiraled out of control, her climax shattering as he drove into her a final time, spilling inside her endlessly.

JONAS ROLLED TO the side, still holding her close.

She sighed. "We should talk about it. About our dreams and what it all means."

"We have. What else is there to say?"

A lot. And she was betting he didn't want to hear any of it. "You said you loved me. You haven't asked me if I love you."

He rose on his elbow and looked down at her. "I assumed you'd tell me if and when you were ready."

"I do love you, Jonas." She put her palm to his cheek and looked into his eyes. The eyes that looked so much like the ones she saw in her dreams. Unusual eyes. They weren't simply brown. They were a hundred shades, ranging from deep gold to flecks of mahogany, to every shade in between. He was a beautiful man, though he'd probably laugh to hear himself described that way.

Beautiful, just as Elijah had been.

"I've loved you from the first time I saw you." She paused and added deliberately, "Over a hundred and fifty years ago."

He went from relaxed to tense in a heartbeat. He got up and pulled on his pants with his back to her. When he turned around the look on his face was clearly readable. Shut down, shut out. His words bore it out. "Claire, don't go there. You know it's impossible."

"I'll admit it's improbable. But—" Jonas snorted derisively and left the room before she could finish. She got up and reached for his shirt since she couldn't find her own. She didn't intend to have this conversation naked. She already felt as if she were revealing too much.

"Would you like a drink?" she asked, following him back into the other room. "A coke or something? I don't have any beer." Come to think of it, a nice stiff drink would be appropriate for what they were going to talk about.

Because she intended to discuss it, whether Jonas wanted to or not.

"Water would be nice."

She grabbed a bottle out of the refrigerator and tossed it to him. He caught it and twisted the top off, drank deeply.

"Past lives," she said. "We've both been dreaming about a past life. Lives that are intertwined. What other explanation is there?"

He paused in mid-sip and glared at her. "Plenty. We're both crazy."

Reincarnation. She didn't know about Jonas, but she'd been thinking about it for some time. Now that he'd told her of his dreams, it made even more sense.

God, reincarnation made sense?

"So you don't believe in people having past lives?" She knew the answer. Until recently, she'd thought it was hokum too. Like her, Jonas was a doctor. A scientist. He wanted everything proved to him. Facts, not fantasy. And he would certainly consider past lives a fantasy of someone's imagination. He wasn't likely to believe in something so controversial, so unlikely, as reincarnation. In fact, she was far from certain what she thought about it all, but she couldn't totally deny the possibility anymore as she had in the past.

"I think it's bullshit."

A nice, unequivocal answer. "Do you really? Still? Even after what's happened to us?"

He paced away, turned, and walked back to her, his expression grim. "Yes, really. Past lives? The whole concept of someone having lived before—not just once but twice—is ridiculous bullshit." He took her hand. "Don't tell me you're buying into it. Because of some crazy dreams we've both been having? Come on, Claire, get real."

"A few months ago, I would have agreed with you. But ever since I started having the dreams, ever since I met you—"

"Yeah, yeah," he interrupted, releasing her hand to wave

his in the air. "We know each other, we're fated to be together. Whatever."

He sounded so disgusted she'd have laughed, except it wasn't funny. She tried again. "Okay, let's look at this logically."

Jonas snorted and took another sip of water. "Yeah, logical. Because there's something supremely logical about being reincarnated."

Claire ignored that and continued. "I've been having these dreams of another life. It feels as if I'm there, as if it's my own life I'm dreaming about. It isn't just Sarah's life, it's mine. The emotions, the feelings are real. Very real. They're *my* emotions and feelings. And I didn't start having them until I found Rachel's journal. Until I met you."

"*Logic* would dictate that if you stop reading the stupid journal you'll stop having the dreams. Maybe you just have a good imagination."

"Yes, but I don't. I never have. And I'm not sure I would stop having the dreams anyway. I told you, now I seem to have them regardless of whether I read the journal. The journal might have been the instigation, but the dreams have taken on a life of their own. A will of their own. That life—the one that took place in 1859—has become even more realistic. Besides, how do you explain our connection if we weren't connected in the past? You've felt it, just as I have. You know you felt as if you knew me from the moment we met. You admitted as much when we went to breakfast that first time."

"No, I didn't. I said you were familiar, like we'd met before. Thinking you've met someone and believing in past lives are two entirely different things." He set his water down and put his hands on her arms, looking down at her. "I'm in love with you now. I don't need to talk about a past connection to know that. Do you?"

"Of course not. But I'm not denying the connection is there, like you are. I have Sarah's eyes. And Bella's," she reminded him. "I'm related to both of them. The woman in my dreams and the girl in yours. We all have the same strange eyes. They're my kinfolk."

He released her, made an impatient gesture. "So what? You're dreaming about a time in the eighteen fifties. And I'm dreaming about a completely different time. As to whether the people in those two time periods are connected, possibly. But past lives? Jesus."

"What would you call it, then? What's happening to us?"

He gave her a dirty look. "I call it crazy-ass shit."

She couldn't help laughing. "Oh, Jonas, I know it seems insane."

"Ya think? It's not funny, either. Calvin Davis, my cousin, was murdered. The killer was never caught."

"I know it's not funny," she said, sobering. "I've dreamed about a lynching, remember? And Sarah, my ancestor, she loved him. She loved the man who died so terribly. It's horrible. Inconceivable."

"Not so inconceivable. Especially not in the South in that time period. A black slave involved with a white woman? I'm surprised they didn't do worse than lynch him. And in the sixties, around here and throughout the South, there was still a huge amount of prejudice about mixed relationships. Just ask my mother or any of her generation. I guess Calvin was lucky to be shot and not lynched."

But there had to be a reason they were seeing these things. "Have you asked yourself why this is happening to us?"

"I've wondered if I have a brain tumor, yeah."

"That's not it. Unless I have one too, and that's too coincidental."

He stared at her as if she were nuts. "For God's sake, Claire, we're talking about reincarnation, yet you draw the line at coincidence?"

"I do in this instance. I don't believe we both have a brain tumor. Or that even if we did it would make us both dream of a past life. Do you honestly think you have a brain tumor?"

Their eyes met. "No. I don't have any symptoms. I don't think crazy dreams are a symptom of a brain tumor. Now mental illness? Maybe."

He walked into the living area and sat on the couch. She followed him and sat beside him. "I don't think mental illness is your problem. Do you?"

"No, but neither do most people who have a problem. Denial is a classic issue in many cases."

"You'd rather think you're mentally ill than admit the possibility of reincarnation? Seriously?"

He jaw tightened. "That's not what I said. I can't deny I've worried about it, though. For God's sake, I'm channeling a kid who died in 1968. Who wouldn't think they were crazy?"

"But you've talked to me. You've seen how we're connected, how your visions and my dreams connect us. How do you explain that?"

"I can't. But I know I don't believe in this shit. And this crap we're talking about is the epitome of woo-woo bullshit. Can you see me trying to explain this to someone else? *I'm channeling a kid from the nineteen sixties.* Not to worry, though. This dude just happens to be one of my past lives."

"What if it's not bullshit? What if it's really happening to us? What if you really were Elijah and Calvin, and I really was Sarah and Bella? What if we're together now for a reason?"

"If you follow through with that analogy, that means we're both fated to die. Too young and tragically."

*Damn*. She hadn't quite gotten that far, but Jonas was right.

# CHAPTER TWENTY

JONAS SAID, "I can't accept that you and I are fated to die because we're involved with each other." Couldn't believe it *yet,* he didn't add, but the addendum was implied. He couldn't believe he was even considering that they'd lived before as a viable theory, but now that he remembered the dreams, now that he connected his dreams to hers, he felt forced to consider the possibility. But Goddamn it, that made him feel like a whack job.

"Even if we're not fated to die, and God knows, I hope we aren't, there has to be a reason for the dreams," Claire said.

"You'd think so." He scrubbed his hand over his face and sighed. "I dreamed about Calvin and Bella last night. I knew what I'd dreamed when I woke up. Bella told him she was pregnant. They talked about getting married, even though they knew there would be problems. They weren't sure if they could legally marry in Texas. And he was worried her old man would kill him if they managed it." He shrugged. "Which is apparently what happened."

"What if her father didn't kill him? Why are you so convinced he did?"

"I'm not convinced. My mother is. She believes the old man bought off the cops. She says the crime was never investigated properly, but most people believe Buster Cantrell killed Calvin Davis. My mother is convinced Buster paid the cops to look the other way, that even if they had found proof of who committed the crime, they buried it." He shrugged. "It's not unheard of. It was 1968. Buster Cantrell was powerful, rich. White. Calvin was a poor black kid. A nobody. She could be right."

"Maybe Buster didn't kill him, though. Maybe we're meant to find out what really happened. Who really killed him. And what happened to Bella's baby? I know Bella died, but what about her child?"

"I have no idea." He thought about it a moment. "You could ask her sister. You said your mother kept in touch with her. Or maybe your mother knows."

She didn't look pleased with that idea. "What's wrong?"

She reached for her water, sipped it, taking her time. Avoiding his gaze, she said, "I haven't told my mother anything about what's been going on with me. She doesn't even know I'm divorcing Glenn. Much less that you and I are involved."

"You're afraid to tell her. Because you're still married? Or because I'm black?"

"Neither." She finally looked at him. Glared. "Don't look at me like that. I'm not *afraid* to tell her. I didn't want to get into it with her about the reasons I'm getting a divorce. And as for you and me. . . . Until tonight I thought you'd dumped me. I thought we'd had a one-night— okay—two- night stand. Why would I tell my mother any of that? Do you tell your mother about every fling you have?"

"I don't have flings. And that's immaterial. You're hedging. You know that's not the case now. Do you intend to tell her about us?"

"Of course I do. But first I have to tell her about the divorce. Glenn is always on his best behavior around her. He's always sucked up to her. She has no idea what he's capable of."

"She doesn't know about the night he hit you?"

Claire shook her head. "I didn't want to tell her. It was all so sordid."

"We went through this the night it happened." He took her hand, patted it comfortingly. "Nothing was your fault, Claire. Your husband was wrong to hit you." She didn't answer, so he continued. "I thought you might have talked to your mother since you're still not talking to Lanie."

"No. I haven't talked to anyone. Except you."

"Maybe you should."

"Well, it sure as hell isn't going to be Lanie."

"You could do worse. She cares about you."

"So much that she lied to me for years. Do you think I'm wrong to be angry at her? After what she did?"

"I don't think you're wrong. I just think your anger is a little misplaced. Lanie made a mistake. She should have told you your husband hit on her when it happened. She owned up to her mistake and tried to explain why she acted the way she did. The person who's never owned up to anything is your soon-to-be ex. He's the one you're really mad at. And you should be. Hell, he won't admit he hit you, will he? Much less anything he might have done prior to that."

"Glenn isn't the point. We're getting far away from the subject."

"What subject?" He said it flippantly, but he knew she'd keep going.

"What if you're having these dreams because we're supposed to find out who really killed Calvin? We're supposed to find out what really happened all those years ago."

"Still too woo-woo for me."

She let go of his hand and got up to pace. "Both Elijah and Calvin were murdered. We don't know what happened to the women they loved, not yet. Well, we know Bella died, but we're not sure about Sarah. And now you and I are together. Maybe we're here together for a reason." She stopped pacing, looked at him, her eyes fervent. "We have to find out the truth."

"So that we can live happily ever after?" he asked sarcastically.

"I wouldn't describe it exactly like that. Maybe we're supposed to find out about the past so we can get it right this time. We can be together and put the past to rest."

"Or, if your theory holds true, we're supposed to be together so I can be murdered. In this lifetime, just as I was in the previous two." Yeah, that was a fun idea.

"Do you believe that? If you're involved with me you're going to die?"

"Claire, I don't believe any of this," he said wearily. "I think it's all horse shit."

"So much so that you won't even consider looking into Calvin's death?"

"I didn't say that." Reluctantly, he told her what he'd been thinking for several days now—since he'd talked to his mother and discovered Calvin's murder had never been solved. "I have an old friend from high school who's an investigative journalist. Emmitt Rickerby. He writes true crime novels. Likes nothing better than to look into cold cases."

"Rickerby? I think I've read one of his books. He's really good, but I remember not being able to sleep after I finished the book. Very scary, considering it was a true story. You really went to school with him?"

"Yeah, he was a good friend back then. We lost touch over the years, but I've been meaning to try to touch base with him anyway."

"Could you talk to him? Ask him to help us?"

"I could see if he's interested. It's sure as hell a cold case and something that might be right up his alley. Calvin died more than fifty years ago. If the police really did sweep his death under the rug, that could bring up a lot of issues. The cops won't be happy. Neither will the real killer if Buster Cantrell isn't the murderer."

"You don't have to tell your friend the real reason you want him to look into the case, do you?"

He laughed. "What, that I think I'm channeling the murder victim? Seriously? No, I don't think I need to let him know about that. I'll tell him about the picture, though, that I'm Calvin's spitting image. And that my mother's still grieving over her cousin's murder. Because that part is true and doesn't make me sound like a whack job."

"You're not a whack job and neither am I. We're having to come to terms with something that's out of the ordinary. Not in the normal realm of our beliefs. That's not an easy thing to accept. Nothing that's happening to us is easy to accept."

"Haven't we talked enough about improbable, impossible things for one night? Can't we table this discussion for another time?"

Claire paused with her water bottle to her lips and slanted him a quizzical look. "What did you want to discuss?"

He reached for her hand, tugged her over and pulled her into his lap and began unbuttoning the shirt she wore. "Nothing. Talking isn't what I had in mind." He slipped the shirt off her shoulders and cupped her bare breasts. "God, you're beautiful. I want to forget all this and make love to you."

"Works for me," she said, and kissed him.

***Rachel's Journal—June 21, 1859***

*I am going to have a child. I have thought so for some time, but I am now certain of it. I've told Ben and he is thrilled. But he has forbidden me to have any more to do with helping the fugitives. I have pleaded with him to no avail. He says I have another life to consider now, the babe's.*

*Sarah is still involved. In fact, Victor's frequent absences allow us to move more people toward freedom than we had imagined when we began our task. I asked Sarah if she thought about aiding her lover. I asked if she would help Elijah to escape and she gave me the oddest look. "I have begged him to go," she said. "But he won't leave me. I think he fears what Victor will do to me. Not that he can stop him. No one can."*

*I asked her to elaborate, but she said she had already said too much. She seems resigned to her lot . . . And yet, she is not. Is she thinking to run off with Elijah? How foolish that would be. Dangerous and foolish.*

*Yet I ask myself if our situations were reversed, what would I do? And I know the answer. I would do anything necessary to be with Ben. Anything I had to do to be with the man I love.*

***June 1859***

"PACK A BAG FOR me, Sarah," Victor said one night. "Enough clothes for a fortnight, at least."

"Where are you going?" While she wasn't unhappy he was leaving, his departure often brought other problems. Such as the overseer being overzealous in disciplining the slaves.

"Hunting. I'll stop by the Hendersons on the way back, so pack something decent for me to wear."

The Hendersons were old friends of her husband's. They held many of the same views as Victor did about secession, war, politics, and the proper way to handle slaves. Sarah couldn't abide them and was always thankful that Victor's hunting trips didn't require her presence. Bad enough she had to suffer their presence when they came to Victor's plantation. At least she didn't have to travel and be trapped with a woman she considered both cruel and tedious.

"Victor, there's something I need to talk to you about before you leave." She'd tried to bring it up before but had always lost her courage. Victor's anger was a thing to be feared, and he didn't take kindly to what he termed her interference in his business. Victor strongly believed that a woman, particularly a wife, should be seen and not heard.

"What is it?" He took a sip of his brandy, but as far as she could tell he wasn't drunk.

"It's about Mr. Bransen, the overseer. He takes advantage when you're gone."

"Takes advantage of what? You? Are you saying he made advances toward you?" He half rose from the chair, his face darkened with anger.

"No, no," she said hastily. "He hardly speaks to me. His treatment of the slaves is another matter. He's so cruel to the slaves. Very cruel. He always finds excuses to whip someone when you're gone. I've spoken to him about it, but he ignores me."

Victor relaxed, sipping his brandy and dismissing her. "The slaves need to be disciplined. I've told you that before. I don't expect you to understand, not the way you coddle that woman of yours."

She might as well tell him the rest. At least he was letting her speak and not dismissing her concerns out of hand. "Mr. Bransen has also made advances to Celia. She's my personal servant and I don't want him bothering her. Please, Victor, will you tell him to leave her alone? I tried, but—" She waved her hands helplessly. Bransen had ignored that request too. Although he hadn't raped Celia, both Sarah and she knew it was only a matter of time.

Victor frowned. "As I said, you coddle her too much, but she's yours to do with what you will. I'll speak to him. Is that all?"

"Yes. Thank you, Victor." She couldn't spare Elijah from Bransen's further mistreatment, but at least she'd been able to spare Celia from his unwelcome advances.

"You're looking a bit peaked," Victor said. "Is there a reason for that?"

"No." He was asking if she was with child. She hung her head, though sorrow was the last emotion she felt. "I'm sorry."

"When you're finished packing you can await me in your room. Damn, if I'd known you'd be barren I wouldn't have married you."

Sarah held her tongue. Nothing she said would make a difference.

His face softened. "Don't take on. You are a beautiful woman. At least I don't have to bed the likes of your sister with her squint."

Something for which Rachel, no doubt, was profoundly grateful. Her sister's squint didn't bother her husband. Ben loved her despite that or any other imperfection. If only Sarah had been so fortunate.

But Sarah had done her duty. As she would tonight and all the endless nights thereafter.

"Yes, Victor," she said, and slowly climbed the stairs.

# CHAPTER TWENTY-ONE

**November Present Day**

JONAS WATCHED Claire as she slept. He knew she'd been dreaming, not simply because she was restless but because she had called out Elijah's name in her sleep. Once he closed his eyes, once he relaxed, he'd sleep. And dream, Goddamn it. Jonas hated being at the mercy of his subconscious. He needed to be in control, and control had never been farther away than it was in his dreams.

*December 1968*

CAL WAS SUPPOSED to meet Bella in the school parking lot by her car. They didn't usually meet at school, but Bella said since they were married now, everyone would know soon enough. She was tired of sneaking around.

So was he. He wanted nothing more than to claim her as his wife and get on with their life. But he didn't mind admitting he was afraid of what Buster Cantrell would do when he found out the truth. Cal was also a little worried about his own mother's reaction, but not much. However much she disapproved, Fay loved him. She would grow to love Bella and the baby, too.

Except she'd have to get to know them some other place. He didn't want to raise their child in Fort Worth. Not with Buster Cantrell around to make Bella's life—and that of everyone connected with her—a living hell.

As he neared the parking lot, he saw her shrinking back against her car, struggling with that bastard, Larry. Cal started to run, but he was still too far away to stop him. Larry yanked her closer. Cal shouted, but Larry ignored him and continued to manhandle Bella. As she struggled, Calvin heard him say, "You can't want him over me. He's colored, for God's sake."

Larry tried to kiss her, but Bella struggled madly, turning her head away. She must have kicked him or bit him because he suddenly let go of her and raised his fist to her.

Calvin grabbed it, turned him, and planted his fist in the son of a bitch's face. "You don't ever lay a hand on Bella again. Understand?"

The wimp had crumbled with one punch, but Calvin wasn't through. He hit him again, would have pounded the crap out of him, but Bella grabbed his arm before he could continue.

"Don't, Cal. He didn't hurt me."

"He tried to kiss you. He put his hands on you against your will. That's hurting you in my book."

"It's all right. Just let it go."

"You'll be sorry for that," Larry spit out, still sprawled on the ground.

"I don't think so." He turned to Bella again. "Are you all right?"

"I'm fine." She wiped her mouth with the back of her hand. "Leave me alone, Larry. I'm Calvin's now. I'll never go out with you."

"What do you mean, you're his?" Larry got up and dusted himself off. "Just what the hell does that mean?"

"We're married. Calvin and I are married and we're having a baby. So you just forget about me."

Damn. Larry was the second to last person he'd have chosen to tell their secret to. "You shouldn't have told him," Calvin said. "He'll go straight to your father."

"I don't care." She looked at Larry scornfully. "You just go tattle if you want. We were going to tell him soon anyway. My father can't keep us apart now that we're married."

"You can't marry a nigger! It's not even legal!"

"People of different races can legally marry now. It's been legal for over a year. Now you take your . . . your prejudiced self out of here and don't come back."

He took off, giving them both a look of loathing.

Cal pulled Bella into his arms, and she rested her head against his chest.

"I understand why you told him, but I think we're going to regret it."

"No one can hurt us now," she said, looking up at him. "We belong to each other."

*November Present Day*

JONAS ARRIVED FIRST at the seafood restaurant where he'd arranged to meet his old friend. He had no trouble picking him out when the man walked in. Emmitt Rickerby had changed very little since high school.

"Jonas? Hey, man, I'd have known you anywhere."

"I'm not sure that's a good thing. Good to see you, Emmitt." Jonas shook hands, reflecting on the friendship he'd let slip since moving so far away. Emmitt had grown up to be successful, but he looked anything but complacent. The man radiated energy.

He'd filled out a little and looked older, but he still wore the same type of wire-rimmed glasses and carried himself with the same serious air. The boy he'd known had been very irreverent, and if his books were anything to go by, Emmitt still was.

He was also a damn good investigative journalist, and Jonas only hoped he could get him interested in Calvin's case. Not only did Jonas not know the first thing about researching a cold case, he had no time to do it.

Emmitt had married his high school sweetheart, and they had three kids. After Jonas looked at the obligatory pictures, he told Emmitt about Claire, and then his mother and the problems he'd been having taking care of her. He figured it was a good lead-in to what he wanted his old friend to do.

"Tell me about this project you think I'll be interested in," Emmitt said after the waitress served their food. "I just finished a book, and while I have other ideas, I'm always interested in new ones."

Jonas had found it surprisingly easy to catch up with him. Though they hadn't seen each other in a number of years, there was no awkwardness when they met again. They had no difficulty picking up where they'd left off. For a man who researched and wrote about some truly horrific crimes, Emmitt appeared unfailingly upbeat. And he was interested in everything, just as he'd been as a kid.

"It might not be your cup of tea. As to whether you'll want to write about it, I can't say. But even if you don't, I'd appreciate some help in finding out what really happened. I promised my mother I'd do my best to find the truth, so I'm stuck." Not to mention, he'd promised Claire he'd look into it, since she was convinced that Calvin's unsolved murder was one of the reasons for his dreams.

Dreams. Bullshit.

He pulled out the picture of Calvin that he'd taken from his mother's house and handed it to Emmitt. "His name was Calvin Davis."

Emmitt studied it for a long moment. "Man. The resemblance is uncanny. I remember you from high school and this guy's a dead ringer for you. Sorry, no pun intended." He glanced at Jonas before picking up his tea. "I assume that's the issue. He's dead?"

Jonas nodded. "Murdered in 1968. Unsolved homicide. He was my mother's cousin. She's never gotten over his death. I found this picture the other day and thought it was me until she told me it was of her dead cousin. She told me what she knew of the story and asked me if there was anything we could do to find out the truth about what happened. So I thought of you."

"Have you talked to the police?"

"No. My mother was working for Roger Dennis back then. The same lawyer she worked for when we were in high school and afterward. She and her boss tried to keep the investigation going all those years ago, but the cops said there wasn't enough evidence to charge anyone. I'm not even sure the case is still open. But I don't know anything about the police department."

"Oh, it's still open. All unsolved cases remain open. The Fort Worth Police Department has detectives assigned to that department and that's all they do. But that said, it might not be the most active case going. It depends on if they have new information or evidence. But they're always open to people coming forward with information, even after all this time."

"So if I—we—found something new, the police would look into it?"

"Sure."

"Even if the cops involved were dirty?"

"Absolutely. I would think most of those involved are long retired, if they're still alive. Fifty years is a long time. Why do you think the cops were dirty?"

"I don't, necessarily. My mother is a different story. She's convinced that Buster Cantrell killed Calvin and paid off anyone investigating. I'm not so sure it was him. Either way, back then no one seemed to care that a poor black kid was murdered in cold blood. Except his family and the girl who loved him."

"The girl who loved him being . . . "

"Buster Cantrell's daughter. His white daughter."

Emmitt gave a low whistle. "I've heard of Buster Cantrell. His name has come up in connection with some of the cases I've investigated. From all accounts, he was a real son of a bitch."

"Apparently. Was he ever convicted of anything?"

"Nope. Very powerful man. I haven't investigated him thoroughly. This is just something I remembered off the top of my head. Why don't you tell me what you know about Calvin's death and we'll go from there."

Jonas told him the story, or as much of it as he knew. Emmitt promised to look into it, see what he could find out from the police department and other sources. He also said he'd try to set up some interviews and include Jonas in them.

He didn't think working around Jonas's schedule at the hospital would be a problem.

"Jonas, is there something you're not telling me?"

"Why?" The only thing he hadn't told him was Claire's theory of past lives, and he sure as hell wasn't touching that one.

"I don't know. I just don't feel like I'm getting the whole picture from you."

Emmitt hadn't gotten where he was without being observant. Jonas had to give him something. "You know the woman I told you I was involved with? Claire Westbrook?" Emmitt nodded. "If we interview anyone, like say, you get the detective on the case to talk to us, she'd like to be a part of it as well."

"Okay. Why is she so interested?"

"Here's the weird part. The girl Calvin was in love with? Bella Cantrell? She was a cousin of Claire's. Her mother is still in touch with Bella's younger sister."

He rubbed his lip thoughtfully. "So Calvin was your cousin and Bella was her cousin. You're right, that is odd. Odd that the two of you are involved now. I assume Claire is old enough that you don't have an irate, bigoted father to deal with. Or that she can tell him to take a leap if so."

"No father. But she has a not-quite-ex-husband. Who's a bigot."

Emmitt was staring at him openmouthed. "Good God, Jonas, you know how to pick 'em."

"Once you meet Claire you'll understand. She's—" He stopped because he couldn't think how to explain his feelings. She was beautiful, sure, but that wasn't why he was in love with her. Part of it, much as he hated to admit it, was that damned connection he felt to her, especially when they were together. "She's worth it, whatever the problems," he finally said.

"I hope so, buddy. Be careful, okay?"

"I will. You be careful too. I wouldn't want anything to happen to you investigating a case I turned you on to."

"BRING THE TEA with you, darling." Evangeline Keaton, Claire's mother, smiled. "Let's sit on the porch since it won't be long until I can't anymore."

Claire suppressed a twinge of guilt. The house and the grounds were too much for her mother to take care of since her father had died. The stables and the lone remaining horse made for even more work, and full-time help was expensive. Evangeline still rode, though not daily like she used to. She liked to say she and Bolo were growing old together. Bolo was an Arabian gelding who detested everyone but Claire's mother. He tolerated his caretakers, but he only loved one person, and that was Evangeline.

But Claire had found a place for Bolo to go to live out his life, not too far out of town. The owner ran what was basically a retirement home for horses, and had assured Claire that Evangeline would be welcome to visit any time and ride him whenever she felt like it. It was the best Claire could do, but her mother wasn't a bit happy about it.

"What did you want to talk about?" Evangeline asked. "You sounded so odd on the phone."

"I'm getting a divorce. And before you ask, yes, I'm absolutely positive that's what I want."

Evangeline didn't look shocked and proved it with her next

words. "I knew you weren't happy, but I didn't know it had progressed so far. Will you tell me what decided you?"

"You knew I was unhappy? You never said anything."

"I assumed you'd talk to me when you were ready. And here you are. What decided you to take this step?"

Claire drew in a deep breath. "Glenn hit me. Beat me, actually. I filed for divorce the next day."

Concern washed over her face. She put her hand on Claire's arm and squeezed. "I'm so sorry. When did this happen? Why didn't you tell me?"

"I . . . I couldn't. It's . . . humiliating."

Evangeline's hand tightened on her arm. "For him, not for you."

"Thanks, Mom. I was afraid you'd—" She stopped, unsure how to continue.

Evangeline leaned forward and put her hand on Claire's knee to pat. "You're my daughter, Claire. Surely you didn't think I'd take Glenn's side over yours."

"Not exactly. But you've always seemed so fond of Glenn, and he's always been on his best behavior around you."

Her mother shrugged, sat back, and sipped her tea. "I never liked him. But you married him and seemed to love him, so I put up with him for your sake."

"Dad never liked him either. He wasn't as good at hiding it as you were."

Evangeline laughed. "No, he made his feelings pretty obvious when you told us you were marrying Glenn." She shook her head. "I'm glad he's not alive to hear this. No telling what he'd do to Glenn. Did you press charges?"

"No. The police weren't very encouraging about that. It was a first offense, there's never been any problems before, on top of that, Glenn is an attorney." She shrugged. "It didn't seem worth it. I just filed for divorce." One bombshell down. Another to go.

"I wish you'd told me you were having such problems. I might have helped," Evangeline said.

"There was nothing you could do. I had to come to the decision on my own." Claire fell silent, unsure how to proceed.

"There's more, isn't there?"

"Yes. Glenn thought I was having an affair. I wasn't. But that's why he beat me up."

"I see." She looked at Claire closely. "You're involved with this man, though. The man he thought you were cheating on him with."

"Now I am. I wasn't at the time. We work together at the hospital. He's a neurosurgeon. His name is Jonas Clark."

"So, you have medicine in common. Will I like him?"

"I hope so. But I have something else to talk to you about. You still keep in touch with Aunt Sophie, don't you?"

"Sophie?" Clearly puzzled, Evangeline asked, "You mean my cousin Sophie?"

"Yes. I need to talk to her. Well, Jonas and I do. Unless you know the story."

"What story? You have me mystified."

"The story about her sister, Bella, and the boy she loved."

"Oh, Claire." Evangeline leaned back and shook her head. "Why do you want to know about that? It's a terribly sad story."

"The boy she was in love with was a cousin of Jonas's." They had decided to tell Claire's mother the same story Jonas gave to his friend Emmitt Rickerby, the investigative reporter. "Jonas's mother was very close to him and the murderer was never caught. No one was even charged. Jonas told her he'd do what he could to find out what happened. Who really killed him."

Evangeline was staring at her openmouthed. "Calvin Davis was black. Jonas is black? You're involved with a black man?"

"Yes. And if you're going to say something racist, save it."

Evangeline drew herself up and glared at her daughter. "Don't take that tone with me, Claire. Simply because I'm surprised doesn't make me a racist."

"I'm sorry. I'm a little touchy about it."

"So it would seem. Do you know the story about Bella and Calvin?"

"Some of it," Claire said. "Why, do you?"

"I know what Sophie told me. And it doesn't make me happy to find you involved with someone of another race. It's a frightening story, Claire."

"I'm sure it is. Calvin Davis was murdered in cold blood and the killer never caught. I don't know what happened to Bella after his death. I know she died. I remember hearing that, but I never knew why. Jonas's mother doesn't know either, only that she died."

"Buster Cantrell all but murdered her. At least that's what Sophie always maintained. The instant she could, she left town and didn't come back until her father was dead. It speaks volumes that he didn't try to stop her. She hated him with a passion."

"What did he do?"

"Did you know Bella was pregnant?"

Claire nodded. "I'm sure her father was livid."

"To say the least," Evangeline said dryly. "Buster Cantrell took her to Mexico. He swore he'd have no mixed race grandchildren. According to Sophie, he drugged Bella and forced her to have an abortion. She died from complications, but

Sophie always believed she died as much from a broken heart as anything."

Claire covered her mouth and closed her eyes, appalled at what she'd heard. God, she'd expected it to be bad, but the story was worse than she'd imagined. "That's a horrible story, but I fail to see what it has to do with Jonas and me." Unless she really was the reincarnation of Bella Cantrell. But Bella's life, her story, was nothing like Claire's.

Yet Claire's life was eerily similar to Sarah's. Complete with an abusive husband.

"This is the twenty-first century," Claire continued before her mother could speak. "Things have changed. There's no reason Jonas and I can't be together. Once I'm free."

"But you're not free. I have a bad feeling about all this. A very bad feeling. You're asking for heartbreak getting involved with Jonas Clark."

Asking for heartbreak. Exactly what Rachel Adams wrote in her journal about her sister Sarah. And look how that ended.

*June 1859*

ELIJAH AND SARAH watched until the three men were out of sight. "Do you think they'll make it?" Sarah asked.

"Mebbe. Long way to go."

"We'll never know, will we? We'll never know if any of the people we help make it to safety or not."

"Can't be helped." He looked at the lake, water shimmering in the moonlight. "This be a good place."

"Yes. It's rumored to be haunted. The lake and the shanty," she said, gesturing at the small structure several yards away. "Victor won't come near it. He's very superstitious."

"Most folks is. The slave women, they talk about this place."

"I've heard them. That's why I told Victor the slave women who were tortured in there haunt it."

"Old overseer lived here."

"Yes. If anyone deserved to be haunted, he did." She fell silent, unwilling to discuss the tales she'd heard of the man. "He was worse than Bransen. I told Victor that one of the slaves was a witch and she had put a spell on this house." She gestured at the shanty, still certain she could hear the screams of long dead women. "I didn't know it really was haunted. I made up the story so I'd have a private place. I found it when we were first married." Before she'd reconciled the dream of her marriage with what the reality actually was—when she'd been looking for a way to end the pain. She'd found the lake and took comfort knowing that if her life became too hard to bear she could end it in the cool water of the lake. "Do you believe it's haunted?"

"I reckon." He shrugged. "That don't bother me none. Those ghosts and such ain't mad with me."

"Good."

"This place be good to move folks through. 'Specially if the master's afraid of spirits."

"That's what I thought too."

"Pretty out here," Elijah said. "Kinda like a dream. Ain't seen nothing like this hereabouts."

"A dream. Yes, it is like a dream. That's why I call it Dream Lake."

He smiled at her. "You go on back now. Master will be lookin' for you."

"No, he won't. Victor went to town. He'll stay in town, with one of his women."

"Does his women worry you?"

She laughed. "Worry me? I'm grateful to them. I only wish they could make it to where he never touches me again."

"It ain't right, what he does to you." His fist clenched. "I cain't stop him. You be his wife."

"You could leave."

"No." He shook his head. "I reckon I'll stay."

As he stared at her, she said, "I could leave Victor. Follow you. We could be together."

"It ain't possible. He'd find us. No tellin' how he'd use you."

"No worse than how he uses me now."

"Dyin's worse."

"Is it? Is it really?" Angrily, she stepped toward him. "Worse than being used again and again by a man with no love, no gentleness in him? A man who takes more care with his horse than he does his wife? Tell me, Elijah, why is death worse?"

"Sarah, you don't know what you're saying. Once you's dead, they ain't no comin' back."

"Do you think I care about that? Do you know how often I've come here and thought of how easy it would be to let the water take me? To walk into that lake and let all my pain and fear, all the suffering I see every day just . . . float away?"

He reached for her, and she walked into his arms. "Don't, Sarah. Stay strong." His arms tightened around her. "Promise me."

She looked up at him. "I can't. If you were to die, Elijah, I would die too. Please say you'll leave. Before Victor or Bransen or someone else takes you from me."

"Iffen I do, you be all alone."

"I'll find a way to follow you. Say you'll go."

He gazed at her for a long, long moment. "I will," he said, resigned and reluctant.

Relief swept through her, and with it, despair. "Then kiss me. We may never have the chance again."

He murmured, "Gonna be damned for this. But—" He bent his head, she rose on her toes, and his lips met hers.

She'd never imagined a kiss like this. Gentle, respectful, but she felt the passion he held back. His lips were soft, so soft. His tongue was warm, magic against hers.

He broke away before she was ready. Nearly flung her aside. "No, Sarah. You want freedom, not me."

"I've never wanted anyone more." Sarah reached for his hand. It was warm and strong in hers. "Lie with me, Elijah. I want to know what it is to lie with a man I love. A gentle man, a loving man. I want to lie with you. Before you go. Because we don't know what will happen, or even if we'll ever see each other again. Don't deny me."

Elijah pulled away, turned his back to her. He gave a tortured groan. "You don't know what you're askin'."

"I know exactly. I need you, Elijah."

"I love you. You know it," he said in a tortured voice.

"There's no shame in our loving each other. Why do you act as if there is?"

"You my master's wife. Ain't no world where that be a happy thing."

She crossed the few steps between them. Put her arms around his neck and drew his head down to hers. "Kiss me. Kiss me, Elijah."

"We both gonna be damned for this." His arms encircled her as he looked down into her face. His eyes were dark, mirrors of his soul. And his soul was tortured.

"No." She put a hand to his face and smiled lovingly. "We'll both be saved."

His arms tightened around her. His lips covered hers, his tongue swept into her mouth. He picked her up, carried her to the grassy spot near the lake. Lay her down and stood looking down at her. The moonlight shimmered over the scene, giving it an otherworldly appearance.

Sarah began undoing the buttons of her blouse. Soon she was naked in the moonlight. Elijah watched her silently. She couldn't tell what he was thinking. Holding out her hand, she said, "Lie with me, Elijah. I want to be touched with love. I want you to touch me, to love me."

He came down beside her and took her in his arms. Such strong arms yet they held her so tenderly. "I do love you, Sarah. More than life."

He kissed her. Made love to her. For the first time since she'd married Victor Lawrence, Sarah felt free.

# CHAPTER TWENTY-TWO

*November Present Day*

RETIRED DETECTIVE Anders O'Connor was a big man. Tall, lean, with piercing blue eyes and a shock of white hair framing a movie star handsome face. Though Emmitt had told them he was in his mid-seventies, he looked ten years younger.

"We appreciate you seeing us so quickly," Emmitt said, shaking hands. "These are my friends, Jonas Clark and Claire Westbrook."

Claire had met both Jonas and Emmitt at the detective's house and hadn't had a chance to do more than say hello. She and Jonas had come together, straight from work. Their schedules had been similar lately, which enabled them to see each other outside of work more easily.

"Not a problem. The Davis case." O'Connor shook his head regretfully. "Not one of our successes, I'm afraid." He ushered them inside, then led the way into his living room, obviously decorated with an eye to comfort over fashion. It looked lived in and very welcoming. "I understand you asked to see the case file, but the cold case detectives denied you access," he said to Emmitt.

"Yes. Since it's still unsolved they didn't want to compromise any evidence. However, they did tell me what they could. Suspects who were cleared and that sort of thing. They also said they haven't had anything new come up since the original investigation."

O'Connor grunted. "I can tell you a little about the case. I've kept up with it through the years. What evidence we had —the gun in particular— was never linked to anyone. No serial number, nothing to identify it." Turning to Jonas, he said, "I know of Emmitt's books but what would your interest in the case be?"

"Calvin Davis was my cousin. I asked Emmitt to look into his murder. My mother was very close to him and has never gotten over his death. I thought if we found out who actually killed him, it might bring her some closure."

"Especially if the murderer is still alive and can be brought to justice," Claire added.

O'Connor turned that piercing gaze on her. "You're no cousin to Davis."

"No, I'm related to Isabel Cantrell. She was *my* cousin."

"You have her eyes," the retired detective said.

"Yes, I've been told that. Jonas and I are both very interested in getting this case opened again."

O'Connor frowned. "It's still open. An unsolved homicide isn't closed until the murderer is caught. It can be, and probably is, inactive, however."

"I didn't realize that," Claire said.

"I should have told you," Emmitt said. "I knew it from

researching other unsolved homicides. Plus, that's another reason the detectives couldn't let me see the case files."

"Let's sit down." O'Connor gestured to the couch. "Anyone want coffee? I just made a fresh pot."

"I'm good, thank you," Emmitt said. Claire and Jonas declined as well, and they all sat down.

"I should tell you right off, Frank Dervish is the man you need. He was the detective who took over the case from me."

"Could I ask why you gave him the case?" Emmitt asked.

"Yes. The simple answer is I was shot two days after Davis was murdered, in an unrelated case. I spent several weeks in the hospital and during that time the captain gave my caseload to the other detectives. He gave the Davis homicide to Frank Dervish."

Emmitt shook his head. "I tried that already. The cold case detectives gave me his name and yours, said you two might be able to talk to me even though they couldn't give me access to the case files. First of all, I had a hard time connecting with Dervish. He resigned from the department a number of years ago, and I got the feeling there was a lot of bad blood."

O'Connor rubbed the side of his nose. "You can say that again. He had to resign or be fired."

"Dervish refused to talk to me, or anyone else for that matter, regarding this crime. He maintains it was a gang-related killing and there's nothing to investigate." He glanced at O'Connor and grimaced. "From some of his comments, I gathered he's not too fond of blacks."

"Oh, he's as racist as they come," O'Connor agreed. "In fact, that's why he resigned, because of that very issue, but that didn't happen until years later. At any rate, by the time I was able to object, Dervish had already decided the Davis case was a gang slaying."

"You didn't believe that," Jonas said.

"No, frankly, I didn't, but I wasn't given a voice in the matter. In the brief time I had the case, I saw no evidence of gang-related activity. But Dervish was convinced of it." He shrugged. "I looked at the files several times over the years, but I was never able to find enough evidence to charge anyone. In my opinion, we dropped the ball on this one."

"Didn't you find that strange? Why was Dervish so convinced the murder was gang related?"

He spread his hands. "I don't know. I found a lot about this case strange. You have to realize I wasn't able to look into it until some time afterward. I spent months in the hospital and rehab. But when I looked into it later, I didn't find much. There were a couple of suspects identified, but they alibied out. I never did think Dervish did much to try to disprove their alibis."

"From what the cold case detectives told me," Emmitt said, "Dervish fixated on the gang aspect and didn't bother investigating anything else." He looked at his notes. "The key suspect was Isabel Cantrell's father. She accused him of the murder point-blank."

O'Connor nodded. "Well, it was 1968, and Buster Cantrell's white daughter had just gotten pregnant by and married to a black kid. If you want to talk racist, Dervish was nothing compared to Buster Cantrell. That man had a hate for minorities. Especially blacks. But then, I'm not too sure he liked anyone, black, white, or anything else."

"His daughter Sophie was his alibi," Emmitt said.

"That she was. Sophie didn't want to give him an alibi. She hated the SOB. But she reluctantly backed him up when Isabel accused him of the murder. Said he couldn't have done it because he was with her. I remember. I took her statement, and Isabel's."

"Did he intimidate her into speaking for him?" Claire asked.

"I don't think so," the detective said. "Not that he wasn't capable of it but there was no need. She told the truth, I believe."

"Could he have paid someone to do it?"

"Yes. Which is what his daughter accused him of next. But Dervish maintained there was no evidence that he did so. Regardless of what Isabel said." He turned to Claire. "You remind me of her, a lot. Your eyes, of course. But something else I can't put my finger on. I remember her, all these years later. She was so broken up about Davis's death. It was a shame. By all accounts he was a good kid, trying to make something of himself. Never in trouble, hard worker." He shook his head. "I never did know what happened to that girl. She disappeared, and then I read her obituary not long after Davis died. I was still in the hospital, as a matter of fact."

"I can tell you what happened," Claire said. "Sophie told my mother. Buster Cantrell murdered her."

"What?" O'Connor half rose. "We never had any evidence of that. All I found was she fell ill and died."

"Cantrell took her to Mexico and forced her to have an abortion. She died a few weeks after that. In my book that makes him a murderer. If he didn't kill Calvin, he certainly caused his daughter's death."

"Damn. I'm sorry to hear that."

"Can you tell us what else you thought was strange about the case?" Jonas asked.

"Before he does," Emmitt interjected, "there's something else odd here, Claire. I meant to ask you earlier but didn't have the chance. It looks like Isabel had an ex-boyfriend. It was unclear whether he was actually a boyfriend or just wanted to be. He was a white kid reputed to be in love with her. According to the detectives he was another suspect. In fact, according to Dervish's notes, he and Calvin Davis got in a fight over the girl earlier that same day. Luckily—or conveniently—for him, he had an alibi."

Claire started to say something, but Jonas stopped her with a look. She realized there was no way they should have known the boy's name. "What did you want to know?"

"This kid who was in love with Bella? His name was Larry Westbrook."

"That's why your name was familiar," O'Connor said. "I don't suppose you're any relation?"

Larry Westbrook. Her stomach clenched. Claire put out her hand and gripped Jonas's tightly. Larry. Lawrence. But how? "Lawrence Westbrook is my father-in-law. He's from Fort Worth and he would have been about the same age as Calvin Davis. But I never imagined . . ." she trailed off. Could it be coincidence? Another Lawrence Westbrook? Not likely. It fit too perfectly.

"Damn," Emmitt said. "This is carrying coincidence a little too far."

No wonder Lawrence had looked sick the day he saw Jonas at the hospital. If he'd known Calvin Davis, he must have thought he'd seen a ghost.

The ghost of the man he murdered?

"ARE YOU ALL right?" Jonas asked Claire as they got into the car. She'd hardly spoken a word since Emmitt had dropped the bombshell. Emmitt had left, saying he was going to do what he could to look into Lawrence Westbrook's alibi for the night of the murder.

"No, not really. I can't believe Lawrence is the Larry Bella talked about."

"Did he ever talk about the past? Do you know anything about those years?"

She shook her head. "I never talk much with him unless I have to, and his past was never anything we discussed. I'm not sure Glenn knows anything, either."

"Is Westbrook's bank connected with Buster Cantrell's? Did he take over when Buster retired?"

"I don't know. It's something we could find out, though. You know how banks change names and owners. But I suspect it is the same."

"O'Connor said the night watchman at Cantrell's bank positively identified Lawrence as driving by the bank during the time in question. Since he worked there, he recognized his car and him driving it. The bank was on the other side of town from Calvin's house, where he was killed, and that gives Lawrence a decent alibi." Even if, as he suspected, the night watchman had lied.

"I wonder if we'll be able to track down the night watchman? What if he lied and we could get him to admit it?"

"If anyone can find him, Emmitt will. But as to whether he'll admit to giving false testimony—" He shrugged.

"If it's true, and Lawrence was involved . . . a lot of things make sense now. Why Lawrence doesn't like me. At first he did, before he met me. The minute we met, that all changed. He used to make comments about my eyes all the time. I finally threatened to forbid him coming over if he didn't drop it. I said Glenn could see him whenever he wanted but I wouldn't unless he stopped."

"Did he?"

"Unfortunately, yes. By then I'd have welcomed a good reason to cut off contact with him."

Jonas pulled into the hospital parking lot to drop Claire off at her car. "I have to take my mother to the eye doctor. She's finally agreed to let me help her and talk to her doctor."

"I hope he can do something for her."

"So do I. He's had her on a new protocol I want to discuss with him. I don't like leaving you like this, though."

"You mean, since I found out my father-in-law might be a murderer?"

He took her hand and squeezed it comfortingly. "It's okay to be upset, Claire."

"I don't know what I am." She was quiet a moment, then said, "I wonder why you haven't dreamed about Calvin's shooting."

"Not that I remember." And he was fairly sure he'd remembered all the dreams by now. "Even if I dream about the shooting and know who the murderer is, we can't prove it." He really didn't want to "see" Calvin's shooting. Not in a dream or anywhere else. Even if it would tell them who the murderer was, he could hardly think of anything less appealing than dreaming about a murder. Especially, in a weird-ass way, his own.

"No, but we'd know what direction to go."

"We already do. Your father-in-law. You really don't believe your soon-to-be ex knows anything?"

She considered that a moment before shaking her head. "No, I don't think Lawrence has told Glenn about any of it. I could be wrong but I just don't see Lawrence admitting to anything, even to Glenn. And Lawrence may not know you're related to Calvin."

"Of course he does. I'm sure he figured it out immediately after he saw me. He wouldn't believe it was by chance I look like him."

"I suppose not. And it explains his weird behavior when he met you."

"Yeah, must have been pretty uncomfortable to see a man who looks exactly like one you thought you'd killed years ago." How strange that they'd all be connected now. Coincidence? Or fate? "I'll talk to you as soon as I finish with my mother."

She leaned over and kissed him before getting out. "All right. I'll see you later."

*WHAT THE HELL was Frank Dervish in such a panic about?*

Lawrence had tried to find out over the phone, but the man refused to tell him. Dervish had insisted he had to see him in person and alone. Was it about the Davis situation or did he simply need money again?

Lawrence knew he should have done something about the asshole years ago. But Dervish had been useful. If not for his handling of the Davis case, Lawrence might be in prison. Lawrence knew he'd had a lucky break when Dervish had been assigned to investigate the crime. He'd met the other cop, the first one, briefly. That one wouldn't have looked the other way, not about anything. But Dervish, well, the man was as prejudiced as the day was long. He hadn't wanted to know if Lawrence was actually guilty of shooting that black bastard, Davis. Or if Buster Cantrell had done it either. No white person was going down for a crime against a black. Not if Dervish had anything to do with it. No, he'd been happy to blame it on gangs and look no further.

Until he'd lost his job at the FWPD, and then he'd come to Lawrence, reminding him there was no statute of limitations on murder. He'd been hitting Lawrence up for something—money, influence, or both—ever since. Dervish could still face prison time for his part in covering up what really happened, obstruction of justice at the very least. But Lawrence was the one who would really be screwed.

Not that he'd ever admitted he'd pulled the trigger. Still, Dervish knew. Even Dervish wasn't that stupid. Otherwise, why would Lawrence have bankrolled him all these years?

"It's open," he called out when the doorbell rang. Bad enough he'd sent his help away. He wasn't getting up to wait on the son of a bitch.

The ex-cop looked bad. Even for a drunk, he looked bad. But that wasn't Lawrence's concern. "Why are you here? What is it you couldn't tell me over the phone?"

"Are we alone?"

"Goddamn it, yes. I sent the nurse away, but she'll be back before long. What do you want?"

"Could I have a drop of whiskey? It's cold out tonight. I'll get it."

"You sure as hell won't. I didn't have you here to feed you my booze. Spill it. What the hell do you want?" he asked him yet again. Was the man ever going to get to the damn point?

"I had a phone call from a true crime writer. Name of Emmitt Rickerby. Guess what cold case he's investigating?" He didn't wait for an answer but leaned forward and whispered, "The Davis case."

No shit, Sherlock. "So? There's nothing to find, is there?"

"N-n-n-o." He didn't sound at all sure.

"Is there evidence? Evidence I don't know about?"

"Well, your alibi was pretty weak. If somebody were to really investigate—" He broke off and spread his hands. "I didn't question that night watchman very closely. Just took his word for it that you were at the bank during the shooting."

Henry Young. The night watchman at the bank. Buster's bank. Buster had paid for Young's son's schooling, college included. In exchange, Young had corroborated Lawrence's alibi. "Is he still alive?"

"I don't know."

"Well find out, damn it. Jesus, do I have to do everything myself?" Clearly he did. Dervish was useless. "He's bound to be ancient, even if he is alive. And there's no reason he'd change his testimony at this late date."

Unless he'd grown a conscience or something equally inconvenient. Still, maybe he had Alzheimer's.

"Never mind, I'll have my assistant look into it." Or he'd google an obit for him. With any luck, the old geezer was dead and buried. "Is that all?"

"Your bruises were documented in the notes. All that about your fight with Davis earlier in the day is documented."

"So? There were witnesses to that fight. It happened hours before the son of a bitch was shot." No one but him knew half his bruises came from that evening, when he'd had the final showdown with Davis.

"It doesn't look good. Gives you motive."

"Motive doesn't matter shit if I've got the alibi."

"I suppose."

He sounded worried, which annoyed the hell out of Lawrence. How hard could it be to find out if the old man was still alive, and if he was, take care of it?

"I googled this Emmitt Rickerby after he called," Dervish continued. "I refused to see him, told him there was no point in looking into a case that should have been closed out years ago. Not that I think he listened. He's black and he has a nose for this sort of thing. I can tell you already, he's thinking he can make this into a racial thing." He sounded disgusted. Lawrence didn't blame him. "It was the sixties, for Christ's sake. One more black bastard dying was nothing. But once he finds out why I resigned, you can bet your ass he's going to look into it even more closely."

"Why should he find out about that? It's old news."

"It's public record. Doesn't matter that the bitch deserved what happened to her, what matters is she was black and I was a white cop."

A white cop who beat the crap out of the black suspect, if Lawrence remembered correctly. Not a very bright thing to do, but Dervish was an idiot.

"Well, don't just sit there," Lawrence said. "What are you going to do about it?"

"What can I do? I don't have any way to stop him. Who told him about this case, anyway? Why now, after all these years, does he pick this case?"

Why now? Jonas Clark had put him up to it. Had to be him. Him and his lover, Lawrence's bitch of a daughter-in-law.

"You need to figure out how to put a stop to this. Now, before it goes further. Rickerby can be discouraged. Once he drops the case it will go back to being just another unsolved homicide." Lawrence got up and walked to the liquor cabinet. Poured out a shot and drained it. Dervish watched him, nearly quivering with desire. Lawrence smiled and poured himself another shot, bringing it with him when he sat again.

"How?"

"I don't give a damn how. An accident, something."

"You want me to kill this journalist? I won't do it. You can't make me. It's not my ass that's in trouble if the truth comes out."

"Oh, really? Obstruction of justice, at the least. Cops, even ex-cops, don't do well in prison, do they?"

"I'm still not committing murder," Dervish said stubbornly.

"Oh, for Christ's sake, who said anything about murder? I just want you to put the fear of God into him. Show him that bad things happen to nosy people."

He wished something bad would happen to that black son-of-a- bitch doctor who had stirred all this up. If he hadn't started looking into a fucking fifty-year-old murder, that journalist would never have poked his nose into the case.

What would have happened if Lawrence had never gone to Buster Cantrell? Never told him what his precious daughter had done?

*"Bella's pregnant."*

*"Pregnant? By who?"*

*"By Davis."*

*Cantrell turned red and threw his glass of whiskey across the room. "Goddamn it! I warned her. I told her she'd better not see him again or there'd be hell to pay."*

*"There's more. There's worse."*

*"What could be worse than my daughter having a nigger's baby?"*

*"They're married. Bella just told me."*

*The old man's eyes nearly bulged out of his face. Lawrence thought he was going to explode right there. "Bullshit. It ain't legal for a white person to marry a nigger. At least not in this state."*

*"It's been legal since last year. I think his cousin helped him. She works for that colored lawyer. You know the one."*

*He rose in disgust. "Jesus H. Christ, I can't believe this. You're sure?"*

*"I wish I wasn't. Bella told me herself, not half an hour ago."*

*Buster took a turn around the room, puffing furiously on his cigar. "Let me ask you something. Do you still want her? Even knowing she's pregnant with a nigger's baby?"*

*Lawrence hesitated, then shrugged. "Yes." It wasn't as if Buster were a stranger to what he was about to suggest. He'd heard rumors, anyway, of women Buster had supposedly impregnated. "There are ways around that. She could get rid of it. Take her to Mexico."*

*"She won't want to do that. She'll have to be forced."*

*"You're her father. You could manage it."*

*Buster sent him a sharp glance. "That's not the only problem. There's still the nigger."*

*"He could be taken care of too."*

*"You talk big but are you up to the challenge?"*

*"Me?" He'd been thinking someone else could do the dirty work. Not him.*

*Cantrell reached into his desk drawer and pulled out a handgun. "Unregistered. No serial number. Untraceable." He laid it on the desk. "Take care of the problem, Larry. Grow a pair and do what you have to do." He left the room.*

*Lawrence picked up the gun.*

# CHAPTER TWENTY-THREE

"HOW IS MACI working out?" Jonas asked his mother when he picked her up. "You haven't complained about her so she can't be too bad." Last he'd heard, his mother had liked the girl, but he didn't know if that had changed.

"Better than I'd thought. She's good about helping me enough, but not too much. She's very easy to get along with. I like her."

"Great, I'm glad. Have you noticed any difference in your eyesight?" Her doctor had high hopes for the new therapy. They were going back today for a recheck and so that Jonas could meet him and talk to him in person. Talking to him on the phone was fine, but Jonas wanted some face time with him.

"Hard to say. I don't think they're any worse." She looked out the window, then glanced at him. "It was a day like today that Calvin died. Gray and dreary. I've been thinking about him a lot since we talked. I still miss him, even after all these years."

There was his opening. "Speaking of Calvin, I wanted to talk to you some more about him."

"Why? What's the point?"

"The Fort Worth Police Department is looking into the murder again. The cold case detectives are looking through the files and are open to any new information. They've never closed the case and now they believe there might be new evidence."

Naomi snorted. "That detective didn't do anything years ago. Why should it be any different now?"

"That was one cop, and from everything I've heard, he was a bad one. He was forced to resign due to racial issues."

"What does that mean?"

"He beat up a suspect. A black woman. It was a number of years ago, but I imagine once a racist always a racist. Could be he didn't do the case justice."

"That's for sure. There was no justice for Calvin."

"I wanted to ask you about Bella. You knew her, didn't you?"

"Of course. We weren't best friends, though. I was afraid of what would happen to Calvin, falling for a white girl. I was right, too." She gave him a sharp look and added, "You'd do well to think about that."

"We've been over this. I'm not talking to you about my situation."

Naomi snorted. "Situation. That's a funny word for it. Suit yourself. What do you want to know about Bella?"

"Some information has come to light that her ex-boyfriend's alibi might not be solid."

"Her ex-boyfriend?" She thought about it a moment. "She didn't have another boyfriend. Only Calvin."

"No, there was someone else. Lawrence Westbrook."

"You mean that Larry fellow? Isn't Claire's last name Westbrook?"

"Yes. He's her father-in-law."

"Her father-in-law? Lawrence Westbrook is Claire's father-in-law? That same white boy who was in love with Bella?" He nodded. "I don't like the sound of that. I always thought he had something to do with Calvin's death."

"I thought you believed Buster Cantrell did it?"

"Mr. Big Shot Cantrell wouldn't have been above having someone else do his dirty work. But they both had alibis. So that detective—what was his name?—said."

"Frank Dervish was the investigator's name. Can you tell me anything more about Westbrook?"

"Like I said, Larry wasn't her boyfriend. He wanted to be, but she never would go for him. He and Calvin had a fight, that last day. I saw it. A lot of us saw it. Larry was furious. So was Calvin. I don't think I've ever seen Calvin so upset. No one heard what the fight was about. But I knew. I saw Larry trying to kiss Bella before Calvin put a stop to it." She shook her head. "That Larry, he was a nasty one."

"Did he know you?" The last thing he wanted was to put his mother on Westbrook's radar. If Westbrook really was a murderer, then Jonas didn't want him anywhere near Naomi. Hell, he didn't want the man near his mother even if he wasn't the murderer.

"Huh, he wouldn't know me from a hole in the ground. A black girl two years younger than him? I was lower than dirt in his eyes. Besides, it was more than fifty years ago. There's no way he'd know me now."

"Let's keep it that way."

"Why would he bother me now?"

"Because you were alive back then. You knew Calvin and Bella. You were Calvin's cousin. You may know more than you think you do. Can the cold case detectives re-interview you?"

"Of course. Do you really think they'll find the killer? After all this time?"

"Stranger things have happened." Very strange things.

CLAIRE WAITED UNTIL they'd eaten dinner and were relaxing for a change to bring up a subject she knew Jonas wouldn't want to talk about. But that was too bad. They couldn't avoid the subject, it was too intertwined with what was going on with Lawrence Westbrook and the whole mystery of Calvin's death.

"I've been reading about past lives."

Jonas shot her an annoyed glance. "God help us."

"Ignoring the subject isn't working. Don't you want to know what I've learned about it?"

"No, but I'm sure you're going to tell me anyway."

She wasn't surprised at his reaction. Annoyed, but not surprised. "One theory for those who believe in reincarnation is that something went wrong in the person's, or in our case, people's, previous life and they have a chance to get it right in the new one."

"I'll say something went wrong. We died. Tragically. Or at least Elijah did, as did Calvin and Bella. You still don't know about Sarah's fate, do you?"

"No, but I'm sure it's bad. I haven't read that far in the journal. And I haven't dreamed about Sarah's death. Just

Elijah's." She'd put it off because she hadn't wanted to know exactly what happened to Sarah.

"Even if I accept your theory, I don't see how it relates to the two of us now. After all, it was more outside forces that kept the two apart, in both time periods. They'd have been fine left on their own."

"Would they? Maybe racism and jealousy weren't the only problems they had. Maybe they didn't trust each other enough. Didn't trust their love enough. Or they debated too long before they acted."

"I think I hear my pager going off."

Claire laughed. "You're not on call. You're really uncomfortable talking about this. Still. Aren't you?"

"Bet your ass I am." He sighed. "It makes me feel like a crazy person."

"Do you have any other reasonable explanation for our dreams?"

"No. But there's bound to be one. Besides, there's nothing keeping us apart now."

"Then why do I feel as if there is?"

"Because you're a worrier by nature. Your divorce is proceeding and should be final before too long, won't it?"

Claire nodded. Unless Glenn managed to delay it again.

"Your ex isn't bothering you still, is he?"

"No, not since he came over to the hotel that time. I think he might have finally figured out I'm serious and there's no point fighting about it because eventually he'll have to give in." At least, that's what she kept telling herself.

"So unless Lawrence Westbrook is the murderer and he decides to kill me because I must be Calvin come back to life, we don't really have a problem. I sincerely doubt he believes in this sort of hooey and I see no reason he should be concerned about you and me."

"I hope you're right." But why was she so uneasy if that were the case? Her nerves were a wreck because of those damned dreams, that's why. And it wasn't hooey, no matter what Jonas said. She brought up another subject she'd thought about but hadn't mentioned. "Jonas, where do you see us going?"

He looked puzzled. "Why should we go anywhere?"

"I mean our relationship. We don't ever talk about it. We said we loved each other but then we dropped it. We haven't made any plans. We never talk about us, except in relation to Calvin and Bella or sometimes Sarah and Elijah. But we never talk about you and me."

"It's hard to make plans when you're still married."

"I'm doing my best to change that."

"Yeah, I know. But until you do I see no point in talking about it."

She gazed at him a long moment. "You don't trust me, do you? You think I'm going to break your heart like that other woman did." She could see him getting more irritated by the minute.

"Don't be ridiculous, Claire. I told you, she didn't break my heart. I don't see the point in hashing over our relationship. We've admitted we love each other. We enjoy each other, we like being together. Why complicate matters any more than they already are?"

"Because I need to know if we're on the same page."

"On the same page about what?"

"Our relationship. Do we both want the same thing or . . ." she trailed off, realizing she sounded needy. She hated sounding, or feeling, needy.

"There's no point in discussing anything until you're free."

Her marital status obviously bothered Jonas more than she'd realized. What was he afraid of? That she wouldn't get divorced? Or that she would?

"Never mind. We don't have to talk about this now."

"Yeah, right."

"No, I'm serious." She held out her hand. "Let's go to bed." Sex might not solve all problems, but she wanted to feel close to him. Being in his arms enabled her to close out the rest of the world, at least for a time. Right now, that's exactly what Claire wanted.

SLEEP WAS HARD to come by. Jonas suspected the talk with Claire had something to do with that. Claire was working, and he was alone in the bed. Alone and remembering what Claire had said. Was he afraid she'd go back to her husband?

He rolled over and pounded his pillow. No sense thinking about him and Claire until her divorce was final. That's what he'd told her, and that's what he meant to do. He closed his eyes and tried not to think of Claire. Instead he thought of Bella . . . and Calvin.

***December 1968***

CAL COULDN'T BELIEVE Larry had managed to find his home, much less showed up there. He'd have thought the little shit would be too scared to show his face in the colored part of town.

"Larry Westbrook. What do you want?" he asked, leaning against the doorjamb.

Larry pushed past him, dragging back the hood of his sweatshirt when he got inside. "I came to give you one last chance to do the right thing. Leave Bella alone. Buster will never let his daughter be with a nigger."

"We're married. Buster doesn't have a say anymore."

"How stupid are you? Buster Cantrell owns this town. He can do anything he wants. Including kill you."

"Yeah, which is why we're leaving. I know you told Buster all about Bella and me. She just called me and told me what he did to her. You really are a chickenshit. Do you know her old man beats her? Any time he wants, he slaps her around. What did you think would happen when you went tattling to him?"

"You're lying. Buster wouldn't do anything to hurt Bella."

"Of course he does," Cal said scornfully. "If you cared about her, you'd have seen the bruises. You know what kind of man he is, but you don't care. You're afraid to take me on yourself, so you let Buster whale on a defenseless girl."

"You're the one who's going to make her live like an outcast. You ought to be horsewhipped for putting your hands on a white girl."

"Get out, Larry. This is none of your business. Bella doesn't want you."

"You make me sick. I'm warning you, you need to get out of town now. You shouldn't have ever put your filthy hands on her. She's no better than a whore now. You think because you knocked her up—"

Cal grabbed him, shook him furiously. "Don't you ever talk about Bella that way."

"Her father will make her get rid of that baby. Do you think he wants a half-colored grandchild? And then Bella will be mine. She'll forget all about you. You'll just be the dirty nigger who knocked her up."

Cal punched him in the mouth. They struggled, Larry managing to land a blow or two but nothing that hurt too much. But Larry kept talking, saying ugly, terrible things about Bella and the baby. Cal punched him again, and again, until he knew he had to stop or kill the bastard. Finally, he let Larry fall to the floor. Panting, he stood looking down at him.

Cal wanted to kill him. But even angry as he was, he wouldn't take a life. Even a worthless one like Larry's. "Get out, Larry. Bella's mine. She and the baby are mine, and you need to forget all about her. Her father isn't going to get a chance to lay a hand on her ever again. We're leaving town as soon as Bella gets here."

Larry struggled to get up. "The hell you are." He pulled a gun out of his sweatshirt and leveled it at Cal. Laughed.

Cal stared at him, unable to believe Larry actually had the balls to bring a gun. But there it was, big as life. He pulled the trigger as Cal rushed him.

Cal fell to his knees, the pain bright, intense. A searing, sharp pain in his belly. *Oh, God.* He put his hand on his stomach, felt the warm blood coming from the wound.

"Now you can go where you belong," Larry said. "Straight to hell."

He tried to get up, tried to say something but couldn't. Slowly, he crumpled the rest of the way to the floor. He didn't see Larry leave. He blacked out, came to later with his head in Bella's lap.

"Calvin! Oh, God, Calvin don't you die!"

"I . . . I . . . " He wanted to talk but nothing came out. He knew he was dying. He was cold, so cold. Something . . . important . . . tell . . . Bella. Tell her, before he . . . died.

"The ambulance is coming. Who did this to you? Who shot

you? Calvin, you hang on. I love you. Do you hear me? I love you so much."

"I . . . love . . . you . . . Bella . . . "

"Don't leave me, please don't die."

Her tears felt like rain on his face. Soft, soothing, warm rain. She was so warm, and he was so, so cold. He felt her love surrounding him. Her beautiful face shimmered, faded as the grayness enveloped him . . .

*I love you, Calvin. I'll always love you.*

# CHAPTER TWENTY-FOUR

*November Present Day*

TWO DAYS LATER, no one had made much progress on the case. With the help of the cold case detectives, Emmitt had tracked down the man who'd given Westbrook his alibi. He was still alive and had agreed to see Emmitt. Emmitt had an appointment to meet the older man that afternoon and had promised to call Jonas as soon as possible after they'd talked, regardless of whether he learned something of importance or not.

Still, Jonas hadn't expected such a quick response when his cell rang that afternoon.

"Can you meet me at my house?" Emmitt asked. "I'm headed there now."

"All right. What's up?"

"I'll tell you when you get here."

Emmitt took Jonas into his study. It was a beautiful room with floor to ceiling bookshelves containing every kind of book, including Emmitt's many research books, all genres of fiction, from classics to science fiction, non-fiction, and the shelf of honor, holding Emmitt's own published books. Jonas counted twenty-eight.

"I had no idea you'd published so many books," Jonas said. "I've read a few of them but not all by a long shot."

"Remind me later and I'll give you some."

"Wouldn't you rather I buy them?" Jonas asked.

"Some of them are out of print." He grinned. "Besides, it's the least I can do if this story turns into a book. I'll give you a signed copy of my newest when it comes out and you can let your friends know it's available, how's that?"

Against one wall were a couple of overstuffed, dark blue leather chairs arranged in what was clearly a well-used reading spot with a floor lamp and side table between them. Emmitt motioned for him to take one chair, and he sat in the other. The huge desk that dominated an already impressive room was a deep, gorgeous mahogany. What he could see of it, that is. Emmitt's laptop computer, notes, papers, various books, and an e-book reader were scattered over the surface.

"What did you find out?" Jonas asked Emmitt.

His friend sat forward, eyes sparkling. "You're not going to believe this. The night watchman recanted his testimony. Westbrook's alibi was bogus. The man who gave it to him admitted to giving false testimony."

"He recanted his statement, just like that? Why?"

"Said he'd had a guilty conscience for years, and now that he's old and in poor health he wants to get it off his chest. My visit and questions apparently convinced him to finally do the right thing."

"What exactly did he say? And what's his name? I'd like to call him something besides the night watchman."

"His name is Henry Young. Buster Cantrell arranged everything. Buster paid for Young's son's schooling and gave him a cash infusion on the condition that he give Lawrence Westbrook an unbreakable alibi for the night in question. The guy was struggling, sick wife, medical bills, a young son on a night watchman's salary, and he couldn't resist. But he said it always bothered him. Especially when no one was ever brought to trial for the crime."

"Still, he hasn't come forward for more than fifty years. Why now?"

"He thinks he's going to die soon and wanted to set the record straight. He said he was going to call the cops and confess. He wants to talk to his son first, but he swore he would contact the police soon."

"Do you believe him?"

"Yeah, but even if he doesn't, I think we can convince the cold case detectives to at least question him again."

"Even so, this still doesn't mean we can prove Westbrook did it."

"No, but now he can't prove he didn't. Without that alibi his defense is a lot shakier. This is good news, Jonas," Emmitt added.

"Yes. But it still doesn't mean the cops can prove Westbrook is responsible for Calvin's murder."

"You're too pessimistic. It's the first break we've had."

"You haven't said, are the cold case detectives convinced it was a gang murder, like Dervish was?"

"No. But there's not a lot of evidence, I gather. Since it's unsolved, I don't really know what they have that might affect the case. They would only give me some of the information in the case files. They wouldn't give me anything they thought might compromise the case, assuming they were ever to find a suspect."

"There should be a way to convince the cops to look into Westbrook's alibi, especially with the new testimony. Damn it, I wish we were able to prove he was there."

"Unless you can come up with an eyewitness, we're going to have to trust the cops to figure it out."

An eyewitness. Calvin knew what had happened. And so did Jonas. The dream that had shaken him so much came back to him with a vengeance.

"Jonas?"

Emmitt's face swam into sight. Jonas blinked, trying to clear his head, more unsettled than he cared to admit.

"What the hell happened, man? I've been trying to get your attention for the last two minutes. You just checked out."

How was he supposed to explain what was happening to Emmitt? Dreams. Channeling a past life. Jesus. Emmitt would think Jonas was a nut job.

But maybe he should talk to Emmitt. His friend wasn't involved, as both Jonas and Claire were. Maybe he could look at the situation more logically, give Jonas a reasonable explanation for these damned dreams. It would be a relief to come up with something, anything, besides Claire's theory that they were reliving past lives. And apparently, doomed to repeat it until they "got it right."

"If I tell you, you'll think I'm crazy. Hell, I think I'm losing it. I'm sure you will too."

"Try me."

Since he couldn't think of a way to ease into it, he just came right out with it. "Ever since I met Claire, I've been having strange dreams."

"Okay. And why is that a problem?"

"They aren't normal dreams. I dream about the past. About

Calvin Davis's life. And it's as if I'm there, in the dream, only it isn't a dream. I think it's what really happened. In 1968."

Emmitt blinked. "You see Calvin Davis's life."

"Yes. And in the dream I had last night, I saw Calvin die. I saw his killer." Not something he'd ever wanted to experience.

"You saw your dead cousin's murder. In a dream. Is that what you're telling me?"

"Yes. And everything that led up to it. I saw Lawrence Westbrook shoot him." *I saw him shoot me.*

Emmitt didn't say anything. He simply stared at him.

"I told you it sounded insane."

Rubbing the back of his neck, Emmitt grimaced. "Not exactly insane. Weird. It's certainly plausible that Westbrook killed Calvin Davis, but dreams about the murder?" He shook his head. "That's a lot to swallow. Why are you having these dreams? Because Calvin was your cousin?"

He wished. "Possibly. But . . . this part's even weirder. Claire thinks—we think—I might be—" He stopped. Accepting reincarnation himself was hard enough, but Jesus, to say it out loud. "We believe I'm Calvin reincarnated. And Claire is Bella."

Behind the lenses of his glasses, Emmitt's eyes widened. "Let me get this straight. You and Claire believe that the two of you are reliving past lives. Specifically the lives of two lovers who died fifty-something years ago." He stared at him a moment. "Holy shit, Jonas, that's crazy."

"I know." He didn't see the need to get into Claire's dreams and her belief that they were also Sarah and Elijah. One past life was hard enough to accept.

"I've seen a lot of strange things during my investigations. Some of them with no reasonable explanation. But I have to admit that someone reliving a past life has never been on my radar. Are you sure?"

"Of course I'm not sure," Jonas said, frustration edging his voice. "It's insanity to even think about something like reliving past lives. But the fact is, I've been having these dreams. The fact is, I know all about Cal and Bella. The fact is, I knew the kid named Larry was in love with Bella. Until you told us, and until I had the dream, I didn't know his last name was Westbrook. I know things I should have no way of knowing. But I've talked to my mother—who knew Calvin and Bella and the whole situation—and the things I've seen, the things I've dreamed about—they're accurate."

"So you think your dream about the murder is accurate too."

"Yeah, I do. But since I can't tell the cops any of this, we have to prove it another way. Maybe breaking Westbrook's alibi will give the cops enough to go on to find out what really happened."

"I think there's a real good chance." He hesitated, then said, "You said you talked to your mother. Maybe all this is simply memories from your childhood. You're remembering what your mother talked about years ago. And you're dreaming about those memories for some reason."

"I've seen Calvin and Bella when no one else was around. Things Naomi would have no way of knowing." Seen them making love, and now, he'd seen them when Calvin died. "I saw Calvin die. I *experienced* his death. I died, Emmitt, more than fifty years ago. My mother couldn't have known all of the things I've seen."

Emmitt looked doubtful, but he didn't argue further. "I'll work on my notes tonight. Kendra and the kids are gone for the evening, so I should be able to get them in order. If Young doesn't call the cops in the next day or two, I'll tell them what I learned and ask that they question him again."

"Let's hope he calls them and comes clean. What are you going to do with all your notes?"

"Write a book, eventually. What else?" He flashed Jonas a grin. "I'll probably leave out the reincarnation part, though."

"Good." He shifted uneasily. "I'm not sure why I even told you." He was already regretting it.

"I'm a journalist, Jonas. My sources are confidential. Just as you'd never break doctor-patient confidentiality, I won't break your confidences either."

"It's not that I don't trust you. Obviously, I do, or I'd never have told you. But bad things seem to happen to people who know too much about this case. I'd hate for you to be drawn into something dangerous. After all, we're talking about murder, and a man who's gotten away with it for more than fifty years."

"If your dream is right."

"So far they have been. I see no reason why this one, the most important one, would be wrong. Assuming you believe in this sort of woo-woo crap," he added with a bit of disgust.

Emmitt laughed. "I have to say, you're about the last person I'd suspect of believing in something like reincarnation."

"Don't I know it."

CLAIRE ANSWERED her cell phone when she heard Jonas's ringtone. "Hi. I thought you were working?"

"I am but I wanted to talk to you. I have a lot to tell you, but I can't right now. Can we discuss it when I'm not on call?"

"Is this about your meeting with Emmitt?"

"Yes. Among other things. I'll fill you in later, but Emmitt saw Henry Young, the night watchman, and the man recanted his testimony. I'll give you all the details later."

"So Lawrence will no longer have an alibi. That's huge, Jonas."

"Yeah. I have to go, Claire, but I'll call you in the morning. You're working tomorrow?"

"No, I'm off the next two days. I'm going to my lawyer's tomorrow morning. To sign the final divorce papers."

He was quiet a moment, then said, "Good. We can talk after you see the lawyer and I get home."

"All right. Call me in the morning when you're off work."

"Other things," Jonas had said. She wondered exactly what that meant. She'd worked all night, and even though she'd had some sleep since coming home, she still felt sleep deprived. She lay down on the couch thinking she'd just close her eyes for a minute.

Could she and Jonas really be reliving past lives? Or was she simply looking for an answer to the unanswerable? She fell asleep thinking about it.

*July 1859*

SARAH LAY WITH Elijah, replete, and wondered how she'd ever stood for her husband to touch her. Victor had never shown her a tenth the kindness, or the care, that Elijah did in simply looking at her. If this was wrong, loving this man, lying with him, then she was damned for a sinner because she would not give him up. Especially not now. Even though it was dangerous for both of them, she'd needed to talk to Elijah. And once they'd found themselves alone, they hadn't been able to resist each other, knowing what they'd had.

"Elijah?"

He rose on his elbow and smiled down at her. His chest was beautiful. Ripples of muscle in dark shades of mahogany. Unmarked, until he turned and she saw his back and the criss-cross of scars marking it. And was reminded of what had been done to him. She couldn't bear to think of it, of the lash of the whip marking that beautiful flesh. All because some men thought they should own others.

"I'm leaving Victor. I can't stay. Even if he never finds out about us, I cannot live with him anymore."

"How you gonna leave? Ain't like you can walk out with nowhere to go."

Impatiently, she brushed aside his questions. "Victor doesn't love me. He feels he owns me, just as he believes it's right to own you, and the others."

"Iffen you could," Elijah said slowly, "where you gonna go?"

"Mexico," she breathed. "And you're going with me."

He'd risen by now and pulled on his clothes. At this he swore. "No, Sarah, I won't. Anybody find out you helpin' fugitive slaves, they kill you."

"So you think I should stay, loving you, you loving me, and the two of us never being able to take more than a moment together? A brief moment of happiness that could be snatched from us in an instant?"

"It don't matter, Sarah. The both of us, we cain't be together." The look he gave her was kind, and despairing. "No place for folks like us. I be a slave. You the master's wife. Ain't nowheres we can live."

"Yes, there is. I told you, Mexico. You know that's where

most of the people who pass through here are going. We could be together there. We would be free, both of us. They don't allow slavery in Mexico."

"Mebbe. So they say. That don't mean a black slave and a white woman can live together there." He shook his head in disgust. "Some places they shoot me on sight. And you—Lord knows what they do to you."

Ignoring his protests, she went on. "I'll dress as a man. I've talked to Rachel and she'll help us. She's going to procure the garments for me. You'll go as my personal servant. My slave. No one will question us."

"Sarah, all this talk, it be madness."

"No, it's madness to stay. We'll have to leave soon, while Victor is away on one of his trips. But that shouldn't be hard. By the time he returns, we'll be long gone. Think of it, Elijah. We can be together in Mexico. Live as husband and wife." Though they could never be husband and wife. Victor would never divorce her, and besides, it would be better if she were simply to disappear with no further word.

"If your husband and his men catch us, we both be dead. You too."

"We have to go, Elijah. The sooner the better."

He returned to the rough bed and sat beside her. "Why now, Sarah? Why you takin' on so now?"

"Because I'm with child. And it's yours." She hadn't meant to tell him this way, but now that she had, she was glad. It had happened the first and only time they were together. Until now.

"A babe?" He shook his head, but she saw hope flare briefly before pain took its place. "The babe be the master's?"

"No." She put her hand on her stomach. "The babe is yours."

"Mine. You sure?"

"Almost certain. My husband can't father children. He never has, not once with all his women. I haven't spoken of it for fear he'd kill me if I implied such a thing." She didn't add that it was urgent she leave before she began to show. Elijah knew as well as she what would happen if Victor found out. That she'd lain with another man would be crime enough. That she'd fallen in love with a slave and was having his child was a hanging offense.

"I'm not sorry," she said, watching him. "I'm glad I'm having your child. To have a babe out of love—that is everything, Elijah. But we have to leave."

DISTURBED BY HER latest dream, Claire woke. She knew it would be hard, if not impossible, to go back to sleep. Sighing, she reached for the journal.

***Rachel's Journal—July 26, 1859***

*Sarah grows more desperate by the day. She was afraid to tell me, but finally I wore her down. She has consummated her love for another man. She and Elijah have lain together. I did not ask how she managed, but she swears she loves him and means to have him.*

*Her husband is hateful, yes. Cruel, abusive. A terrible man. But this course spells disaster. Bad enough she betrayed her vows, but when her husband learns—and he will learn—that she betrayed him with a slave. Oh, God, I dare not think what he will do!*

*I love my sister. I fear for her life. There is nothing I can do to change her course, a path to heartbreak and disaster.*

*Sarah has chosen, for better or worse. I fear the worst.*

## CHAPTER TWENTY-FIVE

LAWRENCE HAD almost fallen asleep when his cell phone rang. Dervish, he saw on the readout. About damn time. "Well?" he snapped into the phone.

"I'm coming over," Dervish said. "If your nurse is there, get rid of her." Before Lawrence could speak a word, Dervish ended the call.

Who the hell did the fool think he was? Lawrence wondered. Dervish thought he could order Lawrence around. *When pigs fly*, Lawrence thought.

Though it went against the grain, he sent the nurse away. God knows what that idiot Dervish wanted to tell him.

A short time later, Dervish walked in and said without preamble, "Henry Young is no longer a problem."

"What do you mean?"

"You know what I mean. I took care of him earlier this afternoon. Just like you wanted."

So much for Dervish's scruples. "Why the change? When I first broached the subject you said you wouldn't do it."

"I thought about it and decided you were right. It was too risky, which I was certain of once I talked to him."

"Had he changed his story?"

"Yes, and he told that damn journalist about it. When I got there, Rickerby was leaving."

"Well, shit, what good did it do to take care of the night watchman if he's already spilled his guts to Rickerby?"

"Do you think I'm an idiot?" Dervish demanded.

Yes, Lawrence did but didn't say it. "What did you do?"

"Rickerby's been taken care of as well. He won't be sticking his nose in where it doesn't belong anymore."

"How did you manage that?"

"I've still got connections. Some lowlife owed me a favor. Sort of like you."

"I don't owe you any favors, asshole. You're in as much trouble as me if this thing blows up."

Dervish had the nerve to laugh. "No way."

"Obstruction of justice, remember?" Dervish knew he was up shit creek. Otherwise, he'd never have gotten rid of Young.

"Obstruction ain't murder."

Lawrence abandoned that argument for the moment. "Did you kill him? Either of them?"

"Henry Young had a heart attack. There shouldn't be any problem. The old geezer was eighty-six. Nothing suspicious about it."

Lawrence grunted. "So you say. What happens if there's an autopsy?"

"I got connections, I told you. What I gave him probably won't show up. It doesn't stay in the bloodstream long. At least, that's what they told me. Besides, there's no reason for an autopsy."

"What about the journalist?"

"Rickerby's either dead or close to it. Seems whoever robbed his house gut shot him. 'Surprised' him at home."

"Good. What about his notes? A journalist is going to have all sorts of notes. And a computer as well."

"I have all that. Notes, computer, everything pertaining to the Davis case. Everything Rickerby found out from Young." He paused and added, "*Everything* is in my possession now."

The son of a bitch was threatening him. Dervish should know better than to fuck with Lawrence. "But you're going to give it all to me, aren't you, Frank?"

He laughed. "Sure. For a price."

"How much?"

"A million should cover it."

"Are you nuts? I can't lay my hands on a million bucks." He could, but he wasn't going to fork over that kind of money to a worthless piece of crap like Frank Dervish.

"Five hundred thousand, then. Should be worth something to you to stay out of jail. Texas has the death penalty, you know. Think about that."

He'd think about it, all right. Think of a way to shut Dervish's mouth permanently. First of all, if the ex-cop had screwed up and there was an autopsy on Young, Lawrence would bet they'd trace something back to Dervish. Either the drug or the fact that he'd gone to see the old man, for Christ's sake. Dervish wasn't smart enough to really cover his tracks. And blackmailing Lawrence—again—after everything Lawrence had done for him over the years. . . . Well, Dervish had asked for it this time. "I'll get back to you. Keep those notes and things close."

"I have them in a safe place. They're not going anywhere." He laughed again. "Don't take too long," Dervish advised. "I'm ready to leave this town for good. The sooner, the better."

Lawrence watched the asshole leave. Let Dervish believe he called the shots. He'd soon find out differently.

The more Lawrence thought about it, the more the idea appealed to him. Only one person, besides himself, knew what had really happened that night more than fifty years before. Although Lawrence had never admitted his guilt to anyone, much less Dervish, why else would Lawrence have paid Dervish off all these years? Even he wasn't stupid enough to believe Lawrence was innocent. But enough was enough.

Dervish's usefulness had just about come to an end. The ex-cop had taken care of the night watchman, but now he was holding Rickerby's notes over Lawrence's head. Long ago, Dervish had overlooked any evidence in Calvin Davis's case that might point to Lawrence's guilt, including a weak and suspicious alibi. And Lawrence had rewarded him. Many times.

Dervish was a liability. If Lawrence gave him the money, who's to say he wouldn't want more in six months, a year? Who's to say he would even give Lawrence everything he had? He could keep notes back, and Lawrence would never know. Not until the asshole demanded more money. No, Frank Dervish was a loose end, and it was long past time Lawrence dealt with him.

Killing Dervish shouldn't be hard. The man was a drunk, and not too bright to boot. Taking him out would be child's play. Maybe not that easy, since Lawrence didn't want to implicate himself. Still, he could think of something. An accident during a drunken stupor. That would be easy enough to accomplish. Getting Dervish drunk was no problem. Hell, all he had to do was flash some green and give him a bottle of scotch to celebrate.

Scotch. Booze and pills could be a lethal combination. What

if Dervish's death wasn't accidental? Suicide. That's the ticket. Dervish was going to kill himself. The man's finances were at rock bottom, had been for years. The hopelessness would finally get the best of him. He'd end it all with a bottle of painkillers and booze.

Getting pills was no problem. Lawrence hadn't used all his painkillers from the accident. He had plenty, surely enough for Dervish, especially coupled with booze.

Lawrence planned to meet at Dervish's place to exchange the notes for the cash. He'd go in disguise so no one would know he'd been there. He'd spike the booze, then put a couple of pills in a baggie and make it look like the ex-cop had gotten them off the street. Oh, yeah, this was going to work out just fine.

Clark was the reason Lawrence was having to concern himself with something that should have been over and done with a long time ago. No one had thought about this crime in years until Jonas Clark stirred everything up again. In Lawrence's book, this "crime" was no real crime. Calvin Davis had deserved what happened to him.

After it was all over, Lawrence could work on Glenn's jealousy. His son was pissed after being cuckolded by his snotty wife and her black lover. And apparently, Glenn wanted his wife back, though Lawrence couldn't figure out why. Claire had always seemed like a tight-assed bitch to Lawrence. Nothing like Bella, regardless of having her eyes.

Claire wasn't important. Lawrence would take care of her, or have her taken care of, later. Right now, Lawrence was going to be damn glad when he could finally put Calvin Davis and all the trouble he'd caused behind him.

SO FAR, JONAS'S night hadn't been too hectic, but the work had been steady. Around midnight, he was headed home to snatch a few hours of sleep when he got a page to call trauma. So much for going home. Knowing he would almost certainly have to return to the hospital, he turned around and headed back, calling in on his cell on the way.

"What can I do for you, Mike?" Jonas asked the trauma surgeon on call.

"I need a consult."

"Okay, tell me about it."

"I've got a guy who has a gunshot wound to the abdomen. He was found unconscious at the scene, but he was bleeding from a blow to the head as well as from the gunshot. The pre-op CT scan of the head showed no obvious intracranial injury. We did a laparotomy and resected a piece of bowel that had been injured. We found no other major intra-abdominal injury. He's in recovery now, and we'd like you to take a look at him."

"I'm on my way back. I'll check his scan and then see him." With any luck, all they'd need was a consult, not another operation.

Fifteen minutes later, he walked into radiology. "You've got a CT scan for me to look at?"

"Yes." The radiologist, Alton Reynolds, pulled up the scan on his computer. "Glad you got here so quickly."

"Oh, why?" Jonas glanced at the computer scan and the name. He did a double take. Emmitt Rickerby. *Rickerby?* Emmitt had been shot? "What the hell is this? Emmitt Rickerby is a good friend of mine."

"That's what I hear. I understand the patient's wife insists you take care of him."

"Get a message to her that I'm here and I'll talk to her as soon as I know something." Oh, Jesus. A gunshot wound. And head trauma. This could be bad. Very, very bad. Jonas forced himself to calm down—to look at the scan objectively, with a doctor's eyes, not a friend's.

Jonas and Reynolds talked about the scan. Thank God, Jonas agreed with the radiologist's initial assessment. He saw no intracranial bleeding. Emmitt had a concussion, but at this point no surgery was needed. When they finished discussing the scan, he asked, "Any idea what happened? How did he get shot?"

"I heard it was a home invasion, but I'm not even sure of that. The wife's in the waiting room, you can talk to her."

"I will, after I see the patient." And after he talked to Mike Sanders again, the trauma surgeon who had operated on Emmitt.

A home invasion. If that were true, why now? Why Emmitt's house? Was it a simple robbery, or did it have something to do with what Emmitt had discovered earlier that day? Jonas wasn't a fan of coincidence, and he had a very bad feeling about this situation. Why tonight of all nights would Emmitt be robbed?

CLAIRE WOKE TO her cell phone ringing. Still groggy from the dream, she recognized the ringtone and answered. "Jonas?"

"Sorry to wake you but I knew you'd want to know. Emmitt came into the hospital with a gunshot wound to the abdomen and a concussion. He's in recovery now but he's stable."

She sat up, suddenly fully awake. "What? Emmitt's been *shot*? How did this happen?"

"A home invasion. The cops don't know much yet, but his wife and kids came home and found him in his study. It's a miracle he didn't bleed out, but Kendra believes that the burglars went out the front door just as she and the kids came in the back. She says the electronics are missing, including Emmitt's computer he used for work and all of his notes. She didn't have time to look at the rest of the house."

"Do you think . . ." she trailed off. Stupid question. Jonas was bound to be wondering the same thing she was. If Emmitt's computer and notes were gone, that made it pretty likely that his meeting with the night watchman earlier that day had played a part in the burglary tonight. "Never mind. We can talk about the details later. Who took care of him?"

"Mike Sanders did the surgery. He said it went well. Emmitt should recover fully and his CAT scan looked good. There was no intracranial bleeding."

"Mike's a good surgeon, Jonas. I'm glad you were able to see Emmitt's scan."

"Yeah. Jesus, Claire, when I saw his name on the CAT scan, I knew it was him. Emmitt Rickerby isn't a common name."

"No, it's not. I'll be there as soon as I can make it."

"You don't need to come. There's nothing for you to do."

"I can be with you. Don't argue, I'll see you shortly."

THE NEXT MORNING, with his doctors' consent, the police questioned Emmitt. That sort of interview usually took place as soon as the victim regained consciousness. However, Emmitt's pain and confusion were too severe to allow it. Jonas had been there all night and knew Emmitt didn't remember much of anything. Jonas hoped he could fill in some blanks for the police.

He caught up with the two cops after they came out of Emmitt's room. He'd met them the night before and earlier that morning when Jonas had cautioned them to be careful in their questioning and not expect too much. Unfortunately, when Jonas had spoken to his friend that morning, it was clear Emmitt had retrograde amnesia covering not only the accident, but the entire day. How long that would last, no one knew.

"Detectives, if I could have a word with you?"

"Sure, Doc. What is it?" Olivetti, the older of the two men asked.

"Did Emmitt remember anything about the crime? Or about the day and what happened prior to the break-in?"

"Not a thing," Olivetti said. "But you told us he probably wouldn't."

"I was afraid of that, yes. He didn't when I talked to him. There's always a chance that most of the day will come back to him, even if the time around the actual shooting doesn't. But in case it doesn't, I wanted to tell you what I know. I met with Emmitt a few hours before the break-in. I'm wondering if his activities earlier in the day could have been behind this robbery."

"Why would you think that, Dr. Clark?" Baxter, the younger cop, asked.

"His wife's been up here and hasn't really had a chance to go over the entire house, but she told me you believe the burglars only hit his study. They took his electronics—computer, tape recorder, cell phone—and his notes. Nothing else. I find that a little suspicious. Don't you?"

The older man shrugged. "Apparently the wife and kids

surprised the thieves. We believe they didn't have time to cover the rest of the house. They wanted to get out before they were discovered."

"Because they didn't want to deal with a woman and two children? When they'd already shot Emmitt? Don't get me wrong, I'm grateful they didn't hurt his family, but I find that odd."

"What's on your mind, Doc?" Olivetti took out his notebook. "You want to tell us what you're thinking?"

"This break-in was no random burglary."

"You sound definite about that." Olivetti glanced at him sharply. "You have anything to back up this conclusion?"

"I believe so. Let's go sit down." He led the way to an empty waiting area, and the three of them took chairs. "Emmitt has been investigating a cold case. The murder of Calvin Davis in 1968."

"1968? That's pretty damn cold, Doc."

"Yes, and recently a few more things have come to light. You can talk to the cold case detectives. They know all about it. Calvin Davis was a cousin of mine, and I started looking into his death because my mother has never been satisfied with the investigating detective's contention that the crime was a gang slaying. I'm hoping to give her some closure. Yesterday, Emmitt talked to a key witness, a man who had given an alibi to a person of interest connected with this case."

He went on to tell the two men about Lawrence Westbrook being a suspect initially, and how Henry Young had given him an alibi for the night in question. Then he related what Emmitt had told him about Henry Young recanting his testimony.

"Has this Henry Young formally recanted? Or is this just something he told your friend?"

"I don't know. You could talk to the cold case detectives

and see if he contacted them. He told Emmitt he was going to." He gave them the detectives' names, but they were already familiar with them since they handled all the cold cases for the Fort Worth Police Department.

"I don't know about you, but I find it suspicious that Emmitt's house is broken into, his notes and computer taken, and Emmitt himself shot on the very day he heard a confession from a witness who lied to the police about a murder investigation. Especially considering the guy whose alibi is no good is still alive."

"It's a theory," Olivetti said, but he didn't sound as if he put a lot of stock in it. "We'll check it out and get back to you, Doc. We'll be back tomorrow. Will you be around?"

"Thanks. And yes, I'll be here. Emmitt's my patient as well as my friend." The two detectives were unconvinced that his theory held any water, that was obvious. He hoped they did a better job of checking out the truth of the situation than the original detective had. They could hardly do worse.

Speaking of that detective, Jonas wondered if Anders O'Connor had ever managed to talk to Frank Dervish. It was possible he would talk to O'Connor even though he refused to talk to Emmitt. But O'Connor hadn't called him or Claire, so it seemed unlikely he'd talked to the man.

The following morning, Jonas got a call from a number he didn't recognize. "Clark here."

"Hey, Doc, it's Detective Olivetti. I have bad news for you. You know that night watchman you told us about? Henry Young?"

"Yes. Did you talk to him?"

"No, and we won't be able to now."

"Why?"

"He's dead, Doc. Died yesterday afternoon."

Dead? Henry Young was dead? "How long after he saw Emmitt did he die?"

"Don't know, Doc. In fact, we've only got your word for it that he even talked to Mr. Rickerby, and if he did, that he was alive when Rickerby left him."

"Are you accusing Emmitt of killing the man? Why the hell would he?"

"We're not accusing anyone, Doc. He was an eighty-six-year-old man with a heart condition, who died of a heart attack. Looks like you're barking up the wrong tree."

"Not freaking likely. There's no way this heart attack was a coincidence." But could he convince the reluctant cops of that fact? The odds of that didn't look good. "Will there be an autopsy?"

"Doubtful," Olivetti said. "The family doesn't want one, and we don't have enough reason to force the issue."

"So you're just going to let a man be murdered—again—without doing anything about it."

"Doc, it seems to me all you've got is a lot of hearsay and innuendo. We've got no reason to believe Henry Young's cause of death was anything but natural. I'll let you know if anything changes. In the meantime, we'll continue the investigation into Emmitt Rickerby's burglary and attack."

Sure they would. Without exploring the scenario that the burglary and attack were directly related to Henry Young's confession, he doubted they'd get very far.

Great. Just great.

# CHAPTER TWENTY-SIX

"WHY DID YOU want to see me, Dad?" Glenn asked when Lawrence answered his door the next morning. "This isn't a good time for me."

Lawrence believed that. Glenn looked like shit and had whenever he saw him lately. Well, it was past time for his son to step up and be useful. "Never mind that. What's going on with that wife of yours?"

He laughed humorlessly. "She won't be my wife for long. I'm due at my lawyer's to sign the final divorce papers in an hour."

"And you're just gonna sit there and take it? Let your woman, your *wife,* disrespect you? She's screwing a nigger. You know it, and yet you've done nothing about it. How can you let him get away with taking your woman? Putting his hands on your *wife*? You'll be a laughingstock."

Glenn shrugged. "Women have affairs all the time. What Claire is doing is nothing new."

"I wouldn't stand for it. I wouldn't take that disrespect."

"What do you expect me to do? Kill her?" he asked flippantly.

"Not Claire. Him. Jonas Clark." Lawrence had thought long and hard about the situation. Glenn could kill the bastard and solve a lot of Lawrence's problems. No one would care about Calvin Davis's death once Clark was out of the way. With Lawrence's help, they could make Clark's death look like an accident. And if Glenn did get caught, well, heat of passion and all that. A good lawyer could work with that. Unlike if Lawrence did it and were caught. No, much as he'd like to, he couldn't risk killing Clark. Not until he'd exhausted all other possibilities.

"Oh, sure. I'll just pull out my gun and shoot the son of a bitch. That'll solve all my problems."

"It would solve one of them. With him out of the picture, Claire might start to see reason."

Glenn stared at him. "You're serious. Are you fucking kidding me? You want me to kill a man?"

"Why not? We could make it look like an accident."

"Why not? Because that's insane. No woman is worth the risk of me going to prison for the rest of my life. Shit, what if they gave me the death penalty?"

Lawrence shrugged. "You're the one who looks like a fool having your wife carry on with a black man. Don't you have any pride?"

"Too much to kill a man over a damned woman. She's not that important." He hesitated, looking at Lawrence closely. "What's going on with you? Why would you bring up murder, even jokingly?"

"If you don't want to man up and take care of the situation, then don't." He should have known the boy would be too much of a pussy to tackle the problem. He might have to do what needed to be done himself. Just like he had before.

"You want Jonas Clark dead, don't you? Why? And don't try to tell me your reasons have anything to do with me or Claire. Why do you want Clark dead?"

"Get over yourself. I was trying to help you regain some self- respect. I should have known better. I didn't raise you to be a chickenshit."

"You didn't raise me to be a murderer either." Glenn stood and walked to the door. Turned around. "You're not going to do something crazy, are you? Like try to kill him yourself?"

"Of course not. It was just talk." Obviously, he couldn't count on Glenn in the matter. And he didn't need his son freaking out, either.

"You're sure as shit talking crazy. What's this about, Dad?"

Lawrence didn't answer. If he couldn't convince Glenn to man up, he would have to take care of the matter himself. Even after all these years, he still felt a thrill whenever he thought about shooting Calvin Davis. Taking care of Dervish shouldn't be hard. Getting rid of Jonas Clark would be more of a challenge, especially to do it and not incriminate himself. But he'd figure something out.

Glenn waited, and when Lawrence continued his silence, he just shook his head and left.

CLAIRE LEFT THE lawyer's office and then pulled out the divorce decree. There it was, signed and sealed. Her divorce was final. She was free. Free to love Jonas, free to never have to see Glenn again. She stuffed the papers back in the envelope, wishing she didn't have to think about Lawrence, but that was a futile hope.

Lawrence Westbrook, murderer?

If only Emmitt hadn't been shot. The lack of information was intensely frustrating. What little they knew wasn't encouraging. When Emmitt had regained consciousness the evening before, he'd been very confused. So confused his doctors wouldn't let him talk to the police until the following morning. By now Jonas would know what had been said, but she didn't know how the conversation had gone. She'd been tied up with her lawyer.

She pulled out her cell, intending to call Jonas.

"Claire, I need to talk to you."

She turned around to see her ex-husband. "Are you kidding me? I have nothing to say to you, Glenn. We're divorced." She waved the papers. "Final papers."

He scowled. "I'm aware of that. I still need to talk to you."

"What's this about?" They'd signed the papers at different times precisely so they wouldn't have to deal with each other in person. She should have known Glenn's cooperation was too good to be true.

"Oh, for God's sake, just talk to me," he said irritably. "You're being absurd."

"Am I? I think I have reason."

Glenn ground his teeth audibly. "If you care about your precious lover, you'll talk to me and get this over with. There's a vacant office right there."

With misgiving, she stepped inside, putting her hand in her pocket to feel the reassuring outline of her cell phone. "What do you want and what does it have to do with Jonas?"

Once inside, Glenn didn't seem to know how to proceed. She watched him pace, mutter a curse. He was never indecisive. Even when wrong, he wasn't undecided. What was going on?

"What about Jonas?" she repeated.

He finally stopped pacing and glared at her. "You're really high on my father's shit list. So is Jonas Clark."

"There's a news flash. So?"

"He's talking crazy. He seems to have more invested in our marriage than I'd ever imagined."

"Define talking crazy." Lawrence, a possible murderer, talking crazy. Not something to inspire confidence.

"Jesus, I can't believe he meant it. But I've never seen him quite like that."

"For God's sake, get to the point. What did Lawrence say?"

Glenn glared at her again, as if this was all her fault. "He wants me to kill Jonas Clark. He came right out and suggested it."

Her stomach rolled. "Why? Why would he want Jonas dead? And why would he expect you to kill him?"

"I assume because he thinks getting rid of Clark will solve my problems with you. But I don't believe that's the reason. He could just be talking. He sounded so cavalier. So matter of fact, as if I could just take care of this small problem and get my life back on track. It was . . . bizarre. I can't be sure . . ." his voice trailed off.

"Why tell me this? Why now? If you're really concerned you should talk to the police."

He scowled. "I'm not turning my own father over to the police. It's just talk, after all. Besides, I'm sure he didn't mean it."

No, he wasn't. Glenn would never have said a word to her if he hadn't been extremely worried. "What was your answer?"

"I said you weren't worth going to jail over. What the hell did you think I'd say? Oh, sure, I'll off the guy?"

He still hadn't answered her question. "So you told me out of the goodness of your heart."

"I told you because if my father does do something crazy I don't want to take the fall for it. I'm not going to jail for a crime I didn't commit, and it would be just like you to try to blame me for it."

"The only thing I ever accused you of was beating me up, and you know damn well that was true. Which makes me wonder why you'd come to me about something like this."

He made an impatient gesture. "For Christ's sake, Claire, I don't want my father going to jail either. If my father is unstable enough to follow through, no telling what could happen. He might get lucky and manage to kill the bastard. Not that I'd cry over that possibility, except for the fallout and how it would affect me. And my father, of course. So I decided to warn you. It's probably nothing."

"If you're so concerned about Lawrence's mental state, you should get him to a doctor sooner rather than later." If Lawrence was the murderer, then she could readily believe he could kill again if he felt threatened. And if he didn't feel threatened, why would he ask Glenn to kill Jonas? She didn't believe for a minute that anything Lawrence had said was casual. Lawrence had been serious. Dead serious?

She needed to talk to Jonas because she had no idea how to proceed with this information. She should tell the police. But she knew they wouldn't put much faith in anything she—the disgruntled ex-wife—had to say about Glenn or his father. Still, she had to tell them. Clearly Glenn wouldn't.

He laughed. "Oh, right. We're talking about my father. You should know him well enough to know he'll never see a shrink. Not voluntarily. He's always said they're quacks just in it for the money."

"Glenn, he threatened to kill a man." And probably already had, at least once. Although she doubted Glenn knew of his father's guilt. Not in light of the current conversation.

"No, he didn't."

"He wanted you to kill a man. Same difference."

"I don't want to discuss this further with you. I've warned you, and you can tell that black bastard you're sleeping with or not. Makes no difference to me." He jerked open the door, turned, and said, "Don't forget, if something does happen, I had nothing to do with it."

Good God. She had to talk to Jonas.

AS SOON AS SHE got home from the lawyer's office, Claire called Jonas, but she got his voice mail. After leaving him a message to get back to her, she looked around for something to do. She was still short on sleep but knew she was too wound up to even make the attempt. She eyed the journal on the coffee table—Rachel's journal that seemed to call to her whenever she had a spare moment. And even when she didn't.

She picked up the journal to pass the time before Jonas arrived.

***Rachel's Journal—July 31, 1859***

*I fear for Sarah's life.*

*Helping an unknown fugitive escape is a far different matter than helping one's sister leave everyone and everything she knows behind. Knowing I will never see her again. I could tolerate that, if I were assured that she and the man she loves (how odd still to me that she loves a slave) could gain their freedom. But I fear something terrible will happen. Is it simply uneasiness or is there more to it? I do not have the sight, yet odd things have happened in my dreams. People long dead have spoken to me in my dreams. People such as my dear, departed mother. Yet on this subject she has remained silent.*

*I have tried to reason with Sarah, begging her to wait. She will hear nothing of it. She is determined to leave when Elijah does. Finally, today, she told me why. She is with child. As my own child grows heavier within me I realize I should have known, no matter how she tried to hide it.*

*Sarah cannot stay, that much is clear. She says there is very little chance the babe is Victor's. She believes he is the one who cannot sire children, no matter that he blames their lack of child on her. So the child is Elijah's. And her pregnancy must be hidden from Victor at all costs. But can she hide it, long enough to get away? God only knows what Victor would do if he knew.*

*No, I know. He would kill her. Is this why I cannot sleep? Why my dreams are so uneasy?*

*And no matter how much I will miss her, I know it is best she goes. My sister cannot have a child of mixed race and give it any sort of life. Not here in Texas. Best they go to Mexico where I hear there are colonies of folks of different races. I cannot imagine a world where that sort of tolerance exists.*

*Perhaps one day, in the future, there will be a world where love is the important element and not the color of one's skin.*

*But that world is not mine.*

"OH, MY GOD, JONAS. Is Emmitt worse?" Claire asked when she opened the door to him late that afternoon. He'd come straight to her apartment from work. She'd never seen him as tired and despondent as he was now.

"No, he's better. Still can't remember anything from yesterday, though." He sat on the couch, weary and dejected. She took a seat beside him.

"Then why do you look so upset? Have the police talked to the night watchman? Didn't he corroborate what you told the police about your conversation with Emmitt?"

He laughed without humor. "No, they didn't talk to him. And they won't now, or ever."

She had a bad feeling, but she asked the question anyway. "Why? What happened?"

"He's dead. Henry Young is dead. Olivetti called and told me before I left the hospital. So unless Emmitt remembers something about that meeting, or about the attack, the cops are treating what I've told them as hearsay. Emmitt needs to corroborate my story. Even then there's no guarantee the police will look on it as a solid lead."

She stared at him blankly for a moment. "Henry Young is dead? How did he die?"

He rubbed a hand over his forehead. "Heart attack."

"That's convenient."

"Isn't it, though. I need an aspirin. My head is killing me."

She went into the kitchen and grabbed a bottle of water, along with the aspirin bottle, bringing both to him.

After twisting the top off the water bottle, he took a long drink, then popped a couple of pills. "Thanks."

"You don't believe Henry Young's death was natural."

"Not for a minute. I think it's too goddamn coincidental to be natural."

"He was old. Did he have a heart condition?"

"Yes. Which is why the cops aren't buying my theory." His

eyes flashed when he looked at her. "Goddamn it, Claire, the man was murdered. I'm sure of it. Everything fits together too conveniently for these to be a random occurrence of events."

She sat beside him, rubbed his arm comfortingly. "It does seem odd that he would die immediately after recanting his testimony to Emmitt. And then for Emmitt to be a victim of an attack the very night he talked to the man."

"Odd is putting it lightly. I asked the police about an autopsy, but they're reluctant to push for it. The family doesn't want it."

"Even though he might have been murdered?"

"No one but you and I believe he was murdered. His family says he's been having health issues for some time now. And he was eighty-six."

"Perhaps we can demand it."

"Maybe. Don't get your hopes up, though."

Hesitant at first, she decided she had to bring up her conversation with Glenn. "There's something else we need to talk about. It has a bearing on all this."

"Can it wait?" He scrubbed his hands over his face. "I'm so tired I can't even think. I've got to get a few hours of sleep."

She knew that feeling of being at the last of your reserves. Jonas looked beyond that point, to utter exhaustion. "All right. Get some rest. We can talk more after that."

She watched him walk into the bedroom, his posture not only weary, but almost . . . defeated. She hated seeing him like this, especially when there was nothing she could do to help him.

Jonas needed to be aware of the threat against him. She didn't relish being the one to tell him. Before he'd come over, she had debated calling the police to alert them to what Glenn had said, but decided to talk to Jonas first. Even if Lawrence hadn't been serious, Jonas and the police needed to know what had been said. If they were fortunate, Lawrence's threats against Jonas, his attempt to coerce his own son to murder Jonas, would force the cops to look deeper into Henry Young's death and consequently, Calvin's death and Lawrence's phony alibi.

If the police ignored this new development, as she was afraid they would do? At least she and Jonas would be forewarned.

# CHAPTER TWENTY-SEVEN

THE LATE AFTERNOON sun streaming through the blinds woke Jonas. He groaned and rolled over, wanting to go back to sleep, but he gave up on that idea quickly. He couldn't stop thinking about what had happened.

Emmitt was in the hospital, a victim of a brutal attack and robbery. And now Henry Young was dead. Jonas knew in his heart the two events were related, and that they could both be traced back to Lawrence Westbrook. He didn't know how Westbrook had discovered Young's plan to recant his testimony so quickly, but he'd bet his last dollar that's what had happened. Even if Jonas hadn't had the dream about Cal's death, he'd believe Westbrook was Cal's murderer, as well as the man responsible for Henry Young's death.

But he couldn't prove it.

He got up and wandered into the next room. Claire sat in the clunky chair beside the couch, reading—what else—her ancestor's journal. When she saw him, she closed it and put it aside.

"You look better."

He went to the chair, leaned down, and kissed her. "I feel better. I want a shower, though, and I don't have any clean clothes over here. Why don't we go to my place?"

"All right. We need to talk."

"Yeah, we do. Would you mind picking up some food on the way? I'm sure I don't have anything to eat in my refrigerator."

"Sure. Chinese okay?"

"Sounds good. Unless you'd rather I pick it up."

"No, I'll do it. I'll meet you there."

A little more than an hour later, Jonas felt like a different person. He was still tired, still discouraged about Emmitt and Henry Young and the cops' seeming intractability in refusing to see a correlation between the two events. Not to mention, their refusal to believe in Westbrook's involvement. But at least he'd had sleep and food.

"You had another dream, didn't you?" Claire said after they'd cleared away the leftovers and were sitting in his living room.

"Yes. And I told Emmitt about it. I talked to him about our theory, for lack of a better word."

"What made you decide to tell him? How did he react?"

"He didn't tell me I was crazy. Which is more than I'd have done if the situation had been reversed." He scrubbed his hands over his face and continued. "Emmitt and I were talking about the night watchman recanting his testimony. We discussed how to convince the cops to look into Westbrook's alibi, and Emmitt commented that unless we had an eyewitness to the crime, we were going to have to trust the cops to figure it out."

"An eyewitness?" She searched his face. "Oh, my God. That's what you dreamed about. Calvin's shooting."

Jonas nodded. "Lawrence Westbrook killed him. So we have an eyewitness. Me. Sort of. Unfortunately, the person who saw it was the victim. And something tells me the cops won't buy our theory about why I'm dreaming these things or the truth of any of this."

"No, they won't believe you." She took his hand, held it, and squeezed comfortingly. "But I believe you. That must have been horrible."

"It wasn't fun." He was quiet a moment. "Bella was with him. When he died, she was there, holding him in her arms." He looked at Claire intensely. "I know it sounds crazy but I felt him. I felt him die, I heard Bella say she loved him. That she'd always love him. Calvin loved her so much." So much that Jonas was starting to wonder if he had his own feelings about Claire mixed up with what Calvin and Bella had felt. But somehow he didn't think Claire would appreciate hearing that, so he kept the thought to himself.

"We can't just let Lawrence get away with it. With murder. Not now that we know for sure. But what are we going to do? Especially if the police don't believe us."

"I don't know." He squeezed the bridge of his nose. "I'll talk to O'Connor. See if he has any ideas how to get the cops to buy into our theory. Or think of a way to get Westbrook to confess."

"Confess? Lawrence? I don't think there's a chance in hell that arrogant bastard will confess."

"Yeah, it seems unlikely to me, too."

"This makes what I'm about to tell you make more sense," Claire said.

"That's right, you said you had something to talk about. You said you were seeing your lawyer today. Is that what this is about?" He had a brief, unreasonable fear that she hadn't gone through with the divorce. He knew it was irrational, knew Claire had been certain what she wanted, but he still couldn't help worrying.

"Yes, it's official. I'm legally divorced. Glenn and I signed the final papers today."

"Good." He couldn't put a name to the look on her face. But she wasn't happy. "Isn't it? Did you have second thoughts?"

"About the divorce?" She shook her head decisively. "Of course I didn't. What I have to tell you isn't exactly related to the divorce. I talked to Glenn afterward. I hadn't planned on seeing him, but he was waiting for me after I left my lawyer's office."

"Did the son of a bitch hurt you?" He wouldn't get away with it if he had. Not again.

"No, nothing like that. At this point I think he's as happy to get rid of me as I am of him. No, he's worried about his father. He thinks Lawrence is losing it. He wanted to warn me."

"Warn you about what?"

"Lawrence tried to convince Glenn to kill you."

Okay, that surprised him. Maybe it shouldn't have, but it did. "Lawrence wants me dead. And Glenn told you this out of the goodness of his heart? Not likely."

"Glenn said if his father 'got lucky' and killed you, he didn't want to be blamed for it. He wasn't about to go to prison for a crime he didn't commit. He said he refused, and his father acted like he hadn't meant it. But he must have, Jonas. Lawrence must think you know something. Why else would he ask Glenn to kill you?"

"I can think of a number of reasons, but suspecting that I know something about the murder does top the list. It's no secret Emmitt and I are friends, or that we've been looking into

Calvin's death, for that matter. Westbrook could be worried about what Emmitt told me concerning Young's testimony. Still, it seems extreme."

"I don't think so. It seems logical to me, considering we believe Lawrence had a hand in Emmitt's attack as well as the night watchman's death."

"Yes, but it's not like he knows I was there. I doubt Westbrook believes in past lives."

"No, but maybe we should tell him."

"Tell him we've lived before?" It wasn't as crazy as it sounded. The fact that Jonas knew exactly what had happened the night Calvin was shot would be bound to shake up Westbrook. The more he thought about it, the more he liked the idea. Jonas smiled. "Maybe we should."

"YOU LOOK SURPRISED to see me," Lawrence said to Dervish.

Dervish swung open his door and stepped back to let him in. "I am. Figured you'd think of a way out of it. Parting with that much cash must hurt. You do have it, don't you?"

"Some of it. You'll get the rest once I get the notes and computer." Lawrence set a black briefcase down on the scarred coffee table and pulled the bottle of scotch out of the paper bag. "Get some glasses. Getting rid of you deserves a drink."

Dervish's eyes lit up at the sight of the scotch. "Don't mind if I do." He went into the kitchen of the small apartment. The place was a dump, not that it surprised Lawrence.

Lawrence set out the scotch bottle on the equally battered small table in the dining room area, making sure he could turn his back to Dervish as he poured. He had his own flask in his pocket and would make sure to give Dervish the doctored scotch. He glanced at the briefcase he'd set on the coffee table, knowing Dervish wouldn't be able to resist opening it.

"How do I know you're good for the rest?" Dervish said, handing him the glasses.

"You don't. Take a look," Lawrence said carelessly, gesturing toward the briefcase.

With his back to him, he heard Dervish open the briefcase and draw in a breath. "Holy shit, that's a lot of green. And this is only part of it?"

"Did you really think I'd hand all that cash over without seeing the goods? I have a note with instructions on how to get the rest." He held up a piece of paper in one hand and Dervish's glass in the other. "Now, where are the notes and computer?" When the ex-cop reached for the glass, Lawrence held it away. "Business first. You've seen the cash. Give."

Dervish jerked his head, indicating a corner of the living room. "It's all there. Now give me the scotch."

The asshole polished off the first glass in one long drink, then held out the glass for more. Lawrence poured him another, took a sip of his own. "I don't have to remind you I don't ever want to see your sorry face again, do I?"

"Don't worry. Me and my money are going to Tahiti tomorrow morning. No way would I risk coming back to this shithole." He drained the second glass in slightly more time than the first had taken.

Lawrence waited until Dervish had polished off the entire bottle, never noticing that Lawrence's own drink came from a flask he'd hidden in his pocket. When the ex-cop was comatose, his breathing labored, Lawrence rose and pulled a baggie out of his pocket, tossing it on the table. He'd crushed one of the pills and left enough in the baggie for the cops to be able to confirm it was the same drug that was in the bottle. He hadn't bothered with forging a note. Dervish had no one he'd leave a note for. In fact, Lawrence couldn't think of a soul who'd miss the bastard.

He picked up the notes and computer and stowed them in a beat-up duffle he'd brought and left by the door, unnoticed by Dervish. Searching the rest of the apartment, he found a small recorder that Dervish had secreted in his bedside table.

*Sorry piece of shit,* Lawrence thought. The recorder was bound to belong to the journalist, proving Dervish was hedging his bets by keeping something back. Pouring himself another sip of scotch from his flask, he took the chair beside the couch and settled down to wait.

Finally satisfied Dervish was dead, Lawrence pulled on latex gloves, washed his glass and put it up, then wiped down everything he'd touched. Not that he was particularly worried anyone would look further than the obvious explanation of suicide. Given the state of Frank Dervish's finances, suicide was a slam-dunk cause of death. But Lawrence hadn't survived as long as he had without being careful.

He put his disguise back on over his regular clothes. In the stairwell, before seeing Dervish, he'd taken off the grubby outer clothes and stuffed them in a bag. Out came the large dingy shirt, the ripped jeans so big they fit over his pants, a fake beard, a grimy ball cap, and a pair of wire-rimmed glasses. No one would associate Lawrence Westbrook, banker, with the bum entering or leaving Dervish's apartment building. The last thing he did was close up the briefcase with the money and put it in the duffle along with everything else.

Hoisting the bag over his shoulder, he looked at the dead man and smiled. "You dumb son of a bitch. That's what happens to people who fuck with me."

He refrained from whistling as he left, careful to keep his gait similar to that of a down-on-his-luck bum. Inside, though, he was happier than he'd been in a long time. Now to take care of Jonas Clark, and the rest of his problems would disappear along with Clark.

*July 31, 1859*

"ELIJAH, WHERE ARE you?"

The shack looked no different than it had the countless times before when she'd been there to help fugitives, or the two times she'd been with Elijah. There was no reason to feel impending doom. She was simply nervous. Then she saw him, and her heart rejoiced. She ran forward to meet him.

"I was afraid you weren't coming."

He kissed her. "Cain't believe it's time. I've wanted this for so long."

"Freedom? Or me?" she teased.

He smiled a bit sadly. "Both."

"What's wrong? Is something wrong?"

"Just a feeling. Don't pay me no never mind."

She shoved aside the thought that in the past it had been best to trust Elijah's "feelings." He'd been proven right more often than not. "Is someone meeting us?" she asked instead.

"No. We walk to the next station. About seven miles from here. From there we rides in a wagon. Where is your clothes? You cain't wear that," he said, gesturing at her dress.

"I was waiting to put them on."

He gathered her hands together and kissed them. "Sarah, I love you. Always will."

"You know I'll always love you too." She searched his face

in the dim light of the oil lantern. "Did you hear something? Are you worried?"

"Always."

"Victor isn't supposed to return for another week. That should give us time to get away. Not to Mexico, but far enough south he won't be able to find us easily."

"Who all knows we's leavin'?"

"Only my sister and her husband. And Celia. But she's on her way to Rachel's even now. I knew she couldn't stay once I was gone, nor would she want to. But Rachel will take care of her." She wished badly that Celia would go with them, but she had refused. Though she hadn't said it, Sarah knew Celia was in love with one of Rachel's servants. "Did you tell anyone?" she asked him.

"Jest the conductor. He gave me directions to the next stop. You'd better get dressed."

Now that the time was here, she was nervous, fearing what could happen. Yet never did she think she was doing the wrong thing. She picked up the pants, and the door to the shack slammed open.

"Goddamn your soul to hell, you faithless bitch!" Victor roared.

Her heart simply stopped.

*November Present Day*

*"NO, NO! ELIJAH!" Sarah stretched out a hand in supplication. "No, please don't . . . Victor, don't do this."*

"Claire, wake up. It's Jonas. Hush, it's just a dream."

Claire woke suddenly, tears streaming, heart pounding. She opened her eyes and blinked as slow recognition dawned. "Jonas? Oh, thank God."

He reached across her to turn on the light, then gathered her to him. "You were dreaming."

She felt him kiss the top of her head. "He found them," she said shakily. "Sarah's husband found them together. She knew they were both going to die."

"It was a dream, Claire. They're all long gone."

She looked up at him, unable to express the torment she'd felt. She still felt. "Not to me. To me it feels as if it happened today. As if it were you and me."

"It was a dream," he repeated, his voice deep and soothing. "Only a dream. You're safe. We're both safe." He took her hand, placed it on his chest. "See, I'm here. I'm real. I'm no dream."

"Hold me."

"I am. I won't let go."

He kissed her, his tongue sliding inside to tangle with hers. She wanted him desperately. Wanted to prove to herself that unlike in the past, the two of them were alive. Lovers. Always. She stripped off her sleep shirt, wiggled out of her panties, watched him pull off his boxers and turn to her. She put one arm around his neck and held him close. Slid her other hand over the warm skin of his chest, feeling the lovely glide of muscles under her palm. His heart beat strong, steady and reassuring.

He kissed her again, and she drowned in the kiss, in the thrill of his touch, the play of their tongues. Drank in his scent, his taste. Her arms tightened around him as she poured herself into the moment. Her heart swelled with love.

Jonas rolled over, pulling her on top of him. He played with her breasts, taking first one, then the other in his mouth. The rasp of his tongue, each liquid pull of his mouth on her nipples sent shivers of sensation coursing through her. His fingers danced over her, sliding in and out, heightening desire. She rubbed against him, smiling at his groan of pleasure.

When she could wait no longer, she took him inside her, gasping at the feel of his hard flesh entering her. He thrust and she squeezed tight, again and again, riding him until the pleasure crested, burst. She kissed him, and overcome, collapsed on his chest.

Eventually she could move. Claire rose on one arm and looked down at him. "Jonas?" He opened his eyes and smiled at her. "I love you, Jonas."

His smile widened. He slipped a hand through her hair, pulled her face down to his. Kissed her, gently, thoroughly. "That's good. I love you too. So much." He kissed her again. She sank into the kiss, wrapped him in her arms as they rolled back over and he made love to her again.

She wanted their love to last forever. But she knew in her heart that it wouldn't. That it couldn't. Restlessly, she went back to sleep. And dreamed again.

# CHAPTER TWENTY-EIGHT

***August 1, 1859***

THEY LYNCHED HIM at dawn.

He struggled, kicking out, then digging his worn boots into the ground as they dragged him toward the tree, the huge oak standing sentinel on the front lawn. But he could do nothing against five men.

*Oh, God, no. No, please,* she pled silently, knowing it was a futile prayer. They had tied his hands, beaten him until she could see the blood dripping from his face and body in the eerie fog of the emerging dawn. Despairing, she put her hand to the window, choked out a cry as they threw him up on the horse and placed the noose around his neck.

*My love. My only love.*

After it was over, when Elijah moved no longer, one of the men turned and strode back to the house. She heard him coming up the stairs, braced herself when he kicked in her door. He held a bullwhip in his hands and smiled that thin, cruel smile she knew so well.

"Now it's your turn," her husband said, and raised the whip.

The whip bit, burned like a fire on her skin, in her soul. She cried out in torment, in despair. She couldn't stop the agony, the bright, hot pain of it. She prayed for darkness, for death.

For her heart had died with Elijah.

*November Present Day*

CLAIRE WOKE, TEARS streaming down her cheeks in the predawn light, and looked at the man sleeping beside her. Her heart turned over, anguish so real, so intense she thought she'd die from the pain of it. *Oh, God. Jonas, what am I going to do?*

She clenched her fists, willing the shaking to stop. The dream. The damned dream that haunted her, asleep and awake. So real, so horrifying. Her helplessness intensified as she remembered watching Elijah die, as she felt the slash and burn of the whip against her bare skin. She knew who he was now. And she knew, with every fiber of her being, that he had died because of her.

Sarah and Elijah couldn't let each other go. And died because they couldn't. Bella and Calvin defied everyone to be together, and paid for it with their lives. Was it possible the only way to save Jonas was to let him go? And if it was, could she find the strength to do it?

JONAS WOKE AND went into the living room in search of Claire. She was reading Rachel's journal again. He wished she'd get over her obsession with her ancestor's journal, but he suspected she wouldn't any time soon. For a long moment he watched her, thinking how right she looked sitting on his sofa, all mussed from sleep, with a cup of coffee beside her. If she hadn't been reading that damned journal, the picture would have been perfect.

"Move in with me," he said.

She jerked like he'd shot her, raising her head to stare at him. "What?"

He walked to the couch and smiled down at her. Reaching for her hand, he repeated, "Move in with me. There's no reason for you not to anymore. I want to be with you, Claire. Come live with me."

Her hand lay limp in his as she gazed at him in surprise. "Jonas, there's something we need to talk about."

"That wasn't the response I wanted."

She pulled her hand away and used it to gesture. "You can't just ask me to move in with you out of the blue. We haven't talked about it, haven't even mentioned living together."

"You weren't divorced until yesterday," he reminded her. "I'm talking about it now. There was no point earlier."

"We need to talk about something else. We need to talk about Sarah and Elijah. And Bella and Cal and how they each relate to the two of us. We can't keep putting it off. Have you thought about why this is happening to us? Our dreams and why we're having them?"

God, not that again. "Claire, you know I have a hard time believing in the whole concept of the two of us having lived before. If I hadn't seen and felt Calvin die, I would say it's complete bullshit."

"But it's not. You know it isn't. My dream last night . . . " Her voice trailed off, then she began again. "I think I've figured it out. Why the two of us didn't work in the past."

"Our relationship didn't work in the past because of jealousy, racism, and prejudice. Pick one or all of the above. Outside forces kept them—or us if you prefer—apart."

"Yes, partly. But it was more. Maybe it was fate, I don't know. All I know is it can't work now either. We can't be together, not in this or any other lifetime."

He frowned, scrubbed his hands over his face. "I need coffee. Particularly if you're going to talk bullshit." He went to the kitchen and poured himself a mug, strong and black, just like he liked it. Took a sip and scalded his mouth. Took another, more cautious sip, and the fuzziness began to recede. What had gotten into her? Dreams, or that damned journal she couldn't stop reading?

He went back into the other room and sat beside her on the couch, setting his coffee mug on the table. He gathered her hands in his and strove for patience. "Didn't you tell me last night that you loved me?"

"Yes. I do love you, Jonas."

"And I love you. You're divorced now. You're free. There's nothing keeping us apart."

Her eyes, those beautiful, unusual eyes, looked so sad. Sad and resigned and brimming with unshed tears. "I wish that were true."

Claire rarely cried. He hated when she did. He tried to clamp down on his annoyance. She had a right to her feelings, even if he did think she was being ridiculous. "What happened? Why have you reached this conclusion? Was it a dream or the journal?"

She jerked her hands away. "Both. Everything. When I dreamed about Sarah's husband finding her and Elijah together—" She broke off and shivered. "It was horrible," she said flatly. "Last night I had another dream, after the first one. I dreamed about the hanging again. Only this dream was longer, more detailed. Elijah died because of Sarah. If she had given him up, let him leave without her, they might both have lived."

"*Might* being the operative word. And not if she was pregnant with Elijah's child. Once she was pregnant there was never a chance for them. Sarah and Elijah died because her husband was an evil son of a bitch. They died because he killed them. Not because they loved each other."

"Sarah and Elijah died because they wouldn't let each other go. Because they got involved in the first place. Because they chose love."

"You're wrong."

"Am I? Think about it, Jonas. Calvin and Bella died because they loved each other too. Lawrence wanted Bella. Lawrence would never have killed Calvin if Bella hadn't been in love with him and carrying his child."

"Calvin and Bella died because Lawrence Westbrook and Buster Cantrell were racist bastards. Cal and Bella died because of jealousy and racism."

"Don't you see, they all died because they couldn't—wouldn't— give each other up."

"No, I don't see."

"Read this."

She handed him the journal, opened to a page near the end of the book. "Read that entry and tell me I'm wrong."

She wouldn't give up until he read the damned thing and probably not even then. In spite of his reluctance, he was curious to see what had affected Claire so powerfully. He started to read.

***Rachel's Journal—August 2, 1859***

*Sarah is gone.*

*I can hardly bear to write the words. Sarah and her unborn babe are both dead. Murdered by Victor Lawrence. He has no shame, no feelings of remorse. I believe he has no feelings at all. Victor is truly evil. He had Sarah and her maid driven into town and dumped at the front door of the store. Sarah was alive, though barely. Her maid, Celia, was not. The bastard had lashed them both, lashed Celia until there was not an inch of her skin that did not carry the mark of the lash.*

*Horrible as his treatment was of Celia, his treatment of his own wife was even worse. He cared not that there was a chance the child Sarah was carrying could be his own. There was the greater likelihood that the babe was Elijah's and that was enough for Victor Lawrence to do his worst.*

*From what little Sarah was able to tell me before she died, Celia betrayed her. Betrayed both her and Elijah, though not voluntarily. When one is lashed to within an inch of one's life, one will say anything to make the pain stop. But Victor did not stop, even after she confessed. He whipped Celia until she died.*

*Victor and his cronies lynched Elijah, early this morning. Sarah watched it from her bedroom window, in agony that she could do nothing to stop them. Then Victor came for Sarah, stripped her, and whipped her. He laughed, taunting her with Celia's death, laughed as he lashed my sister. Victor had one of his minions dump Sarah and Celia on my doorstep, as if they were refuse. The doctor came but he could do nothing except try to ease the pain of my dear sister's passing. But there was no easing Sarah's agony. Not when her dear maid—her friend—was dead, and she the cause. Not when she had watched the man she loved beaten and hanged. Not when she had lost her babe and had nothing left.*

*Sarah blamed herself. She told me if she had never pursued Elijah none of this would have happened. Elijah would never have imagined the two of them could be together. Their love affair was her doing. She would have gone on in her miserable, unhappy marriage and never known what it was like to love a man beyond all reason. Honestly, I believe she wanted to die. With Elijah dead and her child as well, she felt she had nothing left to live for.*

*I know who to blame. That evil man who calls himself Sarah's husband.*

*God help me, but I can find no forgiveness in my heart. Because Victor will not pay. The sheriff answers to him, not to the citizens of the town. Victor Lawrence murdered three human beings and he is smugly certain nothing will happen to him. But I will not stand for that. I will make it my life's work to see that justice is served. God be my witness, Victor Lawrence will pay for his crimes.*

*Sarah and Elijah died for love, but I shall live for revenge.*

"DO YOU BELIEVE me now?" Claire asked when Jonas put down the journal. He had been affected, as much as she had, even though she knew he would deny it.

"Believe that we can't be together because of something that happened more than a hundred and fifty years ago? No. Hell, no. I think your interpretation is flawed. Slavery still existed when Elijah and Sarah fell in love. Calvin and Bella fell in love in the nineteen sixties. The world—our world—has changed a lot since then."

"Are you going to deny racism still exists? How can you?"

"Of course racism exists. But I don't believe the solution is for us not to be together. That makes no sense. If you really believe we're reincarnated, then we have to get it right this time. We have to find a way to be together. Despite racism and prejudice, jealousy or murder. Despite Lawrence Westbrook and what he has done or is trying to do."

"I'm not going to be the cause of your death. Not again." She couldn't bear to think she might have a hand in Jonas's death. If she had to give him up to keep him safe, then she would.

Jonas stared at her, disbelief clearly written on his face. "You won't move in with me."

"I can't. No matter how much I want to, no matter how much we love each other, we can't be together."

Jonas's phone rang. He glanced at it, then said, "It's O'Connor. I should take it. But this discussion isn't over."

"Go ahead." She'd known he wouldn't react well, but she couldn't give him a choice. Her mind was made up. She listened to the rather one-sided conversation Jonas was having with Detective O'Connor. He hung up, his expression grim.

"What happened? What did he say?"

"Guess who's dead now."

Claire simply stared at him.

"Frank Dervish. The cop who took over Calvin's murder investigation when O'Connor was injured. The one who maintained it was a gang slaying. The one we believe was in Westbrook's pocket. He's dead."

"How did he die?"

"Suicide. At least, that's the assumption."

"What does O'Connor think?"

"Same thing I do. His suicide is a little too convenient. Just as Henry Young's death was too convenient."

"You know what this means, don't you?" Claire asked. "Everyone connected with, or trying to look into Calvin Davis's case, is dying or hurt. I'm damned if you're going to be another casualty."

"What are you planning, Claire?"

"I'm going to get out of your life. And you're going to stop trying to prove Lawrence Westbrook killed Calvin."

"No. No way." Adamant, he shook his head. "I may not be able to convince you you're wrong about the two of us, but I won't give that murdering bastard a free pass. If what we believe is true, Lawrence Westbrook not only killed Calvin, he's responsible for two other deaths and Emmitt's attack as well."

"Your life is at stake." She knew it, even if Jonas couldn't admit it.

"I doubt it. But if that's true, running away won't solve anything. And I won't walk away—not from you, and not from the truth about Calvin's death."

"Are you willing to die to prove it?"

"I'm not going to die. But Lawrence Westbrook is going to pay for his crimes."

There was no reasoning with him. She knew conviction when she heard it, and could see it in his face. Implacable. Jonas wouldn't quit until he'd exposed the truth. Expose the murderer, or die trying.

## CHAPTER TWENTY-NINE

LATER THAT EVENING, when Claire had gone to sleep, Jonas called O'Connor. "I'm as sure as I can be that Lawrence Westbrook murdered Calvin Davis. And now he's doing everything he can to get rid of anyone who might be able to implicate him in that murder."

"I don't disagree," O'Connor said. "But we can't prove it. I've been over it and over it with the detectives on both Davis's case and your friend Emmitt's. They're just not buying it. Until they have cause, they can't go after Westbrook. His lawyers would laugh if they tried."

"What if we had proof?" Proof beyond the fact that he'd seen the murder in a dream.

"You got any ideas? Because I'm fresh out."

"A taped confession."

"That would help. It's legal in Texas to tape a conversation with one party's knowledge."

"I know. At least, that's what it said when I looked it up on the Internet."

O'Connor chuckled. "Wonders of the Internet. How are

you going to get him to confess? Not to mention, how are you going to approach him at all? Much less get him to confess."

"I have a plan." Claire would not be pleased to know she had given him the idea.

"Are you going to fill me in?" O'Connor asked when Jonas didn't elaborate.

"You wouldn't believe me if I told you. But I think it will work. I need to see him. Confront him." He planned to drop a bombshell on Westbrook. There had been an eyewitness to the murder. Jonas, in a convoluted sort of way. He had an idea that the things he knew were going to rock Lawrence Westbrook's world. Things no one but Calvin and Lawrence would know. And Jonas.

"I don't know, Jonas. If you're putting yourself in his sights, how do you plan to protect yourself? If we're right, Lawrence Westbrook is a dangerous man."

"I can be dangerous too." Certainly his knowledge of the murder was dangerous to the man's freedom. "I'll set up the meet in a public place. The coffee shop by work. You can be there too, for backup. He wouldn't recognize you if you sat at a nearby table, would he?"

"I doubt it. He met me once, years ago. I've changed since then. What if he won't come? What if he won't confess?"

"He'll come. If for nothing else, to find out what I know. And if he doesn't confess, then I'll have spooked him enough for him to do something drastic. In fact, he's already worried." He told O'Connor about Glenn's revelation.

O'Connor gave a low whistle. "Looks like Westbrook has a screw loose. I don't like the sound of that. "

"Yeah, neither did I. But clearly he doesn't want to kill me himself. Not if he can avoid it."

"Again, if we're right, he has no problem hiring someone else to do the job for him."

"Who's he going to trust? Dervish is dead. Glenn refused. He's between a rock and a hard place now. He'll have to come after me himself or forget it. I don't think he's going to forget it. Not after what he's done so far to save his ass."

"I don't like it, Jonas," the older man repeated.

"We don't have a choice if we intend to prove he's the killer. You haven't been able to convince the cops to move on Westbrook, to try to obtain a warrant or even look deeper into Henry Young's death, have you?"

O'Connor's answer was long in coming. "No."

"Neither have I." Having proven his point, he continued, "I'll need his phone number. It's probably unlisted. Can you get it?"

"Maybe. Why don't you ask Claire? She should have it. What does she say about this plan?"

*Nothing*. "Claire and I aren't on great terms right now."

"Because of this cockamamie idea of yours?"

Jonas had to laugh. "Not so cockamamie. No, it's nothing to do with the plan. She doesn't know anything about that." No, they weren't getting along because of Claire's crazy-ass idea that they couldn't be together. But he couldn't exactly talk that over with O'Connor. "Will you help me?" Jonas asked again.

O'Connor sighed heavily. "You're set on this course, aren't you? No matter what I say."

"I'm going through with it, yes. I need your help, though. I don't want to do this alone." He needed help, if for no other reason than he didn't trust Westbrook one tiny bit. Jonas didn't think the man would try to kill him in a public place, but on the other hand, he couldn't be sure what Westbrook would do when threatened. And Jonas meant to threaten the hell out of him.

"I'll see what I can do. I hope I don't regret going along with you."

"Thanks." Jonas hoped none of them regretted it. But since he didn't believe there was another way to prove Westbrook's guilt, he was going to put his plan into action as soon as he had the man's number. He was off work for the next few days, and there was no time like the present.

And if he had to ask Claire for the number, then he would. Unfortunately, he knew he'd get nothing from Claire until he explained his plan to her. That should be fun.

If Claire refused, he had other avenues. Although Emmitt had no notes and still couldn't remember the accident, he would at least know ways for Jonas to contact a reluctant suspect.

At least Jonas would be acting, instead of sitting around passively waiting for something to happen. Had that been part of Calvin's problem? He didn't act soon enough?

THREE DAYS LATER, Jonas admitted he would have to ask Claire for help getting in touch with Lawrence Westbrook. Both he and O'Connor had tried, but neither could gain access to either the man's address or his phone number. Emmitt's suggestions hadn't worked either. So he decided to call Claire, unsure what he was going to say to convince her to help him. Especially since she'd been stubbornly insistent that she was doing the right thing and hadn't spoken more than a few words in passing to him since she'd decided they couldn't be together.

Fate? It seemed to him if you believed in that sort of thing, then you'd believe that he and Claire were fated to be together. Not so, Claire. Jonas considered the whole thing ridiculous and illogical and settled back to wait for Claire to come to her senses. He didn't dwell on what he would do if she never changed her mind. She had to figure it out on her own, that they were meant to be together.

Normally, he wasn't a big believer in fate or destiny, but recent events had challenged his previous concepts. Challenged everything he believed in, to be honest. Everything he had known to be true was suddenly on shaky ground. He supposed having dreams of a previous life—dreams that were apparently factual—would do that to a person. Even someone as grounded in reality as he typically was.

He ran into Claire at the hospital that day and decided there was no time like the present. "Do you have a minute?"

She looked at him warily, but nodded and followed him into the doctor's lounge. "Is this about a patient?"

"No. I need Lawrence Westbrook's phone number. Do you have it?"

Claire stared at him. "Why?"

"I want to set up a meeting with him and see if I can get him to admit— to me—that he murdered Cal. O'Connor said if I had a taped confession it would help the police proceed."

"Are you insane? What's to stop him from pulling out a gun and shooting you? Again."

"I'll set up the meet for a public place, and O'Connor will be there for backup." She didn't speak, but was obviously unconvinced. "I don't need your approval, Claire. I just need the phone number."

"Why do you think he'll admit the truth to you? Or to

anyone, for that matter? If we're right, he's been running around trying to kill off everyone involved."

"I'm going to tell him the truth. That there was an eyewitness to Calvin Davis's murder."

Glancing around to make sure they were alone, she lowered her voice. "You think telling him you're Calvin in another life will make him confess? I repeat, are you crazy?"

"It's worth a try. If nothing else, I'll spook him some more and maybe he'll make a mistake that will convince the cops we're on the right track. He has to be stopped, Claire."

"Not by you."

"Yes, by me." And by her, if she'd only admit it. "I'm the only person who can remind him of exactly what happened the night he shot Calvin. It's engraved on my memory, and you can be sure he'll remember as well. The arrogant son of a bitch needs to be shaken up. I can do that. I may be the only person who can."

"If I don't give you the number?"

"I'll find a way."

She glared at him for a long moment, then pulled out her cell phone. "I'll text it to you. I haven't gotten around to deleting some of my contacts, so Lawrence's info is still in there. Aren't we lucky?" she asked sarcastically.

"Thanks."

She looked up from the phone, poised to hit SEND. "I have a condition. I want to know when you set up the meeting. Will you call me?"

"Yes." He stepped closer, cupped her face. "You could make this easier and move in with me. Forget your idea that we can't be together."

"If I wasn't convinced I was doing the right thing, I would. I miss you."

He kissed her, short, sweet, and a bit desperate. "Come back," he murmured.

She sighed and put her hand on his wrist, his hand still cupping her face. "I wish I could." Her pager went off, and she stepped back, looking down at it. "I have to go. Call me."

"I will. Don't worry, Claire. Everything's going to work out. This time."

Her eyes looked as sad as he'd ever seen them. "I wish I believed that," she said, and left.

JONAS MADE THE call early that evening, intending to set up the meet for the next day when he was off work. He kept it short. "This is Jonas Clark," he said, when Westbrook answered the phone.

Silence. "What do you want?"

"A meeting. I know something about Calvin Davis's murder I think you'll be very interested in."

"Why would I care about that? I had nothing to do with it."

Jonas laughed. "There's an eyewitness to the murder. If you want to know who it is, meet me at Java Joe's by the hospital tomorrow at two p.m."

"How do I know this isn't bullshit?"

"You don't," Jonas said. "But can you afford to take the chance?" He hung up, satisfied the man would show.

# CHAPTER THIRTY

*DAMN JONAS,* CLAIRE thought. He was the most stubborn man she'd ever known.

He'd kept his word and called her to tell her the meeting was set up for the following day. She wasn't to worry. He had backup. Yes, backup. O'Connor, a retired detective. She liked O'Connor and trusted him, but she'd feel a lot better if some current law enforcement officials were there as well.

But that was the problem. None of the current detectives believed the theory that Lawrence had been Calvin's killer, and that he'd been involved with Henry Young's and Frank Dervish's deaths, if not responsible for them himself. And Jonas was convinced he had to prove it. Jonas was convinced that it was on him to see that justice was served.

Justice. She wondered briefly if Rachel had found justice for Sarah's murder. If so, Claire hadn't read about it yet, but she still had some pages left in the journal. Maybe in the end, Rachel had found justice. Or at least peace.

Claire still had work for another hour. Something was nagging her, something beyond her fear for Jonas and what he was getting into. Something practical, but she couldn't put her finger on it.

Forty-five minutes later, what had been annoyingly just out of reach hit her like a Mack Truck as she was starting an IV in one of her patients. Lawrence knew where Jonas lived. Glenn had used a private detective to follow her, and Glenn said the man had followed her to Jonas's apartment. Glenn had known she'd fled to Jonas after he beat her up. Glenn knew where Jonas lived. It wasn't a stretch to believe Lawrence had gotten hold of that information as well. If not immediately, shortly after Jonas and Lawrence talked tonight.

What was to stop Lawrence from taking care of Jonas now, before the scheduled meeting? Not a damn thing. Would Jonas have thought of that? Would he have taken steps to protect himself now, tonight?

As soon as she finished with her patient, she left the hospital. She dialed Jonas on the way to the doctor's parking lot but got his voice mail. *Hurry*, her mind screamed. Maybe she was overreacting. Maybe she was wrong and Lawrence didn't know where Jonas lived. He couldn't have found the information easily if he hadn't gotten it from the PI or Glenn. That was not only a foolish hope, it was stupid to even think it.

Her heart knew. Jonas was in danger, and she had to find a way to save him. She didn't intend to lose the man she loved for the third time. This time would be different.

*I SHOULD KNOW better than to eat tacos at 9:30 p.m.*, Jonas thought as he climbed the stairs to his apartment. For him they were a recipe for indigestion. As he fitted the key into the lock, he felt something hard jammed into his back.

"Open the door. Don't try anything, or I'll shoot you right here."

*Shit.* Jonas recognized that voice. How did Westbrook find out where Jonas lived? Then he remembered and cursed himself for not realizing it before. Of course the bastard knew. Jonas should have thought of that before arranging to meet with the murderer. But he hadn't, and here he was with a goddamn gun in his back.

"You wouldn't shoot me here. Too public," Jonas said, wishing he had his own gun.

"Don't count on it," Westbrook said, digging the gun into Jonas's back again.

Jonas wouldn't put anything past the crazy bastard. He opened the door, intending to go for Westbrook's gun hand the moment they crossed the threshold. Unfortunately, he didn't get the chance since the man shoved him inside while staying too far away for Jonas to easily get to him.

Jonas turned around to face him. "What do you want, Larry?" he asked, deliberately using his nickname.

Westbrook kicked the door shut behind him. "Lawrence will do. No one has called me Larry in years."

Jonas felt the outline of the cell phone in his pocket. He might be able to dial 911 before Westbrook realized what he was doing. "You haven't been Larry since you murdered Calvin Davis, have you?"

"It wasn't murder. The bastard deserved to die." His gun hand shook as he pointed it at Jonas. "Your death won't be murder either."

Jonas fumbled with the phone, wishing it was easier to dial blind. "I wouldn't be so quick to threaten me, Larry. Not this time. You won't get away with killing me."

"We'll see about that. Take your phone or gun or whatever

you're messing with out of your pocket. Do it slow and easy and toss it on the ground."

*Crap. So much for Westbrook not noticing,* he thought, as he did what the man demanded.

Westbrook laughed. "I couldn't believe you played right into my hands."

Yeah, neither could Jonas. So much for his bright idea of meeting in public. "Can you take the risk? You came to my apartment openly. It's not late. Lots of people are around. What if someone saw you?"

His hand wavered. "You'll still be dead."

"And you'll be in prison. Probably on death row. Why don't we sit down? Talk." He took a seat on the couch, as if he entertained crazy men with guns on a daily basis.

Lawrence seemed confused that Jonas wasn't more frightened. He took the chair, still pointing the gun at Jonas. "Say what you want to say."

"Did Henry Young deserve to die too? Is that why you killed him? Because he was going to recant his testimony?"

Westbrook shrugged. "Dervish killed him, not me. You can't lay that one on me."

"But you told him to, didn't you, Larry? And then you killed Dervish."

He didn't deny it. Instead he scoffed and said, "So what if I did? The man was a useless drunk. He was no good to anyone. You can't prove anything, and neither can the cops. Why do you even care?"

Jonas didn't think it was a particularly good sign the man was admitting guilt. Even though that's what Jonas had wanted, he knew that only curiosity kept Westbrook from pulling the trigger. He had to get the gun away from him, the sooner, the better. He couldn't just rush him. Not without at least a moment of distraction. "I want justice for Calvin Davis. Dervish and Henry Young are all a part of it. And my friend Emmitt. I owe you for him, too, don't I?"

Westbrook waved away Emmitt's attack as if it had been nothing. "Nosy journalist should know better than to interfere in what doesn't concern him."

"Justice concerns everyone."

"Justice?" He laughed. "Davis got exactly what was coming to him. The black bastard knocked up a white girl. He deserved to die. He needed to die."

"The girl you wanted. The girl who didn't want you."

He snorted, looking disgusted. "Bella was too young and foolish to know what she wanted. What kind of life would she have had, married to a nigger?"

*Better than one married to a racist and murderer,* Jonas thought. "Bella knew she didn't want you. She knew she loved Calvin Davis."

"All you know about it is what your mother told you. Naomi was just a kid. She doesn't know what really happened." He paused and said, "Or does she? Is she the one who's got you poking into all this? Maybe I should have taken care of Naomi too. I still can, you know."

No way in hell was this bastard touching his mother. "Naomi doesn't know anything. She still believes Buster Cantrell murdered Calvin. Leave her out of it. I know what happened because I was there."

"You're talking crazy. All this happened before you were born."

A homicidal maniac was calling him crazy. Priceless. "Look at me, Larry. Who do you see? Who do I look like? You knew it the first time you saw me, in the hospital. You looked like you'd seen a ghost. Because you had."

His face reddened. "Calvin Davis died when he was eighteen. Just because you bear a family resemblance to him doesn't mean anything. You're his cousin, after all."

"I don't just resemble Calvin." He leaned forward, holding Westbrook's attention. "Look closely. You can see it in my eyes. I *am* Calvin."

Westbrook laughed, though unconvincingly. The gun wavered. "You're nuts. How can you be Calvin? He died over fifty years ago. I should know. I killed him."

"I know you did. You want to know why I know?"

He gestured with the gun. "Sure. I got nothing better to do than listen to your crap."

Jonas told him about every conversation the two of them ever had, everything the man had done to have Bella for himself and destroy Calvin. He said things only Bella, Calvin, and Larry had been privy to. Westbrook looked sicker every moment that Jonas talked. "I remember the night you shot me. You showed up at my house and told me to leave Bella alone."

*"Get out, Larry. Bella and the baby are mine,"* Jonas quoted. *"We're leaving town tonight, as soon as Bella gets here."*

Jonas waited for his words to sink in. "You shot me, Larry." Jonas touched his stomach where Calvin had been shot. "You left me to die."

Westbrook had paled dramatically. "You can't know. You can't be . . . him," he whispered.

"You shot me and left me for dead. But I wasn't dead, yet. I died in Bella's arms." Any moment now, Jonas thought. Any minute Westbrook would lose it and Jonas could jump him.

Hand shaking wildly, Westbrook aimed the gun at him again. "Then I'll just have to kill you again."

"It won't matter. I'll just keep coming back, haunting you, until you've paid for your crime."

Jonas gathered himself to jump. Someone knocked on the door. Suddenly, the broken man was gone. His grip on the gun tightened. Westbrook was back in control. *I should have gone for it,* Jonas thought. *Too late now.*

A key rattled the lock. Jonas watched the doorknob turn, his blood slowly freezing. Two people had a key, but only one would be out this late at night. Jesus, why did Claire have to show up now? Couldn't she have stayed away a little longer? "Go away, Claire." Please, go away.

"Jonas, Lawrence knows. He knows where you live. I remembered, just now. The first night I came here, Glenn had me followed."

"Don't open the door," Jonas said. But of course, she did.

"Lawrence knows, I tell you," she said as she entered. She stopped short when she saw Westbrook, who had risen at the sound of her voice.

He smiled broadly. "He certainly does. Get in here," he said, motioning with the gun. Claire's eyes widened, but she shut the door behind her. "Now, which one of you wants to die first?" Lawrence Westbrook added.

"I CALLED THE police before I came," Claire said, even though technically she hadn't. She thanked God she had talked to O'Connor on her way over. He had promised to do everything in his power to send the police to Jonas's apartment. She had to trust that he managed to get their attention this time. If only they arrived before it was too late.

With Lawrence looking like a madman waving that gun around, too late might come very soon.

"You won't kill either of us, Larry," Jonas said after

shooting her a sharp glance. "You won't kill me because I'm Calvin. I'll come back. I'll never leave you alone. I'll haunt you until you die. And you couldn't kill Bella. You loved her."

"Bella's long dead. I didn't kill her. Some quack doctor killed her when she got an abortion."

"The abortion her father forced her to have. I bet you had a hand in that, didn't you? And you've felt guilty ever since."

"It wasn't my fault. I loved her. I didn't want her to die."

Claire wasn't sure where Jonas was heading, but she played along. "I talked to my Aunt Sophie, Lawrence. Bella's sister, Sophie. She said their father drugged Bella and took her to Mexico for an abortion. She didn't even know what he'd done until she woke up, sick and in pain. Sophie had to tell her."

"I tell you, it wasn't my fault." He ran a hand through his hair, cursed. "I'd have let her have the kid as long as she gave it away. Damn Buster anyway." He paced, furious, waving the gun as if he'd forgotten he held it.

"You won't kill Claire. Look at her eyes," Jonas said. "They're like Bella's. Because Claire is Bella."

"No! You can't—it can't be true."

"It is true," Claire said. "You loved Bella but you hated her too. Because she loved Calvin, not you."

"Why did she want him? I could have given her so much, but she wanted him." He glared at Claire. "You," he said with loathing. "You always looked at me with her eyes. Reproaching me for something I had no part in."

"You killed Calvin," Jonas said. "Even if you didn't kill Bella, she died because of you."

"No. Buster killed her, not me. He's the one who made her have the abortion." He turned the gun on Jonas. "Shut up! I always hated you. Putting your hands on my girl, getting her pregnant. I took care of you once, I can do it again."

Intent on protecting Jonas, Claire lunged forward, pushing Jonas aside as she cried out, "Don't, Lawrence, don't!"

She heard a *pssst,* the spit of the silenced gun, and staggered back. The pain was sharp. She knew she'd been shot. She couldn't think, couldn't focus. Shock, she realized. Then the pain returned, bright, hot, intense. Claire stared at Jonas and slowly collapsed. He grabbed for her, managing to ease her fall. She heard shouting, words, but they made no sense.

She blinked, slowly her vision cleared, and she realized she was on the floor with Jonas leaning over her. "Goddamn it, Claire. What the hell did you think you were doing? He wouldn't have hit me. He was shaking so much he could hardly aim the gun." Jonas was on his knees beside her, trying to help her. Exploring the wound, talking to her.

"You don't . . . know . . . that . . ."

"I think the bullet passed through. It might have grazed your lung, though. How are you doing? Can you breathe?"

"Not . . . well . . . "

Ignoring Lawrence, who was shouting and waving the damned gun, Jonas calmly took stock. He patted her pocket and found her stethoscope. Pulled it out with a sound of relief.

"God! Hurts . . . " It was becoming harder to talk. Harder to breathe.

Jonas placed the stethoscope on her chest. "Shut up, Larry," he said before giving her his full attention.

To her surprise, Lawrence fell silent.

Jonas listened intently, moving the stethoscope around. Fingers at the pulse in her neck, he told her, "Your pulse is weak and thready. You're not moving air effectively. I don't hear breath sounds on your right side. That's where the bullet entered." He paused, added a curse.

She couldn't breathe. She felt as if a lead weight had fallen on her chest. She knew what was happening, and obviously, Jonas did too.

His next words confirmed her fears. "I think you've got a tension pneumothorax. I've got to do something or you'll die."

Do something? How did he plan to evacuate a tension pneumothorax in the field? He didn't have a chest tube to relieve the pressure. What did he plan to use? Magic? She tried to speak again but couldn't. Grasping for his hand, she squeezed it weakly, her strength ebbing. Their eyes met. *I don't want to die. Jonas, don't let me die. We have so much to live for. . . .* If she didn't die from the gunshot meant for Jonas. She couldn't regret it, though. At least Jonas was safe. Now she had to trust him to take care of her.

Jonas pulled a pen from his shirt pocket. Twisting it apart, he took out the ink cartridge. "It's not a chest tube but it might do the trick. I hope," he added beneath his breath, but she heard him.

Thank God, her brain began to work again after stuttering almost completely to a halt from shock and pain. She felt in her lab coat pocket, thankful she'd come straight from work without changing. Relieved, she pulled out the IV catheter she had in her pocket, left over from the procedure she'd performed just before leaving the hospital.

Jonas smiled when he saw it and dropped the pen. "Hot damn, that's perfect." He took it from her, opened the sterile covering, wiped her skin with the alcohol swab she'd also had in her pocket. Without hesitation, he slipped the catheter between her ribs and pulled out the trochar. Air hissed out, the sound, the feel of it, so damn sweet. The pain eased, and air flowed as she breathed in and out, gaining strength with every welcome breath. Their eyes met, and they both smiled.

"Thank God," Jonas said, bending forward to touch his forehead to hers. "Not that I'm complaining, but why the hell did you have an IV catheter in your pocket? Your stethoscope I can understand, but why the IV catheter?"

She smiled at him again, weakly. "I'm a trauma surgeon. I had to start an IV before I left work tonight. I had a spare in my pocket."

"Lucky us," he said sincerely and kissed her forehead.

"Lucky us," she agreed.

"What's the matter with you two? You're crazy," Lawrence said.

"Hello, pot," she murmured, then closed her eyes. Jonas would deal with Lawrence. She had faith this time.

They'd finally gotten it right.

# CHAPTER THIRTY-ONE

"WHAT ARE YOU doing?" Lawrence asked, waving the gun at him. "Who are you calling?"

Jonas was surprised the gun hadn't gone off again, the way the fool had been brandishing it around. "I'm calling 911," he told him. "Claire needs help. Immediately. She could still die if she doesn't get to a hospital." His phone was still on the floor across the room, so he was using Claire's to call for help.

"If you call 911, they'll send the police. Stop it. Stop it right now."

Jonas glanced at him, but continued, putting the phone to his ear as he waited for the operator to answer. "The cops are already on their way. Remember? Claire called them before she came. Do the right thing for once, Larry."

"What is your emergency?" the 911 operator said.

"This is Dr. Jonas Clark. I have a thirty-four-year-old woman with a gunshot wound to the chest. I need an ambulance immediately." He gave her his address.

"Is she unconscious? Is she breathing?" the operator asked.

"She's conscious and breathing. She had a tension pneumothorax but I evacuated it and now she's breathing fine."

"The ambulance should be there shortly."

"Thank you." He closed the phone and looked at Westbrook.

Westbrook still held the gun, but he seemed nonplussed about what to do. At least he hadn't shot either of them again.

"It wasn't my fault," Westbrook said, sitting down heavily. The gun hung from his hand loosely. "I was trying to shoot you. It's not my fault she jumped in front of you."

*Always someone else's fault,* Jonas thought but remained silent. No sense pissing off a nut with a gun any more than you had to.

"Buster gave me the gun," Westbrook said.

It took Jonas a moment to realize the man had gone back to the past.

"Buster wanted Davis dead. If I hadn't shot him, Buster Cantrell would have. Or more likely, he'd have hanged him." He looked imploringly at Jonas. "Don't you see, it was better I did it. At least his death was quick that way. Cantrell would have lynched him."

Good God, Westbrook took rationalizing to an art form. "What about Dervish and Young? Were their deaths not your fault either?"

He shrugged. "I did what I had to do. Young was old. He'd have died soon. Dervish was worthless anyway."

Sirens filled the air. Jonas decided that was probably a good thing because he couldn't stomach much more of the man. "That will be the cops. Or the ambulance. Or more likely, both. What are you going to do?"

Suddenly galvanized, Westbrook jumped up and ran to the window. "I have to get out of here. Or maybe—" he turned to look at Jonas and Claire. "Maybe I'll hold you hostage."

"You could do that," Jonas agreed. "But you know those situations don't end well for anyone involved. Why don't you leave now, before they get here?"

He looked undecided. "Why don't I just kill you both? Then I'll go."

"That's not a good idea. When I called 911, I also texted a friend of mine. His name's O'Connor. He was the first detective on Calvin's murder case. Dervish inherited the case when O'Connor was wounded. O'Connor knows you shot Claire. He's also convinced you murdered Calvin. After my text, he'll be sure of it. No, your best bet is to get out now." And Jonas hoped like hell the cops got hold of him on his way out. Even if they didn't, he suspected they would pick him up quickly.

"Damn you," Westbrook said, and pocketed the gun. "Why couldn't you just have stayed dead?"

"Not this time," Jonas said as the door slammed behind Westbrook. "Not this time."

CLAIRE FELT LIKE shit when she woke. At first she couldn't remember where she was, but further inspection told her she was in a hospital room. As a patient. She turned her head to see Jonas sitting beside the bed, head down as if dozing. He had several days' worth of beard, and even asleep he looked tired. Good God, how long had she been here?

"Jonas?" she croaked.

His head came up immediately. "Claire." He leaned forward to hold her hand, smoothing his other hand over her hair. "Hey, how are you feeling?"

"Like crap. Hurts."

"Gunshot wounds will do that to you. Especially one that passes through your lung."

"What . . . happened?"

"Do you remember that Westbrook shot you?"

"Yes. What happened after that?"

"You had a tension pneumothorax that I evacuated, and then we got you to the hospital where you had surgery. Mike Sanders resected a small piece of your lung and you should recover fully. You're going to be fine."

"Tired," she said and closed her eyes.

The next time she woke she felt considerably better. Still in pain, though it was better. She was still weak, but a lot less shaky than she had been. Jonas wasn't there, but Lanie was sitting in the chair beside her bed.

"Hey, sleepy. You scared the hell out of us."

"I'm sorry," Claire said. She held out her hand. "Sorry I've been so angry with you. Forgive me?" Life was too short to remain angry with those you love. She understood that now. Lanie had made a mistake. So had Claire. A number of them.

"Nothing to forgive. I was wrong, but I didn't do it to hurt you, Claire. Can you forgive me?"

"Possibly. If you get me some water."

Her friend grinned and poured a small amount into a cup. Lanie added a straw and handed it to her, making sure she could hold it. "Don't drink it too fast," Lanie cautioned.

"Thanks. Where's Jonas?" Claire asked after she'd taken a sip.

"Now that you're definitely on the mend we kicked him out. He'll be back. The man really loves you."

"I know." And she loved him. Was it possible that finally, finally they would have their happy ending?

"Your mother's been here too. She's having lunch with your surgeon. I think they've hit it off."

Claire blinked at that. "My mother and Dr. Sanders? Who'd have thought it?"

"Apparently the two of them. You've had quite an adventure. I don't understand what happened, not even a little, but I gathered that Lawrence Westbrook, your ex-father-in-law, shot you. Apparently, he was trying to shoot Jonas and you managed to get in the way. Somehow it's all tied up with a murder that happened fifty-something years ago."

"Yes. I'll explain later." In a carefully expurgated version. "What happened to Lawrence?"

"The police caught him as he was leaving Jonas's apartment complex. He's in jail, charged with attempted murder. I think there's more, other charges, but you'll have to ask Jonas."

"I'll do that. When is he coming back?"

Lanie laughed and handed her a cell phone. "Call him."

"No need," Jonas said from the doorway. "I'm here." He crossed the room and leaned over her. "I'm not going anywhere," he said, and kissed her.

Claire put her arms around his neck and kissed him back. "Good."

A WEEK LATER, Claire was released from the hospital. They hadn't discussed it, but Jonas was taking her to his place since he didn't think she should be alone until she had fully recovered. Besides, he wanted to be with her. Hopefully, she felt the same. With Lawrence's incarceration, she seemed to have changed her mind about her belief that they couldn't be together.

*Seemed to* being the operative words.

"Glenn called me today. While I was waiting to be discharged."

"Why?" He shot her a glance, but she didn't seem upset.

"To apologize about his father. He's convinced Lawrence is mentally unstable and hopes he'll be put in a hospital for the criminally insane. He isn't happy about it, of course, but it's better than death row."

Jonas snorted in disgust. "Lawrence Westbrook isn't crazy. He should go to prison for the rest of his miserable life. At least."

"No, he's not crazy. But that will be up to the court to decide."

Jonas scowled. "Life in a hospital for the criminally insane wouldn't be a picnic either. I guess I'm okay with whatever happens. Unless he goes free. What about you?"

"He won't go free," she said with conviction. "I'm content to let the law handle it. I think the right thing will be done this time."

"Glenn say anything else?" He glanced at her but couldn't read her expression.

"Quite a bit, actually. He finally admitted what he'd done. He apologized for beating me up. Swore he'd never raise a hand to me again. He even said he'd get help. Counseling." She hesitated, then added, "Glenn wants me to come back to him."

"What was your answer?" He knew, but he also couldn't deny a moment's worry.

Claire put her hand over his on the gearshift. "Not only no, but hell, no. Why would I go back to him when I'm in love with you?"

The tightness in his chest eased. "So you won't complain if I take you to my place? You shouldn't be alone while you recover." And never again if he could help it.

"I was going to ask you if you didn't ask me."

"Great minds," he said.

"CAN WE TALK? I have something for you," Jonas said after dinner.

Propped up in bed again, Claire smiled. While she'd been able to eat at the table, she was still weak enough to be glad to get back in bed. "That depends. Is it something nasty, like that antibiotic you have me on? Or will I like it? Is it dessert? Frozen yogurt?" she asked hopefully.

He laughed a little. "Don't worry, it's not medicine. I'm afraid it's not frozen yogurt, either. I'll go get you some later." His expression turned serious. And oddly enough, apprehensive. "I hope you'll like it."

"Are you going to ask me to move in with you again? Because if you are, the answer is yes."

"No. I don't want to live with you."

Her heart sank. He was through with her?

He pulled something out of his pocket and held it out to her. A ring. A gorgeous round-cut diamond in an old-fashioned, platinum setting. Smaller diamonds encircled the center stone and the band was one of pavé diamonds.

"Oh, Jonas, it's gorgeous."

"I saw this and knew it was the right one. Just like I know

that you and I are right and should be together. Always. Will you marry me, Claire?"

She held out her hand, and he slipped on the ring. It fit perfectly. "Yes," she said, and threw her arms around his neck and hugged him. "Yes, yes, yes."

Jonas kissed her. A kiss of promise, fidelity, possibility. A kiss of love.

MUCH LATER, JONAS brought a book to her. Rachel's journal, she saw to her surprise. "What's this?"

"When I went to get some of your things to bring over here I saw it on your bedside table. I decided to bring it. I don't know why but I read the last entry. You haven't read it, have you?"

He seemed sure of that, and she wondered why. "No. Not yet."

"You need to." He flipped to the page he wanted and waited while she read.

*October 15, 1859*

Claire looked up. "October fifteenth is my birthday."

"I know. Read what she wrote."

She started again.

***Rachel's Journal—October 15, 1859***

*Victor Lawrence died last night. We heard the news from the sheriff himself. It was an accident, and Sheriff Boynton seemed disgruntled that he could not prove otherwise. He would say no more than Victor had fallen down the stairs and broken his neck.*

*We have heard more from the servants. They believe that in the months since Sarah's death, Victor has been driven mad. Impossible as it might be to believe, the slaves swear that Sarah's ghost is responsible.*

*On the fatal night, Peter, Victor's house servant, heard his master shouting, upstairs in his bedroom. Peter went to offer help and Victor demanded, "Do you see her? Do you?" Peter asked who and Victor said, "My wife, damn her soul." He pointed a shaking finger at nothing Peter could see. "There! In the doorway. Go away, Sarah. You won't drive me mad! You won't!"*

*Peter said his master was drunk, that he had been in a drunken state continually since the day he killed Elijah, Sarah, and Celia. Peter said an expression of abject terror came over Victor's face and he rushed out of his room and down the stairs. "No, you're not real, you can't be," he cried. He tripped and fell headlong down the long staircase. Peter said Victor lived for a short while, all the while maintaining that Sarah had killed him.*

*After Victor passed, Peter believes he saw a vision of his mistress, and she whispered, "Justice."*

*I am not sure what to believe. Peter has never been fanciful, and unlike many of the other slaves, does not believe in spirits. For him to relate this tale gives one pause. But I do know that Victor Lawrence is dead, and thus justice has been served for my dear sister and her beloved.*

*For myself as well. My daughter was born early this morning. We shall call her Sarah.*

CLAIRE CLOSED THE journal. "So Sarah and Rachel got justice after all." She smiled at Jonas. "You don't believe it, do you?"

"Believe in ghosts? I've been forced to believe in past lives, but I draw the line at ghosts."

"Such a skeptic."

"Always will be." They smiled at each other. "You know what's odd," Jonas said. "I haven't had a dream—that I remember—since I saw Calvin's death. Or maybe it's not so odd."

"Since Lawrence is going to pay for his crime, you mean?"

Jonas shrugged. "It's kind of a coincidence, don't you think? What about you? Any more dreams?"

"No. Well, not about Sarah. I guess she's at peace. Calvin must be too."

"Yeah, I think they are. Do you think this means nothing woo-woo is going to happen to us again?"

Claire laughed. "I don't know. But I do know if it does we'll face it together. Deal?"

"Deal," he said, and kissed her.

*The End*

## ABOUT THE AUTHOR

Eve Gaddy is the award winning, national bestselling author of forty novels. Her books have sold over a million copies and been published in many countries and several languages. She writes contemporary romance, romantic suspense, romantic mystery, and a bit of paranormal romance as well.

Eve's books have won and been nominated for awards from Romantic Times, Golden Quill, Bookseller's Best, Holt Medallion, Daphne Du Maurier and many more. Eve was awarded the 2008 Romantic Times Career Achievement award for Series Storyteller of the year, and was nominated for a Romantic Times Career Achievement Award for Innovative Series romance.

Eve loves her family, books, electronics, the mountains, and East Texas in the spring and fall. She also loves a happy ending. That's why she writes romance.

Want to hear more about upcoming releases, special deals and other fun stuff? Subscribe to my newsletter .

Find Eve on the Web:

www.evegaddy.net
eve@evegaddy.net

*If you enjoyed Last Shot and would like to hear more about my new releases and special deals, sign up for my newsletter and receive a* FREE BOOK! Free exclusively for my newsletter readers!

Casey Fontaine and Nick Devlin

Can this rooted-to-the-land beauty dare gamble her heart on a man who has never called just one place home?

*Reviews*

*"Casey's Gamble delivers everything I love in a romance novel; passion, suspense and the kind of sweet romance that is addictive. Can't wait to read more titles by Eve Gaddy." Katherine Garbera, USA Today Bestselling Author*

*"Bayou atmosphere so thick you can almost smell the magnolias! You'll be rooting for Nick and Casey to find a love as sweet as the sugar cane she grows--if she survives the threat to her beloved Belle-fontaine." Justine Davis, 5 Time RITA Award winner*

http://newsletter.evegaddy.com/subscribe

# BOOKS BY EVE GADDY

TEXAS TRUE

Texas Forged (Book 1)

Truly, Madly Texas (Book 2)

Texas Made (Book 3)

Texas Cowgirl (Book 4) February 2022

HEART OF TEXAS

Heart of the Texas Doctor (Book 1)

Texas on My Mind (Book 2)

Under the Mistletoe (Book 3)

Heart of the Texas Warrior (Book 4)

DEVIL'S ROCK AT WHISKEY RIVER

Rebel Pilot, Texas Doctor (Book 1)

His Best Friend's Sister (Book 2)

No Ordinary Texas Billionaire (Book 3)

THE REDFISH CHRONICLES

Trouble In Texas (Book 1)

A Marriage Made In Texas (Book 2)
Somewhere In Texas (Book 3)
That Night In Texas (Book 4)
Remember Texas (Book 5)
A Christmas Baby in Texas (Book 6)
Baby Be Mine in Texas (Book 7)
Redfish Chronicles (Books 1-4)
Redfish Chronicles (Books 5-7)

THE GALLAGHERS OF MONTANA
Sing Me Back Home (Book 1)
Love Me, Cowgirl (Book 2)
The Doctor's Christmas Proposal (Book 3)
The Cowboy and the Doctor (Book 4)
Return of the Cowgirl (Book 5)

THE BROTHERS OF WHISKEY RIVER
Texas Heirs by Eve Gaddy and Katherine Garbera (Book 1)
Texas Cowboy by Eve Gaddy (Book 2)
Texas Tycoon by Katherine Garbera (Book 3)
Texas Rebel by Eve Gaddy (Book 4)
Texas Lover by Katherine Garbera (Book 5)
Texas Bachelor by Eve Gaddy & Katherine Garbera (Book 6)

WHISKEY RIVER CHRISTMAS
A Texas Christmas Past by Julia Justiss
A Texas Christmas Reunion by Eve Gaddy
A Texas Christmas Homecoming by Nancy Robards Thompson
Once Upon a Texas Christmas by Katherine Garbera

FREE WITH NEWSLETTER SIGN UP

Casey's Gamble

Romantic Suspense

Last Shot

Cry Love

LONE STAR NIGHTS

Fully Engaged

Cowboy Come Home

Just One Night

Amazing Grace

Midnight Remedy

Too Close For Comfort

On Thin Ice

Multi Author Series

THE AMALFI NIGHT BILLIONAIRES

The Billionaire's Pleasure by Katherine Garbera (Book 1)

The Billionaire's Touch by Mimi Wells (Book 2)

The Billionaire's Bride by Nancy Robards Thompson (Book 3)

The Billionaire's Heart by Kathleen O'Brien (Book 4)

The Billionaire's Lover by Eve Gaddy (Book 5)

RETURN TO CADDO LAKE

Uncertain Past by Ken Casper (Book 1)

Uncertain Fate by Roz Denny Fox (Book 2)

Uncertain Future by Eve Gaddy (Book 3)

Made in the USA
Columbia, SC
28 October 2023

25099711R00214